SAN RAFAEL JACKED

Tom Ellis

LOOSE CANNON ENTERPRISES
Paradise, CA

Ver. 1.0
ISBN 978-1-944476-40-3

Copyright © 2016 by Tom Ellis

Cover images:
Front - The San Rafael Valley Arizona 2014
Rear - The Huachuca Mountains, as seen from across
San Rafael Valley in the Patagonia Mountains
by The Old Pueblo

Print design by Loose Cannon Ent.

-Also available as an ebook-

www.loose-cannon.com

For the Ranchers of the San Rafael Valley, you are the keepers of one of God's most beautiful creations.

And as always
VJRSSP

Author's Notes and Acknowledgements

Nothing in this book is true. It is a novel, fiction, and there is the usual disclaimer in front of the book about any resemblance to persons living or dead so on so forth. The government entities mentioned are real, their employees and those employee's conduct is fiction. I have spelled FBI correctly, and the rest is, you guessed it, my imagination. For the reader to navigate the FBI terms used, I offer the following explanations: SAC, Special Agent in Charge, ASAC, Assistant Special Agent in Charge, HRT, Hostage Rescue Team, sometimes called Super Swat, they are the gold standard of the SWAT world. CI, Confidential Informant that is a snitch that is allowed to remain anonymous. Credentials or Creds, the name given the identification folder agents carry. Bu-car, Bureau car, an FBI agent's assigned government vehicle. Another term, RPG, Rocket Propelled Grenade, a common third world weapon.

The geographic locations in this story are real. If anything the descriptions of the San Rafael Valley are understated. The history of this Valley is correct. There is a sign near the forest service road gives the names of ten ranches in this valley. The three ranches in this book, the Rocking H Bar, the Double B and the CRM are fictional. They are all products of my imagination. Lochiel Arizona is real and accurately described. The closed customs house was there in 2002. I did not mention the bull walking around the dirt streets. There is plenty of livestock in this story.

In the 1962 Movie, *How The West Was Won*, Debbie Reynolds sang a song titled Away. This tune uses the music of Greensleeves. One section of the lyrics, 'I'll build you a home in a meadow,' came to mind the first time I laid eyes on the San Rafael Valley. There is one thing about American West you can't miss seeing, and that it is the grandeur of it. There are many meadows in our Western States. I would like to believe the lyricist for Away once saw the San Rafael.

I lived in southern Arizona from 2000 to 2003. I was able to explore Cochise and Santa Cruz Counties. The San Rafael Valley is off the beaten path. One has to be going there; it's not like you drive by and see it. I found it by accident once and explored it several times from different directions. A friend of mine out for a visit rode along on one of these trips. He made a comment as we passed the Parker Canyon Ranch. 'If you aren't a list person when you move out here, you will be real soon.' It's not the kind of place you can run down to the convenience store and pick up what you forgot on the trip to town!

I attended a 'Spring Fling' one windy weekend in the San Rafael. Ms. Sidney Spencer, one of the five lady ranchers in the valley hosted this event at her Lazy J 2 Ranch. This visit allowed me a first person view of a San Rafael ranch. Sidney introduced me to some guests as a writer and horseman. Her kindness for that introduction was much appreciated. My being either one is subjective. Fifteen years later I remember that visit and the beauty of the San Rafael Valley. I offer many thanks to Sidney Spencer for her review and comments on this manuscript.

The problems on the border between the US and Mexico are valid. I have seen these with my own eyes. My penchant for roaming around the desert alone on horseback was noted by other members of the retired law enforcement community where I lived. One very pointedly reminded me to travel armed. The danger of encountering a drug smuggler was genuine.

The basic plot of this book is an old one; some nefarious person has stolen an innocent person's ranch. A prerequisite was the crook obtain the deed in some immoral manner. SAN RAFAEL JACKED is set in 2008-09 and has all the requirements above. Plus a few more just to make it interesting. Enjoy.

Tom Ellis
St Clair County, Alabama

Contents

PROLOGUE

Lyon Hamilton sat astride a magnificent stallion. The blue eyed honey buckskin was registered as Don Cameron of Lochiel. With a long black mane and tail of the same color, identical black stockings on each leg contrasting with its honey color and black blaze face, the horse turned heads wherever Hamilton rode it. Lochiel was named by an early settler of the San Rafael Valley, a Scotsman named Colin Cameron. Located in Santa Cruz County on the US border with Mexico in southern Arizona, Lochiel was once a port of entry into the United States. A sun-bleached customs house still remains on the dirt main street. There was likely a Cameron in Lyon Hamilton's family tree. He lived and worked on the same ranch several generations of Hamilton's had worked before him. Now, he maintained a small herd of cattle and trained a few horses. Stud fees from Cam, as he referred to the quarter horse, helped pay the bills and the salary of one hired hand.

Hamilton's sister, his only sibling, could tell you who was who in the family tree. She had daughters, while Lyon and his late wife were childless. What would become of the Rocking H Bar ranch and its registered brand were one of the things on Lyon Hamilton's mind as he and Cam rested on a ridge overlooking the ranch headquarters and the evening visa in front of him. He enjoyed sitting up here on the horse and surveying his domain. It reminded him of an old John Wayne movie in which the Duke's character would ride out to a hillside and sit his horse while he pondered the problems of the time. A black and white Border Collie with one blue eye named Jazz sat next to them. Jazz's pedigree was from a championship line of herding dogs. The canine knew his business well and was extremely protective of everything in his purview. Hamilton could see the dust from a vehicle traveling south on the closest farm service road it was probably a Border Patrol agent. The never ending flow of illegals crossing into the USA wasn't usually a problem in this valley. Cochise County to the east and the area west of the Patagonia Mountains bore the brunt of this traffic. A new drug lord south of the border was escalating violence trying to bring Tucson street gangs under his control. The San Rafael Valley, one of the least known and most beautiful places in Arizona was on its way to being trashed by the illegals heading north for entitlements the United States offered them without question. Lyon Hamilton was not pleased with the long-term prospects for his ranch and his home. A home whose deed could be traced back to a Spanish Land Grant.

Chapter One

Carson Bell sat on a bar stool in the casino lounge. It was a small quiet bar where winners and losers came to unwind. Bell was on his monthly overnight trip to Tucson. Ranch business complete he'd stopped in and played blackjack for a few hours. He was up a hundred bucks when he quit. The news played on a TV screen behind the bar. America's President was assuring the country that the border with Mexico was secure. Working on his second drink, the seventy-something rancher was far from being drunk.

"Horse hockey!" He said to no one in particular. "Bartender either change the channel on that TV or turn it off! I can't abide by that lying SOB any longer!"

"Yes sir," the barman answered and promptly used his remote to switch the TV to a sports channel.

A man of average build wearing a black blazer and tan trousers with an open collar shirt spoke to Bell. "I can't say I'm surprised at him saying that. It was the handout crowd that put him in that office. I guess you see your share of that border mess?"

Bell was wearing a western cut jacket and shirt with a bolo tie. His trousers covered a pair of handmade Paul Bond Boots. His dress Stetson hat rested on his head. He looked like a rancher.

"We don't have trouble in the San Rafael. Or should I say trouble known to us? I have plenty of friends in Cochise County that have been dealing with wet backs and drug smugglers for years. Their property gets trashed, fences were torn down. You name it; it has happened over there. The Tohono O'Odham Nation west of Nogales has problems too. And they've got some top-notch trackers on that res. And they find a lot of drugs. But like Cochise County they only get a small percentage of what comes through."

"Why is the area you live in; the San Rafael I believe you called it free from border smuggling?"

"The San Rafael Valley is in Santa Cruz County. The valley is high prairie grass. That sort of terrain doesn't work well for smuggling. No washes and arroyos to hide in on your way north. The Border Patrol works the area all the time. It almost seems like they put them there so they won't catch anybody."

"So your valley is pretty safe then?"

"I suppose so. One of my southern neighbor's is a border ranch. Lyon has cut back his operation a good bit. Just him and one hand run the place. There're several ranches down there single handed by women. Don't think I would mess with any of them. That would be a good way to get shot."

"It sounds like a neat place. I'm new to this area. I don't know my way around. Where is your valley?"

"Take I-19 south to Nogales. Turn left toward Patagonia before you cross the border. When you get to Patagonia, turn right and go south across the mountains. You can't miss it."

"You make sound like it is right down the street."

"Not quite."

The second man laughed and got up from his stool. "It's been nice talking to you. Good luck if you're gambling. And for the record I didn't vote for the son of a bitch either."

"Thank you," Bell said smiling and raised his drink toward the stranger.

A few minutes later the man in the black blazer was standing in front of the casino. The parking valet raised his hand and moments later a dark SUV pulled to the curb. A dull thuggish looking forty-something man with the face of a boxer who failed to duck more often than not got out of the large vehicle and opened the rear door. Once the passenger in the black blazer got inside the truck, the thug closed the door and got back in the right front.

"Where to boss?" The driver asked.

"Take it home Pauli."

"You got it, boss." Pauli Dumas answered as he put the SUV in gear. Dumas aka Porn Dude was a former actor in X-rated films. He was known for his exceptionally large penis and violent temper and banned from the industry after injuring several actors of both sexes. Despite poor table manners, the sexual appetite of a male lion and perpetual hard on, Porn Dude was a computer genius, a talented hacker fluent in Spanish. He typically dressed in too small sweat pants sans underwear to show off his appendage. After an incident in a nice restaurant involving his jumping up from his seat and hunching a bent over server wearing a mini skirt. The boss seldom let him come in any place with women in revealing attire.

The guard thug, Nate Norman aka Numb Nuts was the real muscle if you wanted to call it that. His alias came from his having been kicked in the balls a disproportionate number of times and his lack of intelligence. Numb Nuts was loyal and followed the boss's orders instantly without question. His being foolishly brave helped as well.

As they stopped for a red light, Dumas glanced in the rear view mirror and said, "Looks like a car jacker coming our way boss." A BMW Sedan was in front of the Suburban.

"Run the light Porn Dude. Get us out of here." The boss replied as he drew a pistol from a holster mounted under the rear seat. Numb Nuts was unlimbering a sawed-off shotgun. Dumas shifted the transmission into reverse and backed up enough to go around the Beemer. Dumas drove the Suburban 4X4 to the right of the BMW and turned right onto a side street. Pauli checked the review mirror as Numb Nuts and the Boss watched out the back. A young Latino male stepped up to the

BMW and jerked open the driver's door. Brandishing a pistol, he ordered, and half pulled the driver out of the car. Dumas made a left turn putting the SUV back in the direction it was heading.

"When we get back to the house Pauli, I want you to get online and find out all there is to know about the San Rafael Valley." The Boss said as if nothing transpired.

"Sure thing boss, what's up."

"We are going to jack something bigger than a car."

Ransom Carter, Special Assistant to the FBI Director, knocked on his bosses' door frame. Carter entered when the Director looked up from his desk and nodded.

"I have an interesting intelligence report, Sir."

"Have a seat and share it."

"A first office agent out of Phoenix was visiting Nogales Sonora Mexico on his off time last Friday night. He went into a very popular eating establishment and during his meal, the server came by and told him his check had been paid, and would he please leave. He was given a chit for a free meal because of the inconvenience. Everyone in the place got the same treatment. Our man asked what was going on, and the server said a very important person wanted the restaurant for a private meeting. Our guy asked the waiter if perhaps he could get this person's autograph and was told, El Jefe does not give autographs.

"Once all the customers were outside, our agent crossed the street and watched. Our man recognized W. Ashton Bradford from his academy training and observed Bradford enter the restaurant."

"So we have a credible report of Bradford meeting the most dangerous drug lord in Mexico. Who is our agent?"

"Ernesto Smith."

"I remember that guy from his academy graduation. All his names took up a whole line on his diploma. I commented about that when I handed it to him. He gave me the biggest grin and said, 'Si my father was a gringo.' I almost cracked up in front of the whole room. I checked with the Assistant Director over the academy and found out Smith was in the top ten academically tough as nails and perfect marksmanship scores. He was also known for a wicked sense of humor."

"That would be Ernesto Roberto Xavier Collazo Smith."

"Sharp kid, I suppose he is a native Spanish speaker."

"Yes, his home is Cochise County Arizona."

"Where that Sheriff is on the soapbox about our borders not being secure."

"One and the same. That is why I brought this to your attention. Ashton Bradford meeting with El Jefe does not bode well for law enforcement in this country. The President likes to say our borders are secure. And I believe that Sheriff is right. And Ass Bradford being down there taking advantage of it is something we don't need.

"I checked with Homeland Security and either Bradford has a bogus passport, or he crossed the border illegally. There is no record of his passport being used in the past ninety days to leave the country or reenter."

"Professional Responsibility screwed that one up period. The US Attorney would not even take their case to a grand jury. All we could do was fire that bastard. I don't know how we hired him, to begin with."

"He slipped under the radar. We are our worst enemy with that sort of thing. The IRS couldn't say he was shaking down taxpayers during audits. They were just beginning to look at him when he caught wind of the internal investigation and resigned. With him being a CPA and a law school graduate, complete with bar membership, our people probably peed on themselves to hire him."

"At least we fired him. Glover and company almost let him resign."

"Bradford has been seen in the Tucson area where he frequents casinos looking for high-end prostitutes. I suspect he is involved in human trafficking. I think we need to start an investigation on him. It is justifiable with him being in the company of El Jefe."

"I agree. Assign it to the Tucson Field Office."

"Sir, I believe we need to get a serious undercover operative involved with Bradford. Someone who can make a case against him. I think we should assign Ron Kroll the project."

"Kroll is another one of Professional Responsibilities screw ups. He doesn't need to be an FBI agent, but he keeps squeaking by every time we try to fire him. Ransom you better have a good reason for even bringing that man's name up in this office."

"Yes Sir, what I have in mind will allow us to get rid of Bradford and Kroll both."

"Let's hear it."

"We terminate Kroll, on paper only. And send him to Bradford as himself. Ron Kroll terminated FBI agent. They will be kindred spirits. Kroll is a rogue, but he is without a doubt the best deep cover man we have. Ernesto Smith studied Kroll in the academy."

"Yes, as an example of how not to do things."

"And that is what we need to bring down Bradford."

The Director didn't comment for a few seconds. "If he makes a case on Bradford, how do we get rid of Kroll?"

Ransom Carter looked toward the office door and then leaned forward toward the Director.

"We promise Kroll full retirement when Bradford is indicted or removed from the criminal class. With any luck, they will kill each other."

Chapter Two

FBI Special Agent Ron Kroll sat in his cubical in the Mobile Alabama Field Office. He was going through dormant files checking to see if they were complete and up to the standards of the new Special Agent in Charge, L. Winston Glover. For the past month, the new SAC had made Kroll's life miserable. They had a history. Mr. Glover, to all in the Field Office, was called Skinny Winnie behind his back on good days. Most of the time the sobriquet was even less flattering. Before his banishment to Mobile; Glover was head of the Office of Professional Responsibility at FBI Headquarters in Washington DC. He fell from grace several months after Ron Kroll was sent to Mobile.

For most of his career, Kroll distinguished himself in undercover operations. His success was due to a lot of luck and using the FBI rules, policies and procedures, regulations, and bureaucracy only when necessary. In the post nine eleven worlds, Kroll played by Ron Kroll rules. When a known Muslim terrorist complete with a bomb fell into Kroll's hands he administered a world class beating. The information gained took down a large terror cell operating in Atlanta GA.

The case was thrown out at the Federal Magistrates level. The lack of any witnesses and Kroll's arrest and interrogation procedures were the primary reason. When the Muslim bomber accidentally blew himself, and several colleagues up it didn't help the case either. Skinny Winnie Glover believed Kroll caused that accident.

The zealot Glover tried to get Kroll fired and prosecuted for crimes real and imagined. The harassment levied on Kroll by Skinny Winnie even included an income tax audit for the five previous years. Glover failed in his vendetta against Kroll.

Glover's vindictive investigation into Kroll's version of undercover agent behavior was the result of losing a criminal case against another rogue FBI agent. That agent, W. Ashton Bradford, was terminated, but it was a bittersweet victory for L. Winston Glover. The FBI Director was not a member of Skinny Winnie's small fan club and assigned him as SAC in the Mobile Field Office. The Director saw a chance for Skinny Winnie to screw up and be counseled to retire. The former either forgot or never knew; Ron Kroll was transferred to Mobile a few months before Glover.

All Kroll wanted when he arrived in Mobile was to finish out his last couple of years before retiring without getting on anybody's bad side. Now his nemesis was standing outside his cubicle.

"Special Agent Kroll put on your jacket and follow me to the secure conference room. Now." Glover ordered.

Kroll robotically followed those orders. His mind was in high gear. The office rumor was some bigwigs from Headquarters DC were in town. And the SAC escorting an agent to the secure conference room did not bode well for said agent.

Skinny Winnie opened the door to the conference room and motioned Kroll to enter. Glover closed the door behind them.

Seated at the conference table were the Director and his Special Assistant Ransom Carter. Carter spoke. "Have a seat Agent Kroll."

Ron took a seat across from the two men.

"Glover you are excused. Close the door behind you and turn on the secure light." The Director said.

The Director turned to Kroll. "How is the Mobile office treating you Special Agent Kroll?"

"Things were great until Glover showed up."

"Go ahead and speak your mind, Kroll." Ransom's voice dripped with sarcasm.

"Agent Kroll you are without a doubt the most skilled undercover operative the FBI has." The Director began. "We have a special assignment for you if you are willing to take it. The only good thing I can say about the assignment is you will no longer work for L. Winston Glover. And you will be allowed to retire immediately on completion of said assignment. Are you interested?"

"Sir, with all due respect. I am interested. But I will not accept it blindly. An investigation important enough for you to fly down here must be a secret. You have my word it will stay a secret whether or not I take the job."

"Fair enough. Are you good with that Ransom?"

"Yes, Sir."

"Agent Kroll, have you ever heard of a former agent named Welch Ashton Bradford?"

"Yes, as I recall Glover and his former colleagues terminated him but screwed up the chances of prosecuting Mister Ass Bradford."

"Ass Bradford is probably the best reference to W. Ashton Bradford as he refers to himself. He probably uses the initial W, because he will welch on a bet or a deal. It has come to our attention that Bradford is involved in a criminal enterprise in the southwestern United States. One most likely involving human trafficking and narcotics smuggling. Ass Bradford is a blight on the FBI's record, and we want him doing time in a Federal Penitentiary. I believe you are the man who can penetrate Bradford's organization and make a case we can win.

"The administration is catching a lot of flak over security issues on the Mexican border. There is a county sheriff in Arizona that says the state has to do what the federal government won't do. And having somebody like Bradford down there involved in anything illegal spells disaster. Bradford is smart and he likely sees this border debacle as an opportunity.

It is up to us to stop him before the locals get more information to hand the press about how we ignore the border. Kroll, do you have any comment or concerns at this point?"

Ron Kroll drew in a deep breath before answering. "Sir, I appreciate your confidence in me. Who would I report to?"

"Ransom Carter is in charge of the operation. A Supervisory Special Agent in the DC office will oversee the op and will coordinate personnel and equipment. She will report directly to Mr. Carter. Your backup group will report to her. The local field offices Tucson and Phoenix will provide administrative support and SWAT backup. The field office SAC's will not be totally read on this investigation. These SACs will only know that it is happing in their area of responsibility."

"Who is the supervisory special agent?"

"Havelee Harris."

"It seems you are leaving a lot of brass out of the loop on this investigation. Why?" Kroll asked.

"Ashton Bradford has a network of former agents, and we suspect rogue agents currently employed. We don't want any leaks."

"So myself, my backup team, Havelee Harris, and you gentlemen are the only ones who know what is going on?"

"Yes and we want to limit the size of your backup team. We have some agents in mind for you to choose from."

"How am I supposed to infiltrate Bradford's organization?"

"As Ron Kroll terminated FBI agent."

"So you are going to fire me and give me my job back when I put Bradford away. Gentlemen, again no disrespect intended, but I have been too close to firing to fall for that."

The Director smiled. "Ransom predicted you would say that. I have with me two copies of a confidential document which states that upon the successful conclusion of this investigation you be allowed to retire from the FBI at your present GS rating. The successful conclusion the arrest and indictment of Bradford; or the satisfactory termination of Bradford's criminal enterprise with prosecution not being necessary.

"We will call in a notary to notarize our signatures on this document. Mr. Carter will be witness to our signing this document. We will both have an original copy.

"These documents will state you are employed as an FBI Special Agent. And that all actions regarding your termination this date is a subterfuge for the undercover assignment you are engaged in." The Director paused.

"Ron would you explain how we are going to get Special Agent Kroll in place."

Ransom Carter smiled. "You are going undercover as yourself, Ron Kroll, terminated FBI agent. Adam Hall, the head of security for Gulf Enterprises has been contacted and asked to provide you employment in a Tucson Arizona Casino his company owns but does not advertise it as being part of their empire. The employment will be a sympathy job because of your service to the bureau before the latest incident."

"And what is the latest incident?"

"You roughed up a Muslim who complained about terrorist profiling."

"Oh," Kroll replied with raised eyebrows.

"Before we call for the notary, are you going to accept the assignment or go back to Skinny Winnie?" Ransom Carter asked.

"What is the code name of this investigation?"

"Bad Apple's"

Ron Kroll was quite for a few moments. Apple's was plural, and cruising below the radar until retirement wasn't going to happen either.

"I'll do it."

The documents were signed. Ransom Carter folded Kroll's copy and handed it to him.

"Ron, the Director and myself feel that these documents are the only way to protect you. And the only way you are likely to infiltrate Ass Bradford's organization is to be a fired for cause FBI agent. You will clean out your desk, and SAC Glover will escort you to the personnel office where you will turn in your issue firearm and your credentials. I will go along as well to ensure the ploy works. Glover will believe it is real."

Kroll shook his head and left the conference room. A box was already sitting on his desk. As an unmarried male, Ron Kroll had little in the way of office decoration to take with him. L. Winston Glover SAC, Ransom Carter, and Kroll's Supervisory Agent, a black female, all escorted Kroll to the personnel office.

With a sullen look on his face, Kroll turned in his credentials case and his pistol to personnel. He stepped out into the hallway and Glover said, "You finally got what you deserved Kroll. It has been an honor to escort you through the termination process."

Without word or warning, Ron Kroll knocked Skinny Winnie on his ass. Ron turned without comment and walked to the exit door. He heard applause as the door closed behind him.

A stunned prostrate Glover muttered something about filing charges when Ransom Carter said, "I don't think so Skinny, you asked for that."

The only thing that made the plan to infiltrate W. Ashton Bradford's inner circle work was Ron Kroll's well-thrown punch. Skinny Winnie's decking was FBI legend before quitting time.

CHAPTER THREE

The FBI Gulfstream IV reached cruising altitude; the copilot announced there was no longer need for seat belts. Ransom Carter unbuckled and went to the kitchen area. He came back with two cups of coffee and handed on to the Director. The two men sat in spacious facing leather seats.

"How are you going to placate Glover over Kroll's assaulting him?" Carter asked.

"I'm going to enlist the Attorney General's aid and tell him we don't want the matter prosecuted due to a sensitive need to know undercover investigation. I think the rumor mill will work in our favor as well as Kroll's. We would be extremely naïve to think Bradford doesn't have ears inside the bureau. The AG will tell the US Attorney in Mobile not to indict. Glover will just have to accept that."

"Do you think Havelee Harris is our best choice to keep this investigation on track once Kroll establishes contact with Bradford?"

"Harris is good, but she tends to be unorthodox at times. And she enjoys taking other agents money in shooting contests. Friendly sort of stuff that usually starts with the loser buys lunch. The HRT guys have stopped trying to beat her. They just pay up to get her to go away."

"Are you saying anytime she wants a free lunch she heads down to Quantico?"

"That's about the gist of it. Harris has served on Field Office SWAT teams and has a special sniper rifle assigned to her. A special weapons contractor we use in Alabama, somewhere around Mobile as I recall, built that rifle."

"Interesting, is her head back in the game after her divorce?"

"Yes, very much so. Harris is ready for more responsibility and could very well make a good SAC or ASAC."

"Did Kroll give you an idea of what kind of agents he needs on his backup team?"

"Yes, he wants a Latina female and two African American male agents. He wants the female to be an experienced undercover operative. The black guys having undercover experience would be nice, but their appearance is of more concern to Kroll."

"Do I want to know why he wants that particular mix of agents on his team?"

"He is planning on using a prostitution ruse to get inside Bradford's organization and then to report information learned."

"That's enough, Ransom. FBI men as pimps. What else will Kroll come up with?"

"That would be what we don't want to know. I'm going to give Havelee Harris the agent requirements and go from there. I do want her to have the option of using Ernesto Smith if she finds a place for him. A reward for his spotting Bradford."

"Good idea, maybe he can out shoot her."

"This is likely to wind up in the Tucson Field Office's area of responsibility. How much of need to know do you want them to have?"

"Adele Lane is the SAC out there. She isn't exactly my idea of a team player, and she would micromanage an operation like this. So just give them an overall brief without naming names and refer them to me. Congresswoman Fallon McKay is lobbying me to assign Lane as Congressional Liaison. If this investigation takes off, I will assign Lane to Congress and brief

Quarles her ASAC. I don't think he is ready for the top job yet. I am willing to give it to Harris if the Bad Apple's investigation goes well."

"Good idea, we will probably need to bring the Phoenix SAC into the loop at some point."

"Agree, but let's keep Bad Apple's in our offices for the time being. When they get close to making arrests, we will let everyone in who needs to know."

Rev. Theodis Cleckler invited his visitor to a sitting area in the office corner. The couch, coffee table, and a couple of chairs made meetings more personal. Theo had not seen the attractive silver-haired lady in several years. She was an Air Force wife who once attended his church.

"Lois Thornton it has been a long time. I was surprised to see your name on my appointment calendar." Cleckler took the woman's extended hand in both of his. "It is so good to see you."

"And it is good to see you as well Theo. It has been entirely too long." Lois Hamilton Thornton replied.

"Please sit down. I have fresh coffee if you like?"

"That would be wonderful, thank you."

Cleckler poured two cups of strong chicory coffee and served them on a tray with cream and sugar. He put the tray on the coffee table and gestured for his guest to help herself.

Lois Thornton took a sip and said. "Theo I haven't had Café Du Monde Coffee in years. I was so glad Katrina didn't destroy that place."

"Lois, Café Du Monde coffee is one of my vices. Fishing is the other. How is the General? Enjoying his retirement, I hope."

"Saying the General is retired is a misnomer. He's fine. I expect the time he spends on the golf course is covering up meetings. We have enjoyed being back in the south and away from Washington."

"Where did you all wind-up? Close I hope. I would love to have you back in our congregation."

"We're in Point Clear Alabama. We've only been there a couple of months. It is a bit of a drive for Sunday mornings. But we will make it when we can."

"I know you will. And you will be welcome anytime you choose to come. How is your brother Lyon? I haven't gotten an email from him in some time. And my emails are not answered."

"Lyon is why I am here Theodis."

"What is wrong?"

"I haven't heard from Lyon in six months. With our post-retirement travel and then the move. I sort of lost touch with my brother. I decided to call him a couple of weeks ago, and a stranger answered the ranch phone. He was a very profane person with no manners. Finally, he put someone on the phone he called the boss. This person told me he owned the ranch now, and Lyon had moved to the Fiji Islands. The so called boss was civil on the phone but not helpful. Lyon Hamilton would not sell the Rocking H Bar and move to the South Pacific."

"I agree. My family and I still cherish the vacation we took in Arizona and the time we spent on your awesome family ranch. Lyon always told me God blessed him with being the caretaker of one of the most beautiful places on earth. After seeing it, I believe he is right. How can I help you?"

"I met Lieutenant Jolene Hadfield when she spoke to an Air Force wives group at Kessler Air Force Base. I called the Biloxi Police Department wanting to speak with her. They told me she retired and moved out of state. I know she spoke highly of you and often attended your church. Do you know where she is and how to get in touch with her?"

"I do, and if anyone knows how to find Lyon it is Jolene Hadfield. She doesn't live very far from you in Baldwin County Alabama. If you give me your phone number, I will call her and have her call you." Theodis got up from his chair and walked to his desk. Once he had a pen in hand, Lois Thornton gave him her number. He pushed the button next to Hadfield's name on his speed dial. After four rings the call went to voice mail, and Cleckler left a message.

"Lois, Jolene is really good about returning calls. I hear from her soon. And you will hear from her as well. You referred to her as a lieutenant, she retired as Deputy Chief."

"Thank you, Theo. I appreciate your doing that. How are your family and your boys?"

"Mrs. Cleckler is well, and my oldest is in college at the University of South Alabama. He is staying in a dorm over there. We see him most Sundays, but not all of them."

"Theo, we have to enjoy them while we can. Once they get to college, they are gone living their lives. I hear from my daughters a couple of times a month. And if we are lucky we see them once a year."

"I've heard that so many times. Jerry, my youngest can't wait to leave for college. He received an appointment to the Coast Guard Academy."

"That is wonderful Theo. I bet you and Mrs. Cleckler are proud of both of them."

"We are. Jerry saw what the Coast Guard did during Katrina. He told me that was he was going to do. An old friend of mine, Andy Burns, talked him into applying for the Coast Guard Academy."

After a few more minutes of catch-up chit chat, Lois Thornton got up to leave. Theodis prayed with her and promised to keep Lyon Hamilton on his prayer list. With no more visitors expected, he went to work on his sermon. An hour later his phone rang. Theo checked the caller ID and greeted Jolene Hadfield warmly.

Jolene drove through the gate at Burns place and watched it close automatically behind her. The years since she'd first driven through that gate were the most challenging of her life. And, the most satisfying. Most of that satisfaction was Andrew Burns. Her significant other. At times their relationship was one of the roommates as opposed to lovers. The L word had never passed between them. Of all the guest rooms in Burns house, one was officially her room. She had started out there the first night she stayed over after her troubles at Biloxi PD. After tossing turning and crying, she got up and went to Burn's bedroom. All she said when she slipped into bed beside him was, 'I need to be held.' He obliged every night for the rest of that stay and never made a move to doing anything more. She spent most weekends at Burns, staying in Biloxi only during the times she was on call. The sleeping arrangement went on for six months. On occasions, she would start out in her room, and wind up with Burns. Other times, the most satisfying, were when she went directly to Burns bed. When she worked up the courage to ask him why he never made the move to have sex, his answer brought her to tears.

'I've tried casual sex Hadfield and all it does for me is fill the physical need. It's not going to be that way between us.' When it did, it took her breath away, that time and every time since.

It was an on call weekend when Hurricane Katrina ravaged the Gulf Coast. Jolene was Deputy Chief, and her leadership abilities challenged to their limits. When she finally had time to deal with her destroyed home. Jolene learned from the real estate management company that she owned the house, and her monthly rent payments were mortgage payments. Despite the stress wrought by the hurricane, the companies' long-time secretary explained the situation to Hadfield. Her payments were on direct deduction from her checking account. The management firm forwarded these payments to the mortgage company, CRM Holdings, located in Orange Beach Alabama. CRM Holdings owned fourteen houses in Biloxi and Harrison County. The secretary told Jolene that Raifield Enterprises became CRM Holdings in 1996. The name change was because Mr. Raifield passed away. The managing officer of CRM Holdings was David Cromwell, lawyer, and accountant. He held the same job that he had when he worked for Mr. Raifield. At the direction of the corporation's new owner, four of the fourteen properties were converted to mortgages. And the tenants became homeowners. The woman gave Jolene the phone number of CRM Holdings and apologized for not knowing who owned the company.

Hadfield knew who owned CRM Holdings, and she was mad to the point of being livid! It didn't help the situation when Andy Burns called to check on her and find out how she was holding up. Figuratively she bit his head off, told him where to go, and hung up the phone. Her anger over the matter seethed because she could not leave Biloxi and confront Burns, the owner of CRM Holdings. For Jolene, the situation caused a major rift in their relationship.

Hadfield stopped to see Theodis Cleckler and found him looking out for those who took shelter in his church. He would not take no for an answer when he insisted she rest. A long nap on his office couch did wonders. She was at the point of exhaustion. Theo woke her after dark. He took the time to have coffee with her. Hadfield recalled the conversation as if it were yesterday.

'Chief Jo I've spoken with Andy several times. He is concerned about you. He is sending you a care package with two of our members who went over to Alabama to pick up food. Andy has been busy helping get people fed and sheltered. He did say you were not in the best of moods last time you spoke to him. He knows your house is gone.'

Hadfield was still out of sorts over the house and Burns. She told Theodis that and said more than she should have given the situation. It didn't faze the pastor one bit.

'I understand why you feel the way you do. You and Andy are in a serious relationship. You trust him and have found out he has gone behind your back and done something significant without your knowledge. Chief Jo, you have the right to be upset. I would be if something like that happened to me.

'Andy will help a stranger without reservation. He has always been that way. Andy Burns would buy a meal for a panhandler while his police colleagues would throw the person in jail. That did not earn him a lot of trust among his fellow officers. I've told you how Charlie Raifield saved this church. Andy remembers that, and he helps those in need.

'Just before all of our Biloxi Police troubles I called Andy about helping some of my church families. The cost was beyond our short-term help budget. Three families were going to be evicted from their homes for being behind on their rent. Andy called his business manager, Mr. David Cromwell, and asked him to look into the matter. It turned out that those families lived in houses Andy Burns didn't know he owned. And like you, they had lived in them for years. His orders to Mr. Cromwell were very specific. The management company could not file eviction on any of Burns properties without his permission. Even Mr. Cromwell cannot give that permission. And the rent on properties would be forgiven until the people could start paying again. They would not have to pay the back rent owed either. Andy then told David Cromwell to consider those people to be paying on a no interest mortgage.

'How did your house turn from rental to the mortgage? I don't know. But I suspect it happened during our Biloxi Police troubles. You didn't have a job for a while. I can't break confidences, but if I had to guess, Andy

Burns was behind a lot of the help that came your way. If you were to call David Cromwell, he might tell you how you came to own your house. But then Andy Burns signs his paycheck. So expect Mr. Cromwell not to volunteer Andy as being your benefactor.'

Jolene remembered asking Theodis if it were possible Andy did not know Cromwell had changed her house from rent to mortgage. Cleckler told her that Andy Burns probably told his manager to make sure you didn't lose your home. How Mr. Cromwell did that was up to him. And he would have reported it to his boss. The question was if his boss remembered?

Weeks later, when she finally was able to take time off, Jolene drove to Baldwin County to see Burns. They had spoken via phone since the angry call. But the conversations were casual and civil. She walked in his house and promptly told him they had to talk and talk now. He acknowledged and asked her to have a seat. Burns excused himself for a moment and left her in the living room. When he returned, he carried a large manila envelope. It had her name on the front.

Jolene, something transpired a few years ago that I should have told you. With all that was happening at the time, I overlooked it. It is my fault and my fault alone. When you Biloxi PD fired you, I told David Cromwell to make sure you didn't lose your house. David, if anything is meticulous at following instructions and making a record of it. When he learned you lived in a property, I owned and had lived there before I owned it. He converted it to a non-interest mortgage. He had done this previously when some tenants needed help and had been living in the houses for years. David faxed me a report with that information. I read it and filed it. My copy and his copy are in this envelope. All records on your house and the insurance settlement for it and all funds due you are in here as well.

I suggest you read everything carefully and retain David's accounting services. Unless you are a CPA doing tax work, you will need him. As I understand, you have been living in your office. Jolene, you have a home here as long as you want it. And I am sorry for the distress I have caused you by not telling this a long time ago.'

Burns handed her the envelope and asked she read the contents before making any decisions. Hadfield opened the envelope and began to read the paperwork. When she got to the five figure check from CRM Holdings with her name on it. Jolene decided to forgive Burns imagined transgressions.

She accepted a temporary FEMA trailer offer and eventually sold the lot it sat on after purchasing a condo. Biloxi PD's chief retired and Hadfield agreed to serve as interim chief until a new chief took over. When that chief got settled into the job, Jolene took an early retirement and moved to Burns place. The same real estate management company she'd paid rent to for years now handled her condo.

Chapter Four

Jolene was on her way to meet Lois Hamilton Thornton at a trendy restaurant in Fairhope Alabama. The Nissan 350Z responded with a throaty exhaust roar when she tromped the throttle. Hadfield smiled, she enjoyed the thrill of driving the nimble vehicle. A retirement gift she purchased for herself. Her old Chevy truck was lovingly restored and turned into a hot rod with a new L88 engine under the hood. A couple of Burns' customers did the restoration. The truck attracted people whenever she drove it to fishing tournaments; her Ranger bass boat hitched behind. A walking regimen kept aging weight gain at bay. Her hairdresser kept her shoulder-length red hair dark red. Approaching the big five-oh age, the 5' 7" 135 pound Hadfield still looked good.

The women arrived simultaneously and reintroduced themselves as the host seated them at a private table. They ordered lunch and made small talk before and after the meal. Over a cup of rich New Orleans-style chicory coffee, Jolene got to the point of their meeting.

"Tell me about the situation with your brother. I understand he is a rancher in Arizona."

Lois Thornton sighed, and the expression on her face was troubled. "I like to hope he is still a rancher. But I want to know where he is. I've been trying to get in touch with him for two months. I'm afraid something bad has happened to him. And I can't get any help from anyone in Arizona. I've spoken with the Santa Cruz County Sheriff himself. And he told me there was nothing he or his department could do for me. Lyon's lawyer feels like the sheriff's department is stonewalling me. The lawyer believes something is wrong."

"Theodis Cleckler speaks highly of your brother. Theo and my significant other, Andrew Burns, were in the Marines together. Andy was in the Border Patrol for a few years and was stationed at Naco before he came back to Alabama. He speaks fondly of a valley out there. Tell me about your brother and the ranch."

"Lyon Hamilton is my only sibling, my big brother. He was the rebellious teenager who moved out of our parent's home in Tucson. He went to work on our grandparent's ranch in the San Rafael Valley. Except for three years in the Navy, he has lived on the Rocking H Bar since he was sixteen. That ranch has been in our family since the days of Spanish land grants before Arizona was a territory much less a state.

"That is why Lyon disappearing is so unusual. We would normally talk every couple of months or so. Most of the time Lyon would call me. He would say the same thing every time he called. 'Haven't heard from you in a while Sis just thought I'd call and catch up.' It has been three years since I've seen him. My husband, the General, is not the ranch or farm type. His idea of the outdoors is a golf course. Truthfully, I am not a rancher either. I have three daughters, and none of us enjoyed visits to the ranch. During our more recent phone conversations, big brother seemed concerned about what would happen to the ranch when he passed on. One of my son in laws would like to see it turned into a real estate development. A gated community type thing. Talk like that would probably get him shot in the San Rafael."

"So it is serious ranch country and directions don't include passing a Walmart." Jolene quipped.

"Chief Hadfield, I don't think there is a Walmart within a two-hour drive of the Rocking H Bar. The official address of the ranch is a Post Office Box in Patagonia Arizona. And the ranch headquarters is twenty-five miles or more from that little town.

And the paved road stops five miles south of town. The southern property line is the United States border with Mexico.

"I realized a couple of months ago that it had been awhile since I talked to Lyon. My husband's retirement from the Air Force and us relocating to Point Clear. The birth of another grandchild. I sat down one evening, figured the time difference would be after supper, and I called. A rather impolite man answered the phone and said Lyon Hamilton no longer lived there. After a few minutes trying to pry something out that jerk, he gave the phone to another man who somewhat more civil. This person said he had a quick claim deed to prove ownership. When I asked where my brother was. This man told me he had moved to the Fiji Islands. I asked how much he paid for the ranch; he said, "That was none of my damned business." And he hung up the phone.

"I have a durable power of attorney from Lyon in case something happened to him. I called the bank in Nogales Arizona that has handled his business for years. They would not talk to me, citing privacy rules. I retained a lawyer, David Cromwell in Orange Beach, to work with the bank and Lyon's lawyer in Nogales on my behalf. It is going to take an in-person visit, and I'm not sure I can handle that. Mr. Cromwell advised I contact the district attorney and perhaps a local private investigator to assist me. Chief Hadfield, I want to hire you to go out there and happened to my brother. And if you're significant other, Mr. Burns can go with you I will pay his expenses as well."

Jolene saw the pain in the older woman's eyes. There were a lot of questions Hadfield could ask. The bottom line was, somebody needed to be on the ground out there asking those questions.

"Mrs. Thornton, I will help you. But first I want you to start calling me Jolene. Somebody needs to have boots on the ground out there asking questions. Andy has a friend who recently retired from the Cochise County Sheriff's Department. He was an investigator. I will ask Andy if he will get in touch with him and ask if he will help. We will need someone who knows the ropes locally so to speak. I will also need you to authorize David Cromwell to share information with me. And I will need a limited power of attorney to access Lyon's bank records. Also, do you know if he had a passport?"

"Yes, he got a passport when they started requiring them to go into Mexico. For years you didn't need one. All this Homeland Security business changed that. Lyon would go to Nogales Mexico to fill his prescriptions. I will contact Mr. Cromwell and give you whatever documentation you need. Money is not an object. I will pay whatever you wish for your time and all your travel expenses."

Jolene considered this for a moment before responding.

"This trip will take some planning. I can't give you a date as to when we can leave. You will hear from me by the end of the week if not before."

The gate alarm sounded, and Andrew Burns glanced up at the monitor screen above his work bench. He recognized the Silver Mercedes S-Class approaching his gate. It was the General. Burns activated the auto sensor, and the gate swung open. He knew the General would park in front of the house. Andrew was opening his front door when the trim fit man with short cropped steel gray hair came up the sidewalk.

"Good morning Sir, it's good to see you again."

"Likewise Andy," the General said extending his hand.

Once they were seated on the leather sofas in the living room with its wagon wheel chandelier and walls decorated with knives; the General gazed at the rock fireplace with a large

Moose head above it and Pennsylvania flintlock rifle adorning the mantle. A small bronze cannon on a field carriage adorned one side of the hearth, a brass spittoon on the other.

"Andy, how do you manage to keep this macho living room intact with your lady living in the house?"

Burns smiled. "I gave her a couple of rooms in the back of the house as hers. And a credit card to do what she wanted. That has kept her decorating instincts at bay, so far."

"So far is right. Jolene will want to redo something that doesn't need redoing. Like this room."

"I'll let her build a house before this changes. I wish she would redo the kitchen; it is out of date."

"I've been through that, be careful."

"I trust her to do whatever she want's in there. I just want her to start doing it. I'm not going to tell her to."

"That's good, I would be in the poor house if I let my wife do whatever she wanted. But, she does me the courtesy of asking first. You know she is having lunch with Jolene as we speak."

"Oh, so you have driven over here to warn me of a redecorating conspiracy."

"I wish it were that simple. I understand you worked for the border patrol once in southern Arizona."

Andy smiled again; the General, during his thirty plus years of service he was in the intelligence business and had commanded the NSA. It was possible his retirement was on paper only. Behind his back, he was called General Clout. Something he wielded as necessary.

"I expect you even know the name of the horses I rode."

"Just that you in the horse patrol out of Naco, and you also patrolled the San Rafael Valley when you weren't shooting smugglers on the Mexican side of the line."

"They would send me to the San Rafael whenever dead narco trafficantes turned up on the other side of the fence. I think it was a punishment beat as cops would call it. Boring, nothing ever happened there. I would have volunteered to work the San Rafael all the time. Unfortunately, my wife was sick of Arizona and wanting to come home to Birmingham. I resigned, and we moved back to Alabama. I went back to work as a cop; we got divorced soon after."

"So you liked the San Rafael?"

"A half-breed Apache who was a deputy sheriff in Cochise County once told me my spirit will always be in Arizona. If that is so, it is in the San Rafael Valley. I went back for a couple of years after I retired. I lived near Tombstone in Cochise County. I drove over to the San Rafael a few times. I wanted one of those big ranches when I was in the border patrol, and I wanted one then. And both times I couldn't even afford to ask the price. There was a nice one for sale in 03. I spent hours looking at in on the internet. I forwarded the web information to my accountant and business manager with a what do you think about this message. I could have written a check for the place. But my accountant didn't think it was a good idea at the time.

"I overruled him and bought it. BLM and State grazing leases make up most of the holding. I had the airstrip improved and lengthened to 3500 feet. And I had a hanger built that looks a lot like a barn. Other than those improvements, I left things as they were. All the help or I should say hands as the westerners call them, stayed on. The ranch makes a profit and I put in a liberal profit sharing program for my employees. That was something else my accountant didn't like. But considering I am his largest client, he goes along with me."

"Why didn't you move out there? You obviously like the place."

"I considered it. That valley is nothing more than a small town. The idea that a holding company purchased that ranch and they were outsiders didn't go over well with the locals. Rumor was rife with speculation the place was going to turn into a gated housing development. Ironically, one of the reasons I bought the place was to keep that from happening. At that point in my life, I didn't feel like fighting the outside interloper image.

So I set things up to run themselves. I visit from time to time and speak with my ranch manager weekly. And things were beginning to come together between Jolene and me. I wasn't going to lose another woman over Arizona. That is the long answer, why do you ask?"

"My wife grew up on one of those big ranches and her brother still, runs it. Or at least we hope he does. He is AWOL, and no one knows where he is. The local cops are stonewalling Lois. Lyon's attorney says something is wrong and because the sheriff has stonewalled him. Lois is meeting with Jolene because she heard her speak years ago when we were at Kessler. She is asking Jolene to find her brother. She has no idea I know you."

"Or what all the guns I've built you cost," Burns added. He didn't mention the covert weapons the General commissioned from time to time.

"Exactly I'm one of your confidential customers. And want to be one again. Only this time, I want you to get my brother in law's ranch back. Lois talked to someone named Bradford on the phone, and he claimed he bought it. No way Lyon would sell it."

"So your brother in law would be Lyon Hamilton of the Rocking H Bar Ranch?"

"Yes, do you know him?"

"I know of him. He's one of the top horsemen in southern Arizona. And one of the more vocal ranchers about a holding company buying the ranch next door."

"Would that affect your objectivity in going out there?"

"No. I regret that I didn't make the time to meet my neighbors when I bought my ranch. David Cromwell was giving me hell about buying the place. And the folks that worked it and called it home were not happiest people when the sale happened. I spent the time I had placating them. I would have liked to have met Lyon Hamilton.

"General, the cop side of me has to ask, is there any possibility your brother in law sold the place, skipped out with a bag of cash and is living the high life somewhere?"

"I've asked myself the same thing. The answer is no. Lyon did a Navy hitch and came home to the family ranch. Lois' family has owned that ranch since the days of Spanish Land Grants before the Gadsden purchase. Lyon Hamilton is the American that we military men are pleased to serve. He is a keeper of the land. That church we attended in Biloxi, the one with the African American preacher named Cleckler. Rev Cleckler and his family spent a week out there a couple of years back. Lyon is not living on a beach somewhere. I believe he is dead. I checked Lyon's passport. It hasn't been used for the past seven months.

"I want you to go to Arizona, find out what happened and get the ranch the back. Let Jolene keep my wife informed and out of the line of fire. I will put the weight of my resources behind you and pay whatever price you want. Once you get there and access the situation; I will put a black ops team on standby at Fort Huachuca to back you up.

"I believe your owning a ranch there will make things easier."

"Not in the way you might think. CRM Holdings own's the ranch. Nobody in the San Rafael, other than my hands, know that I own CRM Holdings. My old friend Buddy Russell doesn't know I own that ranch. And that secret has worked well for over five years now."

"You would not still be considered the enemy out there?"

"Probably not, putting a cell phone tower in Patagonia Mountains caused a bit of a stir. But it looks like a tall tree, few folks can find it. And they all liked it.

"I don't have anything going on in my shop right now. General, I will go out there, but not as a rancher and member of the community. It will work better that way. We are going to need some encrypted communications for us to stay in touch."

"I remember Lois saying Lyon was bitching about that cell phone tower at the same time he was saying how great it was. I had no idea you were behind it. And I'm in the intelligence business. I will get you an encrypted satellite phone. It will also allow you to stay in contact with Reid, my black operations team leader. Reid will be collecting reconnaissance information you will likely need."

"Can you keep the Homeland Security at bay if need be?"

"They're easy, and I can keep the other agencies out of your business as well."

"I'll loop in my contacts out there and see what Jolene has to say. Jolene will report sanitized information to Lois. I will report operational info to you. It is important that nobody knows we're out there and what we are doing. I'll get in touch with the time share service my jet is leased to and find out its schedule. We should be on the ground out there within two to three weeks."

"I appreciate your accepting this mission."

"I will keep you informed."

Hadfield thought about the meeting while driving back to Burn's place. As she pushed the remote button to open the gate, Jolene wondered if she would ever think of where she now lived, as anything but Burn's place? When she moved in, Hadfield didn't think it would be a good idea to try and change things in a house that wasn't hers. Still, there was that woman thing about painting walls and hanging new curtains. Most of Burns' house was a world class man cave. Everything else was institutional generic. Guest rooms were complete with white walls and blinds on the windows. The furnishings barely a bed and chest, cheap motels had more class.

The master bedroom was different. The walls were a brown color. And surprisingly Andy had agreed to her buying draperies for the windows. He handed her an American Express card and told her to keep the drapes Southwestern and in the bedroom she called hers, do whatever she wanted. When she tried to give him the card back, he said, "keep it you are an authorized user." His comment about the drapes she chose. "Nice choice" And her room, after she gave the furniture to a thrift store, repainted the room and bought new furniture. "Good work. You could have hired a painter if you'd wanted."

On her way to find Andy, Jolene walked through the large kitchen, which was functional but not modern. She wanted to redo the kitchen. Knowing when to ask Burns could be a problem.

She found him in his knife shop looking at a piece of steel shaped like a blade. There were several hours work left before the project would be complete. Hadfield learned after the first few days spent with Burns, that there were times he could not stop what he was doing for a chat. He was tactful when he explained the need for her watch for a few minutes before speaking. She quietly stood looking at him. Other than the gray hair, Burns had not changed one bit since the night she knocked his front door. She was investigating a missing person, whose body turned up in Burns' lake. Now, Burns would walk with her, hiking the fire lane inside the fence that surrounded his square mile of Baldwin County Alabama. Other times he was on horseback riding the property. She drew a breath; this was a good time to interrupt.

"Got a minute?"

"For you always."

She gave him a peck on the cheek. "Unless you are entering parameters on the lathe using the drill press making a precision cut on a wood stock hammering on a red hot piece of steel the list goes on and on."

"You learned well. How was lunch?"

"Interesting. That is what I want to talk about."

"Good, let's walk down to the pier." Jolene followed him out the door. She picked up a rod and reel which rested against the patio wall. While they walked to the lake, she filled him in on the details she learned. Burns nodded as he listened. One thing was sure about their relationship; he always listened to what she had to say, whether or not he appeared to be listening. When Jolene wanted Andy Burns' attention, all she had to do was ask. Just not when he was hammering on a red hot piece of steel!

He continued onto the pier and sat down on the bench facing the water. She paused at the cleaning table and opened a drawer holding artificial lures and bait. After attaching a plastic worm to the weighted hook, she joined Burns on the pier. Jolene cast the bait into the lake and slowly reeled it back in. It was just seconds before a bass took the bait. He watched while she played the fish for a minute or so and reeled it in. Realizing she was still dressed for lunch in town, he smiled as she danced around holding the rod and the fish away from her body. Jolene got the fish close enough to Andy that he caught the line and removed the fish from the hook. He got up from the bench and released the bass saying. "I've never caught a fish on the first cast."

"That's because you were usually throwing the fishing pole into the lake."

He ignored the comment. Jolene seldom missed the chance to point out fishing wasn't in his skill set and that she knew his proclivity for throwing rods and reels into the water.

"Your description makes the story Mrs. General told you to sound the lot the plot of a B-grade western movie. Some nefarious criminal has stolen the ranch."

"Her name is not Mrs. General; it's Lois Thornton, and her brother is missing. She is worried sick. Something is wrong out there."

"The first problem is that is a border ranch. Santa Cruz is the next county west of Cochise County. Cochise is the county where the Sheriff complaints about our borders not being secured. And with the level of narcotics smuggling going on out there, having a ranch on the US side of the border would be advantageous to a crook."

Burns contemplated the lake. Jolene sat beside him on the bench. He glanced back at her for a moment then looked back at the lake. "If I wanted to get into major smuggling I would hijack a border ranch in the San Rafael." Burns hesitated and looked back at Jolene.

"If that ranch was jacked, Lois Thornton's brother is probably in an unmarked grave somewhere on it. It's always possible he took a bundle of cash and left the country, but given his background I doubt it. Someone needs to go out there and ask questions and be prepared to be ignored and stonewalled.' Burns paused again, 'or worse.

"Hadfield, I expect Lois Thornton has already asked you to go out there and find out what happened to her brother. That is not the kind of place a retired police chief from Mississippi goes poking around asking questions without knowing the lay of the land. There are some serious problems that border right now. A stranger asking questions is not welcome. And, the answers might be as simple as knocking on the door of the next ranch."

"I got the impression from Lois that those ranches are far apart. Not like next door neighbors in a town."

"That is right. My next door neighbor is just across the fence. But it is close to a mile and half by road to get to that neighbor's house. Out there the ranch headquarters are more than any mile and a half apart. What works in our favor is that valley is worse than a small town neighborhood where everybody knows and minds everybody else's business."

"Burns, how do you know so much about the San Rafael Valley?"

"Short answer is I worked that Valley when I was in the Border Patrol."

"Do I want to know the long answer?"

"You need to hear it. Whether or not you want to know it."

"Do tell."

"In 2003 CRM Holdings purchased a ranch in the San Rafael Valley."

"I suppose as the owner of CRM Holdings you were behind the purchase?"

"Yes, and David Cromwell wasn't happy with it either."

"Why?"

"He didn't believe it was a wise business decision. He thought I was thinking with my cowboy side."

"Was it a good decision?"

"As far as the profit David expects from one of our ventures, it was not. However, it does not lose money. It turns a modest profit, and it keeps a pristine piece of God's creation doing what He created it to do."

"OK, usually you tell me when CRM Holdings buys something else to hold. Why didn't you mention buying a ranch?"

"You knew my emotional attachment to Arizona. I didn't want you thinking I was planning on moving back out there."

"Why would you not want to move back there? No, don't answer, that is not a fair question."

"Arizona, cost me one wife, and one other woman. I saw the lowest years of my life there. Buddy Russell says my spirit will always be there. That may be so, but I'm not going to lose another good woman to Arizona."

Burns reached over and squeezed Jolene's hand.

She smiled and kissed him.

"Burns is your ranch near Lyon Hamilton's?"

"I couldn't tell you without looking at a property map of Hamilton's ranch."

"How big is your ranch?"

"Just under twelve thousand acres." He answered sheepishly.

"Twelve thousand acres! Burns that is huge!"

"As far as western ranches go it is kind of small."

"If twelve thousand acres is small, I would hate to see big. Are we going to stay on your ranch when we go out there?"

"No."

"Why?"

"When CRM Holdings purchased the ranch. It was not popular with the community. The ranchers in the valley feared a big company buying the ranch meant the end of the valley as they knew. They worried about subdivisions and other encroachments on their way of life. I wasn't even popular with my ranch hands, at least until after closing. Then they found out the only thing that was changing was the name, the equipment, and their paychecks. The equipment and the paychecks improved. The only real change I made on the ranch was improving the airstrip and building a hanger.

"I made a mistake of not taking the time to go meet the neighbors. But I didn't want any conflict. So I figured leaving it alone was for the best. I am an absentee owner, out of sight and out of mind. Other than my ranch hands nobody in that valley knows me. That's why we're not going to stay on the CRM."

"Is CRM the name of your ranch?"

"Yes."

"OK, what do you purpose doing now?"

"In the interest of full disclosure, Lois Thornton's husband, the General, came to see me while you went to meet her. His request was simple he wants us to go out there find out what happened to Lyon Hamilton and get the ranch back."

"I take it the General is one of your discreet customers whom you do not mention."

"He is that, and he authorizes work that falls under the protection of my security clearance."

"Of which I don't have a need to know."

"Correct."

"I advised her to consider hiring your friend Buddy Russell, the private investigator, to help her out."

"Good advice, that is what I told the General we would do. I need information before we go."

"So you have decided we are going to Arizona?"

"Yes, with planning. You will report to Lois Hamilton. I will report as needed to the General. He will also provide me with clandestine support should the need arise."

"Define clandestine support."

"A black ops commando team."

"Oh, so the law and the Constitution have been suspended?"

"Only when necessary to complete the mission."

"Now I'm being to understand Lois's comment about the General's retirement not being what it seems."

"At times and always behind his back, the man is referred to as General Clout. He can probably get the President on the phone."

"So I'm expected to report the nice, polite sanitized version, and you tell the General what's happening."

"Correct, because getting the ranch back from the bad guys won't be as simple as it was in black and white TV westerns. And will take more than thirty minutes to do."

"You know, there are laws that cover that sort thing. I'm sure Arizona has them."

"They do. And we have the General."

"I would hate to tell Lois that her brother is in the south pacific living it up on the sale proceeds from the family ranch."

"It beats having to tell her he is dead or that he is alive well and in cahoots with the people who jacked his ranch."

Jolene thought about that for a moment before saying, "yeah."

"I also expect that Lois Thornton will need to file a missing person report with the Santa Cruz Sheriff. If they stonewall her on that, Rabun might be able can help. County Sheriffs have a national organization. They network with each other."

"It's hard to believe our Deputy Sundae is now Sheriff Sundae. Do you think he will ever look like a sheriff?"

"In the Hollywood sense of what a sheriff looks like, no. A sheriff looks like a guy who either fooled or convinced the voters into thinking he or she is the best person for the job. Bob Rabun didn't have to fool any voters."

Jolene smiled, "I agree with that." She studied the lake for a few minutes and then turned to Burns.

"What if we have to take the ranch back?"

"Then it gets complicated."

"Why do I get the feeling that is an understatement."

Burns gave her a sad smile. "We don't know what we will find out there. The situation could go sour anytime and turn dangerous for everybody involved. Extreme violence is a way of life with Mexican criminals. I'll give Buddy Russell call this evening and put him to work."

Jolene nodded and cast her line into the lake again. Burns watched. She caught a nice bass on the third cast. He removed the fish from the hook and put it back in the water.

"Burns can I redecorate the kitchen?"

He gave her a quizzical look before he could answer his cell phone buzzed. Andy held up his hand as if to say hold that thought and answered the phone. Hearing his end of the conversation, Jolene realized he was talking to the flight service he leased his jet to for an hourly rate. She smiled and walked back to the house the rod and reel.

Andy Burns listened to Buddy Russell's voice mail message and left the detailed message it requested. Russell recently retired from the Cochise County Sheriff's Department. Burns met the half-Apache Russell when Andy was a border patrol agent and Buddy, a patrol deputy. Russell was an investigator when he retired. He was also a licensed real estate broker. Buddy knew Southern Arizona real estate.

The San Rafael Valley is in Santa Cruz County Arizona. While Russell located his real estate business in Cochise County to the east, he was partners in a private investigations outfit based in Santa Cruz County. His partner was a former Santa Cruz County Sheriff's investigator who also operates a used car lot in Nogales Arizona. Unlike TV shows, PI work doesn't pay all the bills.

Chapter Five

Andrew Burns sat at his workbench when his cell phone buzzed. The number was an Arizona area code and belonged to Buddy Russell.

"Good Morning Buddy, how was the sunrise out there this morning." Burn said.

"The kind that would make you move back here and never leave Cowboy," Russell responded using a sobriquet for Burns the half-Apache had used since the two first met decades ago.

"And with the humidity around that swamp you live in you need to let me sell you a ranch. I don't see how you stand that place. Every time I look at the weather, there is a hurricane or tornado hitting somewhere in Alabama." Russell never missed the chance to comment on his visit to Burns' place a few years before during a once in a lifetime trip to Disney World and its attendant attractions.

"Spoken like a high desert Half Breed. I look at Arizona weather to find out what part of it is on fire. And any ranch you would try to sell me would have a house made out of that pile of mud and branches you Apaches call a teepee."

Russell snorted, "That's a wickiup Cowboy. You would be lucky if I let you buy a line shack an outhouse and a well."

"That sounds good Mi Amigo. It has been too long since I've been out there. It will likely be soon depending on what you have learned."

"The Rocking H Bar has never been listed for sale. And no one has registered a new deed, quick claim or otherwise on the property. According to the tax records, Lyon Hamilton still owns it. And the taxes are due this year and have not been paid. There are no state or federal grazing leases attached to the property. So no BLM involvement. That ranch is 2500 acres of deeded property in a prairie paradise located in one of the worse places in this country. The powers to be in Santa Cruz County have their heads stuck so far up their butts on the border issues that they can see cavities in their teeth."

"Border troubles as bad as your ex-boss says on the news?"

"If anything they are worse. A new cartel kingpin has taken over in Sonora and one of the largest ranch owners on the Mexican side of the San Rafael died. His sons and daughter like the money the cartel throws their way. A lot less work than ranching."

"What did the rancher die of?"

"Natural causes. Hard to believe, but according to my source the truth. The same source used to be my counterpart in Santa Cruz SO. A new sheriff put him on the road. His name is Bernie Cruz alias Burrito Cruz. He was born in Lochiel. There is a Scottish gringo named Cameron in his family tree. He tells me Hamilton is a distant cousin. Burrito says you won't get any help from the sheriff or any of his people. And a lot of the Border Patrol guys look the other way now."

Burns drew in a deep breath. "I hate to hear that. Is this Cruz your PI partner?"

"Yes and he has a used car lot in Nogales."

"He's not one of the TV hucksters advertising Cruz's Cruisers low ride in style is he?"

Russell laughed, "Burrito will love that one. You two will get along well."

"Based on what Jolene has learned, we will likely be out that way in a couple of weeks."

"So you are still seeing that good-looking deputy police chief from wherever around there she's from. The one that fishes."

"Yeah, she took an early retirement and moved in here. I encourage her to keep going to fishing tournaments. It keeps her mind off redecorating the place." Burns said.

Russell laughed out loud. "Yep, that's woman for you, Cowboy. Pretty soon you won't be able to wear spurs in your house. On the serious side amigo, whatever is happening in the San Rafael smells. And it won't likely be settled inside the system either. Between Burrito and me we've got your back for whatever you need to do. I've got a real estate rental listing on the Double B Ranch. It's a casita with a barn and a corral. It was a line shack in the old days. It has an RV hookup and a well. The rancher uses it as a source of income source. He rents it to writers, cowboy wannabes and whoever else. And the good thing, it is across the fence from the north end of the Rocking H Bar. It would put you close to the action. The rancher will do a short term lease on it. And, if you are interested, the guy has a practically new high-end motorhome sitting on the RV hookup at his headquarters. An old couple from Seattle drove it down here. They were terrified of driving it back home. So they put it for sale in place, agreed to pay the hookup rent until it sells or someone is hired to drive home. It's not cheap, but it is an option. It has satellite TV and the internet."

"Take some pictures of it, inside and out. Email me those and the particulars on the casita."

"I will do and one more thing Andy. Don't let that woman get away from you."

Burns disconnected the cell phone and stuck it in his pocket. He walked outside and sat in a chair on his covered patio that doubled as the firing line for his range. He watched the lake and saw Jolene docking her Ranger Bass Boat. He watched her answer her cell phone. He saw one of his tractors moving along the edge of the lake. That one had an eight-foot rotary mower on the rear and a boom mounted four-foot mower for working the shoreline. Burns hired man Wilson Gilmore was driving the tractor.

The 70 something ageless six-foot five-inch-tall mahogany skin color raw bone African American's hair looked like white steel wool. Wilson Gilmore was a paroled murderer. A crime he committed in various degrees three times. After spending 45 years in the state penitentiary. The parole board figured he was too old to cause any more trouble and let him out. No one bothered to explain checkbooks and social security direct deposits to him. Wilson didn't know how to balance a checkbook. He wound up in the Baldwin County Jail for writing bad checks. A sympathetic jailer brought Wilson's plight to the attention of then Chief Deputy Bob Rabun; after Wilson beat a fellow inmate of the same race senseless while the former was working as a trustee. The jailbird victim did not perform work to Wilson's standard. With income accumulating due to no checkbook access, Wilson had funds to make good his checks, which were all written to a large grocery store. Wilson Gilmore liked to feed hungry people, something he'd learned in the prison chapel. Rabun knew Andrew Burns was looking for a hired hand. A call to Andy and the judge set Wilson free on an unofficial work release house arrest at the Burns recently constructed caretakers cabin.

Theodis Cleckler proclaimed the situation a blessing for both Andrew Burns and Wilson Gilmore. Jolene Hadfield, on the other hand, failed to see any blessing in the fact a convicted murderer now lived at Burns place. When Jolene encountered Wilson during a weekend visit shortly after he moved in, the huge black man held a hot cast iron Dutch oven his massive hands with a kitchen towel wrapped around it for protection. When Jolene answered the knock at Andy's front door, Wilson politely explained he had made an apple cobbler for Mister Andy and his lady, and that he needed to sit it in the kitchen.

Burns came in the room about that time and told Wilson to take the pot to the kitchen. When he was out of sight and not necessarily out of hearing range, Hadfield inquired as to who he was. The explanation complete with the admission of murder convictions, almost caused Hadfield to pitch what some southern folks would call a running fit. She didn't. Probably because Jolene realized it wasn't her place to comment. Theodis Cleckler arriving with a church van full of children helped alleviate the meltdown as well. The apple cobbler being the best she'd ever tasted caused a lot of forgiveness. And Wilson explained in a way that only he could when he said.

"Miz Jolene, I's always got along with the white folks. I jus can't stand niggers."

Gilmore finally won her over a few weeks later when he presented her with a model of her bass boat made of popsicle and match sticks. It was painted and detailed right down to the license numbers on the bow. Now all his fines and checks were paid, he no longer reported to a parole officer. The structure of having jobs to do along with a place to live gave him what he needed. He handled the chores and farm tractors with ease. The evil burro had become reasonably tame with Wilson around. He did not drive a truck or car and would not learn. He was picked up on Sundays by a church group, and they returned him before dark. Wilson asked Andy if he could purchase a pair of mules with his money. The long-eared beasts were an interesting addition to the place. As was the large garden Wilson planted after plowing the ground with the mules. The garden had since turned into a forty-acre farm inside Burns' square mile. A farm that provided fresh produce to local people who couldn't afford groceries.

Burns contemplated this and the San Rafael problem. That could easily go from bad to worse, very worse and very bad. He watched Jolene approach and considered her involvement. She would have to share in the all the risks. Was solving the mystery of Lyon Hamilton's disappearance worth the risk? Was it worth the risk for both of them?

Jolene sat down next to Andy. She enjoyed the patio and its view for a minutes before recounting her phone call.

"David Cromwell has gotten all the paperwork from Lois Thornton, and he has been in touch with Lyon Hamilton's lawyer out in Nogales Arizona. That lawyer is J.P. Williams and according to David, he is not happy about Hamilton's disappearance. He is willing to work on her behalf to resolve the issue and inspect the bank records. He will subpoena records and deeds involving the sale of the ranch. He said serving it would be a problem and getting compliance may be difficult. Have you heard from Buddy Russell?"

Burns passed on he learned from Russell.

"How soon before we go to Arizona?" Jolene asked

"I don't have any pressing projects at the moment. A few people are discussing building rifles but no commitments. I got an email from timeshare company this morning. The Citation is due into Mobile Aerospace tonight. So it I've put it on a forty-eight-hour owner priority notice. Hanger space at the Nogales FBO will not be a problem. When I get the information from Russell, we'll set a date."

"Didn't you say the CRM ranch has an airstrip and a hanger? Why not use that instead?"

"The airstrip on the CRM is dirt and even if it weren't the jet won't fit. On the other hand; the MU-2 goes in there quite well. Using the jet is, a misdirection. I don't want anything connecting us to the CRM."

"Sounds good. But what are you going to do with a motorhome when we finish out there?"

"I haven't decided yet. Most likely it will wind up at the campground for sale."

"Is that campground making any money yet?" Jolene asked, knowing it was a property David Cromwell recommended Burns buy. CRM Holdings had grown in acquisitions and income since Andy inherited the original company from Charlie Raifield and changed the name. Business moguls would not have predicted the success of an organization owned by a retired cop and gunsmith. It was the combination of business manager

Cromwell, lawyer, and CPA, along with Burns instinct that made things work. Andy always listened when his mentor, the late Charlie Raifield, spoke about business. The Citation jet was from a company facing bankruptcy they purchased and turned around. When Hadfield learned CRM owned the lodge where she recuperated, it became her favorite perk. The aggravating part was she could only use the place when accommodations were available, which wasn't very often. Burns would not use owner privilege to displace paying guests.

"The campground is doing well. All it needed was to be maintained correctly and kept clean. Fresh paint and advertising make the difference. They get a lot of big motor homes stopping through up there. It being within sight of I-10 doesn't hurt either. David is looking at a hotel franchise now."

"Another place we can't stay at unless space is available?"

"There are several properties involved. I'm not sure it is viable. However, David thinks they are a good investment."

The gate alarm sounded. Burns glanced at his watch. "Looks like my night sight customers are here. A couple of rookies that are starting the police academy next week." He got up to greet his clients.

<h1 style="text-align:center">Chapter Six</h1>

W. Ashton Bradford sat quietly on a bar stool in one of the smaller lounges in the Tucson Casino. He liked the atmosphere. You could carry on a conversation; the gaming machine noise was nonexistent. There was an intimate feeling in the room, a place where one might meet a consort for an affair or a high priced hooker might rendezvous with a client. Ashton was always on the lookout for one of these women. This night, he paid more attention to a man he figured for an employee of the casino's security department. Bradford believed himself an expert on body language and thought he could spot a crook regardless of dress or surroundings. The new guy was a predatory thug with brains. The man casually walked through the bar seeing everyone there and not acknowledging the presence of anyone. There was no prey worthy of his efforts in this room. Bradford liked the vibe coming from the man.

The bartender eased toward Bradford discreetly waiting to speak until the man left the room. "That is the house security supervisor for this shift. He's ex-FBI like most of the security honchos. Scuttlebutt says he didn't leave the feds on the best of terms. His name is Ron Kroll."

Ashton looked toward the entrance as slid a folded fifty-dollar bill across the bar under his fingertips. "Thanks, Fred. Bring me another one if you will."

"Certainly Mr. Bradford," the barkeep said as he caused the bill to disappear.

At 5' 10" in his early fifties, Ron Kroll was in excellent physical condition with the skills of a Hollywood A-list actor. He did not have the classic looks of a leading man. However, Kroll the chameleon could turn into any person he chose to be. Once, he convinced a church congregation he was a humble preacher. A skilled motorcycle rider, Kroll's first undercover assignment was that of a fearsome biker. The gang he infiltrated still hadn't figured out who he was. As an everyday FBI special agent, Kroll was mediocre at best. As an undercover operative, he was the best the bureau had. Unfortunately, he ignored all the rules, the Constitution of the United States, the Bible, the policies of the Catholic Church, and the Baptist convention; and especially the rules and policies of the Federal Bureau of Investigation.

The current gig was the easiest to play, and the most dangerous. All Kroll had to lose was his life and his federal pension. Kroll retained an attorney who was successful in suing the government's alphabet agencies over personnel matters. The lawyer did not believe the FBI would honor the contract and Kroll would have a protracted legal battle to get his pension. The original contract was in Kroll's safe deposit box, and the lawyer had a copy. He awaited Ron's call.

Bradford casually watched Kroll walk toward the gaming floors. A magician was the only person who could fool Ashton Bradford. Ron Kroll was a magician. A call to a bureau contact would begin Bradford's background check of his potential employee. He thumbed through his phone and found Adam Hall's number. Bradford figured Hall for a kindred spirit. A former agent who'd left the bureau for a cushy casino security chief's job.

It took Hall a few minutes to answer the recorded phone. Unbeknown to Bradford, he was the only one with the number. Hall's involvement was confidential. Adam Hall and the Director had gone through the FBI Academy together. They were good friends. Ransom Carter was the only person other than the Director who knew Hall's role.

"Speak," Hall said bluntly.

"You still using all your fancy cameras and spy gear to cheat in your houses poker games asshole?"

"Only when a dumbass dickhead like welch on the bet Ass Bradford is at the table."

"What do you know about an ex-bureau type named Ron Kroll?"

"You give up on foreplay Ass?"

"We are both busy trying to screw the house, why waste time?"

"Kroll throw you or one of your thugs out of a club somewhere?"

"We have not had the pleasure yet. I wanted to get the scoop on Kroll first."

"I vouched for his resume as him not being a thief. It's the only way any house would hire him with his track record."

"What is that?"

"He is a rule breaking heavy-handed bastard who would stomp a confession out anybody. He hates Muslims with a passion and will shoot first without asking questions. He was behind several unresolved killings on some undercover assignments. The Bureau believes he's changed sides and has a ton of cash stashed somewhere. With their typical ineptness, they can't find it. And Kroll is smart enough to hide it. One other thing that should endear him to you." Hall waited to make Bradford ask.

"What would that be?"

"Your favorite internal hitman L. Winston Glover had the privilege of firing Kroll."

"I bet that son of a bitch had an orgasm if he still has balls to have them."

"Well, I'm not privy to what shape his nuts were in when he got to the ER."

"THE EMERGENCY ROOM! WHAT THE HELL HAPPEN?"

Adam Hall knew the hook was in deep, and it was time to set it.

"When Kroll turned in his gun and creds he knocked Skinny Whinny on his ass right in front of everybody."

"What happen then?"

"Kroll strolled out the office with his middle finger extended over his shoulder. And what is really funny, is nobody saw a thing. They said Skinny must have slipped and fallen."

"Now Hall that last part sounds like something that would happen in a police squad room during a civil rights investigation, not in the screw your buddy bureau."

"You're right. The field office was going to prosecute, but I understand the director squashed it. But Skinny won't give it up and will go around the director's back to get Kroll indicted. The bottom line is the bureau wanted Kroll gone and Skinny getting knocked on his ass was good payback for his screwing up the case against you."

"Well, I'm going buy Kroll a drink."

"Bradford, I don't care what side of the legal system you're on, or that you would be a shoe-in on the national Democratic parties' ticket for high office. But take this as a warning, be very careful around Ron Kroll, he is trouble, big trouble. The bureau won't give up on him, a chicken shit assault on an agent charge is not good enough. I know they would like to have your butt indicted and charged. Fortunately, you aren't nearly the prize Ron Kroll is. Be careful around him."

"Thanks we'll talk later." Bradford hung up the phone. Adam Hall leaned back and put his feet up on his desk. He smiled and said, "gotcha" out loud.

Ron Kroll relaxed in the security supervisor's office. He opened the internet on the office computer and promptly went to the Backpage website. He clicked on the escorts link and began to scroll through the advertisements for female companionship. Soon he found the ad, *Penelope Lustful Latina*. He took out his cell phone and called the number shown in the add. The phone rang six times before a female answered with a sultry voice. FBI Special Agent Ivalou Vargas sounded like the hooker she portrayed.

"Hey, Penelope, this your favorite gringo Ron. I get off work in an hour, and I wanna see you."

"Baby I would love that; can you do two fifty?"

"For you yes, and if you dress for me and let me unwrap the package there's a nice tip in for you."

"What you want me to wear sweetie?"

"Tank top with a mini and a hot pink satin thong."

"Oueeee I love it when I have a thong up my crack. I have just the thing. Babe, I'm out on Speedway. Give me a call when you're on the way and I'll give you the address."

"Will do sweetheart, see you soon."

Kroll clicked off the phone and pictured Vargas giving the finger to him by proxy. He knew the hot Hispanic agent could not stand dental floss underwear as she called it. During a clandestine planning meeting between Kroll and Vargas, they plotted the hooker gig as she called it. Ivalou Vargas was an excellent undercover operative and role player. A fourteen-year veteran agent whose youngest looks belied her age. She had the body for a slut suit and heels as she referred to one of the hooker outfits. But getting her to wear it was another story. The trash talk on the phone was for the benefit of who might be listening. Kroll and Vargas developed a series of coded text messages which even a veteran vice cop would believe as hooker and john communications. They would always meet for an incall, hooker slang for the john meeting at her place. The location would be a seedy low-end motel in an area frequented by prostitutes.

Special Agents Desmond Taylor and Mickey Morris played the part of Vargas' pimps and enforcer. The African American agents were perfect for the role and dressed for the part. They would deliver Vargas to the meeting and provide physical intimidation to others. They were also skilled in counter surveillance. A search of available undercover vehicles turned up a Cadillac Escalade with deep tinted windows and wheels & rims worthy of the most discriminating pimp. The Caddy was one of the several vehicles in their stable of rides.

In the text code repertoire, a request for an outcall, the hooker travels to the john, meant extraction was needed. Either a full blown SWAT rescue or a sneaky undercover pickup. The difference was decided by Kroll requesting a specific outfit. Kroll pre-programed his Penelope cell phone with these text messages. Vargas in her Penelope role would not have to put up with real johns calling, Kroll's calls were the only ones her Penelope phone would allow through, all others went to voice mail.

Ron Kroll liked his backup team. They were all good agents, and Ivalou Vargas didn't hurt his eyes to look at either. He liked her attitude.

Vargas received a message earlier from Undercover Operations Supervisor Havelee Harris about Bradford's call to Adam Hall. She placed the add on Backpage. Kroll checked the hooker ads daily. If the Penelope add was there, he knew to call. He could call direct if he had something urgent to report or send a help code. The ruse would be necessary for him to get into town without raising suspicion when he penetrated Bradford's organization.

The pimped up Cadillac Escalade drove by Special Agent Desmond Taylor resplendently attired as a pimp arrived at a low-end independent motel. Real working girls languished around doorways and watched as the car stopped in front of the office.

Ivalou got out and went up to the outside security window that allowed checking in transactions without entry into the actual office. Mickey Morris or M&M as he preferred got out of the Caddy and leaned against it. He glared at all those watching, sending a don't screw with me or my girl message to anyone so inclined. Vargas returned with the room key and pointed toward a second floor room; this development called for a different plan.

Ron Kroll knew when he arrived at the dump the room was upstairs. He spotted the Escalade parked where Desmond or Des could observe everyone moving. Kroll walked to the room; his demeanor suggested he wasn't shopping girls. He already had one. When knocked on the door, M&M opened it and stepped outside. He motioned for Kroll to raise his hands and patted him down for weapons. Which he found and did not remove, for obvious reasons. M&M demanded payment.

"NO, I PAY HER!" Kroll growled loud enough for everyone around to hear. "NOT YOU ASSHOLE!"

M&M answered in kind. "LISTEN HONKEY MUTHER FUCKER, YOU JUS, BE SURE YOU PAYS HER CAUSE SHE WILL SCREAM AND I GOTS A ROOM KEY. AN YOU GOTS THIRTY MINUTES TO DO YOU BIDDNESS!"

Kroll stepped into the room and slammed the door. M&M made a sure everyone saw him looking at his watch. He crossed his arms and leaned against the rail staring at the motel room door.

"M&M is having too much fun with this gig," Kroll said as he sat on a bed. The room had two. Vargas sat facing him on the other. She smiled.

"They both do." She was sitting on top of a folded towel and had another one wrapped around her thighs. Kroll could see her bare legs from knees down.

"Pick a better sleazebag motel next time. This place has probably got lice and HIV on the bed spread."

"Why the hell you think I'm sitting on a towel with another one wrapped around me?"

"Your bare ass is cold?"

"Like hell, Kroll, I don't want to catch anything from sitting on this bed. And for the record, my butt is not bare. I'm wearing shorts and underwear."

"I don't blame you. So Bradford took the bait?"

"Yes, Havelee called and said he got in touch with Adam Hall. Harris says tech support has also picked up queries he made to agents and support staff he is known to contact. Apparently, he has more than a few inside people."

"That is not good. It makes this stunt even more important. Bradford is a known whore dog. He likes his pay to play. You are going to have to give him a come on a preacher couldn't resist. He likes high-end girls. Not the kind hanging in this parking lot. You are going to have to look like you are worth several hundred not twenty bucks."

Vargas extended a middle finger. "UP YOURS KROLL"

"Careful M&M might kick in the door. And I would hate to have staged a fight in this nasty place."

Right on cue, there was a heavy knock on the door.

"LOU YOU ALL RIGHT?"

"YES THIS LIMP DICK CHEAPSKATE CAN'T GET IT UP WITHOUT HAVING A FINGER STUCK UP HIS ASS AND HE WON'T PAY MORE FOR IT."

Kroll tried hard not to laugh at the act. Ivalou was smiling.

"Remind me not to get you on an op where you have to play a cheap ho."

"I'm not cheap."

"Never said you were. Just dress for success and we will bait Bradford."

"Got any ideas about getting Bradford to strike up a conversation with you?" Vargas asked.

"He always sits at the bar. You come in the lounge dressed upscale, sit down and strike up a conversation with him. At some point, I will rescue him from you."

"How much groping, I am I going to have to put up with before you ride to the rescue?"

"That depends on how much you grope him. If he wants to cop a feel tell him to pay up."

Ivalou proffered her favorite gesture at that answer.

"Bradford has a bodyguard with him. The guy sits at a table and nurses a beer while he watches his bosses back. You play up to Bradford, but be classy about it, his little head will kick in. Once you establish contact and start to get friendly, I will send a one-word text to M&M. That will be his cue to come in and act like a badass pimp out to collect the bread and rescue his ho. Bradford's thug will make a move, and I'll take him out of the game. The uniformed security team will escort M&M out and give the thug to the cops. I will escort you out with the admonishment that if you work in my house, you don't work with a pimp."

"I see where you are going with that plan. Bradford gets the idea you will look the other way as long as there are no pimps involved."

"Correct. We know Bradford likes high price working girls. I want him to think I like the same thing. Once I'm inside his circle of trust, you have to stay in the role. I expect some his goons will follow me to our meetings. He has a good computer hacker on his payroll. That is why I want to look like a john meeting a prostitute. When Bradford starts thinking, I'm just getting laid. He will drop his guard."

"What if he wants to get in on the act?"

Kroll considered that for a moment. "We'll cross that bridge when and if we come to it. I don't think he goes for the trashy look you have now."

"Thanks, asshole!"

"You are good enough to change your appearance from a Backpage hooker to a high-end call girl. Should any of his people get a good enough look at you in the casino, I doubt they will make you dressed as you are now. For this bar gig, look elegant, high class. You have to turn heads in the place when you walk in."

"I can do that. Just don't fall all over yourself looking."

"I'll try not to. Be prepared for it to happen in a couple of days. I will text you from my second phone to your other number. One more thing, are we getting any hassle out of the local field office?"

"Yes, Havelee says the Tucson SAC is not happy about not being in the need to know circle. But Havelee says for us not to worry about it. The Director will handle SAC Lane."

"Is Harris still planning on coming out here to run the investigation?"

"Yes, when you get inside Bradford's organization she will be on her way. She also has authorization for another agent on our team. She has her eye on a first office agent in Phoenix. He's a young looking Latino.

"He will work for backup. Maybe other things. We have to play by ear day to day with a job like this."

"Ron, we have your back."

"I'm not worried about you guys backing me up. I'm worried about the chain of command."

"Changing the subject, do you have any idea what Bradford is up to?"

"Based on his background, he is probably good for anything as long as he covers his ass. I expect, with him being this close to the border, smuggling is involved. The big smuggling money is in narcotics. He is either partnered with or looking to partner up with a cartel. And I would also put money on human trafficking. He trolls the casino bars for expensive hookers. So you have to look like you are worth a few hundred."

"Trust me Kroll I'm worth more than that without makeup!"

"I would say you're something money can't buy." He gave her his sincerest smile.

"Flattery will get you everywhere, but high price dinners help."

"Yeah, I will keep that in mind. I think we've covered everything. You can shake the bed and moan real loud for ten minutes or so."

"Ten minutes my ass, ten seconds is more like it!"

"You must be speaking from experience."

"Up yours Kroll." Vargas punctuated the insult with an extended finger.

Ron Kroll was more than impressed, when a couple of nights later, Ivalou Vargas entered the casino wearing a black cocktail dress. The hem stopped several inches above her knees and the topside revealed cleavage. The dress was stunning on her and gave Kroll the impression it was something she would wear for a night on the town and not selected as a high-class hooker outfit. Ron was glad he was available. He thought she might be as well, team banter aside, Kroll liked his colleague.

Vargas perched on a stool a couple of places away from Ashton Bradford. She ordered a drink and went into her Penelope the hooker act smiling demurely at the distinguished looking Bradford. He took the bait like a Billy goat in heat.

"Put that on my tab," he said to the bartender, picking up his drink and moving to the stool next to hers.

"Thank you," she responded followed with a smile and come hither look that made Ron Kroll instantly jealous. From his vantage point in a rear corner, he could watch discreetly. He doubted Bradford knew he was there. Kroll had entered via a staff only door when Bradford and his lackey thug had their backs turned. The goon, Numb Nuts Norman, sat a table watching his bosses back. Kroll figured he was armed and could present a problem as the gig played out.

Bradford did not waste any time. "I'm Ashton Bradford; friends call me Ash. And whom do I have the pleasure of buying a drink?"

"I'm Penelope." She answered complete with a smile, and another come hither look. "Pleased to meet you, Ash." Vargas lifted her drink in a toasting gesture and then took a discreet sip leaving lipstick on the glass.

"If the last name is Cruz you're much prettier in person."

"No," she giggled, "Thank you. I thought you were George Clooney."

That statement got a laugh out of Bradford. "He wouldn't hang out in a sleazy joint like this. And you've got too much class to be in here. Vegas is more your style."

"I'm going to be in Las Vegas tomorrow night. This place is close to the motel, and I thought I would check out the action."

"What kind of action is your pleasure?"

Vargas giggled and fixed Bradford with another come hither look when she answered.

"Pleasure."

"Now that's what I call a lady after my heart," Bradford said with a lusty smile and an obvious look at her cleavage.

Right on cue M&M stalked into the lounge and glared at Vargas's back. Dressed in full enforcer attire, all black with gold chains and menacing look; his sudden appearance caused the unknowing bartender to push his panic button summoning uniformed security officers.

Numb Nuts Norman got up and moved to intercept M&M, who was a few steps from Vargas's back. She smiled and placed her hand on Bradford's thigh halfway to his crotch. Ass Bradford immediately forgot about anything else.

Approaching M&M the goon reached under his jacket. The situation was about to go seriously off-script. Kroll rushed Norman from behind and delivered a vicious punch to his kidney. Kroll spun him around and finished the job with a powerful jab to the sternum. Numb Nuts went to the floor, and Kroll dropped his brass knuckles back into his suit coat pocket without anyone noticing.

Four casino security men hurried into the lounge as Kroll stood up from removing the moaning thug's gun. Ron looked at his employees.

"The one on the floor goes to the cops, along with his gun."

Kroll gave the gun to the closest security officer. "Let the medics look at him and let the cops make the call if he needs the hospital."

Kroll pointed at M&M, "Shake down the pimp if he's packing give him to the cops. If not escort him out. And make sure he gets in his car and leaves the property. Give him a trespass warning."

M&M gave Kroll a belligerent look as the security man frisked him. Finding no weapon, the security officers escorted him outside, M&M played it well, snarling and making threats and daring his escorts to touch him again. Casino EMT's arrived and placed Numb Nuts on a gurney.

Kroll turned to Vargas, ignoring Bradford. "You will thank this gentleman for the drink and leave. Next time you come in here, lose the pimp. Because if I see him again, he is going to be just like the guy who left on the stretcher." Ron pulled a card and fifty- dollar bill from his pocket. He gave them to Vargas. "This will cover a cab and a meal. If you're going to work this house, you don't need a pimp. If you need help getting away from that asshole, call me. You have my card. The security officer at the door will escort you to the lobby door and get you a cab."

Kroll placed his hand on Vargas's shoulder and turned her toward the lounge entrance.

She pouted and said, "you know how to ruin a girl's night."

"Just consider it the penalty for a pimp following you into my joint."

Ivalou Vargas smiled seductively at Kroll as she stuck the fifty and the card in her bra. She stuck her tongue out at him and turned to leave with a security escort. Her swaying her hips got Kroll's attention.

Bradford said, "Thanks for screwing up what might have been a great piece of ass."

"My name is Ron Kroll. I am a house security supervisor. You may have gotten more than you expected. Working girls are going to be in casinos. We keep an eye on them, and we don't allow pimps. We don't want our customers robbed. I'd never seen her before, and we'd gotten notice of Latina chick with a couple of pimps working casinos and mugging their johns. You're a regular, and we take care of our customers. Your tab tonight is on the house." Kroll gestured to the bartender.

"Thank you, Mr. Kroll, I'm Ashton Bradford. I would like to buy you a drink sometime. Now if you have the time."

"Pleased to meet you, Mr. Bradford. I'll take a raincheck on the drink. And if you call that fellow I put down a bodyguard. You can do better. Have a good evening."

Kroll strolled out of the lounge and onto the casino floor. He couldn't get how good Ivalou Vargas looked off his mind.

"I ain't never seen nobody punch like that." M&M offered his fellow team members. The three sat in the bar of the hotel where they stayed in Tempe Arizona. Far enough away from the Tucson casino not to be made by those they hunted. Still close enough to play the game.

"You can drop the hood dialect M&M we're good guys again," chided Desmond Taylor. All three agents dressed casually for the impromptu team debriefing they were holding at a corner table out of earshot of other customers.

Ivalou checked her email when they got back to Tempe and found one from Kroll. It said, '**You looked good tonight. K.**' She smiled.

The two male agents turned their attention to a couple of ladies who were now sitting at the bar. Vargas got up and looked sharply at Desmond and M&M. "Remember you two studs are only make believe pimps. I don't need to explain to Havelee how the two of you got arrested for the real thing."

She high fived both of them, and M&M was treated to her extended middle finger when he said. "You got that right Penelope those two ain't got nutten you ain't got dats hotter."

M&M told Desmond. "That lady can give you the bird quicker than Ron K can knock somebody on their ass."

"I'd of like to have seen that," Desmond said. Ron Kroll reminded him of the late Lyle Thigman.

CHAPTER SEVEN

The rear seats were folded flat in the Chevy Suburban. So Numb Nuts Nate Norman could ride with a modicum of comfort. Numb Nuts would eventually recover from a cracked sternum. And the bruised kidney would heal, maybe. He would not be taken back to the hospital if he continued to piss blood after a day or two. Numb Nuts would either mend on his own or, if he were lucky, be dropped off near a homeless shelter with a few bucks in his pocket. If his luck failed, an unmarked shallow grave waited for him.

They slipped out of the emergency room when the bored cop watching Numb Nuts dozed off. Bradford wasn't worried about the weapons charge or the hospital bill. Numb Nuts registered into the Emergency Room under an alias. Normally W. Ashton rode in the rear seats, with Numb Nuts riding shotgun and Pauli Dumas driving. Tonight, Bradford rode up front. He considered the evening's events and Ron Kroll. Kroll was right; Bradford could do better than Norman for a bodyguard. The question was would Kroll cross the line and be happy with bodyguard duties or would he want a larger role? He was quick as hell with his fists. Numb Nuts had no idea of what hit him. But Kroll was smart, and he and Bradford certainly had a common enemy, L. Winston Glover.

Kroll's assault of L. Winston Glover was factual. It happened. Bradford had other sources besides Adam Hall to confirm it. Those same sources verified Kroll's termination as being real. Another high recommendation was Hall saying he

75

would trust Kroll to work in one his joints. Hall was security chief for a large casino corporation and was as straight as they come. He also knew that having contacts on the other side was just good business. Kroll was the real deal in Bradford's mind. And he was going to recruit Kroll with the zeal of an Alabama football coach after a high school standout.

There was no one W. Ashton Bradford hated more than L. Winston Glover. The professional integrity fanatic almost single handed ruined Bradford's FBI career. Not that Bradford was expecting a long distinguished award-winning run in the bureau. It was more about learning the ropes and where to catch what fell through the cracks. Once as a rebellious teenager his mother asked her first cousin to counsel young Ashton. The cousin was a pipe smoking lieutenant in a suburb police department of Birmingham Alabama, his dear old momma's hometown. Later in his FBI days, Bradford learned the PD his relative worked was more of a municipal night watchman's service than a police department. Before policies and state law disallowed deadly street justice on the fleeing felons; the small agency was known for its officers shooting burglars and providing ass beatings for misdemeanants. The state fire marshal condemned the stingy little kingdom's jail. However, its occupants seldom stayed longer than overnight, if that long.

Bradford vividly remembered the cousin lieutenant's pipe stunk and, most of all, his advice. *If you do something illegal, do it by yourself. That way nobody can rat you out to get their butts out of jail. If you partner up, always make sure the other guy has more to lose that you do.* And the one Bradford liked the most, *If you stole the church and swallowed it when you got caught and the steeple is sticking out your ass. Never change your story.*

All great lessons for a cop or a criminal. For his entire life, Ass Bradford was a more a member of the later occupation than the former. As an IRS auditor, taking bribes was his specialty. During this time, he finished night school for lawyers and passed the bar exam. His having a license to practice law and being a CPA to boot made him a shoo-in for the FBI academy. Luck helped because with creds like his no one bothered to check with some of his IRS supervisors. FBI agents didn't like the IRS any more than the rest of the citizens. They were only handy when the Fine Bunch of Idiots decided if they couldn't get you. They dropped a dime on you to the IRS for special harassment.

It was money, big money that led to W. Ashton's last career change. He was the only one who knew how much. L. Winston Glover's hubris kept him from really learning the score. Ashton planned to show his occupation as a criminal mastermind on the bogus tax return he would file after his current project paid off in the two-digit millions. He would mail the return at the last mailbox before he crossed the border leaving the country for good.

Bradford's thoughts were interrupted when Pauli Dumas farted. It was a loud burst with an instant horrendous stench. Dumas guffawed, "Damn, that was a wet one!"

Bradford was fumbling with the window switch on his door. "What the hell did you eat Porn Dude? I've smelled better sewers. Roll the fucking windows down! You got the child lock switched on dumb ass!"

"Some nasty tacos at a Mexican joint across from the hospital. Man, they were bad." Pauli answered.

Bradford put up with the crude Dumas, whose protruding overbite teeth, rectangular face and wide set eyes and slovenly looks; would make him a shoo-in for the lead part should someone produce a Frankenstein porn flick. The only plus side to Pauli Dumas was his IQ. The man was a genius. His computer skills were world class, and he could hack any system. You just couldn't take him inside a good joint. If there was such an affliction, he was oversexed. The man was always in some state of arousal. Dumas was a sadist; whose table manners were on par with those of a monkey.

"Pauli if you shit your pants. Stop the damn truck get that tarp out of the back and put it on the seat!" Bradford ordered.

"Boss I thought we were gonna wrap Numb Nuts in that tarp if he croaks."

"If he's dead dried shit on the tarp won't bother him."

Numb Nuts let out a loud groan from the back of the truck.

When Porn Dude got the tarp on the seat, they started moving again.

"Listen to me Pauli. Nate is going to be out of action for a while. And you are going to have come inside the casinos with me. Tomorrow you go into town and buy some decent clothes in the right size. And you will buy underwear as well. You will not go up to women wearing short skirts and try to hunch their butts. I'm going to get some salt peter for you take before we leave."

"My mom gave me some that stuff when I was in high school. It gives me the shits worse than bad Mexican food."

"Damn," Bradford muttered and breathed in the desert night air as he shook his head.

Five days later Ron Kroll spotted Bradford on his usual stool at the small bar. Kroll walked over and sat on the stool next to him.

"Bounced any hookers lately Kroll?" Bradford asked lifting his glass toward Jack.

"One last night."

"She look as good as the Mexican chick the other night."

"No, the one last night was on the high end of the skank scale."

"Sounds like the usual choices for this place. Now and then a decent looking one shows up. Never one like that woman the other night."

"Yeah, that one was a real looker. The type I would expect to see in a high-end Vegas joint, not in Tucson Arizona. Her being out of place was the first give away. The pimp showing up was the second." Kroll said.

"Well her looks blindsided me completely," Bradford answered truthfully. "I didn't see the pimp until too late. My brain totally went to the little head."

"That happens to the best of us. I would have made the same mistake with that chick. A word of advice Mr. Bradford. You don't need a bodyguard in this house. If you think different, your man needs to leave his gun in the car. FYI the piece he was carrying showed up stolen when the local cops ran it. It's not my business. And no offense intended, you look like you can afford a higher class thug. A lot of ex-special ops guys out there."

"You're an ex-cop aren't you?" Bradford asked, a knowing smile on his face."

"What tipped you?"

"Only cops say, ran it."

"It takes one to know one."

"You got me there. I was a fed."

"Which letters or were you a secret?"

Bradford laughed. "Never heard it put that way. I was FBI. And you were?"

"The same, FBI."

"How did you get along with the rest of them?"

"The Marshals Service was OK. The DEA too fast too loose. The BATF just hangers on trying to justify their jobs. The Secret Service, everything but the protection detail. I couldn't jump in front of a bullet for the current clown."

"Me neither, what'd you think about our former outfit?"

"Short form, chicken shit."

"Is there a long form?"

Kroll shook his head with a disgusted expression. "The FBI needs an enema. And a king size tube needs to be inserted in the office of professional responsibility." Kroll struck the bar with his fist. "Don't get me started."

"I take it you were asked to resign?"

"I didn't get that courtesy."

"I did, but I wouldn't exactly call it courteous. The bastards were trying to indict me."

"What did you do to rate them trying for an indictment?"

"They claimed I accepted a large sum of cash."

"I'm not going to ask if you did or not. That's not my business." Kroll drummed his fingers on the bar and looked in the back bar mirror as he spoke. "I had the opportunity for three million. But I stomped the rag headed bastard's ass and hauled him to jail and turned in the money. Now I wish I'd took the cash and said Allah be great or whatever. I wouldn't be working in this joint worrying about how I'm going to live the rest of my life. Those bastards got my retirement." He kept his fists clenched on the bar resisting the urge to pound on it again.

Bradford watched Kroll and said. "You look like you need that drink I offered."

"I do," Kroll sighed and motioned to the bartender. "Stoli straight up."

They sipped their drinks quietly for a few minutes. Bradford spoke first.

"I checked you out with some of my old contacts in the Bureau. I've got a couple of questions for you."

"Ask."

"What did it feel like to knock Skinny Winnie on his ass?"

Kroll laughed out loud. "Great! Jumping in the sack with that Latina hooker from the other night wouldn't feel any better. You could do that more than once. Skinny Winnie was a once in a lifetime deal."

It was Bradford's turn to laugh aloud. He hoisted his glass, "I'll drink to that!"

They touched glasses. "You said a couple of questions. What's the second?" Kroll asked.

"I want to why you didn't kick Skinny in the balls while you had the chance?"

"Skinny Winnie hasn't got any balls to kick. He took it in the ass so much from AD's that they probably shrunk back inside."

"You hate that son of a bitch as much I do."

"I wouldn't insult women or dogs by calling him a son of a bitch. There aren't words bad enough to describe him." Kroll spit in a nearby waste can.

Both men finished their drinks. Bradford ordered another. Kroll passed, saying he was on the clock. And he didn't need to be run off for drinking on the job.

As Kroll started to leave, Bradford turned around on his stool and addressed him. It was a slow night they were the only ones in the bar other than the bartender, who was busy at the other end of the bar.

"I can guarantee you five million cash. It could get you killed. You are probably the only person who could get it done and get away clean. I think you hate them enough to do it. Are you interested in coming over to the other side? If you say no, it stops here, and we never had this conversation."

Kroll stepped back and studied Bradford, searching deep into his eyes.

"I'm your man. You know where to find me." Kroll said looking straight into Bradford's eyes. He turned and walked out of the bar into the casino.

A couple of hours later Ivalou Vargas received a text.

Hey Penelope Hope ur Workin Need 2 see U bad.

CHAPTER EIGHT

Andy Burns considered the late Charlie Raifield's fascination with technology and the liberal application of useful gadgets and security cameras that he placed all over his Baldwin County home. Burns, now the owner, figured Charlie would have a ball with the latest stuff. What was there when Andy moved in was now as antiquated as a Brownie camera. Burns would not admit his fascination with the gear was equal to or greater than that of his mentor. There was little in Burns' square mile of Baldwin County that surveillance equipment did not monitor. He could log on to the internet and see what was going on from anywhere in the world. The gate equipment included sound monitoring. Burns got an idea as he looked over the emailed video and aerial photos Buddy Russell sent him.

Russell knew a rancher in the area with a Piper Super Cub he flew off a dirt strip on his property. The rancher took Buddy and his camera on a tour of the San Rafael Valley, overflying the Rocking H Bar in the process. These photos gave Burns an excellent view of the ranch. The video Russell shot with a hidden dash camera when he paid a visit to the suspect ranch under the pretense of shopping for ranch property listings Russell was politely but firmly turned away by the so called owner. The hard looking Anglos in the background caught Burns attention. He zoomed in on one and looked closely at his face. The ball cap and sunglasses obscured his features. The man's resemblance to a customer whom Andy had worked on a pistol for was too close for coincidence. Burns cut and pasted the picture into another file.

Andy watched the video camera pan as Russell was turning around and leaving the property. Burns saw a horseshoe nailed to a fence post. He backed up the video and watched sequence again. The fence post was direct across from the parking area and the front door of the headquarters house. Andy stopped the video and zoomed in on the horseshoe. Once he determined the size of the shoe he fast forwarded to the picture of the ranch thug. One thing was certain, the currently visible crew at Rocking H Bar sure as hell weren't cowboys. Burns emailed the picture to another retired cop he knew who did computer forensic investigations. At least that was what the man's business card said. He built and maintained Burns current system; it was as impregnable as one could have. Another video from Russell was downloading. This footage came from a tiny camera mounted in eyeglasses Russell had worn. Burns watched this with interest. Better pictures of the so called new owner and his help. Andy forwarded all this to the retired computer cop.

Burns went back online and began to search for small wireless cameras with solar batteries. He found what he wanted and placed an order with priority overnight shipping.

Jolene Hadfield entered Burns workshop from the main part of the house. She wondered why he was making detailed measurements of a horseshoe.

"I got an email from the lawyer in Nogales Arizona. He sent me copies of Lyon Hamilton's bank statements. There is a significant amount of money in the bank. It is personal checking and savings, business checking and money market investment accounts. Hamilton is probably a millionaire if you include the ranch's value. There has been no activity on any of the accounts in over six months except for direct deposit Social Security payments and the regular draft for the power bill."

"Has the lawyer been in contact with the so-called new owner?"

"The lawyer says he sent certified letters to the ranch address, a PO Box in Patagonia Arizona. Those letters were returned, marked as undeliverable. He drove to the ranch and was told by the so called new owner to leave. This person would not give him his name. The lawyer tried to file a missing person report with the local sheriff's department. They would not take the report. According to the lawyer, the Sheriff stated one of his deputies went to the ranch and investigated the matter at the request of another complainant. The deputy was satisfied that Lyon Hamilton sold the property and left the country. The sheriff's department says it is a civil matter, and they will not get involved. The lawyer said he was going to file a subpoena for the sale records."

"When are you going to share that information with Lois Thornton?"

"I'm going to call her today. I'm going to tell her to call Bob Rabun and get his agency to file a missing person report for her. I'll give Rabun a heads up."

Burns motioned Hadfield to follow him. They went to the living room, and he sat down in a leather wing chair. She sat on the couch. "What are thinking Burns? You said your friend Russell sent you some pictures."

"Buddy visited the ranch under the guise of having heard it was for sale. He also had a couple of concealed video cameras and an audio tape going. The so-called new owner would not give his name. You are welcome to look at the videos. I've sent them to a source to see if I can get an ID on the perps. This owner and the men with him didn't look like ranch hands. It looked like there were some Mexicans in the background but it is too hard to tell for sure.

"Russell says the guy that owns the adjoining ranch where we are going to rent the casita and pick up the motorhome I bought is uneasy about what's happening at the Rocking H Bar. Buddy feels like we might get more information out of him once we get out there."

"When are we going?"

"Another week or so. I've got more research and prep work to do first."

"That is good. But my question is what are we going to do about whatever we find out there? What agency can we enlist to help? The family lawyer says the sheriff's department is corrupt. The unrest on the border is causing a lot of finger pointing out there, and the state's attorney might not be much help either. The lawyer is going to contact them. If we get out there and find evidence of wrongdoing, who are we going to take it too? There is probable cause written all over this, but nobody wants to look further."

"You can lead a horse to water, but you can't make him drink. Russell says that if anything gets done, we are going to have to do it ourselves. Once upon a time out there, that was a valid concept. Jo, are sure you want to get involved in it?"

She looked directly at Burns. "Lois Thornton needs to know what happened to her brother. We need to help her."

"Even if it means breaking the law to do it?"

"We need to know what we are dealing with and then call the right cops."

"OK, I think you need to take a look at these videos."

After a few minutes of watching the screen. Jolene looked up at Burns.

"So that is what a real ranch looks like?"

"Yes, but those aren't real cowboys."

Burn's cell phone with a text message. **Ck Ur Mail**.

Andy went into his office and clicked on the online computer. The retired cop computer guru came through with his usual efficiency. Burns saw each picture had been culled from the video's and returned to him with a caption. The person calling himself the owner of the Rocking H Bar came first.

Subject: Welch Ashton Bradford, 95% positive recognition, terminated FBI special agent, subject of internal investigation, case mishandled, US Attorney would not file charges against Bradford. The subject is also a disbarred attorney, former IRS audit employee, resigned.

Subject is believed to be residing in or near Tucson AZ

Burns looked at the next picture. Subject: Pauli Dumas 98% positive recognition, former porn actor banned from the industry due to violent attacks and rapes of co-stars. Considered a sadist, and prefers rough sex. Numerous arrests and convictions for assault. Has a genius level IQ and considered and expert computer hacker (not anywhere as good as I am) fluent Spanish speaker.

Burns smiled at the comment. He continued to the next photo. Subject: Nathanial "Nate" Norman, 98% positive recognition, numerous arrests for assault and battery, suspected ties to lower level organized crime. Considered armed and dangerous. Served ten years for felony assault, CA. Below average IQ. Known alias, 'Numb Nuts.'

The fourth subject had two pictures; one Burns culled from the dash video and one from Russell's eyeglass camera. Subject: Ronald Kroll, 65% positive recognition photo 1, 88% positive recognition photo 2, terminated FBI special agent. Expected indictment for assault on a federal agent. Terminated this year Mobile AL field office. Subject recognized as one of the most effective undercover operatives in the bureau. Last known employment was a Tucson casino. Subject no longer employed by this casino.

Burns turned off the email and picked up his handwritten gunsmith log book. He found the name, Ron Kroll eleven months earlier. Kroll had brought in a special Sig pistol for suppressor service. The gun was one Burns had modified under contract for the FBI a few years before. At a casual glance, the pistol appeared to be a standard model P220. A closer inspection would reveal the gun was anything but a stock P220.

Andy leaned back in his chair and considered this for a few minutes. Jolene came into his office. She leaned against his desk and said, "what's up?"

"I got an ID on the Anglos in the Rocking H Bar video. Check this out." Burns turned on his computer again. Jolene read the email over his shoulder.

"That doesn't sound good. Two fired FBI agents in the same place. One about to be indicted and one who apparently got away with something. My question is what the hell is going on?"

"I worked on a bureau pistol for Kroll almost a year ago. It was a special operations gun. Restricted to limited issue for field personnel. Kroll was not one of their super SWAT operatives. I wondered then and wondered now why he had that gun. Of course, I couldn't ask and shouldn't be telling you. It is the security clearance I have to do that type of work for them. Right now I think you have the need to know. And it goes without saying."

She finished the statement for him, "I don't say anything to anybody."

They both considered the implications. Burns spoke first.

"It is possible Ron Kroll is doing an undercover operation, a real deep cover thing. It could be the reason his record is showing termination. That would be a good hoax."

Chapter Nine

Jolene finished pulling her bass boat out of the water and trailering it to the Quonset hut hanger. Burns Piper Super Cub stayed in this hanger along with his airboat, his Go-Devil Boat, and all the tractors used around the place. Bad weather was expected the following day and a possible hurricane landfall within a few days. They were scheduled to fly out of Mobile the following morning for Nogales Arizona. She looked at the small bright yellow airplane. She always thought of it being cute, but steadfastly refused fly in it. When she learned the wings and body were fabric covered, it was not only no, but hell no.

The Cessna Float Plane that once resided in the hanger was now in South America as part of mission resupply service. Burns donated the aircraft to the organization. It was just as well as far as Jolene was concerned. She had flown in that plane once. And that was enough. Burns' lake wasn't a farm pond by any means. From the air, it looked like a puddle, when she realized he intended on landing the float plane in it. After what he called a splash down, or a water landing to some folks. One more of Burns' fleet of airplanes became a non-starter for her.

Jolene would only fly in the Mitsubishi MU-2, turboprop, that Burns keep based at the Bay Minette Alabama airport. He upgraded to that aircraft after Hurricane Katrina totaled his Cessna Twin Skywagon. Burns usually flew the Mu-2 on trips, preferring to leave the Cessna Citation business jet in timeshare service, where the expensive aircraft paid for its self. They would fly to Arizona in the Citation. Burns acquired that airplane three years before. Hadfield was not a comfortable flyer in any aircraft. At least the Citation had a bathroom; provided one called a commode in a closet a bathroom. And the weather forecast for tomorrow wasn't good. Neither was getting up before daylight for the drive to Mobile.

She parked the ATV under the patio cover and walked into Burns workshop. He was wrapping a horseshoe in bubble wrap. Laying on the workbench in front of him were six dried horse apples. Horse shit on his workbench was off the chart for Burns. Hadfield could not stay quiet when he picked up a horse apple with his bare hand.

"BURNS! What are you doing bubble wrapping dried horse shit?"

"If it fooled you, it will certainly fool the bad guys." He answered smiling. Something like that from Burns was merely an amused expression as opposed to an outright smile.

"Are you going to explain or do I want to know?"

"Let's just say for now they are part of my bag of tricks. To be used if the need should arise."

She looked around the shop and saw several hard cases used to transport weapons and a few duffle bags. The bubble wrapped horse shit joined the bubble wrapped horseshoes in a foam filled hard camera case. Hadfield wondered if there were enough rain in Arizona to justify the cases being waterproof as well.

"I don't want to hear any comments about how much I pack after this. That's gear, not clothes; it doesn't fall into the same category. And it is not an invitation for you to have an equal number of bags either."

"Burns!"

"You need to pack tonight. We leave at oh dark thirty in the morning. I want to get out ahead of the weather. We are having lunch with Buddy Russell and Burrito Cruz in Nogales tomorrow."

"Yes daddy," Hadfield said, flipping him off as she left the room,

He wasn't paying attention; Burns was busy putting a military grade laptop computer into another hard case. Besides having a hanger reserved, Burns reserved a full-size SUV 4X4 at the car rental agency. It would be delivered to the reserved hanger before their arrival the next day.

Jolene went back to sleep as soon as she got into the cab of Burns truck. He loaded her three bags and his one. He'd loaded gear the night before. She was sleeping sound enough that she wasn't aware of him buckling her seat belt.

A gentle touch on her shoulder awakened Jolene. The bright lights inside the hanger caused her to close her eyes, then ease them back open. Burns unbuckled her seat belt and laid two thermoses in her lap.

"Coffee to wake you up and for the flight. You need to get on the airplane now. Everything is loaded, and I'm going to open the hanger doors. I've done all preflight checks before engine start. Get a move on it. And use one of the no spill cups on the aircraft for that coffee."

He didn't hear her mumbled comments, which was just as well. Yawning, Hadfield got out of the truck and watched Burns roll open the large door. She stood beside the aircraft steps and waited until he finished opening the door. A tractor was already attached to the tow bar affixed to the aircraft nose wheel. The rain was heavy enough that Burns wore his cowboy hat and a rain jacket. He got on the tractor and called out to her.

"Get on the airplane Jo; there is a nasty storm blowing in from the Gulf. I want to be over Louisiana before it gets here."

She hesitated long enough for him to get off the tractor and come over to where she stood. "Burns it's raining hard."

"Yes, and it will clear momentarily. I don't have time to discuss the issue there is a limited takeoff window coming up soon. I plan to be on the active runway ready to go."

"I don't know this is crazy. Flying in this weather. We can go tomorrow."

"The weather behind this short lull with cancel any flying I do for several days. It is time to go."

He turned and walked back to the tractor. When Jolene heard the tractor motor start, she reluctantly climbed into the airplane. She put her purse on a seat along with one thermos. The aircraft was moving forward, and she hesitated to keep her balance. When it stopped, she stepped into the cockpit and sat in the right seat. Rain pounded the windshield as she watched Burns quickly remove the tow bar.

It was raining harder when he scampered back to the aircraft and climbed in the cabin. She watched over her shoulder as he pulled up the stairs and secured the door. Then he shook his water off his cowboy hat and laid it crown down in one of the seats.

Hadfield didn't make any comment as he methodically went through the aircraft checklists and started the engines. Burns was anal about the checklist, talking was not welcome in the cockpit when he was preparing for flight. He would tell her when to speak, and she was welcome to put on a headset and listen to the conversations with air traffic control. Jolene buckled her shoulder harness and seat belt. She put on the headset and held the thermos like it was a security blanket.

Hadfield was outside her comfortable zone flying anytime and today's weather was not helping any. The luxurious cabin of the Citation eased her apprehension a great deal. But compared to an airliner it was still a small airplane, and it left the ground! The only calming thing was the colorful instrument panel. It was not full of round black gauges and intimidating controls like the cockpits of Burns other airplanes. He told her the airplane had the latest avionic package upgrades, whatever that meant. To her, it looked like a bunch of small computer screens.

Andy Burns contacted the tower for taxi instructions. The rain let up considerably as they taxied to take off position. Jolene felt her heart rate increase as a wind gust buffeted the light jet. The clouds were even more menacing as they stopped short of the runway. She watched Burns tighten his seatbelt and shoulder harness. "Make sure your belts are tight it may be a little bumpy on takeoff."

Before she could answer the radio message she dreaded came over the headphones. "Citation Eight Zero X-ray you are clear to the active for takeoff."

Hadfield tightened her seatbelt and shoulder harness. The rest of the message she put out of her mind as she felt the plane move accelerating as it turned onto the runway. Jolene closed her eyes and put a hand near the seat side pocket that held a barf bag. She drew a deep breath and heard Burns say. "Eight Zero X-ray rolling." The acceleration pushed her back into her seat. She clenched her teeth waiting for the moment it left the ground. It wasn't a long wait, then a thump as the landing gear retracted.

Jolene held her breath until she was light headed. She breathed. She thought of Burns gift for understatement when she recalled the little bumpy on takeoff comment. That probably meant something akin to riding a bucking horse. Andrew Burns was not a reckless pilot. The only time he flew in marginal weather was when he was flying into better weather, soon. Burns believed the adage about there being no old, bold pilots. She trusted Andy Burns with her life, but she was still scared.

"You can open your eyes and breathe now Hadfield. If your pants are wet, you've either peed on yourself or squeezed the stopper out that thermos jug. It's OK to get out of your seat."

The aircraft was in a normal climb. And she saw the clear blue sky. Jolene unbuckled and climbed out of her seat. She went aft to the aircraft's small toilet thankful she didn't pee in her pants during takeoff. Hadfield returned to the cockpit and poured Burns a cup of coffee. She knelt between the seats and sipped from her cup. Burns reached over and squeezed her arm. She liked these impromptu displays of affection.

"We're at thirty thousand feet with a true airspeed of four hundred knots. We have a nice tailwind."

"Are we going straight there or land for fuel?"

"We are nonstop to Nogales. It is well within the range of this aircraft. Flight time a little less than four hours. Weather is good out there it will be little windy, the landing will be entertaining."

"Burns, say something a little more positive please."

"Ok. The approach and landing to Nogales will be rougher than a stucco bathtub."

"BURNS!"

"Enjoy the ride, Hadfield. It will be fun." He leaned back some in his seat and clasped his hands behind his head and stretched.

"What's flying the airplane?"

"The autopilot if I remembered to turn it on."

Hadfield shook head and sighed.

He looked at her and smiled, lightly touching her hand. "Maybe we can wrap this thing up quickly, and I can find I decent horse while we're out there."

"Ok. Can we sightsee?"

"I expect so; there are some artsy places north of Nogales, Rio Rico, and Tubac. You can probably find all manner of dust catchers in those places. And if you remembered your passport we can cross the border to Nogales, Sonora Mexico. I still remember enough Spanish to order dinner."

"Where did you make hotel reservations, or are we going directly to that ranch?"

"The Best Western unless you want the Motel 6."

"No thanks."

Jolene napped on the fold down seats in the cabin. She woke up and read a paperback book for a while and looked out the window every time Burns pointed out a landmark. She was most attentive when they begin descending after passing over El Paso. Hadfield stayed on the left side of the aircraft. Looking at the landscape and realizing she could see Mexico in the not so far way distance. As they got closer and lower, she moved back to the right cockpit seat and buckled up. Still, she watched the ground. After getting clearance, Burns turned the aircraft south and continued to descend. He pointed out the mountain ranges on each side of the Citation.

"Mexico is on the nose." He put the jet in a steep right-hand bank. Leveling out flying west he said. "US Border is below us, welcome to the San Rafael Valley. The ranch in question is on the right side of the aircraft."

Jolene kept her nose almost touching her window as she looked at the valley. She found herself willing Lyon Hamilton to appear on horseback galloping across the ranch below. In a moment the valley was a mountain range, and the small city appeared at the same moment as an Interstate Highway. The aircraft bucked in the wind. Burns was talking on the radio and making rapid adjustments to the instruments with his right hand.

The aircraft was flying north now and descending faster. He made another right turn, and the jet bucked upward and abruptly back down. Gaining and losing altitude with each bounce. Now she could see the runway ahead of the aircraft. It seemed they be thrown back up ten feet for every foot the plane descended. Burns was constantly correcting the aircraft to remain on the runway heading. It bumped up and down quickly as the synthetic voice called out 700 feet.

"Burns," her voice caught as the jet jolted up again. "Burns if we survive this landing can I redecorate the kitchen?"

She saw he was smiling. The voice called 300 feet, she missed the 200 call, and then watched the runway coming up fast as she heard 100 feet. Jolene held her breath. The threshold markings were closing fast. Then came the sudden squeal of the tires. Burns greased the Cessna jet on the runway.

After the roll out they turned off the runway onto the taxiway that takes them to the parking area. A small pickup truck with a large follow sign in bed was waiting on the taxiway to lead them to the ramp.

Wind buffeted the aircraft when it stopped; Andy shut down the engines. Burns put his cowboy hat firmly on his head, and they deplaned. He gave instructions to the linemen to hanger the Citation and bring him the hanger door keys at the FBO office. Two Hispanic men rode the tow tug pulling the aircraft down the ramp. One said to the other in Spanish something that translates: 'I told you only a loco vaquero could land a jet in this wind.'

After transacting the business of getting his airplane housed and signed the papers for the rental SUV, Burns and Hadfield rode back to the hanger and entered it via a parking lot door. She watched as Burns loaded all his equipment into the ample storage area of the Nissan Armada 4X4 the rental company had sent.

Nogales AZ is not a large city. Burns and Hadfield managed to check into their motel and drive to a Mexican restaurant within thirty minutes of leaving the airport. Russell and Cruz met them at the restaurant. Having met Buddy and his family several years before Hadfield enjoyed getting reacquainted. She found Bernie 'Burrito' Cruz delightfully charming. They hit it off immediately. Now and then she would call Burns Cowboy and wondered if she were offending him. Hearing the two westerners refer to him by that handle was surreal. By the time lunch was over the two high desert rats had given her the moniker of Miz Jo. She wasn't sure if she would buy a house or a car from either one of them. But she liked these two former cops.

At Burns insistence, they went to Cruz's used car lot. Parked at the rear of the lot was an old one-ton dual wheel pickup with faded paint numerous dents and one fender a mismatched color. The other was primer and hood another color still. One of rear wheel flares was an odd color also. When Cruz noticed Burns looking over the truck he moseyed up beside him and asked. "Whatcha thinking?"

"The same thing you are. Some Vaquero will buy it as it sets. And with that in mind, I'll give you one-quarter of your asking price to lease it while we're here. You can bring it to the casita after we check in at the Double B."

"That works, we'll settle up on it when we get this debacle sorted out.

"Thank you. If that beat up horse trailer in the back will still roll and haul horses, hook it up and bring it along. Same deal."

The lunch meeting went on longer than expected. Russell and Cruz cited previous commitments and could not make the trip to the Double B. Russell phoned Carson Bell the Double B owner and arranged for Andy and Jolene to visit the following morning. The foursome agreed to meet for dinner that evening and compare notes.

CHAPTER TEN

After an early breakfast, Andy and Jolene's body clocks were still a couple of hours ahead of Arizona time. Burns explained the state did not recognize daylight savings time. While it was in the Mountain Time Zone, Arizona was a time zone unto its self. Jolene enjoyed the morning coolness and the scenic drive. She insisted on stopping to read every historical marker. When they entered Patagonia Arizona, Burns made her happy by cruising the two main streets and a couple of side streets before they followed the two-lane highway south out of town. Soon the paving road turned to dirt and slowed their progress. Hadfield was like a kid pointing out things she had never seen. Before long a wooden sign appeared with an arrow pointing the way to the San Rafael Valley. A few minutes later Burns stopped the SUV, and they got out of the vehicle. Hadfield stood speechless for several moments as she took in the vista before her. Burns walked around the Armada and stood next to her.

"Oh my gosh, Andy this place is beautiful beyond belief!" She turned and hugged Burns kissing him on the lips. Jolene squeezed him tight and broke the embrace. "Thank you, thank you so much for bringing me out here to see this." Hadfield kissed him again this time on the cheek. "You've given up shaving I see."

Burns ignored the comment.

"Of the parts of this world I've seen, I believe God did some of His best work in the American West. This valley is one of His lesser known masterpieces. It is one of the few high desert low grass prairies left. It is a unique ecosystem. Lois Thornton was right when said you could get hung for talking about subdividing this valley. Right now it has a blight and cleaning it up won't be easy or politically correct."

A little while after they got back in the car, they passed another sign post. This one had wooden signs pointing in the direction of various ranches. Jolene smiled broadly at that one saying. "This is not Biloxi Mississippi Andy Burns."

Burns laughed at that one. "It has more lights after sundown. They are a bit higher off the ground and don't run on electricity. Here's our turn." He turned into a road marked with another wooden sign. It read Double B Headquarters and had an arrow pointing up the dirt road.

After about a half a mile they crested a slight rise and spotted a tranquil homestead nestled in a stand of cottonwood trees. A house and several large outbuildings. As they got closer, the pipe corrals begin to emerge from the landscape. Unusual was a large white truck. Its size made Jolene think of a moving van. She realized the white truck was the motor home Burns agreed to purchase. Burns parked the Armada next to a picket fence that protected the yard of the ranch house. He and Jolene got out of the SUV. A tall, lanky man came out of the house. He wore faded jeans and a light colored western shirt. Complete with fake pearl buttons. He put a cowboy hat on his head as he stepped off the porch. What Jolene could see of his bushy hair, it was mostly white, and his weathered face was clean shaven.

"Hello, you folks must be Andrew Burns and Jolene Hadfield. I am Carson Bell. Welcome to the Double B and the San Rafael." He extended his hand to Jolene first and removed his hat. "Thank you Mr. Bell your valley is awesome." She said.

Bell replaced his hat and shook hands with Burns. Turning back to Jolene he said, "God blessed my family, and now He blessed me with the temporary care of His valley. Ms. Hadfield while we ranchers have deeds and such that proclaim us owners of this prairie. We are just very lucky caretakers of it until the next generation comes along.

"Two of my father's great uncles held the original Spanish land grant. They expanded the ranch over the years. When they passed on, the ranch went to my Dad and my Aunt and Uncle. It was passed down to my older brother and me when Dad passed. This valley did not call my Aunt or my sister. Dad and my Uncle bought out Aunt May, and Dad left my sister with a financial inheritance. Len, my brother and myself changed the name and re-registered a brand. Len and his wife ran the place. I ran to the wild blue yonder. I am a retired Air Force officer. Len's son died in a horse wreck. My late wife and I were childless. My sister has daughters, and they have visited once in their life. So now it is just me. I have two hands and a Mexican housekeeper and her husband. One of my hands came from the Rocking H Bar. Come on up to the porch where we can sit and talk."

They reached the porch and Carson introduced Estella Morales. She greeted them in good but accented English and offered fresh coffee. Burns and Hadfield accepted the offer and took seats in old but comfortable chairs on the shaded porch. Jolene could envision generations of cowboys in these same chairs with their boots propped up on the porch rail.

"So you grew up here Mr. Bell?" Jolene asked.

"I did, and I graduated high school I went to the University of Arizona in Tucson, ROTC, and the Air Force for twenty years. I'm a retired a Colonel. I flew O2A's in Viet Nam and then T-45's until I retired. I understand from Buddy Russell you came out here in your plane Mr. Burns. What do you fly? And, I am Carson, not Mr. Bell not Colonel just Carson."

"I'm Jolene, Carson. And I enjoyed the background lesson."

"Your welcome. I didn't want to bore you. But I feel like my guests need to know something about this ranch and the valley."

"And I thank you for the background lesson. Please call me Andy or Burns either one works. We came out in a Citation.

"A CITATION! Burns you're sitting on my porch looking like a cowboy about to beg for a job. And you tell me you flew out here in a Citation. One of those jet shares or something?"

"I lease it to one of those services when I don't need it. It is single pilot rated, so it is demand somewhat. I wouldn't have it if the company that used to own it had done a timeshare lease instead of buying a jet. That aircraft is one of the prime reasons my accountant thought the company was a good buy. Of course, the accountant figured we would sell the airplane. Between my using it and leasing it to the time share service, it breaks even cost wise and turned a small profit last year. The company that formally owned it has shown a nice profit now that their executives fly commercial. It turned out to be a good deal. Jo likes the jet because it has a bathroom."

"Burns that is enough," Jolene said.

"Andy, Buddy Russell tells me he's known you since you were a border patrolman out here. And he said you are a retired cop, did you win a lottery or something?"

An old friend of mine, Charlie Raifield had passed away unexpectedly a few years ago. Charlie left me a considerable amount of money three airplanes and a square mile in Baldwin County Alabama. He taught me how to fly twenty years before I retired. I would commute to his place in a Super Cub. He kept it parked at an airport close to where I lived so I could fly to his place on the coast. We would get in the Cessna twin and fly to rifle matches all over the southeast."

"Russell did say you came into some money. He didn't say how. He also says you are one of the best horsemen he knows."

"I've ridden a horse."

"He said that was the answer I could expect."

Andy didn't answer; he gave Carson Bell the slight smile pleasant look. The old rancher continued.

"You and your lady are going to be living here a few months. So I need to tell you a few more things. First, I'm sure Russell told you the casita has a barn and pipe corral turnouts. Horses are usually welcome over there. Right now there is quarter horse stud living in that barn along with a border collie. Estella's husband Miguel takes care of them. Which amounts to putting out feed and hay and not much else. The horse and dog are dangerous."

"More so than any other stud horse?"

"Yes, let me tell the story.

"The horse and dog belong to an old friend of mine. I've known Lyon Hamilton since grade school. Lyon and the late Manny Collazo from Cochise County were the best horsemen in southern Arizona."

The mention of Hamilton's name peaked Burns and Hadfield's interests. Neither one gave any tell that might have indicated they knew about Lyon Hamilton.

"I knew Manny Collazo; I bought a horse from him while I lived in Cochise County. I hated to hear he passed away." Burns said.

"Yeah, Manny went downhill after his daughter was murdered. Cancer is what got him. I think after his daughter's death he didn't have the will to fight.

"Back in the winter, almost four months ago, Lyon's stallion galloped up to this house one evening about dust. His Border Collie was following right behind him. I've never seen that horse so lathered up. He was under full tack, saddle still cinched tight, bridle and bit in his mouth. Both the horse and dog needed water bad. Miguel, Estelle's husband, came out and took them to the barn. He was able to get the tack off Cam and put him in a turn out pen. Jazz stayed with the horse. Cam would not let Miguel brush him down. Neither Jazz or Cam would not let any of us near them. Lyon's saddle sat on the fence rail with the tack hanging on the horn. If we got near it, both of them would charge the fence.

"I came inside and tried to call Lyon's house. I gave up after thirty or so rings and got in my truck and drove other there. I took my hand Butter Billy Three with me. When we got on the ranch road a rough looking hombre with an AK 47 rifle was standing in the middle of the road. He said Lyon Hamilton didn't live there anymore, and we needed to turn around and leave. I did. Got back here and called the sheriff's department. Best they could do according to the dispatcher was have a deputy come by and talk to me the next morning. I knew something was wrong.

"Deputy Willie Hillman showed up the next morning. That jackass is a real piece of work. He told me he'd been to the Rocking H Bar and that Lyon Hamilton had sold the property fair and square. Hillman said he had seen a quick claim deed, and as far as he was concerned it was legal, and there was not a problem. I asked where Lyon Hamilton was, and Willie Hillman grinned like a lecher and said he went to the Fiji Islands. I asked about the horse and dog. Hillman grinned again and said my new neighbor said I could have them as a gift. He also said I was warned not to go over there again. I asked about Lyon's cattle and the other horses. I was told not to worry about it. Hillman left."

"Did he make a report?" Jolene asked.

"No, he said he would note the contact on his activity report. The sheriff's office will not let you have copies of those reports without a subpoena. And the sheriff himself told me he would have the county attorney fight any subpoena my lawyer might get. Other words it was none of my business." Bell shook his head. His weather-beaten face showed the despair the rancher felt.

"What about the cattle and the other horses," Burns asked.

"Well a couple of days later TR, that's Tobias Rutledge, he was Lyon's hand, showed up here pulling his trailer with both of his horses in it and all his belongings. He had been up to Prescott visiting family for a few days. When he came back, he got the rifle treatment. But it was daylight, and he was crazy enough to demand his horses and gear. Surprisingly some older guy who acted like he was in charge came out. He told TR he was the new owner, and he'd been expecting him. TR said a thug went with him to the bunkhouse and watched him while he collected his gear. TR said his rifle was missing. A few minutes later a thug returned with his 30-30 and told him he could have it when he started out the driveway. TR loaded up his gear and horses. The so-called new owner came out and handed him the rifle. The lever was open, and the man gave TR the bullets and told him not to load it again until he cleared the gate. He asked TR about the other horses on the property and TR told him they were boarders, and there was a list in Lyons office. TR asked about the cattle, and the guy told him not to worry about them, and it was time for him to leave.

"We've watched the place from the forest service roads the cattle knocked down the cross fencing to get to more grass. There a were a couple of water tanks they could use. But if the windmill went down the water wouldn't have lasted long. I've got most of the board horses over here now. I'm not exactly in that business, but I couldn't turn those folks away."

"How many head of cattle are we talking about?" Burns asked.

"Lyon kept around seventy-five head. Here is the interesting part, the new owner showed up over here a month after Cam showed up. He said he knew I had been taking in the board horses, and he wanted to offer me a deal on the cattle. His name is Bradford, and he claimed we had met several months before at a Tucson casino bar. I remember someone who I think was him. I go up there every month. What this fellow Bradford offered was my hands take care of the cattle on the Rocking H Bar. In turn, he would give me fifty percent of the proceeds from the sale. Bradford was adamant that my men stay away from the ranch headquarters area."

"Did you take him up on his offer?"

"Yes and when Butter Billy and TR go over there, someone is always watching from a distance. They ride around on ATV's. None of them approach my hands, but they watch. Something is going on over there. Willie Hillman, the deputy, is in and out. That bastard is as crooked as they come. So he's getting paid off."

"Interesting," Burns said. "When we go over to the casita make sure to show me the property lines. I don't want to wander on to that ranch by mistake."

"Don't worry. I'll make sure you know where you can and can't go."

"Carson, this Cam you speak of is the horse?" Jolene asked.

"Yes, Cam is short for Don Cameron of Lochiel, the horse's registered name. Colin Cameron was one of the early ranchers in this valley, and he named Lochiel for someplace in Scotland. The folks called him Don because of the size of original ranch. And Jazz is the border collie; he is Jazzman of Lochiel."

"If Cam is so obnoxious how do you get him from here to the casita?" Burns asked.

"When we started getting the board horses, some of them are mares. I didn't want to have to deal with Cam and mares in heat. Miguel figured out a clever way to move the horse. He backed the old jeep truck into the barn and stopped it next to the rail where the saddle was. He tied a rope to the gate latch. When the horse and dog were eating, he snatched the saddle off the rail and put in the truck bed. He ran and got in the cab and opened the gate with the rope. Cam and the dog followed the truck over the ranch roads to the casita. Miguel reversed the operation at the barn there. TR had already put out hay and feed in the turnout. He opened a gate using a rope when Miguel drove past it. The horse ran into the turnout, and TR closed the gate. Miguel hung the saddle over the fence, and that was that."

"That was clever. I'm looking forward to meeting Miguel. Carson, we are going to check out the motorhome. Then we can follow you over to the casita."

"That works for me."

Burns and Hadfield drove over to the motorhome in the Nissan SUV.

"That was an interesting story. Do you get the idea Carson is not telling everything?" Jolene asked.

"I do. We'll talk about it when we get to where we are going. Let's look at the RV and make sure it is ready to travel. I'll drive it, and you drive the SUV. Keep your eyes open on the way to the casita."

"Sounds like a plan."

Twenty minutes later, with Carson Bell leading the way in a King's Ranch Edition Ford F250, a three-vehicle convoy left the Double B Ranch. It was five miles on the forest service road before Bell stopped and opened a gate. They followed ranch road behind the gate another mile up a hillside and came to a plateau with a small house and larger barn beside it. Bell parked in front of the house, and Hadfield parked beside him. Carson directed Burns to the RV hookup and spotted for him as he maneuvered the motorhome into place.

"As you know from the information Russell sent you. The casita is an old line shack. The original structure was one room. I added a second room and a bathroom with indoor plumbing when we put in a septic tank. You folks come on inside and take a look."

Burns and Hadfield made the appropriate comments as they toured the small but nicely furnished in the rustic western house. From the house, they could see the barn and the windmill which pumped water into a large tank.

You will probably see my hands, Butter Billy Three and TR from time to time. Miguel comes to the barn twice a day to feed Don Cameron. Estella will come with him this evening and bring you a meal. It's the way we welcome guests on the Double B.

"What kind of nickname is Butter Billy Three? That doesn't sound very cowboy." Jolene said.

Carson Bell smiled. "His real name is William Edward Butterfield the Third. He claims to be a descendant of the Butterfield Stagecoach family. Butter Billy is one of the best windmill men in the valley. He is a damn fine cowboy for his size. You will see where the butter part comes from when you meet him. I've got a windmill broke on the eastern side. He and TR are over there. TR is good with windmills, but he's not in Butter Billy's class."

"I thought stagecoaches were Wells Fargo." Jolene said.

"Carson smiled again. "Wells Fargo wasn't the only stagecoach line in the old west. The Butterfield stage was primarily in the southwest."

"Any ghost towns around here?" Hadfield inquired.

"Sunnyside east of here. It is near Fort Huachuca's old south gate."

"Wow, the history here is cool. At home, it's a green sign called a historical marker. If you can see it, there is a fence around it or somebody charges money to look at it." Jolene said.

Carson laughed again. "Get Andy to take you to Tombstone. It's best-known tourist trap in the state."

"Would you show me the stud horse?" Burns asked.

"He's over to the barn. I'll walk you over there. But don't expect a friendly pet looking for a treat. He is as close to a wild horse as you will get."

They walked the twenty-five yards to the barn.

"What was this horse's disposition before he showed up on your doorstep?" Burns asked casually.

"He was alert, sort of standoffish, not a pet by any means. Cam is a working ranch horse. Lyon worked cattle on him, took him to ranch horse competitions and stood him at stud. I can't figure what caused the change in him and Jazz. Jazz is out of a championship line of border collies. Watching Lyon work cattle with Cam and Jazz, was." The old rancher hesitated, almost choking up.

"Was like art in motion. That horse and dog were world class. Lyon Hamilton was just along for the ride."

The barn had the center run and stall corrals on one side a tack and storage room was on the opposite side followed by large pipe corral turnouts. All of it under one roof.

"Nice barn," Burn said when they entered the open runway.

"Burns Cam and Jazz are in the first turn out on the left side past the tack room. You can see Hamilton's saddle on the top pipe next to the tack room. You need to stay on the right side because if you get too close to the fence both of them will charge the fence and Jazz will try and bite you if you get close enough. They let Miguel come to the fence and feed them. And it took a while for that to happen."

Burns walked to the tack room and went inside. Jolene and Carson Bell stopped, wondering what he was doing. An angry whinny sounded a warning from the corral. Burns came out of the tack room carrying a rag, and a can saddle soap. He walked over to the saddle paying no attention to the angry horse.

Andy admired the saddle. It was a heavy working rig, an A-fork Wade tree, slick seat high cantle. The leather was dark, and tastefully basket stamped, well cared for and dusty.

Don Cameron whined reared his hooves pawing the air and snorted shaking his head. The long tangled mane waved in the air adding to the menacing appearance of the horse. Jazz joined in alternating between barking and teeth bared growls.

Burns hardly glanced at the horse and dog. He began wiping the dust off the saddle. While discreetly raising his eyes toward the equine and its canine backup. The pair decided one more demonstration was in order. It was impressive. Complete with bared teeth and snot slinging with his manhood on display Cameron pawed the air angrily snorting his displeasure. Jazz made a warning attack run advancing half the distance to the pipe fence with his teeth bared and best available growl. Jolene and Carson were impressed enough they backed up. And they were ten feet behind Burns.

Both said, "Burns!"

Andy wiped the saddle and acted as if he paid no attention to the display. The quarter horse circled and bolted toward Burns and the saddle making a sliding stop about ten feet from Andy. The angry dog right beside his giant friend. Don Cameron treated Burns to snorts whinnies head shaking more snot slinging. The stud made a half-hearted rear and dropped his hooves back in the dirt. He glared at Burns baring his teeth. Andy opened the can of saddle soap. Put some on the rag and began rubbing it into the saddle seat.

The horse and dog loudly voiced their opinions about Burns working on the saddle. Neither one moved any closer to the fence. After he had finished the seat, Andy started cleaning the skirt. He would look at the horse and dog now and then while he worked. And it appeared to Carson and Jolene that he was paying no attention to the animals. Who, apparently thought the same thing because they stopped their obnoxious behavior and stood watching Burns. Andy continued working on the saddle. He lifted the saddle off the rail turning so he could finish up the off side. The horse and dog watched from their spot ten feet away.

When he finished cleaning the saddle, Andy returned it to its original position on the fence. He put the rag and saddle soap back in the tack room.

"Nice looking horse," Burns said rejoining Bell and Hadfield at the barn's entrance. "He needs grooming and shoeing. I see Miguel keeps hay and feed up here. I want to meet Miguel, and if you don't mind, I'll take on the feeding duties for Don Cameron and Jazz."

They didn't notice the horse and dog sticking their heads out of the corral watching the stranger walk away.

As they walked back to the casita Bell said. "Burns that is as close as that horse has gotten to a human since he let Miguel unsaddle him. I don't mind you feeding them and don't think Miguel will either. But he will look over your shoulder until he is happy with how you do it.

"Just be careful around that damn horse I don't want a paying guest hurt. I believe Russell a little more about you knowing horses. But I can't get near him and neither can my hired help. I'm taking a chance even letting you around him. With the way, folks sue each other these days."

"I hear what you are saying Carson. Trust me, I value my hide more than you do. We are going to get settled. And we will look for Estella and Miguel this afternoon. I would appreciate your recommendation who has good horses for sale around here."

"I'll get your names, and I'll call ahead with an introduction for you. I'll also have Miguel bring up a couple of well-broke geldings this afternoon along with saddles and tack."

"Thanks, I appreciate that."

They watched Carson Bell leave. He was out of sight before Hadfield said a word.

"Burns you're not going to buy a horse. You are going to ride up to Carson Bell's ranch house on Don Cameron."

"What gave you that idea?"

"That misdirection about horse sellers."

"Remind me never to accuse you of not listening."

"The story of that horse and dog showing up at Bell's house doesn't bode well for Lyon Hamilton."

"No, it doesn't. Nothing Bell has told us sounds good. That guy Bradford is up to something. And I still wonder what Carson Bell is holding back. Russell and Cruz will be here in a couple of hours with that truck and trailer. I want to get the motorhome hooked up and everything ready."

"You want to share your plans for that old truck Burrito is bringing out here."

"Sure, I plan on going over to Rocking H Bar under the pretense of being an out of work cowboy. That truck looks the part. And those geldings Bell is sending over will fit in well for that ruse. I plan on asking Burrito to go with me and do the talking while I look around."

"I guess that is why you have forgotten to shave for the past few days."

"You noticed."

"Hard not to."

<h1 style="text-align:center">CHAPTER ELEVEN</h1>

Ron Kroll rode with Ashton Bradford south on I-19 toward Nogales Arizona and the US Border with Mexico. Bradford drove the GMC Suburban 4X4. He picked Kroll up earlier at the extended stay motel Kroll called home. It was a non-descript place that served transient people. Kroll preferred it because they took cash and he operated off the grid, something Bradford liked. According to Bradford, they were crossing the border for a special meeting at a deluxe restaurant in Nogales Sonora Mexico. They were meeting El Jefe the Sonora cartel boss. One of the most dangerous and ruthless men in Mexico.

"You're quiet Kroll. I like that. But something is on your mind. What is it?"

"Same thing I said when you invited me to this meeting. I don't want my passport recorded crossing the border. I expect those assholes at the bureau have it flagged. And what I do is none of their business."

"You still worried about getting indicted for knocking Skinny Winnie on his ass?"

"Yeah. I would rather cross back and forth under the radar. Don't tell me El Jefe doesn't have a tunnel we could use."

"I expect he has several. He even digs some for the Border Patrol to find. Just keep the five-million-dollar payoff in your head. And remember I don't trust the US government any more than you do. An El Jefe sure as hell doesn't."

Kroll settled back and watched the interstate signs; that displayed distances in kilometers instead of miles. An example of the immigrant takeover of his country. The lights of Nogales shown as they turned off into the town and made their way south. Bradford explained they would park and walk across the border. There was a special parking lot for those doing just that. Complete with a fee to park, even late at night.

"If you're packing there is a lock box under the seat. El Jefe's men will pat us down. We couldn't win a gun battle with them."

"I left it at home," Kroll said sourly.

They left the suburban and walked across the parking lot. Kroll didn't notice Bradford nod to the driver of a beat-up Toyota. Pauli Dumas was discretely following his boss. Dumas would not make the crossing tonight. He would watch the car. When Bradford and Kroll reached the sidewalk to the port of entry, a Mexican male walked up to them.

"Senor Bradford, Senor Kroll follow me Por favor."

They followed the man away from the port of entry and across the street. They walked for a block then turned down a side street. The man stopped and rang the doorbell of an Asian Massage Parlor. A voice asked that they look at the camera above the door. All three men looked up, and a buzzer sounded. A short, plump Oriental woman opened the door and silently motioned them inside. They followed her down a dimly lit hallway to a locker room. Another silent motion for them to enter. She left closing the door behind her. The Mexican locked it from the inside. He turned to a bench in front of a row of lockers. He lifted the end of the bench. Kroll saw the bench concealed a trapdoor. The Mexican gestured for them to enter. They descended a ladder to a concrete floor surprisingly one could walk upright in the tunnel. The tunnel lights were better than those in the hallway above. A rough looking hombre waited in the tunnel. When the door closed above them, the man spoke.

"Silencio Por favor." He gestured for them to follow him.

Kroll could not estimate the distance; he glanced at his watch when they started. Twenty minutes later they stopped at another ladder. This one appeared to go up for several stories. Their guide led the way. Kroll went second; Bradford was last. As they neared the top, Kroll heard dance music. Their guide activated another trap door and climbed out. Ron saw they had entered a small cubical with a chair. The guide held a door open from the outside. Kroll stepped into a Mexican Gentleman's Club. Bradford soon joined him, and their guide went back into the cubical.

A pretty Latina stepped up to Kroll, she smiled and seductively licked her lips as she stroked his manhood through his trousers. The tiny woman, maybe in her teens turned away. Besides her bra, she wore thong panties. Kroll squeezed her round butt. She giggled and wiggled her finger for him to follow. They reached the front of the club and another man, this one in a sports coat and open collar, asked to see their passports. He inspected the documents and returned them.

"Senor Kroll, Senor Bradford, follow me Por favor." They followed him out of the club and down a flight of stairs. Kroll was glad to get away from the loud thumping music. Outside on the street, their new guide waved to a cab waiting down the block. The driver flashed his headlights acknowledging the gesture and pulled away from the curb. A moment later the cab stopped in the street in front of them. The escort opened the back door for Bradford and Kroll. Once they were inside, he got in the front seat. The cab took off. Kroll casually tried to get his bearings.

"Did passport control meet with your approval?" Bradford asked.

"Yeah, you could have eased my anxiety and told me we were going under the fence."

"El Jefe's rules."

"The chicka at the bar checked my gun. She didn't look for a pistol either."

Bradford thought for a moment and then burst out laughing. "If you grabbed her ass look out on the return trip!"

Kroll was not surprised to see there were no customers in the restaurant. El Jefe had the reputation of paying for every patron's meal when he entered a place and then asking them to leave. They got a free meal check for another night. No one complained. A couple of bodyguards searched Bradford and Kroll, and led them to a table where Bradford introduced Kroll to El Jefe.

In person, the short, plump Mexican cartel boss was anything but the stereotype drug lord. He was jovial and smiled easily, an excellent host. Kroll remembered the man was a stone cold psychopathic killer, who favored torture and long drawn out deaths. Rumor had it that El Jefe built a cross where he occasionally crucified those who displeased him.

"Senor Brad, tell me of this border ranch you have purchased." El Jefe asked in surprisingly good English.

"It's in the San Rafael Valley only a few miles from Lochiel. A farm service road that runs parallel to the border runs across the southern part."

"And you feel it will serve our mutual needs."

"Yes, it even came with a large flatbed truck used for hauling hay. The former owner had a long-standing agreement with a hay grower in this country sell him hay. His hired hands would cross the border at the old point of entry at Lochiel and pick up a truckload. There is a large barn on the property used for storing hay. It will serve our purposes well."

"I understand. And you have quarters for drivers can wait for the trucks?"

"Yes, a bunk house. And I also have a cheap source for cargo trucks."

"Excellent, Senor Brad, excellent. Can you handle human cargo as well via the same route?"

"Humans can be transported on the hay truck. It will not be first class seats, but it will work. They can be housed in the barns as well. My truck source can also provide buses if need be."

"I like the way you think Senor Brad. Will Senor Ron be supervising these operations for you?"

"Yes, and he will serve the special project as well."

"Ahhh yes, the special project. Tell me, Ron, what was it like to knock your superior on his ass as Senor Brad tells me you did."

"El Jefe it was better than sex."

"Better than sex with the chicka who grabbed your package in my club?"

"I admire your information sources El Jefe. You know all."

The drug lord smiled in a manner that left no doubt evil lurked behind the friendly façade he was presenting.

"But Senor Ron you did not tell me why knocking this Winston Glover on his ass is better than sex."

"Sex you can have anytime. Knocking a jerk like Skinny Winnie on his butt happens once in a lifetime."

"Why not just shoot him."

"I would have enjoyed doing that. But not in an office with witnesses. I do not wish to spend the rest of my life behind bars. I have enough life left to get even for everything those assholes have done to me. And shooting Skinny Winnie would be too good for him."

"If not shooting, what would be good for this Winston Glover?"

"I suppose one could shoot him slowly. One part at a time?"

"Ahhh, I like that Ron Kroll. How do you say it? I like how you think."

"Yes, El Jefe."

"Perhaps I can help you get your chance."

"I would like that El Jefe."

The crime lord looked at his watch.

"Senor Bradford, Senor Kroll, I must go to another meeting. Your meal tonight and whatever else you may desire," El Jefe smiled at Kroll, "is on the house."

El Jefe got up and left the restaurant. As soon as he disappeared, a waiter arrived at the table with the first course. They didn't even have to order.

"This is excellent, El Jefe does it up right," Kroll said between bites.

"Yes, and you made a good impression on him. He will be checking you out. When he is satisfied, you are in our corner. You will learn about the special project."

"And you know what that is?"

"No, I don't know yet. The money offered is twenty-five million US dollars' cash. Five million of that is yours."

"I would piss on the White House lawn and shit in the lobby of the Hoover Building for less."

Their escort took them back to the club. Bradford wanted another drink and decided on a liaison with a Latina chick who pawed him while he sipped his drink. They retired to a cubical. Kroll hoped the girl who groped him earlier had left for the evening. The last thing he needed was the attention of a Mexican whore. She appeared out of nowhere and straddled his lap grinding her pelvis on his manhood. Lap dances were not unheard of during undercover assignments in the US. Kroll was unprepared for the Mexican style lap dance. The hooker deftly unzipped his fly and was grinding her thong clad crotch on his bare member before he could stop her. When he got aroused; the girl stuck her finger in her mouth and made a sucking motion. Not missing a grinding beat she pointed toward a cubicle. Bradford reappeared just in time with their guide.

The assignment was almost up when Bradford slipped on the ladder. Fortunately for him, he was able to hang on. Finally, they exited the massage parlor on the US side and walked unescorted back to where the SUV was parked.

"Do you mind driving back to Tucson. I've had a little too much booze to be behind the wheel this late at night. I damn near busted my ass or worse on that ladder."

"Sure, give me the keys."

Once they were northbound on I-19 Bradford decided to impart some advice on his colleague.

"Kroll, if you decide to buy Mexican pussy, bring your condom. Porn Dude always said the Mexicans make theirs out bicycle tire tubes. I believe him."

"I keep that in mind. But I prefer to buy mine stateside. I appreciate the rescue. Who is Porn Dude?"

"One of my men. You will meet Pauli tomorrow when you move to the ranch. He used to be a porn actor. He's one gross SOB, but a damn genius with a computer. He speaks Spanish too."

After a few minutes, Bradford was snoring. Kroll drove to an all-night diner across from his hotel. He woke Bradford saying. "Brad we are across from my place. You want to go into this dump and get some coffee."

W. Ashton blinked a couple of times and opened the door. "Good idea Kroll."

An hour later Kroll was in his room. Bradford wrote directions to the ranch on a napkin. Ron promised he would make it down there in a few days. He took out his phone and considered texting Ivalou Vargas. It was three AM that would not go over well. Kroll decided he could report tomorrow and went to bed. Before he dozed off, he thought about Vargas and his abbreviated lap dance. Waiting until tomorrow to see her was the best idea.

It was noon before Ivalou Vargas, in Penelope attire was able to meet Kroll. And he thought she looked exceptionally hot in short shorts and a tank top.

"Aren't you the hottie," Kroll said when he entered the cheap hotel room.

"Yeah, keep thinking that big guy. But my butt's covered and I'm not wearing a damn thong."

"I saw enough thongs last night to do for a while. I thought I was gonna have to call you and ask how to say get off my lap in Spanish."

"Oh, lap dances across the border. Have you gone to the clinic to get checked?"

"I don't think that is necessary." Kroll gave Ivalou the details of the previous night's meeting. She wrote down everything he said, and he made no mention about the strip club lap dance. When they finished, she went over her notes and clarified a few things. She put her notepad back in her purse.

"I will email my report to Havelee when we get back to the motel. You know she will be coming out here now that we have a location we will be working from."

"You and the guys probably need to relocate to Nogales. It is the closest place with motels. Right now we need a heavy duty four-wheel drive pickup with four doors. We all need to drive down for a look at this ranch I'm going to. Bradford says it takes about an hour to drive from Nogales. If I'm going to move in down there, we are going to scout the place as much as possible."

"Why don't I call Havelee right now and see if she can get a truck like that for us."

Vargas made the call and explained to Harris what they needed. She hung and looked at Kroll.

"Havelee is going to find us a truck. She will get back with me asap. She approved us moving to Nogales and told me to book rooms for the whole team. She checked online and said there was an extended stay hotel that didn't look too bad. We'll have to look that over as well."

"Great, how long before M&M starts beating on the door?"

"He won't be they are observing from a different parking lot. I drove my undercover ride down here. It's a beater Nissan that runs a hell of a lot better than it looks."

Kroll was looking a map Vargas spread on the table.

"Our Penelope trick will work in Nogales. I can't see the town of Patagonia having a no-tell motel."

"I can't see it having much of anything," Vargas said looking over his shoulder. She was close enough that Kroll realized she smelled a lot better than the Mexican lap dancer. Ivalou's phone rang before he could formulate a comment.

Vargas disconnected that call and immediately sent a text. She smiled at Kroll.

"That was Havelee; we got our truck. I sent the guys back to Tempe. The motor pool is bringing it down to the motel and will take one of their cars back. Des and M&M say no one-tailed us here."

"Good, it sounds like things are coming together. We can't relax on watching for a tail. It could come from Bradford or El Jefe. I would love to bag that bastard as part of this package. He is not the stereotypical drug lord type. I saw through the façade a couple of times. That is one scary Mexican. He has eyes everywhere down there. He even knew when I squeezed a hooker's ass."

"I need to put that in my report."

"Like hell you do."

"Alright, Kroll come clean about the hooker and the lap dance," Ivalou ordered with a mischievous smile.

He recounted all the details with an aw shucks it happened you know attitude.

"That girl must get a lot of practice. I can't get my zipper down that quick. I would have loved to see the look on your face when she grabbed your cock."

"Try it and see for yourself."

"In your dreams Kroll." She punctuated that answer with her favorite gesture.

"A man can dream can't he?"

"Not on the job with the fabulous bunch of idiots he can't."

"Don't go all feminist on me now."

"Don't go all macho super-agent man and get yourself hurt either. I'm beginning to like you, Kroll. Even if you do get lap dances from Mexican hookers."

He didn't have a smart ass answer for that.

"It appears the Bad Apple's investigation is bearing fruit, no pun intended." Ransom Carter told the Director as part of a daily briefing.

"How so?"

"Kroll has gotten enough of Bradford's confidence that Bradford spirited him across the border for a face to face meeting with El Jefe. He only spoke in generalities, but it is apparent to Kroll there is a criminal partnership between Bradford and the drug load. Kroll believes that in addition to narcotics smuggling they have plans for human shipments. El Jefe is not into running undocumented aliens across the border. So this is likely a white slavery human trafficking operation. The real interesting thing is the mention of a special project. One that Bradford has offered Kroll five million for his part. We will know about this when El Jefe has vetted Kroll. I think we need to have him indicted for striking Glover and making sure it is in the system for El Jefe to find."

"I will handle that with the AG. I don't want Kroll to get busted while we still need him in place."

"That is simple; we don't tell Skinny Winnie where he is."

"Once Kroll establishes himself with El Jefe, I'm going to have the indictment quashed."

"That will work. Agent Harris is leaving for Arizona today. She will be on the ground out there until Bad Apple's concludes. They are setting up shop in Nogales which is on the border. It is the closest place to this ranch Bradford is using."

"Good, maybe this thing will work after all. Catching El Jefe would be good for us. If Kroll makes that happen, I might decide to let his retirement go through."

CHAPTER TWELVE

Jolene sat on top of a wooden picnic table. The table perch afforded her an excellent view of the San Rafael Valley and the Rocking H Bar Ranch. Located in what might be called the front yard of the casita, the table was near a large rock surrounded fire ring. Hadfield was enjoying the morning. She decided the night before they would not cook inside the luxurious Renegade Motor Home. The forty-foot long rolling house suited her perfectly. Burns got the computer system set up while she explored the coach. They would use the computer and sleep in the RV. Meals would be eaten inside the casita or on the picnic table, which was her preference. She sipped coffee and contemplated her surroundings and valley before her. She decided to see what Burns was doing in the barn.

She found him putting shoes on a cleaned up, brushed, and seemingly docile Don Cameron. A well-brushed Jazz lay on the dirt floor watching the process. The horse was cross tied in the barn aisle. The horse whinnied a greeting. Burns spoke but went about nailing a horseshoe to a hoof. It was the last one. Andy began crimping the nails and using a rasp to smooth off the crimps. Once he finished with the four feet, he applied a hoof sealer. As Burns gathered up the shoeing tools. Jolene asked a question.

"Will he let me pet him?"

"I think so just talk to him in a normal voice and pet his neck. And don't act afraid either."

She took a deep breath and approached the horse.

"You are the big beautiful guy, and I bet you know it." She said softly. Don Cameron nickered as she stroked his neck. Jazz got up and walked over to her. She felt his paw touch her leg. She wound up rubbing the horse with one hand and the dog with the other.

"They are both starved for attention," Burns said walking up to the horse on the opposite side.

"What kind of magic did you work on them? Two days ago they were wild."

"I am probably the first person they couldn't intimidate. And I suppose it is a matter of trust. Both of them wanted somebody they could trust. Apparently, they decided that was me. Being a total stranger probably helped more than anything. This big fellow is one the easiest horses I've ever shod. I wish I could have known Lyon Hamilton. He did an excellent these animals."

"I bet Don Cameron and that mare you have at home would make a pretty baby."

"Careful you're beginning to sound like a horsewoman."

"Jo is the prettiest sweetest animal I've been around. Burns, you did a good job of raising and training her. I won't ever forget the first time I saw her. She ran up to that fence and slid to a stop. I thought she was going to fall over. She looked at me as if to say, who are you?"

"I knew she was from a good bloodline when Rabun and the humane society people brought her the Mustang and the burro to the place. I was surprised to find out registration papers came with her. If Lois Thornton will sell me, Don Cameron, I will breed the two of them."

"So you are still convinced Hamilton is dead?"

"Yes, I've believed that since the beginning. And Carson Bell telling the story about this horse and dog showing up at his place validated it."

"When are you going to ride him?"

"As soon as I put a saddle on him."

Jolene watched as Burns put a saddle pad on Don Cameron. The horse paid little if any attention to that. Burns came back with the heavy saddle in hand. He effortlessly sat the forty-pound mass of wood and leather on the horses' back. After buckling the cinch straps, he retrieved the headstall and bit. Don Cameron accepted the bit without hesitation.

Burns unhooked the cross tie ropes and led the horse outside to the large corral. He adjusted the stirrup length. With reins in hand holding a fist full of mane, Burns swung into the saddle. Don Cameron didn't move. Burns squeezed him with his legs and the horse started forward. Andy walked the horse around the corral, turning him and reversing him. After a few minutes, he urged him into a trot. Cameron settled into an extended trot and lapped the corral. Burns nudged him into a lope.

Leaning over the fence rail Hadfield watched. She wasn't much for horseback riding. She rode the mare, Jo. She'd ridden the Mustang a couple of times. She just wasn't comfortable in the saddle and never felt she could control the horse. Burns rode as if he was born in a saddle. Only he grew up in a city and rode his first horse, a pony, in an amusement park. Watching Burns ride Don Cameron reminded her of the first time she saw him ride Major. She could tell Burns was happy. Jolene looked down at Jazz, the border collie sitting beside her. He might as well of been smiling. She didn't hear the ATV approach and stop.

"I'll be damned if I ever thought I would see that." Carson Bell said as he walked up beside Jolene.

"That half-breed Apache Russell wasn't spinning a tale when he said Andrew Burns knows horses. He sits that horse as good as Lyon Hamilton ever did. Damn, I wish Lyon were here to see it."

Burns slowed Don Cameron and walked him to the gate he leaned forward and opened it with the horse sidestepping out of the way. Once the gate closed, he rode over to where Bell and Jolene stood.

"I'll give a hundred dollar's cash for him right now Carson," Burns said.

"Yeah I bet you would. Try that with Lois Thornton and see how quick she tells you where to go. She knows what that horse is worth."

"And I will pay her price and expect her to sell me the dog as well. All she has to say is how much I need to write the check for." Burns got down from the horse and petted Jazz.

"Maybe I should have mentioned that to her this morning when she called me," Carson said.

"Lois told me a real interesting story about a woman detective she hired to come out here and work with a private eye to find out what happened to Lyon. I didn't tell her I'd already met the lady. My question is when were you folks going to let me in what's going on?"

"As soon as we got a feeling for the situation out here and the lay of the land so to speak. When you told us about the horse, I figured I see if could make peace with him first. Jolene works for Lois Thornton. I work for her husband, the General. He is called General Clout behind his back. Our job is to find Lyon Hamilton and to get the ranch back. Buddy Russell and Bernie, aka Burrito Cruz, are working with us. You and your hands are welcome to join the team. But there is a price for that."

"What might that be, cowboy?"

"You know that this valley is full of busy bodies and nosey neighbors. It is worse than a small town. Our business stays on this ranch. Sort of like what happens in Vegas. I'm not going to tell you about any laws I break, which will be a few. And in return, I expect you and your hands to keep quiet about us and what we are doing. We are just a pair of wealthy tourists minding our business and enjoying the culture. Carson should anyone asks about us; we have taken the RV and gone camping, the Grand Canyon comes to mind. Comprede' Mi Amigo?"

Carson Bell looked at Burns for a moment before speaking. "Well, I'm sure as hell glad somebody is taking this serious. I might be seventy-five years old, but I've got one rodeo left in me. Count all my hands in and me. All of them will keep your secrets, and expect the boys to be over here offering to help. And you will find your neighbors to be the same way. Nobody in this valley likes what happened on the Rocking H Bar. And I wouldn't have believed anything you said if I hadn't just seen you riding Don Cameron. Maybe you can ride rope and shoot with the best of them."

"I'm a little slow in the roping the department. I'm going to get my chaps and spurs out of the RV. Then I'm going to explore your ranch. Tell TR and Butter Billy I'll be riding with them to check the Rocking H Bar cattle. Jolene why don't you offer Carson some coffee and fill him in on what we know."

"I can do that. If Carson can drink my coffee."

Burns walked off toward the motorhome leading Don Cameron. Jazz trotted out in front of them.

"Miz Jolene, I think the General has the right man for the job, and he has a good woman behind him. Some things that happen around here have a way of going to the grave with these folks. You know what I'm saying. Let's get some of your coffee. Maybe Lois Hamilton will sell Andy Burns the Rocking H Bar to go along with that horse and dog. He needs a good barn."

"He has one Carson. It's got the prettiest registered buckskin mare you ever laid eyes on in it. A bay mustang gelding, a burro named Jackass and a couple of mules. The mules belong to his hired man and caretaker. Wilson Gilmore plows with them."

"What are the horses' names?"

"The mare is registered as Baldwin County Jo. The local sheriff and humane society removed her, the Mustang and the burro from someone who couldn't take care of them. I saw them the first time three weeks after Andy got them. He said I wouldn't believe how bad they looked. He was still taming the

Mustang, and Jo wasn't quite a year old. The burro's name fits. Andy was pleased when Rabun the deputy showed up with the registration papers for Jo."

"You never said what the mustang's name is?"

"Apache."

"And Burns broke and trained him?"

"Yes, he trained Jo too."

"Do you mind telling me how she came to be named Jo?"

"It's a long story, Carson. Let's get some coffee and I'll fill you in on what we know about Lyon Hamilton, and I'll tell you the story."

"How did you come to meet Andy Burns?"

"One of my missing persons turned up dead in his Lake. I automatically thought Burns put him there."

Hadfield paused and looked across the San Rafael. They stopped at the picnic table. "It didn't turn out that way at all. Have a seat and I'll get some coffee." She disappeared into the casita. Andy Burns rode off on Don Cameron.

Hadfield enjoyed visiting with the old rancher and felt like he would be on their side no matter what. Burns made the right call letting the old man in on what they were doing. She believed Carson Bell would keep his mouth shut. She heard something and looked around from her seat at the picnic table. Two horses were approaching. One appeared to be the size of the Clydesdales that pulled the Budweiser beer wagon. Except it didn't have flashy large feet. The cowboy riding it needed a horse that size to haul him. The second horse, a gray one, was closer to the size of Don Cameron and the rider was a pure cowboy.

"Good morning," Jolene said smiling.

Both cowboys doffed their hats and held them against their chests.

The rider on the gray horse was built like a running back, and extremely handsome. Jolene figured every cowgirl in the county was after him. He spoke first.

Ma'am, you must be Miz Jolene, I'm Tobias Rutledge, everybody calls me TR. On closer inspection, she saw he was older than he appeared, probably close to mid-forties.

The largest one, at least six five and three hundred or so pounds, grinned at her. She said. "You must be Butter Billy Three."

Yes, ma'am, that's me. This big ole horse is named Kenworth. I'm pleased to meet you, ma'am."

"Miz Jolene, Mr. Carson told us Mr. Burns is riding Don Cameron. I've worked around that horse since it was a colt. And I thought Lyon Hamilton was the only man who could handle him. He put me on my butt a couple of times. Mr. Carson also told us why you folks are here. Count me in for anything I can do. Butter here feels the same way."

"Yes, ma'am Mr. Lyon was like family to me. Between him and Mr. Carson, I had two daddies. So it didn't matter that my real one left. I'll do anything I can. I expect you and Mr. Burns will hear from Miguel and Estella too."

"Thank you, gentlemen. Thank you very much. I need to give you both a piece of advice. Don't call Andy Burns mister."

"Ma'am we'll do our best to remember that."

"I can tell you both have wonderful manners. And I love the way you cowboys remove your hats. But please, I'm Jolene or Jo. And both of you can drop the ma'am business."

"Yes, ma'am Miz Jo." Butter Billy said.

"Would you gentlemen like some ice tea? I just made it; it's southern style."

"Thank you, ma'am that would be nice."

Jolene smiled and went into the casita and came back carrying a tray with a picture of tea and three glasses full of ice. She sat it on the picnic table and poured the tea. Both men dismounted and ground tied their horses.

Butter Billy was the first one to take a sip. "Wow, it's sweet, and sure is good. Is that how southern folks make their ice tea, with sugar?"

"A lot of them make it both sweet and unsweet. It gives folks a choice. What kind of horse is Kenworth Billy?"

"Ma'am he's a Belgian. I gotta have one his size; I'm too big for a quarter horse."

"Is he something like a Clydesdale?"

"Yes, ma'am he's a draft horse. He's a couple a hundred pounds smaller than a Clyde, maybe a little more. And he doesn't have feathers on his feet either."

"Feathers, like in bird feathers."

"Oh no, ma'am that's what they call that hair around a Clyde's feet."

Jolene started to say something, but she saw Andy Burns riding up. He stopped Don Cameron and got off, ground tying him like the others.

"Andy, this is TR and Butter Billy Three. They came over to join the posse. I'll go get another glass." Jolene said.

The Cowboys introduced themselves, and both talked about Burns riding Don Cameron until Butter Billy noticed the knife on Andy's belt. TR was studying the rifle scabbard tied to Don Cameron's saddle.

Burns carried the knife almost horizontal on his left hip. He unsheathed it and handed it to Butter Billy handle first. Both men thoroughly examined the knife. Burns observed that neither one appeared to notice his holstered pistol.

"Burns Made," Butter Billy said, reading the etching on the blade. "Did you make this?"

"Yes."

"Wow, you ride Don Cameron and make knives. Mr. Carson says you fly airplanes, how cool is that?"

"If you made that rifle scabbard hanging on Don Cameron you ain't a half bad saddle maker either?" TR said.

"I made the scabbard, but I've never made a saddle. So don't insult a saddle maker by calling me one."

"What kind of rifle are you hiding in that scabbard Mr. Andy."

"One I built. It's a .338 Lapua, I use a 300-grain bullet running around 2700 feet per second."

"You built your rifle?" Butter Billy asked.

"Yes."

"Can we see it?"

"Sure," Andy answered. He walked over to Don Cameron and removed the rifle from the scabbard. He ejected the magazine and pulled back the charging handle to check the chamber. Satisfied it was unloaded, he folded down the bipod and placed the rifle on the picnic table for the two cowboy's inspection.

Jolene handed him a glass of tea. Burns patiently answered questions about the gun. And the knife. He tactfully stayed away from the cost of the items. And didn't mention his airplane was a jet. He was more interested in learning about the Rocking H Bar and when the duo was going to check the cattle. And Mr. Andy would be welcome to ride with them anytime.

Ivalou Vargas checked the towels in the Motel 6 room and selected the one she believed the cleanest. She wrapped it around her butt and upper legs. She sat on top of the second choice towel placed on the edge of the bed. Ron Kroll occupied the only chair.

"Kroll you and your fetish for miniskirts and is a pain in the ass."

"You mean a pain in the bare ass," Kroll said smiling. She flipped him off.

"It's not bare, asshole I've got on real underwear."

"What no thong? What kind of hooker are you?"

"A phony one." A middle finger display accompanied this remark.

"You picked the seediest motel in town so don't complain about the quantity of DNA on the bed spread."

"You could keep that in mind when you made your choices of my attire."

"Hey, we gotta keep it looking real."

"I get any more real looking, and Desmond & M&M are going to have to walk me to the door and stand outside."

"You do look real. Look good too."

"Kroll I'm going to kick your ass."

"Promises all I get is promises."

And another bird. Vargas explained they had found accommodations at the only extended stay motel in Nogales. And it wasn't bad. The Motel 6 was the local hooker haven so it would work for their meetings. She enjoyed the banter but got down to business.

"Havelee Harris is in Arizona. She will be down here in a couple of days. She has to check in with the field offices. I've got her booked into the same motel where the rest of us are staying. It's close to here and not bad for our purposes. It's not as seedy as those places can be. I do know she wants to meet you. She knows how we get in touch. Now, what have you learned about this ranch."

"Bradford laughs and says he made the owner an offer he couldn't refuse. I think they buried the real owner on the property somewhere. Bradford would not part with the kind of cash it would take to buy a place like that and then leave it for the millions he claims El Jefe will pay. I got a chance to look around the so-called ranch office. You already know the place is called the Rocking H Bar. The only name I find associated with it is Lyon Hamilton. We need to know all we can about the ranch and Hamilton. I've lifted a business card and a flyer on a stud horse."

Ivalou was recording the conversation. "I'll get the guys started on the research. We got the GPS coordinates during the drive by recon. Havelee will get them to the helicopter pilots in Phoenix. I think she needs to get the helicopter moved closer. Tell me about the help."

Bradford has a staff of two white thugs and four Mexicans. With me, there are eight people there. Two of the Mexicans left this morning. The white guys are a couple of pieces of work. One is called Pauli Dumas. AKA Porn Dude. I made the mistake of asking how he got his handle. The freak reached inside his sweats and hauled it out. That sure as hell ain't normal. The guy could satisfy a horse. Inbred and gross come to mind.

The other one is Nathan Norman AKA Numb Nuts. That is the guy I put down in the casino bar. He is still recovering from a cracked sternum. I asked him why he was called Numb Nuts. He said it was because he had been kicked in the balls so much he didn't feel it anymore. Bradford told me it was because he wasn't the brightest bulb on the tree. Numb Nuts keeps talking about getting even who sucker punched him. I don't think he knows it was me. Porn Dude is supposed to be a computer genius. We've got to keep our hooker game looking real. In case that guy has a way to get on my phone."

"What about livestock on the ranch?"

"I have only seen dried droppings. Bradford says he made a deal with the neighboring rancher to let his Cowboys look out for the herd. He didn't want anyone complaining about animal abuse. He said they are not allowed to approach the area around the main house. The Mexicans patrol on ATV's to make sure."

Are you going to have any trouble leaving the place for meetings?"

"I told Bradford I would come to work for him, but I wasn't staying on a ranch in the middle of nowhere all the time. I said I had to get laid and party. And working for him wasn't going to happen if I couldn't come and go when nothing was happening."

"Some of those women on Backpage advertise outcalls where they go to the customer. Is it possible we could pull off me coming down there for an outcall? That way I could see the place up close."

"That's an idea; it would have to be when I have the place to myself. Right now I can't see that happening. Besides we are using an outcall text message for the, I need to be extracted help code. And you don't need to show up looking like a hooker with that freak Porn Dude around. Bradford makes the guy wait in the car when they go somewhere. He says Dumas has some freaky oversexed problem and has tried dry humping women in restaurants."

"Yuck!"

"I would say screw this operation and kill him if he put his hands on you."

"Why Ron how sweet and macho." She said sarcastically.

"Ivalou, I like you professionally, and I would like to get to know you personally when this is over."

"I knew you had an ulterior motive for miniskirts and thongs."

"I like your smart ass attitude."

"It's a nice ass too. I know you watch it every chance you get. Do Numb Nuts and the freak ever leave the ranch?"

"Yes, they appear to be Bradford's protection detail. Bradford rides in the back seat of an SUV, Porn Dude drives and Numb Nuts rides shotgun. They are more for his ego than they are guards. Cartel thugs wouldn't consider them a threat."

"Maybe that's why he hired you."

"That is what I'm thinking."

"It sure would be nice to have a good look at the place. Think you could take some phone pictures."

"I will try."

Ivalou looked at her notes and then the time on her phone.

"Well big boy, bang the bed for ten seconds and yell oh baby a few times so the neighbors will think you got some. I need to go. I've got more clients to see, real hombres, not limp dick make-believe cowboys." She put her notebook in her purse.

Vargas stopped at the door and gave Kroll her come hither look. "And I would like to see you when I'm off duty as well." She left the door open when she left the room. Kroll watched her walk away. He heard some catcalls from local males hanging around the motel. The door opened on the pimped up Escalade, M&M got out and fixed the catcallers with a mean glare. Ivalou flipped them the bird.

What a woman, Kroll thought as he watched.

Chapter Thirteen

Burns and Burrito Cruz left the casita at 7 AM. They rode in the old dual wheel one-ton pickup truck pulling a horse trailer complete with a couple of horses. Burns drove. The trailer was beat up like the truck. To anyone looking, they were working cowboys. Their clothes were sun bleached and could stand washing. Both wore sweat stained cowboy hats that had seen better days. Along with the hat, Burns wore wraparound sunglasses and a ragged scarf. Taking their time, and the long way around, they entered the Rocking H Bar ranch road just after 7:30.

Burns spotted the fence post with the horseshoe nailed to it. He stopped beside that post, with the truck blocking anyone from seeing the post from the house. Andy scanned the area for anyone out and about. Both men got out of the truck, and Cruz ambled toward the house in a bowlegged gait that wasn't fake. Despite his years behind a badge, Burrito Cruz was a ranch hand. As Cruz hailed the house, shouting anybody home.

Andy removed the protective cover from the adhesive on the back of the modified horseshoe in he carried. It looked exactly like the one nailed to the post. He quickly and carefully pressed over the modified shoe against the one on the fence. Burns then turned and leaned over the hood of the truck taking in the headquarters house and the surrounding buildings. Recalling the clandestine dash cam videos taken by Buddy Russell, Andy placed everything with his own eyes. A hillside behind the headquarters area. There was also a water tank and windmill that he didn't remember from the video. Burns spotted another horseshoe on the side of the tank.

A familiar man wearing a T-shirt with a casino logo and work pants came out of the house. Burns noticed the imprint of a pistol the man carried in his waistband covered by the T-shirt. Andy shifted his position slightly to access the pistol he carried.

"Morning!" Cruz said.

"It's a good one. What can I do for fellows today?" Ron Kroll replied.

"We need work. Part time all the time whatever you may have. We're good hands and have our horses." Cruz nodded toward the trailer. One of the horses decided it was a good time to show his impatience by stomping the trailer floor. The sudden noise startled Kroll. Cruz gestured with his thumb over his shoulder toward Burns.

"My partner back there is a horse shoe'er to."

Kroll looked at them. His gaze lingered on Andy for a moment longer than it did on Cruz.

"Fellows we have a full crew right now. But I appreciate you coming by here. Is there some place I could reach you if things change?"

Burrito Cruz had anticipated that question and pulled an old feed receipt from his shirt pocket. With a pencil stub, he laboriously wrote his given name Benito Cruz along with a number on it. He handed the paper to Kroll. Kroll thanked him and said he would call if things changed. Cruz added they were going to check with some of the other ranches in the valley. Burns got back in the truck and cranked the motor as Cruz got in. They both waved at Kroll when as Andy turned the truck and trailer around. As they reached the end of the ranch road, Burns received a text from Jolene. He had read it before he turned the truck onto the forest service road.

It's working. White male in the T-shirt is still watching you guys.

"You wanna tell me what is all fired important about that horseshoe you worried with all the way down here, and you don't have it anymore," Cruz said.

Burns laughed and showed Burrito the text. The detective cowboy turned used car salesman and PI looked at it for a few seconds trying to comprehend what it meant.

"SONOFABITCH IT'S A CAMERA!"

"Go to the head of the class. It's a wireless daylight and night infrared solar powered wide angle unit I put in that horseshoe. It transmits to a private web address. I've got a few more ready to put out when we find a place."

"Won't they notice the horseshoe wherever it is you put it?"

"Not likely, I stuck it over one already nailed to the fence. I noticed it when I watched the video Buddy took when he came by looking for a real estate listing."

"I saw that video and I sure as hell didn't see no horseshoe nailed to a fence."

"That's because you weren't looking for one. Bet you didn't see the one on the side of the water tank either."

"Hell no, and this looking for a job scam ain't gonna work twice. How you gonna put one of your fakes on the water tank?"

"First off, it is not a fake horseshoe. I got some old ones out of my barn and put the cameras in them. Put all weather double-sided adhesive tape on the back. I turned on the camera and stuck it on top the existing horseshoe."

"Damn, I gotta see one up close."

"I'll show them to you."

"The half-breed said you were one sneaky cowboy. Anything to you being the real La Migra El Con Riflie?"

"Nothing they ever proved," Burns said. He drove the truck and enjoyed the San Rafael morning.

At the casita, Burns drove the truck around to the barn. He unloaded the horses and turned them out to the corrals. A whinny from the barn told him somebody wanted attention.

Andy was met by the Border Collie, Jazz, as he entered the barn. The dog sat and waited to be petted, which happened. They made their way back to the corral stall where Don Cameron waited his turn. Burns stroked the horse's nose and rubbed his neck. He spoke softly to the big animal.

"I just came from your old home big guy. Nice. I'd be mad too if somebody run me off a place like that. But I expect your fit throwing was more about losing the cowboy who raised you. I thought Major was the best horse I could get. Now that I've met you I know I was wrong. You are the best. And we are going to find your cowboy and bring him home."

Burns laid his head on the Don Cameron's neck; the horse whinnied as if he understood every word said. Andy patted his neck and stepped back. He walked out of the barn and around to one of the corrals. Andy pulled the leather gloves out of his back pocket and put them on. He walked around the corral and selected a few dried horse apples off the ground. Burns went back to the RV and placed the horse apples on the picnic table. Buddy Russell had arrived and was inside the motor coach with Burrito and Jolene. They were looking over her shoulder at the computer screen. One the screen was the Rocking H Bar headquarters house. The old cops were awed by the surveillance camera in a horseshoe.

Burns looked at the screen. "Anything going on?" He asked Jolene.

"No, right after you left the grossing thing I've ever seen happened. Some butt ugly dude, ugly enough to play Frankenstein in porn flick walked out on the porch pulled down his sweat pants and peed off the porch. Is that a guy thing peeing off a porch? Burns I've seen horses standing around with their thingy hanging out, but that freak would put a horse to shame."

"That must have been Pauli Dumas, the failed porn actor, and computer genius."

"There's not any way he can find that camera is there?" Russell asked.

"I doubt it. The retired cop that set up these cameras for me made them hack proof. He is the guy that got the ID information off that footage you sent me."

"I still wanna see those cameras close up," Burrito said.

Burns opened a cabinet and removed the hard camera case. "Come outside; I'll show you some of my toys."

Jolene pointed out a Mexican walking from the barn on the Rocking H Bar. Cruz and Russell watched, Burns went outside to the picnic table and opened the case. He unwrapped a couple of horseshoe cameras and then unwrapped a couple of horse apples. He put these beside the real ones he picked up in the corral. A few minutes later the two PI's and Jolene joined him at the table.

"Horse shoes and horse shit go together," Cruz said.

Burns picked up the horseshoes and passed them around. Russell and Cruz studied them intently. Jolene looked appreciatively at the one she held.

"Burns, I will admit I wondered if you'd hit your head when I saw you bubble wrapping horseshoes and horse apples."

"You got cameras in that horseshit!" Cruz exclaimed.

Burns nodded affirmative, watching as both Cruz and Russell reached for a horse apple. Both of them picked up the real thing.

"DAMMIT THAT'S REAL SHIT!" Cruz exclaimed.

"Glad it wasn't fresh," Russell deadpanned dropping the horse apple."

Burns was laughing now, and Hadfield was having a hard time keeping a straight face.

"I knew you two didn't know shit from surveillance cameras," Burns said.

Jolene giggled.

"Well suppose you pick up the right horseshit and show us," Cruz said.

"Tell me Burrito, do you think anyone we've seen today would pick up horse shit?"

"No, not likely. Not like a couple of dumbass private detectives I know."

"Where are you going to put them and how are you going to get them there?" Russell asked.

"That hillside overlooking the barns and the house. I figured I would put couple there. I want to put another horseshoe on the water tank. There a no dogs on that ranch. We would have heard from them if there were. I can't see that bunch posting sentries at night. So about three AM tomorrow morning I'm going to pay them a visit and put out some cameras."

"What if the freak comes out to pee?" Jolene asked.

"You will warn me via radio and I will hide."

"How am I going to know to warn you?"

"These cameras have night vision capabilities as well. It is the same stuff I use around the place back home. I'll be wearing night vision goggles, and I'm going to solicit Buddy and Burrito to go along as a backup. We'll ride horses over there. I've been over a couple of times with TR and Butter Billy checking on the cattle. I've put out infrared trail markers I will be able to see with the night vision goggles. Once we get to the ridgeline, we will have to mark the trail as we go."

"What if they have someone on guard?" Jolene asked.

"We will know that before we go. You will see the guard on the camera. I don't believe Bradford has brought in anything illegal yet. We drove in the place without problems. No guards on the road or anything. They probably did that until they got comfortable and realized guards attract attention. They have a Mexican male with an AK 47 riding a four wheeler watching from a few hundred yards away while we check the cattle."

"So you think going over there at night is the thing to do?" Jolene asked.

"Yes."

"And what if you have to shoot somebody, or they shoot you?" She said.

"Let's hope I see them first."

Hadfield was not happy with the plan.

"I'm good with it," Russell said.

"Me too," Cruz added.

The Double B hands, TR and Butter Billy Three, showed up later and asked if Burns wanted to ride with them to check on the Rocking H Bar cattle. Russell and Cruz volunteered, and Andy declined, saying too many riders might raise the guard's interest. After the PI's saddled up and the foursome rode off. Hadfield swept the real horse manure off the table and faced Burns as he packed up his wireless cameras.

"Burns are you sure going over there in the middle of the night is smart?"

"The word smart is subjective when used to describe this whole endeavor. If we were smart, we wouldn't be here. Now that we're here, all we have to do is outsmart the crooks and cops. In this case, probably the FBI as well. It's possible they are looking at Bradford and Kroll for something. And it is also possible that Kroll is undercover."

"If he is they went to a lot of trouble to put him there," Jolene said. "You are describing the big picture, quit dodging the question about tonight."

"I've changed my mind about tonight. I've got seven pairs of NVG's, tonight is night vision goggle orientation. I don't know how much experience Cruz and Russell have had with the things. Them being unfamiliar with the equipment adds to the risk. It is a calculated risk, but the odds are in our favor. We'll go to the Rocking H Bar tomorrow night. I doubt they will post guards. What all the thug on the ATV is doing is making sure no cowboy stumbles into what is going on. I think it is worth the risk to put out the cameras. It's a wise move whether or not it's smart, well that's subject to interpretation."

"Well, don't get yourself in trouble or hurt. We are not duty bound to take risks. We are not cops anymore Burns."

"No, we are sophisticated surveillance specialists."

"You're going over there no matter what I say."

"Go to the head of the class Miz Hadfield."

"I won't forgive you if you get yourself killed."

"You will thank me after David Cromwell reads my will."

"Burns!"

"Then you won't have to ask permission to redecorate the kitchen."

"BURNS! THAT'S NOT FUNNY!"

"You will be sitting in that motor coach watching the camera. You will have my back. I trust you. That's why I'm not worried about wandering around over there. I'm going to saddle Don Cameron and ride over to the Double Headquarters and put in a camera. Carson Bell has got a horseshoe or two nailed in the right places."

"Why do you want a camera over there?"

"To see who comes for a visit."

"How are going to put the camera up without him or Miguel and Estella noticing?"

"Bell will to distracted by me showing up on Don Cameron. Miguel and Estella will be too busy watching him. I could walk away with the whole barn, and nobody would notice."

"Burns I'm glad you are honest."

"Thank you, how about researching motorcycle dealers in Nogales and Sierra Vista. A couple of side by side four wheelers might come in handy. No bright colors, I prefer green or camo."

"Will do."

They walked to the barn and Jolene watched him saddle the stud horse. Don Cameron greeted her with a whinny. She rubbed his nose while Burns worked.

Burns swung into the saddle and trotted Don Cameron down the ranch road toward the Double B headquarters.

"Miguel and Estella were beside themselves when I rode up on Don Cameron. Carson Bell just smiled."

"I watched his expression when you rode off. It was sad, almost guilty sad. And by the way, you did a good job of placing the horseshoe camera. A great angle on the front of the house."

"Thank you, wait until you see the pictures you get from the next ones I plant."

Hadfield took a deep breath. "OK, I'm good with it. But I don't like it."

She watched Burns strap a folding camp chair and a tripod behind Don Cameron's saddle. He hung the heavy duty padded bag that held a large spotting scope around the saddle horn. The next thing was the saddle scabbard that held his rifle. He shouldered a backpack that carried his hydration bladder. Burns mounted Don Cameron and looked down at Jolene.

"How do you know when you've hung too much stuff on a horse?" She asked.

"When you land on your ass in the dirt," Burns answered smiling.

"I can't imagine a horse throwing you."

"Imagine it; it's happened more than once." Burns patted Don Cameron's neck. "This big guy thought about it. So far I've stayed ahead of him. But he might put me off just to show me he can."

With that, Burns rode off toward a place he'd spotted earlier. Ten minutes later he stopped unloaded his gear and loosened the saddle cinch. Don Cameron browsed the area for grass to crop while Jazz watched over him and Burns. Andy studied the Rocking H Bar through the spotting scope with a sniper's eye for detail. He carried a pad with him and made notes and sketches from time to time. The SUV left with two men in it. Burns was too far away to positively ID the occupants. He guessed they were Bradford and Kroll.

When Andy rode back to the casita, Jolene told him Russell and Cruz were back and put up the horses. They would be back later in the evening as would TR and Butter Billy, who were bringing steaks and beer.

"Carson Bell had visitors this afternoon."

"They wouldn't have been driving an SUV would they?"

"Yep and it was Bradford and Kroll. Bradford appeared to introduce Kroll to Bell. So Kroll must be the new kid on the block."

"Sounds like it. I'm going to put Don Cam up. I'll be back and look at the footage of Bell's visitors. Did you find some ATV's?"

"Yes, a couple of side by sides with cargo boxes. Both camo. They aren't cheap either."

"I didn't expect they would be. We have time to go over and complete the purchase this afternoon. Where are we going?"

"Sierra Vista. I figured we would need a trailer. There's a place over there with a good selection."

"Good, I knew there was some reason I like you."

"Burns!"

Chapter Fourteen

The four agents met in Havelee Harris' room at the extended stay motel in Nogales Arizona. The supervisory agent was meeting with her team for the first time. After thanking Vargas for the up to date reports and the forwarded videos of the ranch. Harris gave her thoughts on how they would proceed.

"I need to get a handle on the San Rafael Valley and where that ranch is. So we need to drive over there first thing in the morning. You guys have one serious looking ranch truck and another pickup truck in your motor pool so that we will travel in those. Ranching communities despite their being far apart, are often busy body small towns. Everybody knows everyone else's business. We need to visit the other ranches under the pretense of investigating what happened to Lyon Hamilton. We will split into two teams and cover all of them leaving the closest ranch for last. We will meet there and decide if we want to work it with one team or both teams. I understand we have at least an hour driving time to get there from here. So we probably need to leave by seven AM latest. Any questions or thoughts on this?"

"I think we need to dress down, casual, coats and ties will scare those people. And we probably need to be in the valley at seven AM. Those people start work early, and they are not likely to be around their houses much after eight." M&M said.

"Good point. Can everyone be ready to leave by six? We can get breakfast at a drive through."

Everyone agreed. Havelee changed the subject. "Ivalou tell me how your prostitution deception works."

"When we need to meet, I post an advertisement in the escort section on the Backpage website. The phone I use will only accept Kroll's number, and he replies via text. It all sounds like a john meeting a hooker. If he needs to meet, he sends a text asking if I'm working. If he sends a text wanting an outcall and doesn't specify a dress code, that means he needs an emergency backup. If he sends a text with a dress code, that means he needs a quick undercover extraction."

"Where do you meet?"

"We use the Motel 6 here in Nogales."

"Motel 6, why?"

"It's a hotbed motel for hookers."

"Explain your dress code," Havelee said skeptically.

"Boss, you dress like a ho. Tank top and a mini or a mini dress. Short shorts are good, as long as they are tight. I hope you got a thong." Ivalou answered smiling.

Desmond and M&M were trying to keep professional demeanors, but it wasn't working. Havelee pointed at them.

"And what do you two wear to these meetings?"

"He is yo pimp; I am his enforcer. We dress badddd." M&M answered in street dialect.

"Tell me this wasn't your idea," Havelee said to Ivalou.

"It was Kroll's and it works. Bradford has a computer genius on the payroll. That's why we use texts and the Backpage ads. The geek is a real pervert, ex-porn star. And he's surveilled us once and Bradford once. Both times using a different beater car. Des and M&M picked up on them. They did not follow Ron to the last meeting. Apparently; they are starting to trust him. But we have only met once since we've been here."

"I want a face to face with Kroll. When can you set up one of these meetings?"

"To make it go smooth, it doesn't need to be a hurry up and with the distance he travels tomorrow night or the next day might be the soonest. I'll send him a Penelope tease text saying I'm coming to Nogales for a couple of days."

"Oh, so you are Penelope," Havelee said smiling.

"Yeah, Penelope with her hot blond friend. A special on twosomes."

"Girl you wouldn't."

"If you want to get face time with Kroll, you will. I hope you got stiletto heels and a slut suit."

"What we do for the FBI. We probably need to go shopping after dinner tonight."

"Expense it as undercover clothing. And don't forget the thong. Bras are optional."

"Dressing like a whore on the bureau's dime will be fun."

"You better turn out looking hot. We only pimp the best." Desmond deadpanned.

The four FBI agents got out of their cars at the entrance to the Double B Ranch.

"What have you guys come up with?" Harris asked Desmond Taylor and M&M.

"Nothing of substance. Everyone we spoke with knows Lyon Hamilton and no one believes he would sell the ranch and leave without notice. They all say the owner of this ranch,' Desmond pointed to the Double B sign post, 'probably knows more than anyone because his hands are working the Rocking H cattle." Taylor was reading from his notepad.

"We were able to talk to some cowboys from another ranch whose pastures are across the dirt road from the Hamilton ranch. These guys said they've seen armed Hispanic males patrolling the fence line along the road. These guys ride in a side by side ATV." M&M added.

"That's consistent with what Kroll reports," Vargas added.

"We went to every place on the east side of the valley with an open gate. The constant answer was we need to talk to Carson Bell, the owner of the Double B." Desmond said.

"It sounds like the same answers we've been getting. Does anyone have any thoughts on the four of us visiting Mr. Bell?"

"Everyone we talked to said he is a congenial old gentleman. A widower retired military. His deceased brother ran the ranch for many years. Carson Bell has been running it for at least twenty years. Four agents might be of concern to him. We need to decide who is the primary interviewer." Ivalou said.

"I agree,' Havelee answered, 'I'll be primary, Ivalou you are secondary and taking notes. Des you and M&M listen and watch. If you feel, I've missed something. Ask, but I don't want to give Carson Bell the idea we're ganging up on him."

The got into their trucks and started down the ranch road. None of them noticed TR astride a dapple gray gelding watching from a copse of cottonwood trees a hundred yards away. TR put his binoculars back in his horn bag and removed his radio. He lifted the handheld unit and keyed the transmitter.

"Mr. Carson we got visitors on the road. Two trucks, two women in the first one. Two black guys in the second. They have been parked at the entrance talking. Now they headed your way. The women won't hurt your eyes either. The men are clean cut. Most likely they are the FBI people you heard about."

"Thanks, TR, ride on up this way. I've been getting phone calls concerning them all morning. Between the two trucks, they've visited everybody in the valley. I guess they saved us for last."

Carson Bell clicked off and looked up the ranch road. He saw the dust from the approaching vehicles. Carson sat back in his comfortable chair. Estella brought him another cup of coffee. He told her to put on some more and picture of lemonade also. A few minutes later the two pickup trucks stopped in front of the headquarters house. Havelee Harris got out of the passenger side of the truck; Ivalou was driving. With both women out their vehicle, Desmond Taylor exited from the passenger side of the pickup, M&M shut off the motor and got out. They walked toward the four-foot-high picket fence that defined a small yard around the ranch house. They stopped at the closed fence gate and looked toward the porch.

"Open the gate and come on up," Bell said. The agents approached the porch somewhat warily.

"Unless there's a rattler laying out in the yard there's nothing up here that bites," Carson added recognizing the apprehension and noticing the tell a tale bulges of weapons underneath their jackets. Desmond Taylor looked apprehensively at the ground near his feet.

Carson got out of his chair and greeted the agents when they stepped onto the porch. "Welcome to the Double B I'm Carson Bell."

Havelee pulled out her credentials and presented them to Bell. "I'm FBI Special Agent Harris. This lady is Special Agent Vargas; these gentlemen are Special Agents Taylor and Morris."

Bell shook hands with all four of them. He removed his hat when he shook hands with the women.

"Pleased to meet you folks, have a seat and tell me what I've done to get a visit from the FBI. Especially two as pretty as you ladies. The bureau has certainly more pleasant people than the last ones I saw."

"What reason did you have to see an FBI agent Mr. Bell?" Havelee asked.

"Ms. Harris, I was an Air Force pilot. As a young man, I flew Forward Air Control missions in Viet Nam. After two tours

I was transferred to Air Transport Command. Essentially that is the Air Force's airline. I flew T-45's which are Cessna Citation business jets. We would on occasions have FBI agents on our passenger manifests. They were always serious looking types. That was over thirty years ago. They didn't have any pretty ones like you back then. I'm an old white haired cowboy wearing a big hat now. I can get away with saying that." Carson smiled at Havelee.

"Somehow Mr. Bell I don't think you are all hat and no cattle." She smiled back.

"Spoken like a westerner. Are you from this side of the Mississippi River?"

Mr. Bell. I grew up on a ranch in Oklahoma and this valley reminds me of home."

"It should; they filmed the movie Oklahoma near here on the original San Rafael Ranch. The family that owned the ranch donated it to the state. It has been a location for several movies."

"I didn't know that," Havelee answered.

"I'll sit here and talk about the San Rafael all day. What can I help the FBI with?"

"We are looking into the disappearance of Lyon Hamilton.

"Well, it's about time somebody besides me believes he's missing. That idiot sheriff doesn't. My lawyer who is also Lyon's lawyer, J.P. Williams in Nogales, said the sheriff would not take a missing person report. He won't do it because his crooked deputy Willie Hillman went over to the Rocking H Bar and got in bed with those bastards. He's as queer as a three-dollar bill. Pardon me ladies and you gentlemen, I am not politically correct when it comes to crooked cops."

"How long have you known Lyon Hamilton?"

"We went to high school together. Lyon went to the Navy for a hitch. I got a scholarship to go to Arizona State. My brother was the rancher. Lyon came back from the Navy straight to the Rocking H Bar. His grandparents left him the place. I would visit with him when I was home on leave. We got reacquainted after I retired and moved back here. Our wives passed away within a year of each other. Here comes somebody else that tell you about Lyon. Tobias Rutledge, he's one of my hands now. TR was working for Lyon when he went missing."

All the agents turned to see TR ride up to the ranch fence and dismount. He tethered the gray to a hitching post. Vargas was the only one who noticed Havelee's sharp intake of breath. TR opened the gate and walked confidently to the porch. He wore a faded tan work shirt, sweat stained Stetson hat, worn and scraped shotgun chaps over faded Wrangler jeans, and packer boots with riding heels and spurs attached. A large blue plaid scarf was around his neck. A small horizontal sheathed knife wore cross draw fashion on his belt. When he reached the porch, TR removed his leather gloves.

"TR these are FBI agents, introduce yourself." Carson Bell said.

The agents all got up from their seats. Desmond and M&M were the closest.

"Desmond Taylor," Des extended his hand, "Pleased to meet you."

"Likewise, Tobias Rutledge."

"Mickey Morris, Mr. Rutledge, I've never seen a real cowboy. Man, your outfit is just too cool." M&M said shaking hands with TR.

"Thank you, Mr. Morris but days like today it's just plain hot."

The men smiled, and TR stepped over to the women. Havelee, face flushed, almost stuttered when she extended her hand.

"Havelee Harris." She managed to say.

TR removed his hat with his left hand and held it over his chest. He took Havelee's hand.

"Tobias Rutledge ma'am folks call me TR. And if you won't arrest me for saying, you are too cute to be an FBI agent."

"Ivalou Vargas," Ivalou said extending her hand.

TR shook it and said. "Ivalou and Havelee, those are the two neatest girl names I've ever heard. Mr. Carson, did you check these ladies' badges? They are just too pretty to be cops."

"TR, you aren't old and white haired like me, you might get handcuffed for saying that."

Havelee reached in her jacket pocket for her credentials and fumbled the move dropping the creds. Red faced, she reached down for them. TR was faster; he scooped up the folder first. Opening the credential wallet, he examined the picture.

"You're better looking in person." He said handing Havelee her credentials.

"Th-thank you," she said blushing like a school girl.

"Desmond, why don't you and M&M interview Tobias. I see some chairs on the other end of the porch." Ivalou said giving Havelee time to regain her composure.

The agents and the cowboy walked to opposite end of the verandah. Havelee whispered, "Thanks," to Ivalou. Carson Bell noticed Harris' reaction and heard the exchange.

"I see you are a bit taken with my cowboy Agent Harris." He said with a wry smile.

"Speechless is more like it,' Ivalou said as she calmly picked up the interview.

"When did you learn Mr. Hamilton was missing?" She asked.

"Several months back when a valuable stud horse he owns showed up right where your car is parked. The horse was saddled and all lathered up from running hard. Lyon's Border Collie was standing beside him in the same shape as the horse. Lyon would never let Don Cameron out like that. My ranch hand got him unsaddled and settled in a corral. I tried calling and got no answer that evening. I drove over there the next morning. I was greeted by AK-47 carrying thugs and told in no uncertain terms not to come back. I called the sheriff. That jackass Hillman went over there to investigate. He came back here and told me Lyon Hamilton had sold the ranch and moved to the Fiji Islands. Hillman then told me the new owner said I could have the horse and dog as a neighborly gesture. Because his help treated me rudely. An AK-47pointed at you is a little more than treated rudely. Hillman also told me I would be arrested for trespass if I ever went back over there."

"Do you still have the horse and dog?"

"Yes, you can't sell a horse like that in this state without papers. And this so called new owner didn't bother to send the papers. The dog is the same way. He is out of a championship line of border collies."

"I gather from your tone you don't think the new owner is a legitimate rancher."

"No, I don't. Bradford is his name, and he hasn't got a clue what a ranch is all about. I ran into him a couple of times in a casino bar a few months before Don Cameron and Jazz showed up over here. I had a little too much to drink the first time I talked to him, and I was grousing about that moron in the White House saying our borders are secure.

"Bradford showed up a few weeks later and said he would let my cowboys work his cattle and split the profit at sale time. He said my men could come over and check the herd, but they have to stay away from the main house and barns. That is not a problem because the herd is on the east side of the ranch. The scary part is there is always an AK47 toting guard watching from an ATV when my guys are over there."

"How many hands do you have Mr. Bell?" Havelee asked getting back in the game.

"Three, TR, Butter Billy three, and Miguel. Estella, Miguel's wife, is my cook and housekeeper. Here she comes now."

Estella came out of the house carrying a tray with cookies, lemonade, tea, and coffee. She sat the tray on the table between them. She smiled, went back into the house and came out with a similar tray for the group on the other end of the porch.

"I don't want to hear about or see any of this; no thank you, professional nonsense out of you ladies or your men on the other end of the porch. Help yourselves and if you don't, you can leave." Bell said as he poured a glass of lemonade.

The women politely indulged. Havelee glanced at the far end of the porch and saw Des and M&M were partaking as well.

"What kind of name is Butter Billy three?" Ivalou asked.

"His full name is William Edward Butterfield the Third. He is one of the largest cowboys you will find in the saddle. He rides a saddle broke Belgian gelding he calls Kenworth. And he is one of the best windmill men in southern Arizona. I constantly get calls for him to fix somebodies windmill. He's over in Cochise County today working on one.

"Clarify something for me," Havelee asked. "Who are Don Cameron and Jazz?"

"Lyon's quarter horse stud, Don Cameron of Lochiel, is Cam's registered name. The dog's registered name is Jazzman of Lochiel. Lyon called the horse Cam or Don Cam. Miguel is one of the best vaqueros this side of the border. He barely got the saddle off Cam before the animal came unglued. All anybody can do is put feed and hay in the corral. That animal went from manageable too wild on his run from the Rocking H Bar to here. The dog is the same. Both of them raise hell charge the fence and everything else. I've never seen a horse act that way."

"You said you still have them?"

"Yes, I still have them, but they are not in one of these barns. Lyon boarded horses for folks. This guy Bradford ran all the borders out. There were thirteen of them. Ten of them are here now. I took them in. There are three mares in the lot and being ranch raised you ought to know about studs and mares in heat. Miguel was able to trick the horse and the dog into to following him to another barn on the other side of the ranch. I've got printed information on him with pictures that Lyon gave me if that will help you."

"That would be great."

Bell returned and handed a color printed flyer to Havelee.

"Wow, he is drop dead beautiful! A honey buckskin with blue eyes, gosh I love that mane! And his tail almost drags the ground." She said looking at the picture. Vargas was looking over her shoulder reading the flyer.

"That horse gets five grand to get some!" She exclaimed when she saw the stud fee. Bell stepped back inside the house, and Vargas whispered to Havelee.

"I bet TR doesn't charge near that much."

Havelee swatted at Vargas with the back of her hand saying, "I guarantee he hasn't got one long enough to charge that much either."

"Girl you have a dirty mind."

"That's the pot calling the kettle black."

Carson reappeared before the agents could even giggle. He took his seat and handed Havelee some pictures of Lyon Hamilton riding Don Cameron and some pictures of the horse's different offspring.

"I know why you don't believe Lyon Hamilton is missing. No horseman would sell out and leave an animal like this to run off under saddle to another ranch.

"Mr. Bell, has anyone working on behalf of Hamilton's family, a private investigator maybe, been by here inquiring about Mr. Hamilton?" Havelee asked.

"I talked to my lawyer, of course, I told you he was Lyon's lawyer as well. J.P. Williams in Nogales told me Lois Thornton, Lyon's sister, contacted him a month or so ago in regards to Lyon and what was going on at the ranch. She asked for recommendations about private investigators out here. J.P. gave me her phone number and address in Alabama. Lois' husband is a retired Air Force General. Last time I saw them, he was in line for another star."

"Would you give us that information sir? We need to contact Mrs. Thornton."

"Sure, if you will excuse me again." Carson Bell went back into the house. It appeared Desmond and M&M were finishing up. Bell returned with a piece of paper containing Lois Thornton's information."

"Mr. Bell, thank you for your time and the refreshments. We will do our best to find out what happened to Mr. Hamilton. And we will likely be back to see you." Havelee said.

"I couldn't be so lucky that either one of you would come back to see an old man like me. But if you call ahead of time I'll make sure TR is here to see you."

Havelee blushed she noticed that Desmond and M&M were now standing shaking hands with TR. She and Vargas walked toward their car. Havelee stopped to look at TR's horse. He was a muscular dapple gray quarter horse with a big powerful rump. The saddle was a working rig, slick seat high cantle, doubled rigged. A lever action rifle in a saddle scabbard, a lariat was tied down next to the saddle. Horn bags, a cantle bag, a pair of fence pliers hung in a holster made for them. She was patting the horse's neck when TR appeared beside her.

"You ride?"

"Not in the past few years. I grew up on a ranch. I know how."

"Hop up there I will adjust the stirrups when you get your seat."

"I can't ride today."

"Yes, you can. I'll give you a boost."

Her special agent's poise went away, and she raised her leg. TR caught her foot in one and calf in the other. She didn't have time to hop on the other leg before he hoisted her up. Once in the saddle, he adjusted the stirrup length until she was comfortable.

"If he comes back without you, I'll come looking," TR said and patted the horse's neck. Havelee turned him away toward the ranch buildings.

Desmond and M&M walked up and stopped beside Vargas. All three were watching Havelee ride the horse. She was walking him in a circle.

"You guys can head back to town if you like," Vargas said.

"And miss seeing her bust her ass. Not a chance." M&M said.

Havelee changed directions with the horse and trotted him down the ranch road. Her blond hair moved in the breeze. She sat the trot like a veteran cowhand. Once she was out of site Vargas commented, "I'd of fell off before I got to the barn."

"I wouldn't have got up there in the first place. I'm not getting on anything that has four legs and is bigger than me." Desmond said.

"Personally, I prefer two wheels. I wish I had my scooter here. This motorcycle country." M&M added.

They heard the horse's hooves on the dirt and turned to see Havelee canter the gray down the driveway. She pulled him in a slide stop, turned and walked him to the hitching post. Harris vaulted out of the saddle and landed lightly on her feet.

"That was fun, thank you." She said to TR touching him on the arm.

"You are welcome back anytime; he is one of my working horses. You can ride him or the other one. And Mr. Carson's got a string of nice geldings too. I love to show you the ranch."

Havelee took a card from her pocket and wrote a number on the back.

"My private cell number is on the back. We will be working out of Nogales for the foreseeable future. Give me a call. I'll take you up on your offer." She smiled and touched his arm again.

Turning back toward her vehicle Havelee was relieved to see Desmond and M&M were back in their truck. She got in the passenger side. Ivalou got in the driver's seat and started the car. Once they started down the ranch road, she looked over at Havelee.

"When you gonna get laid girlfriend?"

Harris flipped her the bird. "Vargas you been undercover as a whore too long."

Ivalou laughed.

Jolene and Andy walked with TR and Butter Billy back to the old Jeep FC170.

"We appreciate you guys coming over and bringing the steaks. That was some of the best meat I've ever eaten," Jolene said.

"You are welcome ma'am you sure know how to grill them. That is San Rafael Valley Grass feed beef. It comes from another ranch here in the valley. The lady rancher sells it in local stores." TR answered.

"That was some fine cooking Miz Jo; you need a chuck wagon." Butter Billy said.

"Thank you, it was nothing fancy. Estella can out cook me in a heartbeat."

"You guys need to come to Alabama and let her grill some bass for you." Burns offered.

"Never been there. You get many tornados where you live?"

"We get a lot of watches and warnings hurricanes are a big worry as well. We live a few miles inland from the Gulf. I sure like this truck. Think I could talk Carson Bell out of it?" Burns said.

"You'd have to Miguel to keep it running. And Estella probably wouldn't move to Alabama."

Burns laughed. "I don't think they've made these things since the fifties. I would like to drive it before we leave."

"Now we can make that happen."

"OK guys, thanks for bringing the meat. We will do it again. Let us get back to Burrito and Buddy."

They walked back to the fire ring in front of the casita. Russell and Cruz were sitting beside a nice fire.

"Think those boys could help us any?" Cruz asked.

"Probably, I believe we can trust them. It worries me that TR is making eyes with that FBI agent, Havelee Harris. I build a rifle for her once. And I wouldn't put it past her to use her charms on TR. I don't want him spilling the beans about us being here and what we're doing."

"I think TR is just looking for a roll in the hay. Havelee is mixing business with pleasure. TR said he didn't bring up our being here to the agents who interviewed him. And when I invited Carson over he said he didn't tell them either. Lois Thornton mentioned TR when I first talked to her. Lyon Hamilton thought well of him as a hand. And wanted to ensure TR always had a place on that ranch." Jolene said.

"You need to contact Lois and tell her to expect the FBI to show up on her doorstep," Burns told Jolene.

"I will. Tell me again how you plan to install those camera's tonight." She answered.

"Indian style with a half-breed Apache leading the way."

"Indian no fight at night spirits bad." Russell spoofed.

"Going to be just like your ancestors stole horses in the dark."

"Heap dark tonight no moon to light pale face's ugly mug."

"Are you sure you won't get lost," Hadfield asked.

"Not with Half Breed leading the way."

"Indian have heap good headlights on the jeep. Not get lost in the dark too many bad spirits. Rechargeable Maglight Indians best friend."

"Maybe Indian have too much fire water. No more beer for you tonight."

"Indian carry two Maglights and canteen of good whiskey," Russell replied. "Paleface carry fake horse shit."

"Tonto Russell will not need his Maglight," Andy said.

"Kemo Sabe mean pale face is a dumb shit. Injun always carries Maglight." Russell answered.

"You can put your feather in the headband of the night vision goggles Injun."

"Indian grew up with indoor plumbing. Can't find the outhouse in the dark without Maglight."

Hadfield was enjoying the repartee, but it wasn't helping her misgivings about the endeavor. Even with Burns telling her there was a black ops commando team backing them up.

The trio left for the Rocking H Bar shortly after two AM. Burns rode Don Cameron, Russell and Cruz followed in the newly purchased ATV's. When they reached the Rocking H Bar, Burns rode ahead, keeping in touch with Buddy and Burrito via radio. Jolene sat in the RV watching the front of Rocking H Bar Ranch house on her computer screen. The green tint made the scene look spooky. A horse whinnied in the corral, and Hadfield jumped.

Jazz scouted ahead of Burns and Don Cameron. The dog seemed to understand the mission. The small party got within a couple of hundred yards of the hillcrest overlooking the ranch headquarters. Burrito Cruz clicked his radio twice. Burns knew Cruz would wait ready to ambush anyone who might be chasing Burns and Russell should they run into trouble. Russell stopped just short of where the ranch road crested the hill. Both Russell and Cruz carried modified AR-15's Burns brought from Alabama. The weapons were suppressed and capable of firing a full auto three shot burst.

Burns got off Don Cameron and crept to the top of the hill. He lay flat on the ground and studied the ranch house and buildings. Everything was dark, no one stirred. He moved back to Don Cameron mounted and rode the crest parallel to the ranch. When he found the location overlooking the barns and bunkhouses, Andy dismounted carrying a couple of horse apple cameras.

Stealthy Burns placed the cameras and activated them. He clicked his radio mic four times. It was almost a minute before he heard Jolene answer. Her voice was clear but low in his ear piece. "Cameras working, good resolution on the barns, and the bunkhouse. I can see the door clearly."

Two sets of two clicks told Burns that Russell and Cruz also copied. Andy mounted up and rode back to the first point he selected. After dismounting he crept down the hillside, stopping once to place another horse apple camera. When Hadfield verified it was working, Andy moved to the critical part of the operation. He was downhill from his horse and in the open. There was no moon only stars. Russell got out his ATV and went to the hill and stopped where he could give cover fire should Burns run into trouble.

Burns reached the water tank and unslung his rifle. As he gave a series of clicks and then realized Jazz was standing next to him. At this point, he could not risk giving commands to the dog. He hoped the dog would warn him should anything move. He carefully moved around the tank until he found the horseshoe stuck on the side. Carefully balancing his rifle Burns removed the horseshoe camera from his waist pack and then removed the tape protecting the adhesive. He turned on the camera and carefully placed over the existing horseshoe. Andy heard Jolene's voice through his ear piece.

"Camera is working there is a dog that looks like Jazz taking a dump right in front of the porch steps."

Burns looked and smiled. Jazz finished his business and trotted over to Burns. Andy rubbed the dogs head and then moved around the tank. Jolene began breathing again when she heard the clicks indicating Andy was mounted and on his way back.

She was outside waiting when she heard the ATV's approaching. Jolene walked over to Burns when he rode up.

"This has been the longest three hours of my life." She said. Don Cameron nuzzled her neck. Hadfield stroked the horse's mane glad Burns couldn't see the tears in her eyes.

Cruz and Russell bunked in the casita. They were all having coffee in the motorhome the next morning. Burns connected a computer to the large TV, and they all watched Kroll come out on the porch with a cup of coffee, followed a few minutes later by Bradford. Numb Nuts walked out of the door and stood on the porch. He held a cup of coffee. A few minutes later Porn Dude came out of the house shirtless wearing gym shorts. He walked barefoot down the steps and out in the yard. Willie Hillman appeared on the porch similarly attired.

Jolene shook her head. "I know what's coming now."

Pauli reached in his shorts for his penis and realized he was standing in dog shit.

"Maybe that will teach him to use the bathroom like everybody else," Jolene said watching Porn Dudes antics as he hopped around the yard on one foot.

"Teach him to wear shoes too," Russell said.

"Notice who's in bed with them?" Cruz asked.

"Yeah, Willie Hillman. Why am I not surprised?" Russell answered.

"Tell me about Hillman," Burns said.

"He started out with Tucson PD, got through the academy but didn't make it out of training before they cut him loose. Sierra Vista hired him; he lasted six months before he moved to the Patagonia Marshalls Office. It took a year there before he was asked to resign. Nogales PD was next, two months before he was asked to leave. The guy is bisexual and hung like a horse. He's probably playing I'll show you mine if you show me yours with shit foot there." Cruz said gesturing at the TV with his coffee cup.

"Hillman was welding fence pipe when the current sheriff got elected here in Santa Cruz County. The sheriff ran off all the good folks and kept the bad. Hillman has lasted longer here than anywhere else. It's because the Sheriff keeps him working down here out of the most populated areas. Out of sight out of mind. I expect Hillman just hasn't been caught at anything yet. I hope when he does he brings down this current sheriff with him."

"Why is that?"

"He's bought and paid for by El Jefe. That damn drug lord contributed to the sheriff's campaign fund even. The biggest billboards and the biggest signs get you elected around here. Hell, you don't even have to lie much."

"You considered running against him?"

"Yeah, but I can't run against El Jefe's tax-free cash."

Chapter Fifteen

Ron Kroll, Ashton Bradford, Porn Dude, Numb Nuts, and their visitor Deputy Willie Hillman, were all drinking beer on the front porch of the ranch house.

Kroll and Bradford listened to the thug's trash talk and Hillman's macho responses. Kroll wondered how the man got a police job. His phone buzzed with a text message.

Hey baby got a special for the next 24h 2 Girls for $$$ hot blonde friend loves wearing thongs OXOXOX Penelope

"SHIT" Kroll announced.

"What's up," Bradford said taking the proffered beer from Hillman. Kroll took one from the drunk deputy.

"Thanks, Willie. My favorite hookers got a girlfriend in town tomorrow. Doing a two for one."

"YOU MEAN SHE DOES TWO OF US FOR THE PRICE OF ONE" Porn Dude yelled. "WILLIES OFF TOMORROW WE'LL REAM THEM BITCHES GOOD"

"This ho travels with two mean ass pimps. PD and they'd probably shoot your ass on sight when they see your crank. Can't have the merchandise stretched outta shape." Kroll replied.

"Hell Kroll you don't wanna share."

"Correct good buddy; I don't want you nowhere around her," Kroll said with malice.

"Pauli you buy your pussy in Nogales. I can't have the heat with you damaging a whore this side of the border." Bradford said.

"Shit boss you ain't no fun."

"Willie you say you off tomorrow?"

"Yeah, Mr. Brad whatcha ya need?"

"How would you like to ride up to Tucson with me Porn Dude and Numb Nuts. We need to bring some trucks back. Ron will drive us up there. Payday is a couple of hundred each."

"I can handle that. Nogales here I come."

"HOT DAMN" Porn Dude yelled.

Numb Nuts belched.

Porn Dude and Willie went inside to watch a porn flick. Numb Nuts went to the bunk house to watch a soccer game with the Mexicans. Kroll and Bradford sipped their beer on the veranda. It was much quieter now.

"Those idiots would go crazy without satellite TV," Bradford said.

"I'll buy that; there ain't a damn thing to do at this place."

"Yeah, but the payday will be worth it. After you drive us up to Tucson, you're on your own for a day or two. The Mexicans are hauling product up from Mexico tomorrow. They will load the trucks tomorrow night, and the drivers will leave the next day. We will stay out of the way for this first run. In case the DEA and the Border Patrol are watching too closely."

"I've only seen one Border Patrol truck since I've been here. And it was in the daylight. I haven't seen anything on these roads after dark. Hearing that Sheriff talk I expected a couple of thousand Mexicans to come running by every night."

"Yeah, you would think so. But it doesn't happen here. That's why I got this place. If tomorrow's load gets out, there will be one more of this product, and then a live load will come through. We'll have to be around for that one."

"Live load?"

"A shipment of women, and you will need to keep a close eye on Porn Dude while they are here."

"I can do that," Kroll answered.

Ron Kroll was trying to keep from staring at the mini skirt clad Havelee. The woman was hot and didn't realize the view she was treating him to. She was sitting in the only chair. And exposed the black satin thong she wore every time she moved. Kroll figured Ivalou dictated the hooker dress code. And she was extra hot as well. And seated next to Kroll on the edge of the bed. A towel in place as usual under her bottom.

"Kroll, I wasn't wild about this hooker gambit you and Vargas use to meet. But I will admit, it works. We heard a few catcalls walking in here."

"I hear 'way to go gringo' when I walk back to my car. I always have a satisfied smile on my face."

Vargas blushed slightly and elbowed Kroll.

"Ouch! You have to keep up the charade."

"What is happening at the ranch?"

"I believe they are bringing a large shipment of narcotics across the border. In the next couple of days. Bradford gave me a thousand bucks and said, 'have a good time, don't come back for at least two maybe three days.' Exact words. He and his goons left when I did. I last saw them getting on northbound I-19."

"Any chance they doubled back to check up on you?"

"It's possible, but I doubt it. Bradford seemed anxious to leave the ranch."

"I've gotten all clear texts from Des and M&M since we've been here," Ivalou added.

"So what makes you think something big is up?"

"El Jefe flew in yesterday afternoon."

"Expand on that please."

"A helicopter brought El Jefe to the ranch. He conferred with Bradford and left two middle eastern types with AK47's at the ranch. They moved into the bunkhouse. After El Jefe left Bradford decided everybody was leaving."

"El Jefe just flies across our border when he feels like it?"

"Not really, Bradford said the balloon was down."

"Do you have any idea what the balloon being down means?"

"No."

"The middle eastern connection bothers me as does El Jefe flying into our country like he owns it," Havelee said.

"Kroll one of your reports said you had met Carson Bell, the owner of the neighboring ranch. What's your take on him?"

"That he's sorry he was drinking and running his mouth in a Tucson Casino bar."

"Why do you say that?"

"Because Bradford bragged about the conversation. He said it gave him the idea to hijack a border ranch in an area where there are no apparent border problems."

"So you don't believe he bought the ranch from this Lyon Hamilton?"

"No, I suspect Hamilton is dead and buried somewhere down there."

"You feel like something bigger than narcotics is in play here. Do you think we could catch El Jefe on this side of the border when this happens?"

Kroll had hesitated before he answered. He was thinking about the question and was totally distracted when Havelee flashed him a look at her crotch.

"I think all we can hope for is to stop whatever they have planned. And try to catch Bradford before he crosses the border. We can't mount the typical surveillance operation like we can in a city. HRT could do it. But I don't think Headquarters will send them out here on a wait and see what happens operation. And the more people that get in the loop, the more chance Bradford hears about it. The man has connections inside the bureau. Catching El Jefe would be pure luck. Taking him out would the best we could hope for."

Kroll thought for a minute or two before answering. Havelee heard on of her cell phones beep and excused herself to the bathroom.

"Are you enjoying the view you're getting of Havelee's thong?" Vargas asked.

"Yes. You could at least give her some competition."

Kroll wasn't expecting Ivalou to lean over and give him a quick kiss on the lips. And an equally quick flash of her hot pink thong.

"I'm staying in at the Best Western tonight. I'll text you the room number so you can pass it on to Havelee." Kroll said.

"Like hell," Vargas replied giving him a jab in the ribs with an elbow. "And, you can forget it, she got the serious hots for a cowboy on Bell's ranch."

"No shit?"

"She even rode his horse. And the way she's squirming around in that chair flashing you; I think she's got riding him on her mind. Talk about lust at first sight. And that cowboy stud was thinking the same thing."

"At least she will be close by if I need help."

They heard the bathroom door open, and Havelee walked back to her chair.

"Ivalou you have anything to ask Ron while we have his undivided attention."

"No, but if we stay in here much longer, the guys will go pimp on us and start knocking on the door."

"They do get into the pimp thing don't they," Havelee answered.

Kroll left the room first and waved at a group of Mexican males who watched him leave. He gave hard looks at Desmond and M&M. Kroll went to his car and drove to the Best Western. He checked in for a two-night stay.

Havelee watched the performance discreetly from the window.

"Think we need to get Des and M&M to walk us out?"

"No, they will stand outside the car and look mean. We walk out and tell the hombres in their dreams."

"I know one damn thing. I'm not ever wearing a thong again. I can't sit still with it up the crack of my ass."

"You gave Kroll plenty of free shots. It was bothering him."

"I could tell he was uncomfortable about something. You mean I was flashing him?"

"Big time girl. Every time you moved Kroll got a look. He was watching you like you watched that cowboy TR."

"Come on I didn't think I was that obvious."

"You weren't too bad. But if you'd been wearing that slut outfit Mr. Bell would have stroked out. I bet TR will want to show you the barn next visit."

"Vargas you have a dirty mind. I was going to ask him to show me the barn. But that will have to be the second date. He's coming in town tonight and taking me to dinner. Text the guys and tell them we're on our out."

"Maybe he can get up in time to drive back to the ranch and clock in."

After checking into the motel, Kroll went out to dinner. He texted a number, and a smiley face to Vargas' Penelope phone and promptly forgot about it. Back in his room, a leisurely shower was in order. After that, Kroll laid down on the bed to see what was on TV. There was a discrete knock at his door. Not expecting anyone he wrapped a towel around his nakedness, grabbed the Burns modified SIG pistol and walked softly to the door. The thought of looking through a peephole and being shot dead by an El Jefe assassin occurred to him. Kroll stood to the side of the door and called out, "who is it?"

"It's Ivalou open the door before I chicken out."

Kroll glanced at the peephole and saw her standing away from the door holding up her credential folder. "Are you alone?" He asked.

"Yes, Damnit! Let me before somebody sees me!'

He checked the peephole again and saw see her favorite gesture. Ron took a deep breath and opened the door. She stepped in closed the door behind her and locked all the locks. She sat her purse on the table and removed her jacket. Kroll watched as she carefully removed her Glock and placed it next to her purse.

"Do you always greet women in your motel room wearing a towel around your waist and a pistol in hand?"

"Only when I'm not expecting them."

"Oh, if you weren't expecting me I'll leave."

"Don't! Please stay. I'll get dressed."

"Good, you don't need to dress on account of me."

Ivalou stepped over and kissed him full on the lips removing his towel at the same time. He led her to the bed and put his pistol on the night stand.

"You finally decide you weren't going to need that." She said as she stroked his member and at the same time she unbuttoned her blouse. Kroll was busy undoing her jeans. The only thing she said when she stood naked in front of him was.

"Turn back the sheets. I know this is a nice joint, but I still don't trust motel room comforters. And Kroll, I don't do one night stands."

"I don't either."

Sated after a second round, they lay entwined in the other's arms and legs. Ivalou rested her head on Kroll's shoulder. "I figured Havelee's outfit primed your pump, and I was right." She said nibbling at his ear.

"It was your outfit the first time I saw you."

"My outfit or Penelope's?"

Kroll lightly pinched her butt. "You. Penelope let me see more of you."

She snuggled against him. "Kroll, no man has turned me on like you do. Why do you think I sit on a towel when I've got my Penelope outfit on?"

"So you won't catch crabs off the bedspread?"

"KROLL!"

"How did you get the boss lady in a slut suit?"

"Took her shopping and picked it out for her. She has no idea of how much she showed you. Poor Desmond and M&M had to keep their heads turned. I was afraid M&M would wreck the Caddy."

"Honestly, I think she knew what she was doing."

"Maybe, but I think her mind was on TR the cowboy. That phone call was from him. He's coming to town and taking her to dinner tonight."

"So you two have advanced past the agent and supervisor agent to girl talk."

"Yep. That wrangler is a hunk, and he went right for Havelee, and she opened the door. I don't think I could like somebody that might track horse shit into the house."

"So you're a city girl then?"

"Not really, It's beautiful down there, but too far from civilization. Now that little place went through to get there; I could like."

"You talking about Patagonia?"

"Yeah, that's it."

"It looks peaceful. When this is over, I've got to find a place to settle down and be a retired FBI agent."

"So you are going to retire?"

"Yes, that is the deal, stop Bradford and they will let me retire. They even gave me a notarized contract saying that. And I have a lawyer that will make sure they abide by it. They've tried to fire me too many times."

"All the records say you got fired. The contract is probably smart. But can we get Bradford?"

"They are moving a large shipment of marijuana out of the ranch in the next couple of days. That's why Bradford told me to leave for two or three days. And he left with his thugs too. He did tell me he has human cargo coming through, and I think we might do something with that. He says my job is to keep an on Porn Dude. Bradford is afraid he will screw up the merchandise."

The remark earned Kroll a jab in the ribs.

"You're good at that, remind not to piss you off."

Vargas smiled demurely. "I'll run that by Havelee when you get more information. Do you still think something bigger is going down like a terrorist attack?"

"Absolutely, with a bunch of AK-toting ragheads on the place. They've even got an RPG or two. We could probably make a case on that. But I think they have something bigger in the works, and they will stage it out of that ranch. That is when we move in. However, we might not get much time to act. I wish there were someplace closer to for you guys, and we could have a SWAT team on standby."

"With Havelee screwing the cowboy she might think us moving to that ranch is a good idea. There are some RV hookups there. It is possible; I mention it. We will still have to come to town to play Penelope."

"Or have a quickie in the barn."

"There will be waiting list for the barn. Havelee has it staked out already."

"She must be in heat big time over that cowboy."

"Yeah, they got it bad for each other. Almost as bad as I have it for you, Kroll. And I'm not letting you get away. So don't go do something stupid like getting yourself killed."

"I like a woman who says what's on her mind."

"Good."

Ivalou untangled herself and got out of bed. A few minutes later she came out of the bathroom and put on her panties. "For the record Kroll. I like this kind better than those thongs in your fantasies. They cover my ass."

"And a nice ass it is. My fantasies about you don't have anything to do with thongs."

She put on her bra and began to dress. Ivalou sat on the bed and touched Kroll's bare chest. "Just so you know Kroll, I'm serious about this is not being a one-night stand for me. If it is that way for you tell me now, and it will never happen again."

He kissed her. "Lou, you aren't a one-night stand woman. I want you to keep coming back."

"Me too, but we have to be careful."

"We will be."

He walked her to the door and stood behind it naked as she slipped out. Ivalou turned back and smiled sweetly. "I think I like the naked look. Maybe with the pistol too."

Kroll watched her leave. When she was safely in her Bu-car, he closed the door, and leaned against it. "Wow." He said to the empty room.

Lois Thornton answered the FBI agents' questions under the watchful eyes of the General. She made no mention of Burns and Hadfield being in Arizona. What the FBI didn't know would not hurt them. And to the General's thinking they did not know very much. This federal fishing trip only verified what he already knew compliments of Andy Burns. At least the FBI showed some respect since one of the agents was a supervisor.

"So based on what you have learned from your private investigator. You believe your brother has met with foul play and did not sell the ranch to this person Bradford." The Agent asked.

"That is correct."

"And this investigator, a Mr. Russell searched all the real estate records and could not find a sale of the ranch?"

"That is correct."

"Why is it that your brother is reported missing by the Baldwin County Sheriff's Department and not the sheriff's department in that county, uh, Santa Cruz County?"

"The Sheriff out there refused to take the report. He told me my brother was not missing. Our Sheriff Rabun called him, and that man told Sheriff Rabun to worry about policing his county and not Santa Cruz County Arizona."

"We will speak to Sheriff Rabun before we return to Mobile. I appreciate your being candid with us."

"You never did say why the FBI is interested in my brother in laws disappearance." The General said.

"We were asked to follow up on information on his missing by the local field office. The request was to verify specifics about

Mr. Hamilton and the ranch. I can't say why Tucson wants that. And if I knew, we wouldn't be able to tell you."

"Can we expect full disclosure when you conclude your investigation?" The General asked.

"It's possible you might be briefed on the aspects which involve Mr. Hamilton and his ranch."

"Unless you have any more questions for Mrs. Thornton and myself, we have plans for lunch. Good day gentlemen."

They watched the FBI men leave.

"It doesn't appear they have a clue about Andy and Jolene being out there."

"And they don't have the need to know either."

"Just like we don't know what they are doing. Are you planning on leaning on the Director to find out what they are planning?"

"Not unless they screw up. Which is likely."

Jolene and Andy watched the computer screen. The cameras were perfectly positioned providing excellent video of the Rocking H Bar. A gang of foreign males loaded marijuana bales into the old box trucks delivered to the ranch by Bradford's thugs. Unless it were prayer time, distinguishing between Mexicans and middle easterners was difficult. El Jefe's helicopter made several daring fence top level flights across the border, discharging two or three heavily armed men each trip.

"Burns remind me never to complain about your flying again after watching that helicopter."

"You mean you wouldn't want frequent flyer passes for El Jefe Air?"

"NO! And I wouldn't want to be that pilot either if he crashed that helicopter."

"If he crashed it and got out alive, El Jefe would kill him. If he died in the crash, El Jefe would dig up his corpse and kill him again. Then go kill his family."

"I don't know what's scarier for this country Mexican drug lords or radical Islam."

"We will find out soon, check the feed on the rear horse apple camera."

They watched as some males spread out prayer mats facing east.

The General went to his study and reviewed the images and reports from Burns. Burns concluded with the presence of heavily armed obviously Muslim males arriving in El Jefe's helicopter and the visit by the drug lord himself. There were two issues, smuggling, and terror. The General quietly passed the word about the trucks and the three routes they would likely take out of the San Rafael.

Chapter Sixteen

TR and Butter Billy Three were repairing a fence between the Double B and the Rocking H Bar pastures. Both men were working off horseback because there were no ranch roads of trails near this section. A fence stretching tool broke and Butter Billy returned to headquarters to get a replacement. TR continued to work. His horse was enjoying cropping grass despite his hobbled front legs. TR heard an ATV approaching from the Rocking H Bar pasture and checked the location of his horse. Tobias' rifle was on his saddle when he saw the side by side ATV gaining speed and coming his way. TR moved toward his horse and the rifle.

A burst of automatic rifle fire came from the ATV. TR's horse bolted the moment he reached it. Even hobbled the gelding could quicker than his owner. And the burst from the nearby machine gun caused the equine to ignore Tobias' shouted whoa. TR stumbled as he tried to grab the horse.

From the ground Tobias Rutledge watched his horse flee carrying his rifle. TR heard a voice behind him yell; "ALLAH AKBAR INFIDEL WILL DIE ALLAH AKBAR."

TR struggled to his feet looking for a place to hide. The ATV crashed through the loose fence wire. The passenger fired another burst from an AK-47 rifle. The rounds missed TR striking the ground fifty feet away. TR ran in the opposite direction and dived into a low area that would provide some cover.

Butter Billy Three topped a rise on his way back to the fence when he heard the ATV approaching. He spurred his huge gelding Kenworth forward. The massive horse reached full gallop, and Butter Billy pulled his rabbit-eared double barrel 12-gauge cowboy shotgun from his saddle scabbard. The big cowboy managed to shoulder the weapon and cock both barrels and stay astride the charging Kenworth.

The bursts of fire didn't cause the horse to waver. Butter Billy's accidently firing both barrels did. Kenworth proved the saying you could shoot a gun off the back of any horse, once. Butter Billy was airborne and about learn the pitfalls of his other dream, riding saddle broncs in a rodeo.

Andy Burns' charge to the sound of the guns was not as dramatic as Butter Billy's. Burns watched the incident unfold from a ridge three hundred yards away. He'd dismounted with his rifle when he first noticed the ATV. The crosshairs of his scope were aligned on the driver when the passenger begin firing. Andy shifted his aim as Butter Billy galloped onto the scene reminiscent of the cavalry in a B western.

The extra-large cowboy hit the ground with all the grace of feed sack falling off a truck. Burns aimed at the now slowing ATV. The passenger was clutching his chest. No one was in the driver's seat. He lay on the ground with blood pumping from his throat. Butter Billy wasn't moving. Andy hastily mounted up and spurred Don Cameron to the scene.

TR recovered and was yelling into the ranch two-way radio he carried and ran toward his partner. Between panicked transmissions, he is calling out to Butter Billy.

"Butter ya got the bastards! Wake up Butter! Wake up!"

Don Cameron slid to a stop as Andy dismounted and trotted to the prostrate Butter Billy Three, who was lying flat on his back and moaning. Jazz ran toward the ATV growling.

"Stay still Butter. TR is calling for help." The radio hissed static each time TR released the transmit button.

"I must have broken the radio when I hit the dirt, Andy. Carson should have answered by now." TR said.

"Let me see the radio," Andy said reaching for the small portable unit. TR handed it to him and spoke to Butter Billy."

"You alright Butter?"

"Kenworth threw me! Where is he?"

Andy examined the radio and turned the frequency knob. He handed it back to TR.

The cowboy pushed the transmit button. "Carson!"

"What do you need TR?" The rancher answered.

"Mr. Carson a couple of assholes wearing those Arab head rags charged me shooting a machine gun from an ATV. They came from the Rocking H Bar. Butter got 'em both with his shotgun. But he got bucked off. He's hurt. We need some help out here!"

"I'll send Miguel in an ATV and call that jackass sheriff of ours. How bad is Butter Billy?"

"He's conscious and asking about Kenworth. Jackson ran off too. And he is hobbled. Both of them are probably on their way back to the barn. Probably be smart to get the medic helicopter out here. Butter is hurting too bad to get up."

"Give me your GPS coordinates?"

TR fished out his handheld from his vest pocket. He mashed a few buttons and read off the figures to Carson Bell.

"Got them I'm clear on the radio, keep yours turned on I'll get back with you."

TR got his cell phone out next and texted Havelee. Burns was photographing the scene and the dead men. When the cowhand finished texting his FBI agent girlfriend; he turned his attention back to Butter Billy, who was trying to get up but hurting too bad to do so.

Burns walked over to TR and put his hand on the cowboy's shoulder. "You've got things under control be careful what you say to the cops. And I wasn't here, comprende?"

"We got you covered Andy."

"Yeah Andy, will you find Kenworth for me?" Butter said with difficulty.

"I'll do my best big guy."

Burns mounted Don Cameron and cantered back over the ridgeline. When he reached a point where he could observe unnoticed, he dismounted and loosened the cinch on Don Cameron and let his reins fall to the ground. The horse was ground tied and would not wander away. Burns got his binoculars out of the saddlebag and began to watch the scene. The medical helicopter landed fifteen minutes later. The medics went to work on Billy Butter. They were loading him up when Carson Bell arrived riding an ATV. He spoke to the EMT's and ducked his head below the turning blades and stepped into the cabin to speak to Butter Billy.

"Butter you are in good hands. They are taking you to the Sierra Vista hospital. I passed Kenworth on the way over. He's cropping grass I'll catch him and take him back to the barn. Don't worry about your horse and I'll call Bonita for you."

All the big Wrangler could do was mutter thanks and give his boss a smile.

Bell stepped back and along with TR watched the helicopter take off.

"Miguel will bring the sheriffs people out here. Are you alright?"

"I thought I was a goner for sure. Jackson, my bay horse, ran right off, hobbles and all, with my rifle still in the scabbard. All I had was my knife and those bastards had machine guns." He gestured to where the ATV sat still running with its front wheels caught in a ditch.

"One of is laying over there. And there's one in the ATV. You should have seen Butter Boss; he comes charging in here on that big old horse like John Wayne. Except Kenworth didn't take kindly to both barrels on that shotgun going off above his head. I've never seen a draft horse buck. I sure wouldn't have wanted to be in that saddle when it happened. Butter hit the ground hard. But he saved my life. I texted Havelee and told he what happened. She said she was on her way."

"Good maybe the FBI can find out what the hell happened out here. Have you seen Burns this morning?"

"Yes, sir he rode in right after it all had happened he had a mean looking scoped rifle in hand. He would have got those bastards if Butter hadn't got a lucky shot. He talked to Billy and me. He asked me to say he wasn't here."

"You don't say anything about him to your FBI agent girlfriend either."

Havelee exchanged several texts with TR. When she was sure he was OK, she called Ivalou Vargas.

"I got a text from TR a few minutes ago; there was a shooting incident at the ranch. Two are dead. They appear to be middle eastern males. The cowboy they call Butter Billy was injured when his horse threw him. The locals are in route. Can you contact Kroll and see what he knows?"

Vargas knew Kroll was still in town; they were going to meet for lunch later in Rio Rico.

"I'll send a text code on the Penelope line that asked him to call me."

She grabbed the other phone and texted:

I have a new thong I want to model for you. It's hot, like me. OXOX Penelope

"He will call back on this line. I think we need to let the locals handle this and see what happens. And I don't think I would tell them I was FBI either."

"I agree, but I'm worried about TR. I like that cowboy."

"Yeah I saw lust, at first sight, when he got off that horse girlfriend. Do you think he will tell the cops he's got an FBI hottie with a thong?"

"No, he won't! He doesn't care for the local sheriff at all. And I'll get even with you for that thong trick you pulled on me with Kroll. Girl, you got one coming."

"I thought you enjoyed that. You flashed poor old Kroll enough."

"Kiss my ass, Vargas."

"The Tucson SAC might do that; I won't."

"How have you gotten this far in the FBI without getting written up and sent to sensitivity training?"

"I'm a Latina, and we're special. Kroll's calling let me get back to you."

"I hope you aren't calling to break our lunch date. I would be upset." Kroll said when Vargas answered.

"Not a chance sweetie, that's a high priced joint I have in mind."

"You would look good in a fast food place."

"You'd better say as a customer and not an employee. I've said do you want fries with that enough in this lifetime."

"I'm in Nogales ordering a pair of boots. What's up?"

"Oh, spending Bradford's money I see."

"You got that right. The only way I can afford boots like these. What's going on?"

"Havelee got a text from TR there has been a shooting at the ranch. Two of the middle eastern types charged the fence shooting. One of the cowboys got them first. You have any thoughts on why?"

"No, I haven't been there in two days, and I don't think Bradford went back. El Jefe is shipping dope, and he didn't want us around the ranch for whatever reason. I'll listen when I get back tonight and see what's said."

"Any suggestions?"

"Yeah, we don't need to be involved. Let the locals handle it. If Havelee wants to know more, she should put on her tightest cowgirl jeans and take off to the Double B worrying about her boyfriend. She might wind up getting laid in the hayloft."

Vargas giggled. "I'll tell her you said that."

"Tell her to wear her thong."

"I thought that little wildcat was going to whip my ass for that trick."

"See you for lunch."

Vargas got Havelee back on the line. "Kroll hasn't been back to the ranch since he left. He doesn't know if Bradford went back or not. He doesn't think so. He is for our staying out of it and let the locals handle it. He did suggest you trot your butt down there wearing tight jeans and your thong. And play the worried girlfriend. He mentioned something about a hayloft too."

"Flip that asshole off for me next time you see him. I know he hasn't had any hayloft experiences, or he wouldn't have suggested tight jeans."

"Sounds like the voice of experience."

"Flip yourself off as well. I am going to go down there and play the worried girlfriend."

"I would suggest you tip TR not to say you are an FBI agent. He needs to let the other ranch folks know as well."

"Will do. I'll keep you in the loop. I'll brief Desmond and M&M before I leave."

TR's phone buzzed with a text message.

I'm on the way. Don't tell local sheriff I'm FBI, let the others know this 2. Do not talk to the news media Hav.

He discretely showed his phone to Carson Bell, who nodded. They were both watching the Sheriff's detective and

Deputy Willie Hillman tramp around the scene. The detective was taking pictures. Hillman was on his phone.

"What's going on Willie?" Ashton Bradford said calmly into the phone.

"Brad, two ragheads started shooting at the Double B hands. They were in an ATV with the Rocking H Bar brand painted on the front. What the hell you want me to do? These dead assholes are wearing them Arab scarf things around their heads."

"Where are these so-called ragheads now Willie?"

"They dead as hell, one of the cowboys shotgunned them!"

"They're probably in hell Willie. I'm in Tucson for a little gambling and drinking. I gave my Mexicans a few days off. I suggest you check my ranch and see if my two ATV's are there. With all the wetbacks crossing the border these days you can't be too careful. Those two probably stole it from the barn shed. I would appreciate you making a report and seeing that the machine gets back to the barn. And Willie I appreciate your calling about this. You are a fine police officer."

"I'll do that, Mr. Bradford. I don't think your ATV is damaged much. And I'll check your ranch too."

"Thank you, Willie."

Bradford disconnected the call and said, "dumbass."

The bartender asked if he needed another round. Bradford thanked him as he dialed El Jefe's phone.

Bradford recounted what Hillman had told him in a circumspect manner, which warned El Jefe that the deputy would be prowling around on the ranch. The drug lord invited Bradford and his colleague Senor Kroll to a late dinner that night in Nogales.

Vargas and Kroll were enjoying lunch when his text message tone sounded.

Meet 10P 2nite border lot dinner same place Ash

"I hate to mix business with pleasure." Kroll handed Vargas his phone. She read the message.

"I know I don't need to say this, but be careful. And I need to text Hav and let her know what's happening."

Havelee read the message about the meeting in Nogales Sonora Mexico. She was waiting for Miguel to pick her up in the ATV. She saw TR's bay gelding standing at the barn saddled next to Kenworth, the Belgian gelding that belonged to Butter Billy. Havelee walked over to the horses and saw the bay wore hobbles. She removed the hobbles and unsaddled the gelding. It took some effort to remove Kenworth's saddle. Havelee managed to get the massive draft horse saddle on the ground by simply pulling it off the horse's back instead of lifting it. Kenworth didn't move during the process.

She worked up a sweat tending to the horses. She put them in stalls and gave them hay. She was filling the water barrels when she heard the ATV's returning.

TR walked over to the barn and hugged Havelee.

"I'm sure glad to see you." He said.

"And me you. I put your horses up. I suppose the Belgian is Kenworth, Butter Billy's horse?"

"He is thanks. We are going to the hospital in Sierra Vista to see him as soon as the sheriff and the coroner's people get out of here. Miguel is going to take the jeep truck out with the coroner to pick up the bodies. Carson is mad as hell at Willie Hillman. He drove out to the scene in a sheriff's truck and broke an axle. That guy with Carson is a detective. That's his car by the coroner's van."

"TR, who is Willie Hillman?"

"He's a dumb ass deputy the sheriff hired. He's as crooked as a sidewinder rattlesnake and likes boys as much as he likes girls. Probably likes boys more because no self-respecting woman would have anything to do with him."

"So he is still at the scene?"

"No, once we got the Rocking H Bar's ATV out of the ditch. Hillman insisted on driving it back to the headquarters. He said, and I quote 'Ash wanted him to do it.' That sack of shit, pardon my French, is in bed with those bastards. I know it."

Carson Bell walked over to TR and Havelee. The detective got in his car and left.

"Good to see you again Agent Harris." The rancher said removing his hat when he spoke.

"Thank you Mr. Bell, and I'm off duty so drop the agent part. I was worried about TR."

"Well, you have certainly dressed for the ranch this visit. It looks like you have been working the barn."

"She put up Jackson and Kenworth," TR said.

"You'll make a hand Miz Havelee," Bell said.

"Thank you, what's happening with the homicides?"

"The coroner is going to rule justified as self-defense in both deaths. Our great sheriff's investigator and deputy have decided those two crossed the border illegally and stole the ATV from Rocking H Bar. Hillman believes nobody is home over there. He is taking the so-called stolen ATV back over there. I don't know how he is going to get back. The investigator told me he wasn't going over there to pick him up. The detective is, what do they call it? A homophobe or something. I called the sheriff and said that torn up SUV needs to be off my property before dark. They are sending out a towing outfit that specializes in off-road recovery. Miguel believes our Jeep FC170 will make it out there, and he will take the coroners people back to get the bodies." Bell answered.

They watched the old Jeep pickup leave as Bell continued.

"Bonita, Butter Billy's girlfriend, says he has several broken ribs and a concussion. They want to keep him overnight for observation. I figure when they get the bodies out we'll ride over there and see how he is doing. I expect we can find some grub while we're there. It will be my treat. Miz Havelee it will be after dark when we get back I would prefer you accept the hospitality of my guest room rather than you driving back to where you are staying."

"Thank you, Carson, I will take you up on that."

"Let's go sit on the veranda and see if Estelle can rustle up some of her lemonade."

The whole crew from the Double B went to Sierra Vista and visited Butter Billy Three. He was still addled a bit and didn't believe the lithe Havelee was able to unsaddle his horse. When TR assured him she did it correctly, and Kenworth was well, the big cowboy was happy. Later that night Havelee visited TR in the bunkhouse, slipping back into the ranch house at first light.

Willie Hillman got lost trying to find the Rocking H Bar headquarters. The ATV ran out of gas. He wandered about the San Rafael on foot most of the night. A rattlesnake bit him at some point. Willie was not well liked by his colleagues, and no one gave a damn about him being missing. A Border Patrol agent heard shots fired as dawn was breaking. He found Hillman lying next to a farm service road with his legs caught in a barb wire fence. He was almost out of ammunition. Willie was not exactly known throughout the southern Arizona law enforcement community for his stellar abilities as a cop. The Border Patrol agent summed it up when he said to Hillman.

"I hope you were saving the last bullet for yourself Willie."

Chapter Seventeen

Kroll and Bradford were patted down for weapons in the massage parlor before they ever entered the tunnel. The hombre doing the shakedown was macho and didn't check either man's crotch area. Kroll breathed easier when they made it through the strip club without getting accosted by a Latina dancer. Getting groped by a stripper would have revealed the Keltec P-3AT .380 caliber pistol resting in the protective cup pouch of the athletic supporter he wore. This meeting with El Jefe worried him particularly after the incident at the ranch. The searcher also missed a large folding knife secured in his sock against his Achilles' tendon.

El Jefe greeted them at his table in the back of the restaurant. Once again they were the only patrons. After they had were seated, another man joined them.

"This is Emran, my associate from the middle east." The drug lord said with a wave of his hand. Emran glared at Bradford and Kroll.

"Emran is troubled by today's events involving his soldiers, Si." El Jefe continued.

"Emran was to instruct his soldiers they were guards this day, not killers of gringos. That will come another day. Emran's soldiers were anxious to kill Americans. This action might have caused us a great financial loss and set our timetable back, causing great danger to Emran's associate's plans. Emran's numero dos has been sent to your ranch to ensure such stupidity does not happen again. Emran is not sorry this happened."

One of El Jefe's minders stepped behind Emran and strangled him with a garrote. The man struggled almost upsetting the table. El Jefe calmly pushed it out of the way as he watched Kroll and Bradford. Emran's sphincter muscle gave way with an odorous blast. Two more bodyguards wearing rubber gloves assisted the strangler in removing the corpse.

"Emran has been replaced. Si" El Jefe said. The drug lord's cold eyes contrasted with his smile.

Kroll sniffed and waved his hand in front of his face. "Whew! It must have been something he ate."

El Jefe burst out in laughter. "I knew I liked you Senor Ron! You have a sense of humor. Dinner is on El Jefe this night. No worry, they did not remove him by way of the kitchen."

The return trip was through a different tunnel and exited into a tattoo parlor. Bradford and Kroll were a block from the parking lot.

"Willie Hillman saved our asses on that screw-up. El Jefe sent along a bonus for him." Bradford said.

"Ash, Hillman doesn't strike me as the brightest light on the tree. I'm surprised he didn't screw things up worse." Kroll said.

"You're right. But Willie did call me and ask what to do. I told him we were out of town, and no one was home at the ranch. Some illegals must have stolen the ATV. We are going to have to make peace with Carson Bell somehow."

"I wouldn't unless he reaches out to us."

"Why do you say that?"

"There was no mention on the evening news about anything happening. The only crime mentioned was in Tucson. We are out of town. We don't know anything. If we go to Bell, it looks like we knew something. Let him come to us."

"Good idea, I'm going to drive back to Tucson and grab a room. Are you going that way?"

"No, I'm going to stay here and check out the action on Backpage."

"Wear a raincoat. No telling what those women got."

"Will do, let me know when everybody heads back to the ranch."

Kroll went back to his room at the Best Western and drank a beer while he contemplated calling Vargas. It was two AM. The strangulation he witnessed was bothering him. He's managed to keep his head in the game while it was happening. Now he wasn't sure. He picked up his cell and dialed Ivalou's personal number.

The phone ringing woke Vargas, and it took her a moment or two to realize which phone it was. She reached for it and fumbled with it while she turned on the light. A call from Kroll, this time of night, wasn't good.

"Ron, what's wrong?"

"I know it's late. But I need to see you. Just put some clothes on and come over."

"Be there in fifteen." She clicked off and threw on some clothes. She took a couple of minutes to brush her teeth. Ivalou put a band around her hair and a baseball cap on her head. She grabbed her purse and pistol. Nineteen minutes after the call, Kroll answered the door and let her in. He did not look good.

Vargas sat beside him on the small couch. She held one of his hands in hers as he recounted the dinner across the border.

"I've seen some garbage undercover. It was always a tossup with me as who was worse, biker gangs, mobster made men or middle eastern terrorists. They all made me wanna puke. That business tonight is without a doubt the worst I've seen. There is not a psychological definition that defines El Jefe. Someone needs to take him out of the game."

"Ron, you can't do that. You are still an FBI agent. Regardless of what they say you are; you are not an assassin. And with the bodyguards El Jefe travels with it would be suicide. Do even think that way."

"Lou they have something terrible planned, that we have to stop." Kroll got up and went to the same fridge and took out another beer.

"We need to be face to face with Carter. Get Havelee to arrange it. And we need to meet tomorrow. You guys have to be closer to the ranch."

Kroll drained the beer and went for another. Ivalou walked up behind him and put her arms around his torso and just held on while he drank the beer.

"My contacts in the coroner's office have sent prints and photos to all the federal databases and Interpol." Burrito Cruz said.

Russell and Cruz were sitting at the picnic table outside the motorhome with Burns and Hadfield. They were drinking coffee enjoying the early Arizona morning.

"I'm having a hard time with the lackadaisical attitude of a double homicide by the sheriff's department," Jolene commented.

"It reminds you of the good ole boys back in the good ole days in Alabama," Burns added.

"Not just Alabama, that sort of stuff was everywhere," Russell said.

"What is the deal on the border patrol finding that sheriff's deputy Hillman?" Burns asked.

"He's in the hospital. Unfortunately, his injuries are not life-threatening. Apparently, the dumb ass got lost driving that ATV back to the Rocking H Bar. He walked around all night and got snake bit. My sources tell me it was a dry bite." Russell answered.

"And four box trucks full of dope just drove off to points unknown," Jolene said.

"El Jefe carried the day," Cruz said. "Do you think it's possible those ragheads did that as a draw off?"

"I don't know, whether it was or not, it worked. I will say this, the next load of dope isn't going to get away." Burns said.

"What have you go in mind?" Russell asked.

"Destroying it."

"I don't know if my heart can stand watching another nocturnal visit to the Rocking H Bar," Jolene said.

"That will happen."

"Oh shit."

The FBI team used the Escalade as a conference room. Desmond drove while M&M kept watch from the right front seat. Havelee, Ivalou, and Kroll rode in the rear seat. The dark limo tint kept anyone from seeing them. Havelee sat in the middle. She was not going along with Kroll's desire for a face to face meeting with Ransom Carter.

"I will report everything you have said to Mr. Carter. Getting a face to face meeting with him is not going to happen. He will not fly out here because you want to talk to him. Granted you have a unique situation with the assignment, but it is not enough to demand the Director's special assistant fly across the country to see you. I believe you are right that a terror attack is being planned and will involve Bradford and El Jefe. But until you come up with more hard evidence other than illegal immigrants from the middle east; Carter will not commit the resources. You are looking at all we've got. I've been promised another agent from the Phoenix Field Office when he winds up something he's working on. But there is no timeline on the when that will happen."

Kroll started to say something. The is phone buzzed. He looked at the screen and held up a finger for silence. Bradford was calling. Kroll held the phone were Havelee could hear Bradford.

"Kroll."

"Ron, Brad here I need you to pick up two drivers in front of that massage parlor we use in Nogales. They are our friend's men. They will have on white polos and University of Arizona ball caps. They are on their way now. Bring them to the casino lot in Tucson. These guys are on their way now. How long before you can get there?"

"Between twenty and thirty minutes, I am pulling into Patagonia now. I've got to turn around."

"Call me when you are headed this way with them."

"Will do." Kroll clicked off.

"Got any idea of what is going on?" Havelee asked.

"Only what you heard. I suspect another load of narcotics is involved, and they are staging the trucks at the ranch for load out."

Vargas was able to hear the conversation also. She spoke up. "We have a good chance to get eyes on with Bradford's people and some good intelligence."

Desmond pulled into the Best Western Parking lot.

"What are you thinking Ivalou?"

"We trail Ron then pick up Bradford's crew at the casino."

"I know Bradford's SUV from when we first staked him out. M&M and I could head on to the casino and get eyes on with the SUV." Desmond offered."

"There is a big parking lot at the Border crossing for people who walk across. And the main road back to I-19 is one way and has several parking lots. The massage parlor is the one with the tunnel. I suggest Ivalou get her car and get eyes on the front of that building. Havelee you make the loop and find a parking space on the northbound side where you can pick up my car." Kroll said.

Ten minutes later Ivalou found a street side parking space and eased her car into it. She got out with a tourist sized purse and went to her trunk. She was able to photograph the two men Kroll was picking up. They walked out of the parlor after she opened her trunk. She rummaged around in the trunk until she saw Kroll's car drive up. Vargas closed her trunk and got behind the wheel of her car. She radioed Havelee Kroll was moving.

With five minutes, Havelee and Ivalou were alternating between leading and following Kroll's vehicle north on I-19. Ivalou knew a different route to the casino and got off before the I-10 interchange. Havelee continued west on I-10 when Kroll exited. She got off at the next exit.

Ten minutes later M&M was able to get photos of Bradford talking to Kroll who remained in his car. Just before that M&M got pictures of Porn Dude and Numb Nuts. Bradford, ever the big shot was photographed getting in the back seat of his SUV with Numb Nuts holding the door. Soon the large Suburban pulled out into the roadway with Kroll following. Moments later Ivalou was on their tail.

Thirty minutes later Bradford's vehicle pulled into the dusty lot in a warehouse district. He stopped in front of four box trucks. The rough looking vehicles with obvious damage to the cargo boxes were former rental trucks sold off once more when they were well past their prime. Vargas and Havelee photographed Porn Dude Numb Nuts and the Mexicans each getting into a truck. Bradford and Kroll chatted a bit then went to their cars. Bradford left first, and this gave Kroll a chance to send a surreptitious text to Vargas.

Trucks 2 ranch

She called Havelee with the message. Desmond and M&M were already in route. They would change vehicles and park in Patagonia near the state highway south to the San Rafael. M&M

would photograph the trucks as they went through the small town. Havelee was on her phone to TR, she was going straight to the Double B and planned to be waiting near the ranch road entrance to the farm service road in one of the Double B vehicles. She would photograph the procession of trucks from that point. Ivalou would follow Kroll and report. She would stop in Patagonia.

Bradford was driving his SUV and headed straight back to the casino. Kroll stayed with the trucks. Ivalou stayed with Kroll.

One they were on I-10 her phone rang. It was Kroll.

"I'm following the trucks to the ranch; then taking the Mexicans back to the massage parlor. Bradford is staying Tucson, and I'm going back to the Best Western in Nogales for the evening."

"Got it. Havelee grabbed the chance for another night at the ranch with her cowboy. She's on her way there to photograph the trucks from the road. Any idea of why the change?"

"No, El Jefe alluded to having a shipment ready for drivers coming from another destination. I suspect more of our middle eastern friends will drive the trucks. The ones on the ranch now are guards. We won't be allowed to hang around during the loading process. And I think they are too smart to go cowboy hunting before this shipment leaving."

"Could this be the big one Bradford has talked about?"

"No. We are still waiting for a shipment of women before the big one. These trucks could be for the women. I don't know. I'll be making a Penelope call in a few days when this gets sorted out."

"I'll notify Hav and pick you up on the route back to the massage parlor."

Vargas clicked off and called Havelee. After passing on Kroll's information to the supervisory agent, Ivalou listened to Havelee's plans.

"I'm going to ride with TR tomorrow when he checks the cattle on the Rocking H Bar. I want to get a feel for the place, and maybe I can find an observation point somewhere on the Double B. I'm going to feel out Carson Bell about our moving to his ranch for the duration of this investigation. We would be a lot closer to Kroll if things went sour."

"I think Ron would like that. We will have to tweak the Penelope plan some to make it work. I don't think the Escalade would fit in very well in that valley."

"The guys still have that pickup. We can rent a storage building for the caddy if need be."

"Why don't we play it by ear for the time being but be ready to move to the ranch. I'll pick Kroll up when he comes back through Patagonia. I'm going to enjoy that little park area in that town."

"That is a pretty little town. I understand Bird watching is a big attraction there."

"I'm a big city girl LA is home for me. I think I could get used to Patagonia if I ever retire and settle down."

"I could get used to the San Rafael Valley."

"Girlfriend I think you are in lust with a San Rafael cowboy."

Havelee laughed, and they both clicked off.

"Havelee Harris is getting to be a regular visitor at the headquarters house. And the bunkhouse after dark" Jolene said after reviewing camera footage from the Double B headquarters.

"That's not surprising after the interaction between her and TR the day the team visited the ranch," Burns answered.

"Do you think it's a case of mixing business with pleasure or she is genuinely interested in TR. He is a nice guy. I would hate to see him brokenhearted when she moves on to another investigation."

"TR is good people. Havelee is a ranch raised cowgirl, and they know how to break hearts. I expect Havelee is mixing business with pleasure and is wanting to use the Double B for a surveillance base. We know Bradford is bad. They visited every place in the valley asking about Lyon Hamilton. They have sent agents to see Lois Thornton. I don't know if they realize who her husband is. I suspect Kroll is undercover as himself, a disgruntled terminated FBI agent and they are after Bradford. With El Jefe on the radar, they may be trying to land both fish. Bradford and his gang took off when it came time for the last dope shipment. Four more trucks came in yesterday, so they are up to something. It will be interesting to see if Bradford and his crew shows back up today. And if Kroll is with them."

"I hate the idea of you sneaking back over there in the middle of the night with all the new guards. But, putting a tracker on Kroll's car might answer the question of who's side he is on. Buddy and Burrito could follow the tracker."

"That is a good idea. Bradford is still not posting guards at night. And I have a couple of trackers. If Kroll shows up today, I'll put a tracker on his car tonight."

"Provided they don't start posting guards," Jolene emphasized.

"I'm going to put on a pot of coffee. Cruz and Russell are turning off the farm service road."

"You ignored my guard's comment."

Burns poured water into the coffee pot and turned on the machine. He went outside to meet the private eyes.

"For a make-believe cowboy from down south, you don't make bad coffee," Russell commented when the group sat down at the picnic table.

"Apache's wouldn't know good coffee if it spilled on them," Cruz said.

"Mexican flavor tin cup of water cattle walk in with old horseshoe and call it coffee."

"If it were left up to you two it would be coffee grounds boiled in a pot with eggshells," Burns said.

"TR has a new helper riding the Rocking H Bar herd this morning." Buddy Russell commented.

"Blond and cute, she sits a horse well. I had a nice view of her crossing the farm road. It looks like they took the long way to that section the herds grazing." Cruz said.

"And she was paying a lot of attention to the Rocking H Bar side of the fence."

"When are you two gumshoes going to get some up to date information. Miguel told me that when he brought a load of hay over this morning."

"Does Miguel think TR will get pussy whipped into telling about our operation?" Cruz asked.

"That is always possible. But TR thinks he's pumping her for information."

Jolene laughed. "Burns you could have used a better choice of words."

"What do you guys think about putting a tracker on Kroll's car and following him when he leaves the ranch?" Burns asked.

"Red neck southern cowboy way behind the power curve. Indian have a tracker on city boy's car since he spent the first night in town."

"Yeah and they've got a pretty slick operation going. FBI blondie isn't the only special girl agent in heat. The Latina is Kroll's girlfriend. I don't think the Harris woman is aware of that either. They use an elaborate prostitute scam to meet and swap info. The women show up dressed like hookers in mini dresses with their butts hanging out."

"No way,' Jolene said, 'not Havelee."

"Yes ma'am, her little fanny was hanging out the bottom of her skirt, that butt crack underwear showing off both cheeks."

"I would have to see that to believe it," Jolene said.

"Turn on your computer," Russell said, holding up a flash drive.

Cruz went on with his narrative. "They meet at the Motel 6 and the two black guys dress like pimps and drive a black Escalade. The Latina has met Kroll several times. Kroll has been followed by Bradford's thugs twice. They have stopped following him, so I suppose he has earned their trust. The real winner is that Kroll stays at the Best Western when he overnights in town. The FBI team stays at the extended stay. The Latina agent sneaks out and visits Kroll at night. She's hot in a slut suit. It must have got to him. The real kicker was yesterday. They all met in the Escalade then split up in different cars. Kroll picked up two Latino males near the border in Nogales and took them to Tucson and met Bradford. The went across town and picked up four trucks. Bradford's crew drove two of them, and the Latino's drove two. The FBI team followed them all the way. I expect the trucks are now at the Rocking H Bar. Kroll came back to town and the Latina agent picked up following him in Patagonia. They shacked up all night at the Best Western."

"You guys shadowed an FBI operation?" Hadfield asked.

"Indian have a video to prove it," Russell said holding up the flash drive again.

"I thought you two didn't do the sleazy divorce stuff," Burns said.

"Not much, Indian stay in practice by following FBI. Indian prime pump by looking in windows with the camera."

When Burns and Hadfield quit laughing. Andy got serious. "I knew it was a good idea to get you two involved."

"I second that," Jolene said.

"It's obvious Kroll is undercover. And they have a well-planned op going on."

"The operation is not well backed up. Kroll is out on a long thin limb." Russell said.

"Are we going to act as discreet back up for Kroll?" Cruz asked.

"Let's see how this is going to play with the trucks they brought in yesterday," Burns said.

Later Burns mounted on Don Cameron watched Havelee scouting for a place to observe the Rocking H Bar. He used his binoculars to look at the horse she was riding. Havelee carried the rifle he built years before in scabbard attached to the saddle. TR did not offer to lead her to the property included in the casita lease. Andy got out the satellite phone and made a call.

While he was out Jolene texted Andy, saying she was going to explore some of the shops in Tubac and Rio Rico. She would stop for groceries before returning to the casita. He was pleased with how quickly she acclimated to southern Arizona. Burns hooked up the horse trailer and loaded Don Cameron. Jazz jumped into the trailer with the horse. Burns left the casita and headed east toward the Huachuca Mountains.

Pleased to find no one camped at any of the forest service sites, Burns found a shady place to park his rig. He unloaded the horse and mounted up, traveling east on trails. He skirted the edge of an unoccupied house and entered the Sunnyside ghost town from the west side. Riding Don Cameron down what was once the main street of a religious sect copper mining town; Burns looked over the sagging buildings and the exposed foundations. He could understand why the town's founder chose the place. After leaving the town, he guided the stallion to the dry creek bed and heard Jazz growl a warning. The horse's ears perked up. Andy reined in and watched. A man wearing a camo uniform stepped from the tree line. He carried a small black hard case. Burn's knew there were several others watching. He dismounted and walked toward the soldier.

"Mr. Burns?" The soldier asked.

"Yes."

"I'm Reid. The General told me you need this equipment, and I will brief you on our operations this far."

"Correct, let's see what's in the case."

They squatted down, and Reid opened the case. The contents secured in protective padding. Reid quickly briefed Burns on their operation. "Once the timer is set these things work as advertised. They get very, very, hot; you could probably set concrete fire with these things."

"That is what I need, are the timer's accurate?"

"It is a mechanical timer, not a clock. Twenty-four hours or less they will ignite within three minutes of the length of time set. Set them for over twenty-four hours they will ignite within an hour of the setting. But they will ignite. The General wants me to brief you on our prep for backing up your operation. We have a dedicated drone overflight every twelve hours. The flash drive I will give you has all the video from last week. Give me a secure email link and I will send them daily. There is a separate file with the soil excavation information you wanted. We can support any incursion you make. We have made four recon missions already. I've found your trail markers. The General tells me you have surveillance cameras on the ground. Can I get a feed from them?"

Burns removed a sim card from his shirt pocket. He exchanged the sim card for the flash drive. "Everything you need to access my cameras in real time is on here. There are files with photos of all the targets. We identified Ron Kroll as deep cover FBI agent this morning. He is on our side."

"Does the FBI know you are reading their mail?"

"No. Based on the recent arrival of large trucks, I expect another narcotics load is coming soon. So be prepared to cover an incursion to sabotage these trucks."

"Law enforcement is not interdicting them?"

"Law enforcement didn't get the last load and the General tipped the DEA and Homeland. The FBI knows these trucks are on the ranch. And they know there is a smuggling operation. I think something bigger is coming, and they are letting the drugs go through to catch the bigger prize. I suspect a terror op. Eight middle eastern males have crossed the border in the past week. Look at the download files from those cameras; you will see what I'm talking about."

"Very well, Mr. Burns, we need to get back through the gate before the MP patrol comes around. I don't like to attract attention. Nice looking horse and at some point, I would like to see that rifle you have the General talks about."

"Mr. Reid you are welcome to see it and shoot it anytime."

Burns watched Reid disappear back into the tree line. Andy mounted up and rode Don Cameron back to the trailer using a different route. He wondered if it would be possible to link up with Kroll. He discarded that idea as soon as he thought of it. The FBI didn't like anyone playing in their yard; they didn't invite. And the invitation to play was limited to watching from the sidelines. Burns read the online editions of all the local newspapers daily. Tucson Arizona had its share of gang-related violence. And if the news was accurate the gangs were at odds with El Jefe; who wanted to control their turf from south of the border. Andy took out his cell phone and texted Jolene.

P/U 12 cans black spray paint cheapest $

Burns considered his plan while he rode. Once back at the trailer, he loosened the saddle cinch and loaded the horse. The drive back to the casita was uneventful. TR was waiting patiently on a bench in front of the barn. His horse tied to a nearby fence rail. Burns waved at him as he stopped the truck. TR met Burns at the trailer and watched him unload Don Cameron. As long as

Burns was around the horse and dog were docile around other animals and humans.

"Andy, we have a problem," TR said as he watched Andy unsaddle and the stud horse.

"Is the problem about five four blue-eyed and blond?"

"How, did you know?"

"I watched you and her ride out to check the Rocking H Bar cattle this morning."

"We didn't see you and she weren't missing much."

"She has a good eye for detail. But she wasn't looking for me either. What is the problem?"

"She wants to move her team to the Double B to be closer to the Rocking H Bar. They are watching the place for some reason. Havelee won't talk about her investigation as she calls it. I've gotten myself hung up over that little gal. I think she feels the same toward me. But that FBI side of her is hard to get around. I hope she's not playing me."

"I had my heart broken over a cowgirl once. And it hurts. Tobias my advice is to approach with caution. That woman is armed and dangerous. And FBI agents tend to be FBI agents first and foremost."

"Carson told her about Don Cameron. She hasn't mentioned wanting to see him yet. And that could be a problem for what you are doing."

I don't need her nosing around. She will take one look at Don Cameron and know someone has been riding him. That woman knows horses."

"That's right. Havelee rides as good as any cowboy I've seen. I guess you can say she rides ropes and shoots with the best of them. That is a mean looking rifle she carries."

"I can attest to the fact she shoots well. I built that rifle."

"How did you wind up building a rifle for Havelee?"

"She was assigned to the Mobile Alabama office a few years back. I do special weapons work on contract for the FBI. Her issued rifle needed an overhaul. She helped Jolene during a really bad time. So I returned the favor when I built Havelee's rifle."

"Wow, I would love to have the kind of relationship with Havelee, that you have with Jolene. If I can ask, why don't you marry her?"

"Tobias, that is a question I can't answer. I hope you and Havelee can work through the FBI thing and have something. And I hope she's not playing you."

"Thanks, Andy. Now, what are going to do about her seeing Don Cameron? Why don't you just tell her why you are here?"

"That is where this gets complicated TR. The FBI doesn't play well with private investigators. Lyon Hamilton's sister hired us to find him. The FBI is investigating the so-called new owner of the ranch. Harris would love to know what we know and would arrest us in a heartbeat for interfering with an FBI investigation. That is why she doesn't need to know we are here."

"What about Don Cameron?"

"We take a wait and see on that. Did Havelee tell the sheriff's people she was FBI when she came over after that shooting?"

"No, and she texted me telling me not say anything either."

"OK, we have determined the fellow Kroll on the Rocking H Bar is an undercover FBI agent. Her not mentioning being FBI means they have an active investigation involving Bradford and Rocking H Bar. I appreciate you guys keeping quiet about us. That helps what we are doing. Let Carson in on what I just told you. If Havelee remembers, Don Cameron, ask Carson to tell her that he moved the horse to a better facility for its safety. She will understand keeping an unruly stud horse being a problem."

"I'll talk to Carson this evening. She's gone back to Nogales, and she has to go to Tucson tomorrow. I'll hear from her when she's back in Nogales."

Burns watched TR ride off. He slung the rifle case over his shoulder and walked to the motorhome. Jolene drove up in the rented SUV as he got to the motor coach. Burns put down his rifle and helped her with the groceries.

CHAPTER EIGHTEEN

Supervisory Special Agent Havelee Harris, reported to the Tucson SAC Adele Lane and was shown to the secure conference room. Harris was scheduled for a secure link video conference with Ransom Carter, Special Assistant to the Director. While they waited for the link connection with FBI Headquarters, SAC Lane pointedly engaged Havelee.

"Special Agent Harris, your investigation could be better served by this field office, if you shared what you are doing. The classification is unprecedented."

Before Havelee could respond the link became active, and the tech left the room. Ransom Carter's face filled the screen.

"Ms. Lane, you are correct in Special Agent Harris' investigation classification being unprecedented. It is that way for a reason, and Agent Harris will not be sharing any information with you until the Director authorizes your need to know. You will continue to ensure your teams are aware of a special investigation and to respond as backup should the need arise. When we are prepared to serve arrest warrants, you and your people will be briefed. Until such time you will continue to support Special Agent Harris' administrative requests. Do you have any questions regarding what I have just told you?"

"No Sir, but I would like to be on record as opposing this highly unusual classification of what is obviously an important investigation happening within the area served by this field office. I believe I should have a need to know."

"Your statements are noted and will be made known to the Director. You may excuse yourself from the secure area."

The SAC left the room and locked the door behind her.

"Agent Harris, I commend you for your performance under difficult circumstances. SAC Lane has brought enormous pressure on the Director for her to be read in on the Bad Apple's investigation. We will do this when arrests are imminent. I've read your reports, and unfortunately, Ron Kroll hasn't provided enough evidence to make a solid case against Bradford. We have examined aerial photographs of the Valley and the ranch in question. We have determined that HRT sniper teams could infiltrate the area for a long time surveillance. However, we cannot justify such surveillance at this time. When Kroll gives us more information, we will act on getting teams in place. We cannot get a military drone overflight at this time either. The presence of large trucks is simply not enough probably cause for these efforts. Bradford and El Jefe being present when narcotics are being stored and loaded on to the trucks would be enough cause for the support you want. Kroll needs to get precise information as to when this is likely to happen, and we will respond at that time. We can't field such resources on the contingency that it might happen soon. The addition of a viable lead to a terror attack would be cause to launch the resources you need. Havelee, simply put, the Director wants more evidence before he moves against Bradford. The Phoenix SAC assures me that Agent Ernesto Smith will be available in a couple of weeks."

"I understand sir."

"Good, you and your people are doing a good job. Perhaps with the addition of Smith on your team we can move forward at a quicker pace."

The Ransom Carter closed the secure connection on his end. And the tech came back in the room to shut down the equipment. Havelee sat at the table considering her options. It was painfully obvious; the Director was not going to commit expensive resources to anything that wasn't already signed sealed and awaiting delivery. She put her notes back in her briefcase and left the room. Harris left the building and drove back to Nogales. As she drove, she pondered the chances of Kroll being recognized should they all meet for a planning session.

Ron Kroll suggested they meet somewhere east off of I-10. They wound up at a restaurant in Lordsburg, New Mexico. The agents secured a round table in a small private dining room.

"So what you are saying is the Director and his buddy Carter have their heads stuck up their asses. And we are on our own without backup." Kroll said.

"That is one way of looking at it," Havelee said.

"I spent yesterday with Tobias Rutledge, the cowboy who worked for Lyon Hamilton in the Rocking H Bar. We moved the ranch cattle to another section. I spotted one guard on a four wheeler watching us. I only saw him once. We found one of the ranch ATVs near where we first picked up the herd. It was out of gas. TR said it was the one used by the two men that attacked him. Deputy Sheriff Willie Hillman attempted to return it to the ranch headquarters. I understand Hillman was found caught in barbed wire fence east of where we found the ATV. He was dehydrated and suffering from a snake bite. TR said the ATV was out of gas. He removed a wire from the electrical system so it will not start. So they are down one ATV. TR said there was only two. The four wheeler and the side by side with the bed on it."

"That is consistent with what I've seen on the place. I noticed the four wheeler in the usual place near the ranch shop when I was there with those trucks. There is a big four by four

Ford one ton and the ranch flatbed. The Mexicans are keeping those busy making border runs for grass."

"Too bad you can't get pictures of them unloading that stuff," Vargas added.

"El Jefe's thugs won't let anybody get close to the barn when they bring the stuff in. That's why I was told to leave. They make Bradford's bodyguards leave as well. I suspect they're hauling marijuana across the border as we speak."

"Are you saying they bring the stuff across in broad daylight?" M&M asked.

"Yes, they cross the border at Lochiel with a flatbed truck loaded with hay. Except it's not all hay. You pay enough people to look the other way, and daylight doesn't matter. I think they are planning to use middle eastern males to drive the delivery trucks as a way getting them further into our country. Figure where the dope is going, and you have the location of the next terrorist attack. There may very well be weapons and explosives in those hay trucks. But we are screwed as long as Washington won't give us the support we need."

"When you were playing cowgirl did you find any place we could set up surveillance from ourselves?" Desmond asked.

"There is a part of the Double Ranch that Carson Bell leases short term that appears to have the elevation necessary to see the headquarters area of the Rocking H Bar. He said the area I asked about is rough terrain and practically inaccessible. That is why I asked for an HRT sniper team for surveillance. And you know the answer to that."

"Yeah tell them the time and day the bad guys will be there with a thirty-day notice and HRT deploys," Kroll said sarcastically. "Do you think you could get a covert camera out of them I could install when I go back to the ranch?"

"That I can do," Havelee said.

"What do you plan on doing with this guy Smith when you get him?" Kroll asked.

"Ernesto Smith looks like a Mexican cowboy. I'm going to station him at the Double B. He can drive the big pickup we have and keep an on the Lochiel crossing as well as the traffic at the Rocking H Bar."

"That is a good idea. The best one I've heard so far."

After tossing around the idea of moving to the Double B and ways they could keep what they were doing secure. The agents left the dining room. Havelee paid the bill and thanked the proprietor. She paid no attention to the Mexican sitting at the counter eating a piece of pie. When they all got back in their cars and left. Burrito Cruz finished his pie and paid his check. He ambled out to a worn looking pickup truck and called Buddy Russell.

"They're all headed back west."

"Gotcha, I'll pick them up at Wilcox."

Andrew Burns studied the videos from Rocking H Bar. The trucks were loaded awaiting drivers. El Jefe's helicopter had not made the low flying border crossing in forty-eight hours. The Aerostat radar balloon was up. Obviously, the radar balloon's presence kept the drug lord away. Andy decided the trucks could not sit loaded much longer. He called Cruz and Russell, then sent a message to Reid. Only Burns and Hadfield knew about Reid and his black ops team. And Jolene wasn't sure they were real. Andy stretched the story about them being there when he planted the cameras. They would deploy in a position that should anything go wrong, Burns and the private eyes would be able to escape. Still, it was a risky move; Jolene was not happy.

"So I get to sit here and watch the cameras. And hope your radio works when some terrorist with an AK walks out of the bunk house." She said.

"Russell and Cruz are deployed to cover me in the event someone comes out and discovers what is going on. That will give me a chance to escape. You have the most important job of all. You are the lookout; you will see them first. The General's team will be covering all of us."

"I don't like it. We need to call Havelee and tell her what we know. You need to stop before you get hurt. Burns, you aren't a nineteen-year-old Marine crawling around in the jungle anymore. Please don't do this."

"There was a line in a movie once about recognizing one's limitations. I know what mine are. This plan is a calculated risk. The last load got out of there without a problem, and our government didn't stop it. I'm going to make sure these trucks don't get through. And your job is to let me know when trouble is coming."

"Four trucks full of dope should be handled by the cops. Call in an anonymous tip to the DEA. Just don't go over there on a midnight raid. Burns that idea is crazy."

"If the DEA wouldn't act on a tip from the General. They sure as hell won't act on an anonymous phone call. The General gave them everything we had on the last trucks."

"I still don't like it."

"Your feelings are duly noted."

Burns left the motorhome. And set to work preparing his equipment. A couple of hours later Jolene came up to him and hugged him.

"I'll be your lookout, Burns. But if you get hurt I'll never forgive you."

"Thanks, I trust you to watch our backs."

The trucks were left parked between the headquarters house and barns on the Rocking H Bar. For Burns, it was a straight line ride to the blind side of the vehicles from the forest service road. It was 2:30 in the morning and there was a quarter moon. No clouds, just stars. He was in touch with everyone via a headset to a communications radio clipped to his belt. Tucked securely in a high ride holster was a 45 caliber 1911 pistol, a Burns' modified special ops design with an integral suppressor. It didn't make any noise, neither did the rifle in the saddle scabbard. The late Lyle Thigman's favorite blackjack was in his pocket, and a stout doubled edged spear pointed Burns Made knife in a belt sheath. He wore black clothing and his dark leather chaps.

Andy Burns could wreak havoc on anyone who discovered him near the trucks. The horse and the dog would raise the alarm. Russell and Cruz riding in a camo colored ATV wearing night vision goggles and following infrared markers Burns had posted previously during his clandestine visits to the Rocking H Bar. Cruz packed his favorite firearms. Russell carried his pistol and a suppressed Burns rifle with a night vision scope. Everybody was hoping none of the bad guys woke and went outside to take a piss. If they did and spotted Burns, they wouldn't have time to put it back in their pants. Russell and Cruz were not aware of the black ops team covering them.

Burns cantered Don Cameron past the Rocking H Bar ranch road. He had continued another hundred yards before he reined in the horse. Andy checked with Jolene, and she reported there was no movement around the ranch. Burrito gave the same report. Burns got off Don Cameron and did something that would make a rancher cringe. He cut the fence. Burns made sure the wire was safely out the way before he remounted and walked Don Cameron toward the trucks. The vehicles were between him and the buildings.

Burns pulled his night vision goggles in place when he got close to the line of parked trucks. Now with green-tinted vision, he examined the trucks parked on the other side of a cross fence. A gate was beside the vehicles. Burns rode over to the gate and leaned down from the saddle and silently opened it. Don Cameron stepped sideways allowing the gate to swing past. Andy cued the horse forward, and it would not move. He heard a low growl from Jazz.

Andy quickly searched the area ready to react. No one was around the trucks. He looked down and saw a rattlesnake slowly slithering across the ground searching for a meal near the open gate. Andy dismounted quietly and stalked the snake. In a quick move, he bent over and grabbed the reptile behind its head. Burns walked to the closest truck and opened the unlocked passenger door. He deposited the three-foot-long Diamondback on the floor and quietly closed the door. Remounted he rode Don Cameron beside the first truck. He clicked his mike button twice and listened for responding clicks from Jolene and Cruz indicating all clear.

After hearing the clicks, Burns stood up in the saddle and climbed onto the truck body roof. He went to work with his knife and cut a hole in the plastic roof skylight. He activated the timer on the incendiary device and dropped through the hole. It fell between the marijuana bales. Then Burns crawled to the front of the truck and examined the roof seam for cracks or damage. He found three good places and enlarged the openings with his knife.

Andy silently dropped off the truck roof onto Don Cameron's back. The horse didn't move; Burns walked the horse to the next truck. One down three to go.

Burns finished the last truck and was still on the roof when a rapid clicking sound came over his earpiece. Somebody was heading his way. He lay flat on the truck and listened for Burrito to tell him what was happening. One male from the bunkhouse was walking toward the trucks. He stopped the light a cigarette and answer the call of nature. Cruz provided a whispered play by play of the man's moonlight stroll. Andy lay flat on the truck roof. Don Cameron and Jazz were quiet.

The man ambled down the side of the parked trucks, not looking at anything. He got to the back of truck Burns was on. He crossed behind the truck to the side where the horse and dog remained silent. When he turned down that side, he was facing Don Cameron's impressive rump.

Before his mind to could figure out what his eyes were seeing. Two steel shod hooves connected with his chest. Jazz bit him in the crotch and hung on with a violent shake of his head. Burns looked over the side of the truck roof and watched the show. The man never made a sound. Andy called off Jazz with a stage whisper then dropped off the roof onto Don Cameron's back. Burns removed a can of black spray paint from his saddle bag. He tagged the sides of the trucks and rode off.

A phone ringing awakened Pauli Dumas; it was a call from one of the Mexican ranch hands. It took him a few minutes to figure out what the man was saying. Porn Dude called Bradford's room and woke up his boss.

"Boss, one of the Mexicans from the ranch just called. One of the Arabs is dead. And the dope trucks have been tagged by gang bangers."

"What the hell are you talking about Pauli?"

"We got a dead raghead and the trucks been spray painted with gang signs."

"When the hell did that happen?"

"Last night."

Bradford was interrupted by his cell phone ringing. He looked at the screen and the current number for El Jefe.

Ron Kroll was sleeping soundly next to Ivalou Vargas. His cell phone began to buzz.

"Kroll," He said sleepily.

"Ron, you're closer to the ranch than I am. Get down there and find out what's going on. One of the jihadists is dead, and the trucks are painted with gang graffiti. El Jefe says one of his men speaks English."

"OK, I can do. Are you going to start that way?"

"No, and you will have to leave as soon as you call me back with what is happening. El Jefe says the shipment can't go until late tonight. He says something about the balloon being up and his helicopter can't fly across the border."

"OK, I'll call you when I know something."

"Call me when you get to the ranch."

Kroll clicked off. He got up from the bed and watched Vargas sit up yawn and stretch.

"What the hell was that all about." She asked getting out of bed and reaching for his shirt to hide her nakedness.

Kroll was pulling on his pants. Vargas went to the bathroom.

A few minutes later she returned. Kroll took her place in the bathroom. It didn't take him as long. He stopped by the sink and brushed his teeth. Ivalou got dressed by the time he finished.

"So what's up?"

"Bradford called, said El Jefe called him. There is a dead jihadist, and the trucks have gang graffiti on them. Bradford wants me to find out what's happening.

"You may want to wake up Havelee and the guys. They can follow in that pickup truck at a discrete distance and photograph from the service road. I hope this doesn't turn into our needing backup, but I want them close. Get back to your hotel and get ready. Dress like a mean ass take no prisoners Latina for this gig."

"Got it," Ivalou said giving him a quick peck on the cheek as she went out the door.

Ron Kroll walked alongside the old yellow trucks and read the graffiti.

CINCO CINCO SEIS

556

VE RAPIDO EL JEFE 556

MATAR EL JEFE 556

Kroll examined the corpse as he took out his phone. He snapped a few pictures of the trucks and the jihadist's corpse. Then he called Bradford.

"I think the raghead got kicked by a horse. It looks like two horseshoes imprinted on his chest. And something bit him badly on his package. Not much blood so the kick probably killed him quickly. I'm texting you pictures of the trucks and the body. No one knows what happened. The dead guy was known for getting up in the middle of the night to go piss. He probably walked up on whoever sprayed the trucks. As high up as the writing is they were probably on a horse."

"Well, tell those assholes to use the tractor to bury the guy and you get the hell out of there. I'll call El Jefe with the bad news.

"Those FBI agents had a field day photographing those trucks on the Rocking H Bar," Cruz said. He and Russell had followed the agents from Nogales. The two PI's went on to the Casita. Jolene was watching the computer screen showing the camera feed.

"Bradford must have called Kroll to come investigate. That was a gutsy move letting the Latina agent ride with him. Even if she did stay in the car." Burns said.

"Bradford's SUV is still in Tucson," Russell reported. "Kroll stays in Nogales and the Latina agent sneaks over to his motel every night."

"Nothing like fooling around while undercover," Jolene said.

"I just hope those trucks get out of this valley before they catch fire," Burns said.

"That will be funny as hell if the FBI shares with the DEA and they come bust everybody involved," Cruz said.

"And the trucks catch fire while all that is going on," Russell added.

"We don't need a wildfire in this valley. Even if it does get blamed on the five fifty-six gang." Burns responded.

Chapter Nineteen

The four marijuana-laden trucks left the Rocking H Bar at 4:00 AM. The drivers were promised martyrdom in the land of the Great Satan after they completed their deliveries. None spoke any English past a few basic phrases. And their directions were crude maps. Each map warned them to avoid Sierra Vista Arizona and its most prominent landmark, Fort Huachuca. All four jihadist wannabes promptly got lost. Due to their lack of sleep from a nighttime border crossing and immediately being put in trucks and told to drive. The men quickly found places to park their trucks for a nap.

Haji Zabeeb almost screwed up the mission early on. He found a pull off spot within one hundred yards of Fort Huachuca's rear gate. The wind wasn't blowing in the right direction for the MP's manning the gate to notice the pungent smell of burning pot. Andy Burns incendiary devices worked as expected. Holes in the wooden floor board of the cargo box provided enough airflow augmenting the missing skylights. Cracks in the seams did the rest. The illicit cargo was steadily turning into a glowing furnace. At some point in the trucks life, another cargo shifted and punched a hole through the front of the box into the cab. The hole provided another outlet for the heady fumes. And, enhancement for Haji's restless dreams.

The bales in the other three trucks ignited in a similar fashion. Though not as hot has Haji's truck yet, the pending disasters awaited movement to fan the flames.

Aashif Qaadir woke up before the other drivers and somehow managed to get his truck out of the valley and on I-40 toward Tucson. The vehicle would run 75 miles an hour. The speed caused a bellows effect on the already glowing bales. Aashif was not affected by the burning marijuana. His cab was tight, and he paid no attention to other motorists trying to warn him his truck was on fire. He was approaching Casa Grande when three state trooper cars surrounded his truck and forced him to stop. Qaadir could not figure out why they dragged him out of the cab and onto the ground. He understood the handcuffs, however. In his country, this usually mean an execution was happening soon. The troopers quickly realized this was not a Mexican driving a truckload of burning dope; when Aashif Qaadir began reciting Muslim prayers.

Jabir Tabrez realized he was going east on I-10 when he should have been traveling westbound. He slowed then hit the brakes hard as he considered a U-turn across the median. Jabir sped up and then slammed on the brakes again when a likely look spot came in view. It wouldn't work, and he hit the gas. The third abrupt braking pissed off a passenger Tabrez didn't know he had. The rattlesnake sunk its fangs into Jabir's calf. He screamed and lost control of the truck. Witnesses said it fishtailed and ran off the road going end over end once before it struck the bottom of Davidson Canyon. The snake slithered out of the wreckage as the marijuana bonfire of Davidson Canyon began. Jabir died on impact.

The Tabrez wreck and fire got the most attention and blocked I-10 in both directions as emergency services responded. A group of eastbound motorcyclists out for an early morning run to New Mexico were closest to the pot conflagration. They were enjoying it. This bunch was higher than any nearby tree when a pissed off firefighter arranged for them to get around stalled traffic. They merrily gunned their bikes eastbound.

A few miles ahead of the stoned bikers Fadil Naadir was not feeling any pain either as he entered I-10 eastbound. Fadil didn't care which way he was going. His truck was running wide open at 65 miles per hour. The speed caused the hot coals of marijuana to blaze at the same time the stoned bikers reached it. The motorcyclists realized they were following a five-ton pot pipe.

Haji Zabeeb's weed enhanced dreams the erection in his pants led him to believe he was driving a suicide bomb truck. This idea morphed into reality in his pot deadened mind the same time an old TV remote slid from under the seat during a hard stop. The red button would detonate his load, and the promised virgins would be waiting. Haji finally found a paved road that went toward the forbidden town of Sierra Vista and Fort Huachuca. The Fort was his target, and his erection reminded him of the promised virgins. Zabeeb stood on the gas and ran three red lights at major intersections in his quest for paradise. Pot smoke belching truck attracted the attention of the Sierra Vista Police.

A couple of motorcycle officers intercepted the truck when Haji stopped and yelled at a senior citizen pushing a grocery buggy he'd almost run down. Incredulously Zabeeb yelled, FORT BOMB PARADISE VIRGINS ALLAH AKBAR!

The senior pointed in the direction of the fort. Haji gassed the truck making a left turn onto Fry and a straight shot to Fort Huachuca's main gate.

One of the motor cops asked the senior citizen what the driver said.

"He's a fucking raghead, and he's going to blow up the Fort! You need to shoot that bastard before he does it!"

Warning of a terrorist attack in progress went out over the police frequency. The local cub newspaper reporter monitoring the police scanner went wild notifying every media outlet on Facebook and the Associated Press wire service.

Zabeeb's truck was not running as well as it should. In his zeal for paradise, Haji shifted it into low gear. It was still going fast enough to keep the cargo box fire stoked. The police chase was turning into a drug induced parade of cops and everybody whose olfactory nerves were working. The rolling bong easily knocked a couple of squad cars aside, and the officers emptied their pistols into the truck.

"ALLAH AKBAR!!" Haji shouted every time he came close to a group of people.

The main gate was where the action would be. The MP First Sergeant gave orders to the security team to lock and load. One MP sat the M249 Squad Automatic Weapon on a bipod in the front window of the guard house. Another loaded a belt of ammo into the weapon. The two female MP's assigned to the post took aim down Fry with their M4 carbines.

The four-lane Fry Blvd intersected Buffalo Soldier Trail in front of Fort Huachuca's main gate. The First Sergeant used the traffic signal control to stop traffic on Buffalo Soldier Trail.

An alert police sergeant ordered his officers not to get in front of the truck as Zabeeb bore down on the gate. "Back off! Back off the truck! The MPs will open fire on it when it crosses Buffalo Soldier!"

Two police cars accelerated to the intersection in front of the main gate and stopped their cars blocking traffic. The cops bailed out and took cover behind their cruisers.

The First Sergeant noticed the young MP on the SAW was turning blue from holding his breath. The older man laid his hand on young Military Policeman's shoulder and said.

"Easy son, just breathe. Fire on my command. Aim for the driver. He is coming in range now. Standby."

Haji saw the main gate dead ahead and readied his TV remote. He said whatever prayers his marijuana inhibited brain function could remember. Haji commenced screaming "ALLAH AKBAR!" out the window of the truck at everyone watching with a camera phone.

Zabeeb sucked in one last breath of the powerful smoke. He let go of the steering wheel closed his eyes and pressed the red button.

The truck would not track in a straight line without someone steering it. A bump in the road didn't help either. The smoking vehicle veered to the right and crashed into a stone wall smashing the radiator. The momentum carried it partway over the wall before coming to a stop. The impact opened the seams of the cargo box. Flames erupted as more air fed the burning marijuana.

The driver's door came open when Haji smashed against it. The would-be martyr fell out.

"Safe your weapon soldier. Clear it and stand down." The First Sergeant ordered the MP on the machine gun. Watching the man on the ground by the burning truck the First Sergeant directed to two women forward. "He doesn't appear to be wearing explosives approach with caution. Police are approaching as well."

The two women MPs moved forward covering the jihadist. A male and female pair of Sierra Vista Police Officers moved in also. If Zabeed hiccupped, the cops and MP's would shoot him into a bleeding pulp. The two MPs aimed their carbines at the prostate terrorist. The male cop patted him down and checked for injuries. Other than a red mark on his forehead there were no visible injuries. More cops moved in. The first two pulled him away from the burning truck. The two MP's raised their weapons. Haji moaned, and the cops lifted him to his feet.

Stunned and very much under the influence Haji thought he was in paradise. One of the MPs was close enough he recognized her as a woman. He managed to say something about uniformed virgins and groped the MP's crotch. She laid Haji out with a quick jab.

"Virgin my ass," she said as the First Sergeant arrived.

"Nice punch soldier." He said.

"Thank you, First Sergeant, my brother fought golden gloves he showed me a thing or two."

At that moment Haji started to get up again, and the female cop Tased him. Zabeed started hunching his hips upward as the current hit.

"The stupid sonofabitch is air humping virgins," the MP said.

"Be advised the Fire Department is waiting for verification of explosives before they come any closer." Dispatch radioed the police sergeant.

"It appears to be a couple of tons of marijuana burning. And the crowd is getting higher than a democrat's tax hike. Tell them to put this mess out. Before we have a street dance."

Traffic at the eastbound I-10 Border Patrol checkpoint near the Arizona-New Mexico line was light. The fire at Douglas Canyon was still causing a backup. The Border Patrol agents noticed their drug K-9s getting fidgety. They started to whine. One agent caught a whiff of pot in the air. All of them saw the faded yellow box truck pulling off the interstate too fast and belching smoke like a steam engine. A motorcycle gang was following the truck. The riders were zigzagging and popping wheelies.

The truck slid to a stop and did not quit rocking before Fadil Naadir opened the door and got out. The now flaming truck continued forward and veered into a parked patrol vehicle.

Naadir, smiling broadly and speaking Farsi unrolled his prayer rug pointed it east and knelt down saying his prayers. Four bikers joined him.

Burning marijuana trucks and the failed terrorist attack on Fort Huachuca led the noon news broadcasts around the country. Havelee and Ivalou watched the news intently. Kroll watched it on a TV at the small café in Patagonia where he was eating lunch. His phone buzzed with a coded text from Penelope. It was urgent that he call her. The phone rang with an incoming call from Bradford.

"Kroll, have you seen that shit on TV about the burning trucks?"

"Yeah, I'm watching the news now."

"Do you think they are the trucks from the ranch?"

"Probably, but I'm not going to call the cops and ask."

"Man you are funny. You must have had your comedian pill this morning."

"Well, Ash I really can't say about the trucks. I just don't know. You have pictures of them. One for sure, there is a rat in your partner's barn. Somebody sold out those trucks. If I'm correct, those tagged numbers belong to a Tucson street gang. I've seen them on the news and in town."

"I have too. Don't go back to the ranch until I call and tell you. Shack up with a whore. Come to Tucson and get some cash if you need it. El Jefe will figure out he has a snitch, and there be more bodies at the ranch."

"I'll be in Nogales waiting for you to call."

Kroll hung up and paid his check. He called Vargas on the way back to Nogales.

"Bradford and company are not coming back to the ranch today. El Jefe is probably on the war path."

"Havelee is wondering if the trucks on the news are the same ones from the ranch."

"Probably, Bradford called earlier and said we could start back to the ranch. A human shipment is due in the next day or two. We have to be there for that. He called just after I got your text and told me to hang out in Nogales until he called. He thinks El Jefe has a snitch for the gang in his organization."

"I would hate to be the snitch. Since you're planning on coming back to town, Havelee will want to have a debriefing sometime this afternoon."

"I'll be available. I think we should either meet at a truck stop in Wilcox or the eastbound rest stop in Texas Canyon."

"Sounds good I'll let you know."

El Jefe was not the only one unhappy with the burning dope trucks. The General was livid. He appreciated Burns' successful sabotage mission. He was not happy with that the fact the previous four trucks got clean away. The General got on the phone to a Washington news source. Clips of the pot burning trucks led the evening news segments about the DEA director having an affair with a staff member.

Ransom Carter and the FBI Director enjoyed the evening news reports of their upstart counterpart's new difficulties. Both of them wondered who the unnamed source was. The Director worried if the same source knew of his mistress.

<h1 align="center">Chapter Twenty</h1>

Jolene observed the flatbed ranch truck cross the border at Lochiel and return an hour later with the usual load of hay. Or so it appeared. What piqued her interest was the time frame. It was an unusually quick turnaround for the expected load of dope. Maybe it was a makeup shipment for those lost to fire. When the truck unloaded at the barn, she saw it was not. Jolene grabbed her phone and called Burns.

"Are you where you can get a look at the Rocking H Bar barn?"

"I can go up the hill and use the spotting scope. What's going on?"

"The hay truck just unloaded a dozen or so women from across the border at the barn. I'm thinking human trafficking."

"I think you are right."

"They didn't even bother to unload the hay bales on the sides. They just put the tarp back on and are leaving now. I bet they are going back to get another group."

"Let me know if they cross the border."

"OK."

Burns pondered the conversation as he rode Don Cameron to an observation point. Once in place he lay behind a powerful spotting scope and studied the Rocking H Bar headquarters area. A male with an M16 casually stood guard at the barn door. Whether the man was Mexican or, middle eastern was a guess. The two races could pass for the other anytime. Two more men patrolled the ranch armed with AK47 rifles. The weapon of choice for aspiring jihadists. The suburban SUV was gone. Yesterday Bradford's two thugs were using the tractor to bury bodies. Apparently, El Jefe had loyalty issues with his help and laid off five employees. Only the car driven by Ron Kroll was visible.

Burns turned the scope toward the bunkhouse and studied the door. It had a wide single barn style door that swung outward. A board was used to secure the bunk house door from the outside. Burns spotted a two by four used for this task leaning against the door frame. At angle off the bunk was the workshop. A building with a double doorway with no doors. If they posted any, this would be where the night guards would hang out and sleep on the work bench. Movement caught his eye, and he saw the barn guard ambling toward the shop.

The next vehicle to arrive did not come under cover of darkness. It was a heavy duty Japanese pickup truck of the type often seen on the evening news used by third world armies. It carried a weapon mount in the bed. Three men got out of it and removed bags from the truck bed. Once they stored their gear in the bunkhouse, they returned to the truck. Two climbed into the bed and proceeded to mount a heavy machine gun on the tripod. The other passed out AK 47 rifles to the two in the bed and kept one for himself.

Burns called Jolene. "Did that light colored pickup cross the border at Lochiel?"

"Yes, with three men in the cab. The flatbed is crossing now. And Havelee Harris just showed up at the Double B headquarters. She has her team with her."

"Keep me posted."

"What do you think about the women?"

"Springing them from the trap they are in."

"I figured as much. I'm sure you've noticed what that pickup has in the back."

"It appears they are taking guard duty a little more serious."

"Are you sure that is a good idea. We have a video of El Jefe's men killing five people yesterday. I expect that was due to your graffiti."

"Good idea or not it is the right thing to do. We'll watch the guard mount tonight. I want to know how alert they are."

"Burns, why don't we let Havelee in on what's going on?"

"She has an undercover agent over there who can do that."

"Burns."

"Keep an eye on things." He disconnected, not wanting a discussion. Andy got up from the spotting scope and went to where Don Cameron stood. Burns removed his encrypted satellite phone from a saddle bag and called Reid.

Havelee Harris along with Ivalou Vargas, Desmond Taylor and M&M sat on the Double B headquarters veranda. Carson Bell and TR sat with the agents.

"Mr. Bell, we need to use your ranch as a surveillance base and staging area. We have reliable information the drug trucks that burned came from the Rocking H Bar. Having my team close by we can photograph the operation and take them down before the next shipment leaves."

"Agent Harris you have been an overnight guest here several times. I suspect you and TR are courting," Bell said.

TR and Havelee both blushed at the comment. The other agents managed to keep straight faces. M&M picked that moment to roll his eyes toward the ceiling.

"You will be dealing with some mean hombres and once you catch the current bunch. The FBI will be gone. And I still live here. And another bunch of mean hombres will move in.

And those drug lords have long memories. I don't want to wake up in the middle of the night with one of them fixing to cut off my head. I know you've been rubbernecking around every time you've been down here, seeing what you could see. TR thinks you are pretty good hand on a horse. I don't know if any of you would be worth a hoot busting bales or fixing a fence. Right now I can't see my way to allow your crew to move in here. I'll talk it over with TR, and now that Butter Billy is getting around a little better I'll include him. We want whatever is happening over there stopped. But letting the FBI have free rein of my ranch. I don't know. I'll give you an answer in a couple of days."

Havelee thanked Carson Bell for his time and the agents left the ranch. Bell and TR sat quietly and watched them drive off. The men in a pickup truck and the women in a car.

"I haven't told her about those dudes warning me off the herd this morning," TR said.

"Tell me about that again. We didn't have much of a chance to talk about it."

"I was riding toward the section the where the cattle are grazing, and I heard machine gun fire. I looked up on the hill, and one of the guards was pointing his rifle at me and the other pointing motioning me back in this direction. I turned around quick and loped back to the Double B."

"Have you seen Burns this morning?"

"No, I haven't. Mr. Carson, I appreciate you not getting too much into to Havelee and me seeing each other. She doesn't share FBI business with me, and I don't share ranch business with her. I was worried that she was just using me to snoop around the Rocking H Bar. And I grant you she is doing that. But I got the feeling there is more to our relationship."

"What are you going to say when it's over, and she goes back to DC or where ever she is from?"

"I don't know. I've been lost ever since those dudes told me to leave the Rocking H Bar, and Mr. Lyon disappeared. This valley is my home, and I always thought of the Rocking H Bar as where I would live out my days. Probably as only a ranch hand. But it is nice to dream about calling it mine one day."

"I know Lyon was concerned about the future of the Rocking H Bar. His sister and her kids didn't want the place. He was considering your future as well. Like I worry about Miguel and Estella and Butter Billy. And of course now you. I'm not getting any younger. And I don't have any relatives to leave this place to."

"I understand that Mr. Carson. Miguel Estella and Butter Billy are all good people. They have ridden for your brand a long time. I haven't. Don't get me wrong; I do appreciate your taking me on and your concern about my future. But I don't believe I've earned a home here like I had on the Rocking H Bar."

"TR I understand what you are saying. You and Lyon came over here to help as much as me, and my folks went to the Rocking H Bar. So, what I decide about this place is not your concern. If you aren't going to need the Jeep for anything, I'm going to take it over to the casita to see Burns. I want to talk to him before I let the FBI in this place. Your sweetie can come visit you of course."

Jolene heard the old Jeep truck approaching from the ranch road. The road was more of a trail than a road. Buddy Russell and Burrito Cruz arrived a few minutes earlier. Jolene to put on a pot of coffee. Burns was on his way back.

"Looks like Carson Bell," Jolene said.

"I sure would like to buy that truck from Carson. I could make a bundle on that thing." Cruz offered.

"You will have to get in line behind a bunch of folks," Russell said.

"All of you will have to get ahead of Andy. I think he's going to make Carson Bell an offer for that Jeep that he would be crazy to refuse." Jolene laughed. "Right after he gets the papers on Don Cameron."

"Lyon Hamilton's sister ought to give him that horse nobody else can get near it much let less ride the damn thing," Cruz said.

"Apache got better sense than to ride that horse," Russell added.

Bell stopped the Jeep next to the motorhome. He got out of the truck and walked over to the table.

"Good morning Carson you are just in time for coffee," Jolene said.

"Jolene you sure aren't particular about who you hang around with." Carson said gesturing toward the two PI's."

They all joined in a laugh as the Cruz and Russell shook hands with Bell.

"Where is Andy Burns this morning?" Carson asked.

"He is on his way back here. He has been watching some new activity on the Rocking H Bar."

"Speak of the devil and he shows up," Russell said as Burns trotted past the motorhome toward the barn. He got off Don Cameron and loosened the saddle cinch. One the horse was secure in the shaded barn he joined the group.

"Good Morning." What brings our landlord over this way?" Andy said cordially.

"We need to parlay and seeing who your guests are; I expect they are in on whatever it is you are up to," Bell answered.

"That pretty little FBI agent TR is sweet on wants to station herself and her agents on the Double B to surveil the Rocking H Bar. I don't want to know what all you are up to in that regard. But I don't want the FBI getting in your way either. Personally, I think you will get to the bottom of things before they do." Carson Bell said.

Burns and Hadfield looked at each other and then at the rest of the group. They picked up the subtle nods of ascent from Russell and Cruz.

"The FBI doesn't know we are here and what we are doing. And we have resources the FBI doesn't have or should I say can't use because of legal constraints priorities so on and so forth. With that said. I hate to interfere with a cowboy's love life. Your friendly feds don't need to be around here."

"I'll stall them for a while, and the politely say no. I like to see TR with that woman. She's a cowgirl alright. But I don't want him getting hurt. I hope she isn't using him."

"I wouldn't put that past her. I hate it for TR; he's a good hand. And I appreciate him keeping quiet about our being here."

Hadfield went into the trailer and came out with cups and carafe of coffee. She sat everything on the table and told them to help themselves.

Carson Bell related TR's incident with the guards earlier in the day. "Something is going on that they don't want anybody but them over there." He said.

Everyone was quiet for a few minutes. They all were thinking about the implications of the guard's actions. The small talk turned to weather and then ranching. After finishing his coffee, Carson Bell took his leave. The group watched the old rancher leave.

"Got any idea why they warned TR off the ranch?" Russell asked.

"Might be because their dope burned up?" Cruz asked.

"Bradford's people came back to the ranch yesterday morning. His goons went to work with the tractor burying the ones El Jefe killed. I guess he figured the Mexicans ratted him out to the five fifty-six gang. That is his answer to the dope trucks catching fire. They brought in a technical with a three-man crew this morning. They are taking guard duty serious for this next cargo."

"Are you talking about one of those terrorist pickup trucks with the machine gun in the back?" Cruz asked.

"Yes."

"What is the cargo?" Russell asked.

"Women, there have been four loads already this morning. The women are a mixture of races, Asian, Latino, Caucasian. I'm thinking they believe they are coming to this country for jobs. Except the jobs waiting for them are as prostitutes. I've seriously considered blowing the whistle on this operation. But I think the women will be moved again before the FBI can get their act together and do anything about it. We are going to rescue those women."

"Cowboy fell off a horse. Hit head. Cowboy talk loco." Russell said.

"To make this work we're going to have to involve Miguel and Estella. Butter Billy if he's up to it. We need TR, but I'm worried about his FBI girlfriend. And Carson Bell needs to know about it."

"What are you planning?" Russell asked.

"We hookup that big cattle trailer parked by the barn. Come in on the ranch road off the southeast corner. Turn it around on the hill above the barn. Sneak down there and let the women out. Load them in the trailer and bring them back here. Then we sort out how to best help them."

"Easier said than done, Andy. When do you plan to do it?" Cruz asked.

"Tomorrow night."

"What is keeping us from getting blown away?"

"The same thing that kept that from happening when we sabotaged the trucks."

"And that is?"

"Stealth and a black ops team that is on call for us at Fort Huachuca."

"Are you saying we had a bunch of badasses ready to haul ass over the Huachuca Mountains and rescue us?"

"No, they were waiting for us on the ranch. One of the operators wondered why I couldn't do any better than a fat ass Mexican for help."

"NO SHIT! YOU HAD BADASSES OUT THERE IN THE DARK!"

"No shit compadre."

"SON OF A BEACH" Cruz exclaimed hyping a Mexican accent for all it was worth.

"Cowboy not as dumb as Apache thought."

Cruz and Russell offered up contacts in the volunteer social services area to help relocate the women from the proposed temporary camp at the casita. People that were really good at keeping their mouths shut. When the PI's left, Burns found Hadfield staring at him with a cop look to beat all cop looks; she was not happy.

"Do you realize what the hell you are thinking about doing?" Hadfield said coldly.

"I do and I every expectation of pulling it off."

"And you are going to use those same so-called commandos that hid in the dark looking over your shoulder while you planted firebombs in those trucks. Commandos I've yet to see."

"Yes and I expect you will see them tomorrow night."

"And why is that?"

"Because they will take out the machine gun truck. The truck is in front of the cameras. You won't miss them."

"Burns you're a piece of work. The bedroom in the RV is mine. No, the whole RV is mine. You are living in that cabin or the barn I don't care. I've got to sort this out on my own."

Jolene walked back to the RV went inside and closed the door.

Andy smiled and went to attend to Don Cameron. The horse understood.

The plan started to come together later that afternoon. Burrito Cruz paid a visit to a Nogales war surplus store and came out with four dozen cots and five dozen gray wool blankets. Estella went grocery shopping. Buddy Russell went to a large sporting goods outlet in Sierra Vista and purchased two large camp stoves six propane tanks and several large cooking pots.

Cruz reported back that the volunteer services would be at the Casita to pick up the women the morning after their rescue. These people were in touch with other groups more than willing to aid in saving these females from the life that awaited them. What amazed the PI's and Burns, was the ability of these people to keep a secret.

Butter Billy's girlfriend, Bonita came with him. The stout woman was carrying her AR-15 and plenty of ammunition. She announced that she was going with Butter Billy. A rapid exchange in Spanish erupted between her and Cruz. Burrito turned to the others and said, "she's going, or she will shoot us all."

Burns walked over to Bonita and politely asked if she would consider carrying a different weapon. Bonita indicated she would consider it. Andy went to the storage compartments on the RV and unlocked one. He pulled out a black case and motioned Bonita to follow him. Behind the barn was an earth bank with a nearly vertical slope. Burns opened the case and removed a modified AR rifle. He handed it to Bonita along with a magazine of ammunition. Andy pointed toward a discarded piece of lumber laying against the wall.

He watched as Bonita expertly loaded the weapon and fired. She hit the board ten times out of ten shots and smiled brightly at the short rifle. It didn't make any noise.

"Bonita, push the safety switch up." He said.

She looked at him quizzically and then followed his instructions. The safety selector moved to another position. Burns pointed back at the board. Bonita aimed and squeezed the trigger. The rifle fired three rounds full auto and the board split in two. She proceeded to fire at each half board and split them as well. Bonita squealed in delight. She cleared the rifle making it safe and hugged Burns giving him a peck on the cheek.

"Si, mine." She walked off carrying the rifle in search of Butter Billy.

"I think she just traded rifles with you," Russell said.

"Yeah, I doubt she'll want to give it back."

"That's a suppressed machine gun; it could be a problem down the road."

"It's a ghost, no numbers."

"Oh."

"Look at the ones you and Cruz are using."

"Indian understand. Indian dumb sometimes."

They walked back the picnic table.

"What are your plans for the gun truck?"

"I'm going to leave that to the black ops, guys. They will take out the crew and steal the truck. They are also going to cover the service road at the ranch entrance to stop any large transport vehicle coming into the ranch."

"Indian glad badass dudes doing the heavy lifting."

"Once we get the camp set up. Estella will fix dinner for us. Burrito has a detail after dark. Butter Billy and Bonita will practice driving the truck and trailer using night vision goggles. I've given her some IF light sticks she can ground guide him when he turns that around on the hill above the barn."

"What if they decide to move the women tonight?"

"The black ops team is already in place along the service road. If transport shows up, they will stop them. And we go hell bent for the barn." Burns paused and looked across the valley. "And we hope we can get them all out."

Russell nodded his ascent then asked. "Are you going to let TR in on this?"

"I want to, but I don't want Havelee Harris, and her team involved."

"Maybe the three of us should talk to him. I wouldn't mention the black ops team. And while we are on the subject your lady isn't happy with this operation either."

"True, and she knows the FBI will likely screw it up because it has to happen quickly. So she is between a rock and a hard place with the whole thing. Once she gets her head around what we're doing, she will come around. I like TR, and he knows what we are doing here. I don't think we can risk taking him along on this caper. He will probably find out about it later. It will be easier for him to keep his mouth shut then." Burns said.

Ron Kroll was able to slip off for an ATV ride around the Rocking H Bar. Deputy Willie Hillman returned to duty a couple of days before and was hanging around the ranch. As soon as Kroll saw bars on his phone, he sent a Vargas a text. A few minutes later Vargas read the message and called Havelee. She in turned called Desmond and M&M. Within a half an hour they were meeting.

"OK, Kroll has advised something is going to happen late tonight or tomorrow night. I believe it will most likely be in the early morning hours. So be prepared with water, snacks and for sleeping in the trucks. I'm going to call TR and tell him we are going to camp out on the ranch road. I will ask him not to tell his boss. I hope the big guy they call Butter Billy is still at his girlfriend's place. Any questions?"

"Will TR go along with not telling Carson Bell. And more important is will he stay in the bunkhouse?" Ivalou asked pointedly.

"I'm going to impress on TR that we are not invading the ranch. And when I say it is FBI business he will stay away. He understands that. Any more questions?"

"What time are we moving out?" M&M asked.

"No later than five thirty. That will give us time to get through Patagonia and be in the valley by dark."

All the agents shook their heads affirming their readiness for the task ahead.

Havelee called Tobias Rutledge.

"I've got a favor to ask, and it involves FBI business, comprende?" She said after the usual greetings.

"If I can help you I will."

"We need to be close to the Rocking H Bar tonight and tomorrow night. We will park on the Double B Ranch Road near the entrance. We will be there all night both nights. And your boss doesn't need to know about it."

"Hav, he probably wouldn't care about you guys being all the way out there. You're over a mile from the headquarters house. But I won't tell him."

"I appreciate that, and I don't need any midnight cowboys riding up the road either."

"I understood the FBI business when you said it. Besides tomorrow is a work day for me. It will be daylight before I get out that far. Would you want me to wake you guys up or bring you coffee?"

"No smartass. We will be awake and gone before the sun gets up."

"Hav, where are you going when you finish this job?"

"I don't know. Probably back to DC where I'm assigned. I'm working a screwed up investigation out here. It is the type of thing that could leave me asking Carson Bell if he needed another hand. Why are you asking?"

"Well, I like you. And I don't want this to go away."

"TR, I don't want it to go away either. There is a supervisory opening coming up in the Phoenix Field Office. I am going to apply for it. Provided this current case doesn't put me in line for an early retirement."

"Well, Phoenix is closer than Washington."

"Listen to me sweetheart. I've been taken with you since you rode up to the house that day. I don't want you thinking that I am using you. Because I am not. I want us together. That is why I'm looking into the Phoenix opening."

"OK babe, that makes me happy."

"Good, catch you later. Maybe I can come for a visit this weekend."

Havelee hung up the phone.

Jolene was still mad at Andy. She came over to where Estella was putting dinner out for everyone and got a plate and took it back to the motorhome. Estella and Miguel would go back to the ranch house, and she would serve dinner for Carson Bell, TR and her husband, Miguel. Butter Billy and Bonita were going to camp out at the Casita in case things happened early.

Burns phone buzzed with a text from Jolene.

FBI in 2 vehicles car & truck parked Dbl B entrance rd.

Burns thought about this for a few minutes when his satellite phone buzzed. It was Reid.

"We have eyes on two females in a truck, two black males in a second truck. Parked inside the entrance road to the Double B Ranch. They appear to be law enforcement. Advise"

"We have them on camera. They are FBI. If this thing goes down, they don't need to be on the scene until we get the women out. They are not the enemy. Can you slow them down?"

"Yes, we have a gadget for that sort of problem."

"Elaborate unless it is classified."

"When activated their cars, radios, and phones get fried. In short, they are walking and not calling."

"Trade you a rifle for one of those gadgets."

"No deal it's seriously classified."

The phone clicked off.

"Something up?" Russell asked.

"FBI has a stake out at the Double B Ranch entrance. Carson Bell likely doesn't know they are there."

"He doesn't know you have cameras looking at him either does he?"

"No."

"This could screw things up."

"No, not really," Burns said smiling, thinking how much he would like to see Havelee Harris and company walking to the Double B with hat in hand looking for a ride.

El Jefe's well-planned extraction of the women might have embarrassed the FBI team, had the drug lord hired an intelligent nonalcoholic driver. The moron was drunk, driving an ancient school bus and came into the valley the wrong way. A narrow one hundred eighty-degree switch back turn doomed the old the vehicle. A rookie border patrol agent found the bus and the driver the next morning.

Sonora's drug king was livid all day and threatening to fly to the Rocking H Bar and kill everyone involved. The Aerostat balloon languishing high above the Huachuca Mountains, it's electronic eyes seeing everything that flew toward the USA, was the only thing that kept him from it.

M&M and Desmond were relieved to see daylight. They scrambled to recover M&M's trousers from the truck bed via the sliding rear window over the back seat. Sometime during the night M&M correctly figured Havelee and Ivalou were sound asleep. He carefully stepped out of the cab to urinate. The moment his feet hit the ground, he heard an angry buzzing sound. Desmond already terrified of the wilderness night yelled snake. M&M pissed in his pants trying to get back in the truck. He spent the rest of the night bare ass in the back seat of the truck. His pants and underwear laid out to dry in the truck bed. Both men gripped their Glock pistols fearful of huge rattlesnakes breaking into the truck. Desmond peed in a cup, and M&M took careful aim at the window when Des lowered it to pour out the waste. The commando team videoed the whole incident.

It was a long hot day in the San Rafael. Jolene stayed cool in the RV and didn't venture outside. Burns and the rest of the crew went over the plan until they knew every move the other person would make. Reid forwarded the video of the FBI agents to Burns encrypted laptop. Russell just shook his head. Cruz laughed until he hurt. The PI's and Burns retreated to the cool darkness of the casita, and it's evaporative cooler. They all took a long siesta, awakening in time for dinner.

Havelee Harris was amused at Desmond and M&M when they reported for duty that evening. Both men were wearing tall snake proof boots with their trouser legs stuffed into them. Both carried several plastic bags from Walmart.

"I don't think the boots will create a new look in pimp fashions." She said.

"Pimps don't have to pee in the company of rattlesnakes either," M&M responded.

"Hopefully, something will go down tonight. I will commit us to this on this stake out unless we hear something definite from Kroll. I know it is not comfortable out there. But at least it is not cold."

"We're good to go," Desmond said.

Vargas gave an affirmative nod. She was unusually quiet. Havelee figured it was concern about Kroll. He had not communicated in over twenty-four hours.

They drove to the San Rafael mostly in silence. Harris texted TR and told him they would be back in place all night.

Jolene watched the FBI agents park their vehicles and settle in for the night. Burns raid as she was beginning to think of it was going to happen in the wee hours of the morning. Conversations between them were civil and short. She was pleased that some serious backup support was close. She texted Burns that the agents were back in place. A few minutes later he knocked on the outside of the RV and then entered.

"We are going over there tonight and get those women out. Jo, you are our eyes over there. We are counting on you to tell us if anyone is moving."

"I can do that. But what if this thing deteriorates into a shootout? This raid rescue or whatever you call it is nothing but vigilantism, and you are breaking the law. I know you think it is the right thing to do. I hope you have considered the consequences should this thing blow up in your face."

"I have, and the means justify the end. We have covered every contingency, and if I didn't think we could make it happen, I wouldn't be doing it. By your count, there are sixty women imprisoned over there. They close the barn door and have an armed guard. Those women are captives; they are prisoners. If the FBI were planning to move on this, there would more than four agents sitting a few miles away. Kroll has alerted them, or they wouldn't be there. If you see anything that indicates a full-scale FBI operation, let us know, and we will get the hell out of there. And they won't be any wiser."

"I wish I could let Havelee in on what we are going to do. But I agree with you about trusting her not to interfere and not to arrest us."

"Just let us know if she comes charging in with the cavalry."

"I will. And Burns, be careful."

"I'm always careful."

CHAPTER TWENTY-ONE

Two hundred yards southeast of the hillside overlooking the Rocking H Bar. Burns checked in with Jolene via radio. She gave an all clear. The half-moon lit the high prairie; the night visions goggles functioned perfectly, giving Burns team a green-tinted view of the landscape. Andy switched his radio to Reid's frequency. The commandos were positioned north to south in an L shape around the Rocking H Bar compound. Their team on the service road reported no activity. Reid's people had eyes on Burns group and the ranch compound. Andy transmitted a single word message to both units.

"Showtime."

Andy rode Don Cameron south of the compound. He dismounted and tied the horse to the trunk of a cottonwood tree. Jazz stood guard on his equine partner. Burns slung is rifle across his back and rechecked the rest of his gear. Burrito Cruz drove up in an ATV. Andy unloaded two large dyed black pillow cases with the open ends securely closed with wire ties. He heard Jolene's voice in his earpiece.

"The perverted dude came out of the front of the house. He peed and is now walking toward the barn."

Burns clicked his mic in acknowledgment. Burns began the two-hundred-yard hike to the compound carrying the pillow cases. Another message came through his earpiece.

"Trailer ready."

Ron Kroll found keeping Porn Dude away from the women was a full-time job. Ass Bradford threatened the oversexed mutant with a painful death if he molested any of the females. Kroll dozed off fully clothed in his bed. Numb Nut's snores subsided, and the ranch house was quiet. The creaking sound of someone walking on the wood floor awoke Ron. He rolled out of bed and went to check Pauli Dumas's room. Porn Dude wasn't there.

Burns was half way to the barn when Jolene called again.

"The pervert took a woman out of the barn. The guard is with him. They are heading toward the building diagonally across from the bunkhouse."

Burns acknowledged with a mic click and continued his trek toward the compound. No plan completely survived once it started. Securing the bunk house was his first objective. The news that a second person was out and about wasn't good, being forewarned would allow him to deal with it. *Bless you, Jolene* he thought.

"Technical is going down," Reid reported. Burns acknowledged. He knew a three-man team would assault the truck with silenced submachine guns. One commando would steer while the other two pushed the truck down the ranch driveway until they could safely start it up and drive off. The jihadists guarding the vehicle would not survive.

Andy Burns was creeping along the opposite side of the barn toward the bunkhouse when he heard Jolene's voice.

"Burns! Two little girls just ran out of the barn. The smaller one tried to go toward the bunk house. The larger one grabbed her and pulled her up the hill toward the horse apple camera. They must have stepped on it because I lost the picture. Ron Kroll came out of the house and is walking toward the barn."

Andy acknowledged and paused at the northwest corner of the barn. He could see the south side of the bunk house and only part of the south wall of the shop. He carefully walked up the side of the barn and looked around the front. No guard. He gave his mic three clicks. Burns quickly moved to the bunkhouse as he watched Kroll walk into the open door of the shop.

Burns froze by the side of the bunkhouse waiting to see if his quick sprint attracted any attention. He stepped to the front door pulled spray can of oil from his pocket and doused the door hinges. Burns eased the door open. He cut the ties on the two large pillowcases he carried and threw them inside. Burns closed the door and placed the two by four across the brackets on the door frame, effectively locking everyone inside. A commotion in the workshop drew his attention.

Kroll went outside and started toward the barn. He didn't see the guard near the barn. Ron found the man standing in the workshop doorway fondling his self while he watched something inside. A single light was on in the shop, and Kroll saw what was happening. For an instant, he thought it was Ivalou Porn Dude was raping. The woman was a doppelganger for the female Special Agent. Ron spotted a tattoo on the victim's limp arm. Ivalou didn't have body ink.

Kroll smashed the guard's skull with his brass knuckles. The man dropped his M16 and collapsed. The clatter did not phase Porn Dude. He was busy raping and choking his victim. Ron Kroll picked up the cattle prod he'd seen on an earlier visit. He was too keyed in on Pauli Dumas to notice Burns slipping into the building behind him.

Porn Dude's bare ass was elevated as he stood on his tip toes humping and choking his victim. Kroll pressed the switch on the cattle prod and rammed the shock stick into Porn Dude's balls.

A bull with its testicles hung on a barbed wire fence couldn't have made the sound Porn Dude emitted during this violent colitis interruption. He fell to the floor grasping at his privates as Kroll pinned them to the floor while applying the current.

Burns accessed he woman and saw her pupils were fixed and dilated. Her facial expression showed the horror of her last moments alive. Porn Dudes bellows were waking those in the bunkhouse. Andy removed Lyle Thigman's blackjack from his pocket and choked up on the spring handle. Burns touched Kroll on the shoulder. The undercover agent spun around, and

Andy smacked him on the forehead with the leather covered lead end of the blackjack. It was lights out for Ron Kroll.

Dumas was still conscious and holding his injured package as he squirmed around the concrete floor. He was in no shape to see the blow coming. Andy pocketed the blackjack, and the first scream came from the bunkhouse. Seeing the door was still secure Burns jogged to barn and removed a spray can of paint from the side pocket of his trousers. Andy tagged the barn doors.

NO PUTA EL JEFE MUERTE 556

Buddy Russell, Burrito Cruz and Bonita, all fluent Spanish speakers were quietly herding the women out of the barn and up the hill, where Butter Billy Three waited with the Double B Ranch truck and cattle trailer. He would follow Cruz's ATV's driving with the help of night vision goggles navigating the rough ranch roads using night vision goggles. Buddy would follow on his ATV and Bonita would ride in the trailer, as they hauled their precious cargo to safety.

Burns turned and jogged into the night. The first shots rang out inside the bunkhouse followed by more screams and curses. Whoever built the building put the electrical box with a cut off lever on the outside. Andy switched off the electricity moments before he'd opened the door and pitched in the open pillow cases. The lights would not come on. And six very angry rattlesnakes crawled out of the pillow cases.

"Egressing now, negative contact with juveniles." Reid's voice said in Andy's earpiece. Burns clicked the mic as he spotted the Cottonwood where left Don Cameron and Jazz. Burns heard Jazz whine. Burns checked the dog, and he heard another sound.

Andy pulled down his night vision goggles and spotted a little girl maybe thirty feet away sitting on the ground, crying. Mindful of scaring the child more he removed the goggles and the face mask before he reached her. She said, "ido madre." Burns recognized the words, Spanish for mother gone. A burst of full auto M16 fire rang out, the child screamed leaping into Andy's arms.

Mounted on Don Cameron with the crying child in his arms Burns cantered into the night. She paid no attention to the goggles he put back on. The Jazz growled and ran forward. Andy heard another girl's voice, this time, a mixture of Spanish-English and something else he didn't recognize. He saw the images of a child fending off a coyote who was trying to get something she held. Burns shot the coyote with his silenced 1911 before Jazz could attack.

He reined in Don Cameron next to a girl perhaps nine or ten years old. The child he held continued to cry. The older girl held a small animal in her arms. The coyote was trying to make it a meal. Burns took off the night goggles once more and looked at this child. She handed him a small kitten. Andy managed to hold on to it, and the smaller child as the girl jumped up grabbed his leather chaps and swung herself onto Don Cameron behind Andy. Once seated she reached around for the cat. Andy noticed the fur ball had a very long tail.

Kids night and a mountain lion cub, He thought. The girl behind him wrapped an arm around him and held on. "Vamonos!" She said.

Burns shook his head and urged Don Cameron into a canter. He would follow the ranch road the others had taken. There was still a long way to go in the dark before he would turn Don Cameron north and follow a trail of IR markers. Burns clicked his transmit button three times to let the others know he was on his way out. Even with all that was happening he heard the click code from the trailer crew in his ear piece. They were safely ahead of him.

"Burns! Find those little girls!" Hadfield yelled into the radio.

Andy clicked his mic button again, unaware the child riding behind him broke the antenna a second before while she was grasping his belt for a better hold.

Burns and his passengers had ridden for another quarter hour before he slowed Don Cameron to a walk and begin scanning for markers. He noticed Jazz run ahead and then saw the shapes of cattle. Burns reined in and stopped. There was enough moonlight in the distance that he could see the cattle spilling out into the service road from a gate Russell and Cruz forgot to close.

Andy heard the dog barking and knew he was pushing the cattle into a group. Once the cattle were on the road, Burns would have to turn them north. And do this in the dark with the assistance of one border collie a stud cow horse and night vision goggles. With two kids and a mountain lion cub along for the ride. The smaller child cried herself to sleep and was resting against his chest. Burns loosely held her.

The child riding behind him punched Andy between the shoulder blades and demanded, "agua!"

Burns removed a water bottle from a horn bag and handed it over his shoulder to the girl.

"Gracious vaquero." She said.

"You're welcome Cat Brat." He replied and heard a soft giggle.

Part of the cattle had started north on the service road. Jazz ran south and turned the rest of them. Burns tried his radio and could not raise anyone. He reached into his shirt pocket and brought out the cell phone. No signal.

She will be pissed off now, He thought, putting the phone up. He remembered the encrypted satellite phone in his saddle bags. He removed it and called Jolene's phone. She didn't answer; he left a message. He relaxed in the saddle, held on to the small child and let the dog and horse move the cattle.

"Damnit! I can't raise Burns on the radio or his cell phone!" Jolene said to Russell who was standing in the RV with her watching the confusion at Rocking H Bar.

"We heard his coming out clicks. Maybe his radio went out and cell phone service down there is spotty. Those idiots at the Rocking H Bar sure as hell aren't following him."

"I'm still worried about Burns." She said.

The sound of automatic fire got both Ashton Bradford and Numb Nuts out of bed. Half-dressed they ran out of the ranch house. And hit the ground when a burst of gunfire came from the bunk house. There was barely anything to deflect the AK47 rounds fired from inside the darkened building. The bullets chewed through the uninsulated walls and into the night. Rounds ricocheted off the concrete floor; their destination, to whom it may concern. There were screams and prayers in both Farsi and Spanish. In a sixteen by twenty-foot building with no lights, nine scared undisciplined men with automatic weapons and six pissed off rattlesnakes was a combination for disaster.

Numb Nuts drew his Glock and began firing from where he lay. The thug emptied the pistol into the walls of the bunkhouse. He missed the structure ten times. Six rounds got inside, and two hit his cohorts. One fell on top of a snake and was bit five times. With Numb Nuts out of ammo, the only thing he and Bradford could do was hug the dirt.

Ron Kroll was addled and his mind foggy. He knew someone hit him and that was it. Conscious enough to realize bullets were flying around above him, he huddled behind a blacksmith's forge, and an anvil mounted on a huge log base. Porn Dude was still out cold.

The gunfire subsided when the ammo ran out. Only moans and occasional screams sounded from the bunkhouse. Bradford came into the workshop and found a confused Kroll, still trying to get his head straight. Porn Dude was another matter. He was still out, naked from the waist down with his flaccid member laying across a cattle prod between his legs. The dead woman and Kroll with a rapidly swelling forehead left little doubt in Bradford's mind as to what happen. More shooting started and Bradford carefully looked out of the shop. Apparently, Numb Nuts had found another magazine for his pistol and was blazing away at the bunkhouse.

"CEASE FIRE YOU STUPID SON OF A BITCH!" Bradford yelled.

Numb Nuts sheepishly complied.

While he was a crook with little regard for anything other than money, Bradford remembered his FBI training. Using a flashlight, he studied the bunkhouse closely before approaching and spotted the two by four securing the door. During a careful walk around of the building, he spotted the breaker box with the thrown switch. Bradford turned it back on. Amazingly one light was not shot out.

Kroll walked unsteadily from the shop. He'd found a lantern.

"Hey Kroll, see if there is a rope in that shop. We need to open the bunkhouse door." Bradford said.

After a few minutes of looking while struggling with dizziness and foggy vision, Kroll found a rope. He figured out what Bradford wanted and after several tries were able to loop the rope around the two by four. Ron heard the buzzing snakes inside the building as well as more moans and screams. He moved to a corner stretching the rope behind him. On Bradford's signal Ron jerked the rope, flipping the two by four out of the brackets. The door opened because of the weight of five men leaning against it. Their bodies fell to the ground. One rattler slithered around the bodies. Numb Nuts opened fire on the snake causing Bradford and Kroll to dive to the ground behind the bunkhouse. Numb Nuts ran out of ammo again. And the snake kept going.

Bradford dispatched Numb Nuts into the ranch house with instructions to bring the double barrel shotgun that leaned in a corner. And a box of shells for it.

It took Numb Nuts three trips to get the right shells for the first shotgun he found. With birdshot loaded in both barrels Bradford figured he couldn't much more damage. The injured that were mobile climbed into the bunks away from the rattlers. Bradford dispatched the snakes. He told Numb Nuts to load the men that were still alive in the back of the farm truck. Then drive to Nogales and dump them in front of the ER. Numb Nuts got lost and two hours later shoved the bodies off the truck in the parking lot of the Sierra Vista hospital.

Lanterns and electric lights lit up the area around the casita. Estella and Miguel were working an improvised chow line to feed all the women. Two buses with social workers that arrived before dark sat nearby. These people milled about talking to the women as did Russell and Cruz. Hadfield was beside herself worried about Burns, who wasn't back and was still not answering his phone. Carson Bell showed unexpected an hour before. TR rode in on horseback thirty minutes later.

"Carson," Russell said. "We have learned that these women paid money or have promised to pay fees out of wages earned for their transportation to the US and promised jobs. What these people don't know is a life enslaved in prostitution awaited them. We know that Deputy Hillman knew about it, and we felt we needed to get them out before their transport showed up. We could not rely on the feds to react quick enough to save them. So Andy Burns came up with a plan, and we pulled it off."

"So I have a bunch of illegals on my ranch, and my hands are feeding them. And you have buses and vans ready to move them out at first light."

"The vans are from organizations that deal with battered and exploited women. I'm not going to speak to the legality of this." Russell answered.

"I'm glad you did it." Carson Bell said. "TR is pissed off about not being included. But I understand why you didn't invite him to the party. I wouldn't have either. That little blond FBI woman would have him spilling the beans in a heartbeat. TR did tell me his FBI girlfriend and her helpers are staking out the service road from my driveway. They were out there last night and are there right now. I expect they were too far away to know what is going on."

"That is good to know," Russell said, not letting on they already knew.

"We know we got out all the women except one. And there are two missing children. Burns is probably looking for them. But we can't raise him on our radios, and he is not answering the phone. We have at least an hour to first light. Cruz and I are going looking then."

"Butter Billy and Bonita showed me how to work these night vision goggles," TR said as he walked up to Russell and Bell. "I'm going to ride the service road all the way to the southeast section gate on the Rocking H Bar. It I haven't spotted Burns by then, I'll follow the ranch road back toward the

Rocking H Bar headquarters. Cruz says Burns has marked trails with something that shows up in these goggles. And I'm not going to tell Havelee either. At least let me help find Andy."

Russell looked at Cruz and Carson Bell, Jolene had joined them and heard what TR said.

"OK, TR you ride south on the east service road. We will take one of the ATV's and ride west on the north road until we get close to the west service road. We will turn back before we get to the FBI's stakeout. We will leave one ATV here for Jolene and Butter Billy to use. They will be our backup. Let's ride," Russell said.

TR nodded and went to where his gray gelding waited. He swung into the saddle and trotted down the ranch road into the darkness. Cruz and Russell followed in the ATV.

"Those men will find Andy." Carson Bell said to Jolene.

"I know Carson and if anybody can take of themselves out here. It is Andy Burns. But damn it, I'm worried about him."

"Cell phones work fairly well up here on the north end of the valley. They don't work as well in the south. I would tell you to keep calling. If he has those kids and that other woman with him, he is going to be slowed down. Anybody that could do what he's done so far can certainly get back here."

"I hope so."

Cruz and Russell could travel faster than TR. They were on their way back to the casita when TR came up on the first cattle in the herd. He moved off the road and let them pass watching the animals. In a few minutes, he got a glimpse of a dog working. He figured it was Jazz. TR begin moving south along the side of the northbound herd until he spotted a horse and rider.

The child riding behind him was turning into an impatient pest. Burns had given her an energy bar he carried in his saddle horn bag. The younger child remained asleep nestled against his chest. He reached into his shirt pocket and removed his cell phone. He saw two bars and sent a text.

In route with cattle. Hav 2 girls 1 cat. 1 female dead at Ranch

Jolene was eating a delicious egg dish Estella prepared when her phone buzzed. She read the text.

"He's OK! He has the girls!"

A few minutes later Russell and Cruz returned to the casita and learned the news. Buddy went over and spoke a social worker everyone referred to as Pastor Jimmy.

"We've heard from our missing man. He has the little girls. But the missing woman is dead. I don't know when he will get here; he's on horseback. We will get the girls to you later."

"Praise the Lord those children are safe." Pastor Jimmy said. "I have learned the missing woman is the youngest child's mother. Lupe is the girl's name. The older child is an orphan the smugglers picked up in Mexico. Her name is Larcena, and she is Native American. They don't know which tribe. Both girls speak Spanish well; I don't know about English. We need to load up and get moving soon. I want to be on the pavement heading toward Nogales before the first Border Patrol units start moving."

"We'll take care of the kids. Thank you for your help Pastor."

"It is a blessing to help. Please convey my thanks to the gentleman that organized this effort. There is a special place in heaven for men like him."

"I will do Pastor."

TR moved his horse beside Burns and Don Cameron as they followed the cattle.

"Looks like you have passengers."

"Cat Brat that's TR go ride with him. He probably has a meal or two in his saddle bags." Burns said moving Don Cameron closer to TR's horse.

The girl gave the long-tailed kitten to Burns and reached over to TR. She grasped his extended hand and easily swung over to his horse. Once she was behind TR, Burns handed him the cat.

"Burns this is a mountain lion cub," TR said as he examined the furry creature with the long tail.

"It can't be very old. The mother is dead, and Cat Brat rescued it. I rescued her and it from a coyote. I should have let the coyote have them both."

This remark resulted in the child sticking her tongue out at Burns. She rummaged through TR's saddle bags until she found a couple of wrapped sandwiches. Which she proceeded to devour, like the coyote planned to do to her kitten. Burns watched this and to the kid's credit, she put the sandwich wrappings back in the saddlebags.

"Hope you don't get hungry or you have more sandwiches to eat. I would have stopped at McDonalds and fed her, but there is not one around here."

TR laughed and handed the kitten back to the little girl.

"I hope she doesn't get sick off yesterday's sandwiches." He said.

"She speaks Spanish and something that sounds like Indian to me. She knows more English than she lets on. All the one I'm holding does is cry and sleep. I have a feeling her mother is dead back in the Rocking H Bar's workshop. I think the one you have was turned loose in the desert for being a brat."

TR laughed again. "The rest of them made it back OK. They will have left by the time we get there. Burns, I understand why you didn't include me. I would have been glad to help. And this secret stays with me."

Andy nodded ascent.

"What has the cattle got to do with your plan."

"Nothing. I think my Half Breed Apache forgot to close the gate behind him or left it open so his relatives could rustle the cattle. I'm thinking the pasture nearest the casita is as good of a place as any for them."

"I've been thinking about driving them up there myself. Until the dude with the rifle chased me off the other day. And that certainly is a serious looking rifle you got hung across your back. Did you use it on any of those assholes?"

"Not yet."

TR's horse picked up the pace to head off a couple of steers that moved away from the group. Burns was amazed to see how well the little girl stayed on behind TR as the horse worked. Don Cameron picked that moment to move after two more that went off to the right. Burns grabbed the saddle horn to steady himself.

CHAPTER TWENTY-TWO

Havelee Harris' team of agents finished another night sitting in the San Rafael Valley waiting for a vehicle that didn't show. The weary team trudged into their respective rooms and proceeded to crash. Desmond and M&M were dead to the world. Ivalou Vargas sleep fitfully worried about Kroll. He had not answered any coded Penelope messages, and Vargas personal cell phone did not ring. Havelee slept soundly for three hours. The motel phone ring woke her. It took a moment for her to realize it was a phone call.

"Hold for Tucson SAC Lane." An impersonal voice announced when Harris answered. Havelee tried to get fully awake before the grating sarcastic sounding voice of Adele Lane came on the line.

"Agent Harris you will immediately detach two of your agents for duty with Tucson PD Street Gang Task Force. I have made several attempts to contact you via your issued cell phone. It is a policy violation to have that phone out of service."

Havelee hesitated a moment before replying.

"Harris I expect an answer for you."

"Excuse me, ma'am; I was with my team on an overnight stakeout."

"That is not my problem. I have ordered you to send me two of your agents. They need to report forthwith to the Tucson Field Office for a briefing."

"Ma'am, no disrespect intended, but my team doesn't work for you."

"Harris, your team is deployed in my area of responsibility. And I assure you that it will not be in your best interest to go over my head to Headquarters. Seven street gang members got shot last night; Tucson PD suspects this was the work of a drug cartel headed by individual known as El Jefe. Your people are working near the US border on some top-secret investigation. Whatever knowledge your agents have gained will be useful to this task force. Now wake up and get your people in route. And before you start calling Washington, I'm going to warn you once again not to buck me on this. My authorization comes from the Assistant Director."

Havelee listened as the phone clicked off. She walked into the kitchen area of the extended stay motel room and started the coffee pot. Mentally she calculated the time in Washington and feasibility of calling Ransom Carter this early. The only thing she was sure of at the moment was watched pots never boil.

Reluctantly, after a downing a half a cup of coffee, Havelee called Desmond Taylor and Michael Morris, M&M. Twenty minutes later looking none the worse for the wear, the two agents were knocking on her door. Havelee though ill of how quickly men could get ready as she opened the door.

"We'll do what we can to help," Desmond said after hearing the orders to report ASAP to the field office.

"Lane strikes again," M&M said.

"I will follow up with DC and try to get you guys back soon. Unfortunately, I don't think it will do much good. Lane has a point. While she doesn't know the target of our investigation, we are working the border. Good luck with it and keep me in the loop as much as possible."

Later in the morning Havelee was able to get in touch with Ransom Carter.

"Agent Harris,' The Special Assistant to the Director began. 'I have an email regarding the temporary re-assignment of your two agents. I've spoken with the Director, and we concur that SAC Lane and Tucson PD have priority. You, on the other hand, are in more of a watch and wait mode. As you said, the human trafficking pickup didn't happen as expected and Kroll hasn't checked in. He has gone off the reservation so to speak in the past. The Director and I believe Kroll has done something like that now. For the time being Ron Kroll is on his own out there. You and Agent Vargas continue surveillance of the ranch where Kroll is thought to be. If that rancher Bell will let the two of you move on to his place, you are authorized to do so. You need to be aware that if there is any escalation of violence gang violence in Tucson, you and Vargas will be recalled to assist in that investigation."

"I understand Sir if I may ask, will there be any backlash from SAC Lane regarding my calling you."

"Lane expected you to call. And you have acted in a professional manner in doing so. Harris, you understand the big picture here. I will tell Lane that you are completely on board with these changes. And that you will forward any information you may learn from you undercover operation, that might be of use to the gang task force."

"What if Kroll checks in with information we can act on?"

"Advise me ASAP anytime day or night. I will decide how much response we can provide. I need to go now Harris."

"Yes Sir, what if Kroll needs help?"

"Use your best judgment."

Carter hung up the phone. Havelee realized she was out on a long thin limb. And Ron Kroll was at the end of it. She finished another cup of coffee and called Vargas.

El Jefe was not in a good mood. His bodyguards carried the idiot who hired the bus driver to a fenced area behind the luxurious estate in southern Sonora. El Jefe walked outside to a patio and took a chair next to an ornate table as he watched his bodyguards work. A servant brought him a glass of wine.

The bodyguards stripped the man to his briefs. His T-shirt was stuffed in his mouth to squelch the screams that would be forthcoming. The terror in his eyes gave El Jefe a modicum of satisfaction as he watched his guards throw the man down on the heavy timbers that formed a cross. El Jefe knew of no reference to compare his cross to the ones used by the Romans. His worked very well. The Romans would have been proud to have one as well constructed. The man writhed in pain when the guards drove the first large spike into his palms. El Jefe wasn't sure where the Romans drove their spikes, so he instructed his men to use one in the palms and one in the wrists. Each foot would get a spike as well. He didn't want his victims to fall off and break their necks. The only people El Jefe killed quickly were the messengers that brought him bad news. It was the least he could do, after all; the news wasn't their fault.

His guards expertly drove the spikes using heavy sledgehammers. Missing would likely crush the body part. El Jefe believed in giving his staff the finest tools available. A small man wearing middle eastern dress stood nearby watching the process with obvious pleasure. He was clearly one of El Jefe's favorites, if not the most favored. This Iraqi once worked in Sadam Hussein's torture chambers. The little man burst into tears of gratitude when El Jefe once presented him with a brand new deep cycle DieHard truck battery and heavy gauge jumper cables. Recent business dealings with the terrorist organizations called for a trusted interpreter. The little torturer provided this service with accurate answers. Which, at times, led to the execution of his countrymen who lied to El Jefe. Other times resulted in El Jefe getting to watch the little man use the battery and jumper cables. The little Iraqi certainly knew the most sensitive parts of the human anatomy.

The guards rigged the block and tackle and pulled the cross upright. The Iraqi quickly stepped over and yanked the T-shirt from the victim's mouth before the cross became vertical. El Jefe smiled at the screams. And at the thought of dressing his guards as Roman soldiers for these events. They were loyal men would do so immediately if commanded. El Jefe worried about offending their masculinity by ordering them to wear something that resembled a skirt. To El Jefe Roman soldiers were macho. Somehow two thousand years changed what looked macho to his guards.

A servant brought a cell phone to El Jefe. He could see the fear in the man's eyes as he took the phone from him.

"How are you this fine day Senor Bradford?"

"Not well El Jefe. We were visited by the five fifty-six gang again last night."

El Jefe's expression changed to anger. "THE PUTA'S! WHAT HAPPENED TO THE PUTA'S?" He yelled.

"One is dead; the rest of the women are gone, they were stolen by the five fifty-six gang. I have ten dead men here. They stole the machine gun truck as well. I have texted you a picture of the message they painted on the barn."

"Bradford those bastards have cost me money. How are they finding out what we are doing?"

"We can't ask the Mexicans you sent; they are dead. Only one Iranian or whatever he lives barely. He doesn't have enough English or Spanish to converse. I suspect the turncoat died in the attack."

"How did they get the women out of your barn and off your ranch?"

"I suspect they trucked them across the pastures."

"The guards, what happened to the guards?"

"They were killed with silenced weapons. Another guard had his skull smashed."

"Bradford, our final shipment comes from our middle eastern friends this week, as soon as the balloon goes behind the mountain. It will come and so will many guards. They will have your payment in cash. Use good men to keep this from being fucked up. Comprende?"

"Si El Jefe Si."

"Good I will deal with those thieves in Tucson, they will be no more!"

El Jefe threw the cell phone at the cross.

The drug lord cursed and threw his wine glass. He got up and kicked over the chair and the table. A bodyguard returned with the servant.

El Jefe looked at the hapless household worker and saw the urine dripping from his trousers.

El Jefe pulled his Colt Government Model 1911 from his waistband. The ornate dark blue 38 super caliber weapon carried both gold and silver inlays and engraving. The pistol's grips were silver and inlaid with a gold Aztec symbol. El Jefe racked back the slide chambering a round.

He shot the servant between the eyes.

Securing his pistol, he motioned for his Iraqi torturer. The man trotted over and bowed to his master.

"Ubay bring me Malmud! I need a bomb pronto!"

"Si El Jefe Si," the torturer said as he bowed profusely backing away, before turning and trotting into the estate.

Ron Kroll knew he wouldn't win any beauty contests with his purple and red swollen face. One look at the prostrate Porn Dude made Kroll think he got the better of the deal from whoever hit them. Dumas lay on his bed wearing only a T-shirt. He was moaning and holding an ice pack under his swollen testicles. They were bluer than his face.

"How the hell are you Pauli?" Bradford asked as he pulled on a pair of leather work gloves. This move made Kroll wonder what the former FBI agent was doing. Bradford pulled a pair of metal cutting shears from his back pocket and grabbed Porn Dude's penis.

"NO BOSS NO NO DON'T BOSS NO PLEASE NO DON'T BOSS PLEASE!"

Bradford held Dumas' tool in one hand and opened the shear with the other. He put the open blades around the base of Porn Dude's dick. The man squirmed and tried to move away, Bradford held tighter and pushed on the blades.

"Listen to me you stupid oversexed son of a bitch. You killed one of El Jefe whores and let a damn street gang sneak up on us. If you thought with your brain instead of your dick, we wouldn't be in deep shit with El Jefe. One more fuck up and you are going to have the shortest pecker in Arizona. Do you understand asshole?"

"Yeah, Boss! Please get those things away from me! Boss, I'm sorry Boss I won't even jerk off anymore Boss please!"

"Just remember asshole. You won't have anything to jerk if you do this shit again."

Bradford gave another yank and shoved with the shears for emphasis. Dumas screamed.

Kroll shook his head and left the room. He encountered Numb Nuts in the hallway.

"Did the boss cut off Pauli's dick? He said he was going to."

"No not yet, but if he doesn't keep it in pants, he will lose it," Kroll said relieved he didn't have to watch it happen.

Numb Nuts looked disappointed when he said. "Well, that won't happen either. That man has only two toys. His dick and one of them damned computers. Don't know which one he likes more."

Kroll walked outside and sat on the porch waiting on Bradford. Whoever hit them last night was good, and it was an operation planned with military precision. Ron Kroll didn't think for a minute that a Latino street gang did it.

Bradford came out of the house and sat down next to Kroll.

"Ron I kind of wish you had killed that stupid son of a bitch last night."

"Ash I wish I had been a few minutes earlier. I might have interrupted what was happening."

"Those fucking gang bangers are smart. I remember seeing intelligence reports that said a lot of them had military training. They are bold. I just don't know who the hell told them we are here. It has got to be someone in El Jefe's camp."

"I've seen the military training reports also. I don't know if it extends to the planning it took to pull off what they did. My head has stopped spinning, and I'm seeing without blurring. I'm going to take the ATV for a ride around the ranch. Those bastards couldn't have done this without leaving evidence of some kind. I want to know who we are dealing with."

"Good idea. The big one happens as soon as the balloon goes down. El Jefe told me to expect it and a lot of guards. He doesn't want any mistakes."

"What the hell are we doing then, just providing him a base of operation?"

"That and a guide to deliver the package."

"Who is the guide?"

"You and it is worth five million US dollars in cash, a way out of the country and a new identity."

"Throw in another hundred and I'll cut Dumas's dick off for you."

Bradford guffawed.

"I need that oversexed bastard's computer and Spanish skills a little longer."

"Ash have you ever considered El Jefe might be planning on double crossing us. Look at what has happened. First the trucks now the women. That bastard has got to be pissed."

"Yeah I have. But to double cross us, El Jefe has to double cross a middle eastern terrorist group who is paying me twenty-five million to ensure the package gets delivered. El Jefe is getting twenty-five million as well. That is a lot of cash to lose just to double cross, someone. Money is El Jefe's bottom line."

"Mine too, but I hate to trust that bastard. Or a bunch of ragheads either."

"El Jefe is a bastard alright. I think the ragheads have better business ethics. We will be careful."

"When do I learn where I'm going?"

"When everything gets here. You might want to say goodbye to your whore in Nogales pretty soon. When this starts, I'm collecting everybody's phones. Hope you understand, but I can't take any chances."

"I would do the same thing. Don't worry about it."

"Well make sure the ATV has enough gas in it. I would want to see you walking around lost like that dumb ass Hillman."

"You got that right," Kroll said as he got up.

Buddy Russell drove up to the Double B Headquarters house. The oldest of the two girls was enjoying the attention of TR and Carson Bell, whom she started calling Abuelo the moment she met him. Russell entered the fenced area and walked up the steps to the verandah.

He watched the child feeding the mountain lion cub with a bottle. The oversized kitten was sucking greedily.

"This kid decided me and Miguel are her grandfathers and Estella is her Abuela," Bell said.

"She named the cat Pepe and me Daddy," TR added.

"Her name is Larcena Sells and is full blood member of the Apache Nation. She has a birth certificate in the back pocket of her jeans. She showed it to me earlier, and I called the San Carlos Reservation office. She is a known orphan; her parents died several years ago. She was last known to be living with a relative in Mexico. He, according to some of the rescued women, apparently sold her to the smugglers that brought her to the Rocking H Bar. Where, as you've heard she managed to escape along with a younger Mexican child known as Lupe. Andy Burns found them both in the desert, where Miss Larcena here was fighting off a coyote for that cat. Whose mother, according to Burns is dead. He spotted her body, while he was rescuing Larcena. Miss Larcena is twelve years old," Russell said.

"Are all the women gone now?" Bell asked.

"Yes, they are in three separate shelters. One of the pastors has a contact in the immigration service. The pastor says there won't be a problem getting any of them green cards. The children might be a little more difficult, but with someone to take of them, it can happen."

"Good because I'm foster homing both of the little girls. The young one is already calling Miguel and Estella Abuelo and Abuela. I'm her gringo Abuela." Bell said.

"Burns says Lupe's mother died from being attacked and raped. The attacker was one of Bradford's people," Russell said.

"Yes and I hope Burns hit the son of a bitch hard enough to kill him. For that matter, I wish he had taken out all of those bastards while he had the chance."

"Between us, and no one else, I suspect he probably will before this over. Federal, state and local law enforcement aren't going to help."

"Works for me, I'll pay for his bullets."

"Speaking of federal here comes our favorite FBI agents or at least my favorite," TR said.

Russell turned around and watched Havelee Harris park behind his truck. She and Vargas got out of their truck and walked to the porch.

Harris forgot her special agent demeanor and hugged TR. Larcena watched this. The lion kitten finished its bottle, and she proceeded to hand the bottle and the cat to Carson. Then she went over and hugged TR, who picked the child up.

"Who do we have here?" Havelee asked looking at the scruffy little girl who needed a bath and clean clothes.

"Larcena Sells, a rescued orphan who I intend to adopt. She is an Apache and is twelve years old."

Larcena reached for Havelee's hair. She stepped closer so the girl could reach it. Larcena examined Havelee's blond locks intently. Blond hair was something novel to the child.

"Prieta." She said, releasing Havelee's hair.

"What did she say?" the agent asked.

"Pretty, she thinks your hair is pretty.

Larcena spoke to TR in rapid Spanish and then looked at Havelee smiling.

"What did she say?"

"She said I needed to marry you so you could be her mother."

Havelee blushed. Larcena pointed at Ivalou and said something to TR in Spanish.

"I hope she is not suggesting bigamy," Ivalou said smiling.

"No,' TR answered. 'She says you look like her friend Lupe's mother. And Lupe's mother is with Jesus."

At that moment Estella and Miguel came from inside the house. Lupe was between them and saw Ivalou. The child screamed and ran toward Vargas.

"MADRE MADRE!"

Lupe jumped up, and Vargas managed to catch the girl and lift her into her arms.

"I'm not your Madre sweetheart." The Latina agent told the girl. Lupe took Vargas arm and pushed up the light weight jacket sleeve. She intently examined Ivalou's bare arm.

Tears gushed from the child's eyes when she sobbed. "No mi Madre."

Vargas bit her lip and blinked away tears as she hugged Lupe in her arms.

"I think somebody needs to come clean about what is going on," Havelee said as she realized everybody had a guilty look except her and Vargas.

No one responded right away. Havelee walked over to a wicker couch and sat. Vargas carrying Lupe sat next to her. Larcena recovered her kitten from Carson Bell and snuggled in between the two agents.

"Talk, now," Havelee ordered.

"Myself and a colleague assisted by Billy Butterfield and his girlfriend Bonita, rescued fifty-nine women and these two children from a white slavery operation last night. The youngest child's mother was found dead, apparently at the hand of one of the traffickers. The women are safe in local shelters. Mr. Bell has agreed to keep the children in foster care here at the Double B Ranch." Russell said.

Harris didn't respond right away. Larcena handed her the kitten and said, "mi Pepe." Havelee held the cat and stroked its tan coat. The long tail and the color caused to her realize she was holding a purring mountain lion kitten.

"I don't suppose these women were in a barn on a neighboring ranch?"

"I don't remember where we found them. Only that we found them Special Agent Harris." Russell answered.

"And these children are my adopted granddaughters," Bell added.

"They are our adopted nieto," Estella said forcefully.

Miguel nodded his ascent.

"And I'm going to raise this one as my daughter come hell or the FBI. And if you don't like it Harris you can have my gun and creds now." Ivalou said, tears flowing freely down her cheeks as she hugged Lupe.

Havelee continued to pet the cat who was now asleep in her lap. Larcena laid her head against Havelee's arm.

Everyone was looking at her waiting. Havelee raised her head from watching the kitten she continued to stroke with her right hand. She took Larcena's hand in her left.

"After I graduated from the FBI academy my proud daddy hugged me and said, 'Hav sweetie the only thing I can tell you, is always to try and do the right thing.' I think that is what everybody here is doing. So the FBI is not going to get the chance to do anything else. I will help, not hinder."

"Does that mean you will marry TR?" Larcena asked looking hopefully at Havelee.

"I didn't get a chance to tell you she speaks English," TR said coming to the rescue.

"She is fluent in the Apache language as well," Russell added, backing up TR.

"That young lady is something we will discuss at another time." Havelee leaned over and kissed Larcena's cheek.

"Mr. Bell, we asked you if we could use your ranch for surveillance. It has gotten critical; we get an answer." Havelee said.

Vargas' Penelope phone buzzed. She pulled it from her jacket pocket and read the text message.

Women are gone unknown who moved them suspect 556 street gang. Unknown their source. Terror threat in progress!!! Expect suspects and gear to X border next time the balloon is down.

"It has gotten real critical," Vargas said handing the phone to Havelee.

She read the message and handed the phone back.

"Estella put on extra plates for all our guests and make sure the other two guest rooms are ready." Carson Bell said.

"Thank you, Mr. Bell."

"Just sneak out to the bunkhouse and discuss that child's needs."

Havelee blushed again. Vargas managed to send a text and still hang on to Lupe.

GOOD GUYS NOT 556

"Burns, you scared the hell out of me this morning."

Andy Burns was napping on the couch in the RV when Jolene decided he'd slept long enough. He yawned stretched and sat up looking around for his boots.

"I'm sorry. My radio antenna got broken. I called on the satellite phone and left you a message. I texted you as soon as I had a cell signal."

"You left me a message?" Jolene grabbed her phone and started punching buttons. They both listened to Burns message.

"Burns what are you doing with a satellite phone? It has a blocked number."

"That is how I keep in touch with the General and the black ops team."

"BURNS DAMNIT! I LIVE WITH YOU I SLEEP WITH YOU. WHEN IN THE HELL ARE YOU GOING TO INCLUDE ME IN EVERYTHING YOU DO?"

"Sorry, with everything involved, I forgot about the sat phone. I almost forgot it last night. When you calm down, we will talk."

Burns got up and left the motorhome. He walked to the barn and went in the tack room. He came out and went to work cleaning the saddle he used. He didn't pay any attention to the time as he worked. Don Cameron snorted, and Jazz got up and trotted to Jolene who came into the barn. She petted him, then walked over to the corral fence and stroked Don Cameron's neck.

"Burns we've had this conversation before. I know it is hard for you to share. And you certainly try to. This whole situation is hard to comprehend. We are now involved in people smuggling. You clobbered an FBI agent. You haven't shot anybody yet. At least anyone you told me you shot. I feel like a voyeur watching all these cameras. It's not like watching the stuff we used in the police department. And you are twisting the tail of one of the meanest human beings in this hemisphere. And on top of all of that. You scared the hell out of me last night when you didn't show up with the rest of them.

"Now I know at least you tried and left a message I didn't find. But damn it this is harder than I expected." She teared up.

Burns stopped cleaning the saddle and took her in his arms. She put her head on his shoulder and cried.

"I know you don't know how to use this word Burns, but I love you. Please don't scare me again."

He squeezed her tighter. And Don Cameron stretched over the fence and nuzzled her neck and shoulder.

Burns reached up and touched the horse's nose with his fingertip and pushed him away.

"She's mine bonehead, go eat some hay."

Havelee and Larcena visited TR in the bunk house. The Apache child enjoyed their company. And Pepe was tolerated by the adults. When Larcena dozed off, Havelee waited until she was sound asleep to ask about the cat. Pepe slept soundly in the chair with Havelee.

"What are we going to do with this thing?"

"I like the way you make that our problem."

"I like we. TR I've told you, I don't know what the future holds, but I'm going to try to get transferred out here somewhere."

"It can still be we. Me you and Larcena."

"You are smitten with her aren't you?"

"And you're not, sitting there petting her cat."

"You're right. How big will this thing get? But I guess the question should be will it stay tame or get wild?"

"I've never heard of anyone raising one of those things. Best we can hope for is that it when it gets to eating on its own, it will learn to hunt. And not kill anybody's livestock for a meal.

Releasing it in the wild, probably up on San Antonio Mountain, is what should happen. Hav, they hunt those things around here. People pay the locals to guide mountain lion hunts. I would hate to see it have to live in a pen. But damned if I want to be the one to take it away from her."

"That investigator Russell thinks the Apache Council will go along with me adopting her. I'm going to make every effort to do so. It's love at first sight. Just like with you."

TR smiled. "I'm getting this picture of Special Agent Havelee Harris putting the cat out every night at her Washington DC condo."

"That would be hysterical. Pepe prowling around at night eating gang members."

Later Havelee carried Larcena and the cat in her arms back to the ranch house. She correctly figured that Lupe was sleeping soundly in the bed with Vargas. The two agent stakeout of the Rocking H Bar ended the next morning with the Tucson SAC ordering them back to be part a bomb task force. El Jefe's middle eastern allies would manage to kill eighteen people with a truck bomb just before daylight. Only a third of that number were five fifty-six gang bangers.

The news the following night would show a White House press conference with the President assuring the citizens of Arizona their borders were secure.

Chapter Twenty-Three

The FBI agent's attention did not waver as they listened to the Tucson PD gang unit boss. The Tucson and Phoenix agents filled the conference room past capacity.

"We feel like the attacks of four nights ago were in response to the recent marijuana truck burnings. Graffiti that survived the fires appeared to be hate messages and warnings directed at El Jefe. We know the five fifty-six gang has been at odds with him since he took over the Sonoran drug and smuggling operations early last year. The quantity of marijuana lost in those truck fires was significant and a serious hit on El Jefe's bottom line. We understand from reliable sources in Mexico there have been no large purges in El Jefe's organization. Just his normal killing rate for subordinates."

A hand shot up in the group. The cop acknowledged the agent.

"Captain, would you elaborate on that last statement?"

"Certainly, El Jefe, like all drug lords does not put a premium on human life. In contrast, a lot of them have family and loyal lieutenants. El Jefe has a very small circle of loyal employees; he is the most brutal of the drug lords. He comes across as friendly and at the same time sit down for dinner while he watches his men crucify someone who has displeased him. The only people he kills quickly are those who have the misfortune of giving him bad news. El Jefe kills the messenger.

"There have been rumors, nothing concrete about a cross-border alliance with a former law enforcement officer. Description of this person ranges from him being everything from an assistant CIA director to a taxi cab inspector. We have no indication this is anything but a rumor.

"The forensic reports on the truck burnings indicate a military incendiary device with a mechanical timer was used to start the fires. These things are seldom if ever seen outside the special operations community. There were no traceable pieces recovered.

"The drivers are all middle eastern and claim not speak English. Through translators, they all said they were given passage to our country in return for driving those trucks to Las Vegas. All of them claimed to have been blindfolded and brought into this country in a vehicle. And they were sent out in the trucks at night and told to drive north.

"It is hard for us to believe the five fifty-six gang has the smarts to interdict and destroy that large of a load. Those guys don't have the brain power for that sort of action. I believe someone planted a red herring and with this recent bombing El Jefe took the bait. I understand you guys have forensics from the bomb. If there is evidence of an IED, there is reliable information from Sonora that El Jefe has middle eastern associates. I believe the first killings were in response to the truck burnings. I ask if anyone has any information as to what might have pissed El Jefe off enough for a bombing response?"

SAC Lane took the floor and thanked the Tucson Captain. "OK, take an hour to eat and catch up. Harris and Quarles remain here."

Havelee sat quietly as the others left the room. Quarles, the Assistant Special Agent in Charge or ASAC of the Tucson Field Office did the same. To Havelee the man clearly wanted to be someplace else. He wasn't the only one.

"OK, people we have a secure link to the Director and his Special Assistant Ransom Carter online in two minutes. Harris, Carter tells me you handled the reassignment of your agents in a professional manner and not going over my head as I expected you to do. To not to blindside you, I am going to ask the Director to order you to reveal the depth of your investigation and the target of that investigation. This terrorist bomb trumps your need to know excuse."

Havelee nodded. Lane was putting on a show for her ASAC. The communications tech announced ten seconds and left the room. She turned on a secure meeting sign in the hall and locked the door on her way out.

The Director was seated with Carter to his right in a nicer and smaller conference room. He did not waste any time with perfunctory greetings.

"SAC Lane, you have done a good job putting this investigation together. Thank you. At this time, you are on temporary assignment to the Office of Congresswoman Fallon McKay. The Congresswoman specifically asked for you as her liaison on a forthcoming project. I hope you have kept ASAC Quarles in the loop because he is now in the hot seat. Lane, you are excused, see your administrative assistant for your travel arrangements. Check-in with Mrs. Wilson in my office first thing after lunch tomorrow. Mr. Carter or I will have a few minutes to brief you on your new assignment. Have a good flight."

The look on the Directors face was one of don't ask questions. Lane mumbled thank you and got up from the table and left the room.

"Quarles, Phoenix SAC, and his ASAC are now connected to this conference. Gentlemen Supervisory Special Agent Harris, who is sitting quietly for the moment beside ASAC Quarles, works directly for me and is tasked with an investigation that reports only to me. Besides myself, Ransom Carter is the only person who knows about this investigation other than Agent Harris' team. You, gentlemen, are now allowed to know what is going on. Consider this Director's Level Need to Know. You will not provide anyone else with specifics of this investigation. Understood?"

A series of Yes Sirs came from the FBI managers.

"I listened to the Tucson Gang Unit Captain's briefing. The rumor about El Jefe having a former US law enforcement official is true. That former official is the single worst hiring mistake the Bureau ever made. W. Ashton Bradford is the target of Agent Harris' investigation. She is working with a very creditable confidential informant, who will remain anonymous. Agent Harris, brief us on what you have so far."

Havelee spoke without using notes or a computer for reference.

"Our CI has attended dinner meetings with Bradford and El Jefe on two occasions. These meetings took place in Nogales Sonora Mexico. Bradford and the CI crossed the border illegally and returned the same way. Bradford is operating out of remote ranch near the border. When El Jefe has a major shipment crossing, Bradford leaves the ranch along with his bodyguards and our CI. Our CI hasn't seen the marijuana because of this. What he has seen amounts to two different convoys of surplus rental company box trucks arriving at the ranch. He has seen the presence of armed guards that patrol the ranch building area and at times the ranch perimeter.

"There is a herd of cattle on the eastern sections of the ranch. Bradford made a deal with the owner of a neighboring ranch for that rancher's Cowboys to take care of the herd in return for half the profits of the sale of these cattle. When the Cowboys are checking the herd, there is an armed guard on an ATV watching from a distance. I have ridden with these cowboys on several occasions and observed this myself. My team has established a rapport with the elderly rancher of the neighboring ranch. This gentleman grew up in that valley and knew the missing owner of the ranch Bradford occupies. Bradford claims he purchased it with cash, and the rancher is living it up tax-free in the Fiji Islands. We don't believe this. The CI thinks Bradford hijacked the ranch and killed the rancher. There is a tractor with a front end loader on the property and has dug more than one grave since the Bradford El Jefe alliance.

"According to our CI, there has been some heavily armed middle eastern males take up residence on the ranch. Our CI hears the language spoken and sees the daily use of prayer rugs. There is a staff of Mexicans as well. And these people keep disappearing. It is possible El Jefe's recent staff purges happened on this side of the border. Our CI states burials are carried out using the ranch tractor.

"During the meetings with El Jefe and Bradford our CI has frequently heard reference to the big shipment. There was also a shipment of females we believe victims of human trafficking. Our man saw the women. They disappeared, and evidence of gang interference, tagging on a barn door, was seen by our CI. Whether this five fifty-six gang could pull this off or not, somebody removed a large number of women from that ranch. Right under the noses of the guards and Bradford. So El Jefe using a bomb to retaliate is probably not too far-fetched. I've put out inquiries to INS regarding a large number of females and so for no one knows anything. So this could very well be a gang we are not aware of that is pointing the finger at the five fifty-six crew to draw attention away from them.

"Our last communication with the CI was during the day that the bombing occurred. He specifically said a terror event was being planned and will happen soon. I wish he could be more specific. We sent a tiny surveillance camera in with him. It is unknown if he has been able to deploy it. The CI's primary contact agent will continue to monitor cell phones for his messages. She will advise me immediately should we hear from him. And in turn, I will brief you, gentlemen."

"Thank you, Special Agent Harris. Are there any questions?" The Director asked.

"Sir,' the Phoenix SAC began. 'Would it not be advantageous to reassign Agent Harris's team to her and put them on that neighboring ranch for surveillance. I realize we have our hands full with the bombing, but this CI of hers saying a terror event is eminent. I think we should be close to him."

"So noted, and if we receive communications from him as to timing and possibly the arrival of El Jefe himself we will do so. Right now I want all our boots on the ground in Tucson to sort out that bomb. I've gotten four calls from the White House. I will say this. Agent Harris, advise your team to stay in the loop together, and if the CI needs help, they drop what they are doing and head that way."

"Thank you, Sir, if may say. That ranch is a good two hours from here driving. Perhaps we could get a helicopter on standby?"

"Phoenix has the helicopter. They are authorized to move it to Tucson. Is there anything else?"

"Yes Sir,' Havelee said. 'During his last communication, our CI said the terror event would cross when the balloon was down. Do any of you gentlemen have any idea what that may mean?"

"How does he communicate?" The Phoenix SAC asked.

Havelee looked at the man on the TV screen as she answered.

"Sir he communicates via text messages. Occasionally voice. He and my lead agent have a text code system they use to arrange meetings and to communicate. The specific text was terror op X when balloon down."

"I've always heard the phrase as when the balloon goes up," Ransom said, speaking for the first time.

"I was thinking the same thing." ASAC Quarles added.

"Agent Harris do you know if X means anything specific in the text code your agent uses?" The Phoenix ASAC asked.

"It does not sir; we believe the X means crossing."

"OK, I want a bomber in jail in the next forty-eight hours. This conference is over." The Director said. With that the screens when black.

Harris looked at Quarles. He let out a long breath. "Can't say I'm unhappy to see Lane leave. But I'm thinking I just got screwed."

"I think our CI is the one getting screwed. I would appreciate your following up on that helicopter as soon as you get the chance. I know you are going to be busy. We'll all do our part up here. And we'll commute from where we are staying in Nogales. That way we will be close if anything goes down at night."

"Good idea, and if you would get me some GPS coordinates for that ranch. I will try for a drone mission over it. Don't know if I can get one, but I'm going to try."

Havelee was already typing on her computer.

Quarles consulted his computer for a few minutes. "Harris, I'm giving your team back to you. You and your team will be assigned the area of I-19 all the way south to the US Border. That will put you close to your investigation should things start back up there. I feel like there is a link between what your team is doing and this bombing. Keep as close an eye on that ranch as you can. We have a considerable number of gang contacts Nogales, so have your people work them.

"OK, let's get everyone back in here. I want you to brief the rest of the group on your investigation, without using the targets name. I don't feel like that exceeds the Directors need to know requirement. Are you good with that?"

"Yes, I am."

After giving a more sanitized recap of her investigation, Havelee posed the when the balloon goes down question to the group.

A young Latino agent in the rear of the group raised his hand. Havelee recognized him; she endured his calling her ma'am with good grace.

"Ma'am there is a radar balloon at Fort Huachuca it is part of the Aerostat system. It covers a wide section of the border including Arizona and New Mexico. The balloon is reeled in for maintenance and repairs. If the ranch you speak of is in the sight of that balloon. I think that might be the reference."

"Thank you, Special Agent Smith. Introduce yourself to those who are lucky enough not to know you." Havelee said smiling.

"Smith,' the young agent said with a bright smile. 'Ernesto Roberto Xavier Collazo Smith, my mother married a gringo. Everyone calls me Ernie."

Havelee laughed with the group. "The ranch is in the San Rafael Valley Ernie. Is that close to your balloon?"

"Si, if you had looked up and east when you were riding the range with the cowboys you have seen it."

Havelee could feel herself beginning to blush. "Ernie do you know that valley well?"

"Yes, I grew up in Cochise County which is east of Santa Cruz County where the San Rafael Valley is. That valley is home to one of the most beautiful quarter horse studs in Arizona. My family has bred several mares to him."

Havelee turned to Quarles, "I want Ernie on my team. Can I have him?"

Quarles answered. "Special Agent wise ass Smith, Report to Supervisory Agent Harris after this meeting."

"Si! Muy Gracious ASAC Quarles!" Ernie said with a huge grin.

The meeting concluded. Havelee asked Ernie Smith to sit with her while she called Ransom Carter on a special number. She quickly gave her reasons for having Smith assigned to her right then and not in two weeks. She asked permission to read him in on the need to know."

"Permission granted, Smith is a member of your team for the duration of this investigation. Good choice Harris, keep in touch."

With the call over Havelee got up and locked the conference room door and turned on the secure conference light.

"Special Agent Smith, what I am about to tell you is classified Director's need to know only. You may not divulge any of what I tell you without the express permission of the Director. You may only discuss this investigation in general terms with other agents. The exception being myself and your fellow team members. Who are, Special Agents, Ivalou Vargas, Desmond Taylor and Mickey Morris, aka M&M. Special Agent Smith do you understand what I have told you?"

"Yes, ma'am Ms. Harris."

"Ernie you call me ma'am one more time and I will shoot you. My name is Havelee."

"Si! And I will not bet with you about shooting either."

"Too bad, I like free lunches."

"Si, you would not like buying my lunch every day."

Havelee gave him a look that said you are on buddy and get ready to lose. Ernie smiled brightly. She began the briefing. Ernie Smith's expressions went from serious too sad when he heard the whole story.

"That is the story, Ernie. What do you think?"

"It makes me very sad to have to believe Senor Lyon Hamilton is deceased. He was the first gringo outside of my father's family I ever met. He was a great horseman and rancher. His stud Don Cameron of Lochiel throws wonderful offspring when he mates with my family's mares. I believe you are correct that Bradford has killed Senor Lyon. I was taught about Ron Kroll's undercover operations at the academy. I was disappointed to learn of Mr. Kroll's termination. Now I understand the need for that deception. Thank for making me part of your team. What do you need me to do first?"

"Do you have access to an old pickup truck and a horse trailer? You will have to have a horse too."

"Si."

"Good, we will outfit the truck with a radar detector that conceals a camera. You will play the part of an out of work cowboy. And I want you to drive into the Rocking H Bar pulling a horse trailer with your horse and ask for a job. You have to look like a cowboy. You won't get hired, but you get a look around and some good video. I need you down there tomorrow morning. When you leave the Rocking H Bar, drive north to the Double B Ranch, and I will meet you there. You are going to be a Double B cowboy."

Jolene sat in front of the computer screen and watched the beat up pickup with and old horse trailer pull into the Rocking Bar. It stopped in a place with a perfect view from the horseshoe camera. It was like an actor driving up to the mark. A young looking Latino cowboy complete with a dirty straw cowboy hat scuffed boots with spurs attached. She wondered how they got out of their trucks without busting their cute butts when they drove wearing spurs. This one looked like the real thing ready for work. And it was seven o'clock in the morning. Early for the Rocking H Bar thugs, of whom there were fewer. She could almost hear the cowboy calling out is anyone home. He stood still giving her a view of his wrangler clad backside. She was tempted to zoom for a better look when Ron Kroll walked out on the porch.

Hadfield watched him approach the cowboy and shake hands. They spoke for a few minutes, and Kroll shook his head negatively. The cowboy must have asked for a job, she thought. Kroll was pointing north and talking. He shook hands once more with the cowboy. Jolene watched him get back in the truck and make a wide looping turn as he got the pointed back toward the ranch road.

Jolene got up and poured another cup of coffee. She checked the camera on the Double B Ranch for the first time that morning, wondering how long it would take the out of work cowboy to get there. She noticed people sitting on the veranda. She zoomed in and recognized Carson Bell and TR. A woman sat with her back to her, and the little Apache girl was next to her. It didn't take much to recognize Havelee Harris. Jolene felt like a voyeur as she'd watched the romance between the blond agent and Tobias Rutledge develop. The addition of Larcena Sells, the orphan Apache girl, Burns rescued appeared to sweeten the mix. Hadfield had noticed the three of them together several times. Video surveillance was intrusive. The Latina agent came on the porch with the other child. They looked like mother and daughter. Something they couldn't be for real. But the resemblance was uncanny. Both girls wore new clothes, and their hair nicely groomed.

The cowboy drove up and stopped his rig. He got out and walked up to the porch. Harris stood up and begin introducing him. Jolene texted Burns to come to the motorhome. When Burns arrived, he looked at the recording of the cowboy's earlier visit to the Rocking H Bar. Andy zoomed the camera in on the dash of the truck as it turned around.

"Real cowboys don't have fancy radar detectors. They can't afford them, and their trucks usually won't go fast enough to need one." He watched the footage of the truck arriving at the Double B and Havelee introducing him.

"I expect that cowboy is an FBI agent. I don't think Kroll knows it. That would depend on his having noticed the radar detector. He stood outside and watched guy leave. If he saw it and made the connection, he will figure it out."

"So you think the radar detector is hiding a camera?"

"Yes and I am going to send the best shot we have of our new player to my computer guru for facial recognition."

Havelee was surprised to learn the Rocking H Bar cattle herd was now at the Double B Ranch. With the introduction of Larcena into her life and the obvious lack of details regarding her rescue, Harris realized no one mentioned the cattle.

"Well, somebody left a gate open, and they did what cattle do when they suddenly find and open gate. They go through it in search of places to graze. Fortunately, someone pointed them north on the service road. We are holding them in our southeast sections for the time being. I wanted to move to the southeast section of the Double B. But when the guard waved me away last time I was there, I forgot about trying to do that." TR explained."

"Could we get away with moving them back onto the Rocking H Bar now. It would give us access." Ernie asked.

"We can try, but when the guards come looking, there could be trouble," TR said.

"We don't know if they have guards out," Havelee said. "It might be worthwhile to move a few head over there and see if attracts any attention."

"That pasture was overgrazed after Lyon went missing. And it hasn't recovered enough to support more than a dozen head. And I wouldn't want them there more than a couple of days." TR said. "They belong in the northwest or southwest section. We were told to keep them on the east side of the ranch."

"Do you think Mr. Bell might consider paying a call on Bradford about making that change?" Ernie asked.

"He was adamant about our not letting cattle on the west side. That is because he knew he was going to be up to something. He wanted us watching after the cattle so no one would complain and draw attention to whatever he is doing. Ernie if you want to saddle up we can ride the northwest fence line, and you can get a feel for what the place. You can ride that horse you're hauling around can't you."

"Si maybe you help me put these saddle on it. I've never done that." Ernie replied in a hyped accent.

"You two sort that out and I'll saddle my horse. I want to see if Ivalou came up with anything on the video from your radar detector." Havelee said. A few minutes later she found Vargas advancing the video frame by frame on her computer screen.

"Learn anything?"

"Ron has two black eyes. His injury appears to be a two or three days old. Probably consistent with the time frame of the rescue. He is walking OK, and I don't think he was paying a lot of attention to the dashboard of the truck. I think he wanted Ernie out of there. I'm looking at this so called bunk house. The door is wide open which is not right, too many critters can get in that way. There are numerous places that may be bullet holes on the front the north side and what I can see of the roof. They look like bullets were going both ways, inside out and outside in.

"If you look closely at the area in front of the doorway, there are what appears to be drag marks and the large dark spaces with darkness in them. These dark spots may be blood. If it is something or somebody has bled out. And there are several spots like that around that area. I'm thinking the bunkhouse or whatever that building is played some part in a gun battle. Other than seeing Ron come out of the house, his car and Bradford's SUV there are no signs of anyone else on the property. There is a tractor with a front end bucket on it and a large flatbed truck that appears to have carried hay.

"There is also what appears to be spray paint tagging on the barn. I can't read the letters."

Havelee looked over Ivalou's shoulder for a few minutes, then phoned Desmond Taylor.

"Des, when you and M&M finish that interview, Check the local PDs for gunshot victims. Start with the ones closest to the Rocking H Bar. Do not call the Santa Cruz Sheriff. I don't want him to know we are working in his county. Try Sierra Vista as well."

"What did you think about Ernie's observations?" Ivalou asked.

"They pretty described everything you saw in the video, except the possible bullet holes. I don't think Ernie could have seen those with the naked eye. You have to zoom in to see them. He thinks there is probably only Kroll, Bradford and the two thugs around the place. The Rocking H Bar cattle got out when whoever moved the women forgot to close the gate. We know they TR warned away from the cattle a few days ago. Do you thing we would accomplish anything by trying to put a few of them back. The only place Bradford wants the cattle will not support the whole herd. And only a dozen or so for a couple of days. It would give some idea of guards."

"As long as we don't provoke a shootout we should be OK. Who is going to do it? TR and Ernie?"

"I thought I would ride with them."

"Three cowboys for a dozen cows might be thought of as too many."

"It's not like cowboys are watching."

"Good point. Have you given any thought as to who might have removed the women?"

"As far as Larcena and Lupe are concerned, how much do we want to know?"

"I'm not letting Lupe go to any foster care. And I think you feel that way about Larcena. Russell said he would help us both get them in the system. But he so much as said questions aren't welcome as to how he does it."

"I feel the same way you do. Carson Bell trusts Russell. We should do as well. Oh, Shit!"

"What?"

"TR and Ernie!" Havelee answered almost running out the door. Vargas quickly checked to ensure the girls were with their adopted Abuela Estella and ran after Harris. They both got to the corral in time to watch TR boost Ernie upon the horse he'd brought along. Ernie proceeded to do a header off the other side landing on the ground in an almost too neat tuck and roll. TR shook his head and rolled his eyes. Havelee ran up next him followed by Vargas.

"Ernie are you OK?" Vargas asked as she went to check on him.

"Si just no air. I knocked some if out when I fell off that beast."

Ivalou's mother instincts kicked in, and she helped the fallen agent, who looked genuinely distressed, sit up and breathe.

"I know he is an FBI agent he showed me his badge. He's got the right look, but a cowboy he ain't. He could barely figure out how to open the trailer door. And unloading that horse was almost a disaster. I think he needs to drive an ATV not ride. He didn't have a clue about how to put on a saddle. I thought anybody who ever watched TV knew the saddle horn faces the front," TR said

Havelee watched Ernie stumbling and leaning first on Vargas and then on the horse. He practically wrapped himself around the horses' rump as he staggered back to try it again. The horse stood still as a statue during all this. Just like it knew what was happening and what part to play.

"He even got his chaps on backward this guy hasn't got a clue." TR lamented.

Ernie tried to mount up again. He wound up falling and sliding underneath the horse as he caught his arm in the stirrup. Ivalou went to help out and only managed to give him an impressive massage with her breasts as he accidently turned at the wrong time. The usually smiling young Latino now displayed a clueless pained countenance as Vargas helped him to his feet.

TR went over and managed to hoist Ernie into the saddle, without him falling off the opposite side. With a big smile, Ernie held the reins. The smile lasted until the horse bolted forward into a trot almost unseating the cowboy. Ernie twisted rocked turned squealed and managed to avoid falling off by narrow margins, not once but several times as the horse trotted around the barn and corral area. He was screaming 'whoa' an 'alto' all the time. Finally, the horse stopped, and he realized he didn't have his gun.

"Where is my Glock pistol?" He shouted, hamming up a Mexican accent. "It's fallen from my holster! It's fallen in horse shit!"

"He didn't have the damn thing to start with," TR said disgustedly.

"I'll look in his truck," Vargas said sorry for the young agent and wondered if Havelee lost her mind when she asked for him. If he knew so damn much about this valley; why couldn't he ride a horse?

Ivalou found the gun, and Ernie sat proudly on his steed. His grin was so infectious that the women could not stay angry at him. TR was not as enchanted.

"Ivalou why don't you follow along in the ATV. In case El Agentio falls off his horse and has to be driven home." TR said.

Havelee saddled the gelding of her choice and smiled to herself. She rode beside TR and Ernie followed barely able to guide the horse and coming close to falling off a couple of times. The horse took it all in stride. Ivalou followed hoping the young agent would not get hurt badly.

"Hav, forgive me for saying this, but that guy is a horse wreck waiting to happen. His seat in that saddle looks like a monkey fucking a football. Pardon my language but FBI Special Agent or not he is going to get hurt. Ask him to stay away from the cattle with that horse. If he can do it," TR said.

Havelee assisted TR as he cut out a dozen head of cattle. Ernie sat proudly on his horse smiling. Ivalou watched from the ATV. Once TR and Havelee started the herd moving Ernie and Ivalou fell in behind them. It took close to forty-five minutes before TR opened a gate from horseback and Havelee urged the cattle onto the Rocking H Bar. The others followed through, and TR closed the gate. He was far enough behind and unable to respond when a steer bolted from the small herd and ran west. Ernie still smiling touched spurs to his horses' flanks and the animal burst forward at full gallop in pursuit of the errant steer. Ernie leaned forward in the saddle, undid the lariat tied to his saddle and shook out a loop. He was spinning it around his head when the horse closed in throwing range of the beast. Ernie threw his loop expertly, and it fell effortlessly over the bovine's head. The FBI vaquero sat back in his saddle and dallied the rope around his saddle horn as his horse lowered his haunches and slid to a stop. The 700-pound steer was jerked backward to the ground. It jumped up a few seconds later and followed a grinning Ernie and his horse back to the group.

Ernie smiled as he shook the lariat off the animal's neck and re-coiled it next to his saddle. He looked at the others. After securing his rope, he removed his hat with a flourish and bowed to the women grinning. Looking at TR he said,

"I learn fast no?"

"Damn jackass," TR muttered as he rode off after the herd.

Havelee smiled at Ernie and went after TR.

"You got us all Ernie. Where'd you learn to ride like that?" Vargas asked.

"I started riding so young that they laid me on the saddle seat to change my diaper."

"I believe that."

"I worked my way through college as a rodeo clown. I fought bulls and did a comedy routine with Amigo here."

Ernie turned the horse and cued it to bow at Ivalou. She laughed once again. He tipped his hat and cantered off to the west and rode along the raised hill ahead of the herd.

"Damn young pups, that goofball Ernesto had me believing he didn't know which end of a horse the shit comes from," TR said still grousing about being had.

"I would have liked to of seen the look on your face when he went after that steer. But I was too busy watching a real cowboy work. If I stay in the FBI, he will be in my squad."

"What do you mean if you stay in the FBI?"

"I am vested in the retirement program, and I'm at the top pay scale. I can leave and freeze my retirement until I reach my sixties. My next step is into management. And I don't know if I'm chicken shit enough to make that move. I could teach at Quantico, but that is in Virginia. The daughter I am going to adopt, and cowboy I love are here in Arizona. I have compromised the FBI by not pushing to learn what happen to those women. I've learned a lot about myself since seeing Larcena for the first time and meeting you."

TR reined in and turned his horse toward Havelee. "I think I am supposed to have a ring or something for this. But there's not a store close.' He removed his hat. 'Havelee Harris, will you marry me and let Larcena be our daughter?"

Havelee urged her horse close to his, she leaned over and lightly kissed his lips.

"Tobias Rutledge, when this investigation is over. I will marry you. And together we will adopt and raise Larcena."

Ivalou, who was following them and the cattle, while she watched for Ernie riding in the distance. Ivalou wondered about Kroll and what he was doing. She thought about how he would take to Lupe.

Vargas didn't know that Ernie, who just rode out of sight, was about to meet Ron Kroll for the second time this day.

Ernie pulled Amigo to a quick stop when Ron Kroll pulled the ATV across their path. An M16 rifle was in a rack on the machine's handlebars.

"Cowboy I told you this morning we don't need any help! If you went to work for Bell and are looking for our cattle, you will find them further east. You are off limits! Turn that nag eastbound now." Kroll said with menace. He noticed the smiling Latino cowboy wore a holstered Glock. And he just sat on his horse smiling at Kroll.

"I am very pleased to meet you Mr. Kroll; I am Ernie Smith."

"How the hell do you know my name? I didn't tell it to you this morning."

"I knew who you were this morning. If you permit me, I will identify myself correctly. I have to reach into my saddle bag for my folder. Please don't reach for that nasty looking assault rifle on your handlebars or for the Burns modified Sig you carry. My horse Amigo will rear and strike your head with his hooves. He is wearing steel shoes; they will hurt your head. And I do not wish to bust my ass when he does it."

Ernie produced his FBI cred pack and opened it for Kroll to see.

"If you please, Mr. Kroll, I am Special Agent Ernesto Roberto Xavier Collazo Smith. My father is a gringo like yourself. I have admired your career since we studied it at Quantico. I was disturbed to learn of your termination. Supervisory Agent Harris told me differently when she read me into her team yesterday."

"Where in hell are Harris and Vargas?"

"They are a quarter a mile behind me, maybe more if Agent Harris hasn't gotten kissy face with her boyfriend the wrangler they call TR. He doesn't like me very much."

"I wonder why.' Kroll said sarcastically. 'Vargas is not riding a horse is she?"

"No, she is enjoying the day in an ATV. She will not have any trouble following me. She appears quite taken with you and jealous of Havelee's love life with the cowboy. Oh, they both have semi-adopted children now. Two little girls who I understand were rescued recently in the middle of the night. I hear her machine now. I will proceed south to keep watch over you and her from your colleagues should there be any following. And Mr. Kroll you should remember to duck. Your eyes look very bad."

Ernie galloped off as Vargas was arriving. She stopped in front of Kroll's machine and was getting out of hers as he dismounted his. They embraced and kissed passionately. After a few minutes, they came up for air.

"What happened to your face? You look horrible!"

"I was knocked cold by an unknown person a few nights ago. I awoke damn near in the middle of an intermural firefight. I think the asshole that slugged me is the same one who put a two by four across the bunk house door after he threw a couple of pillow cases full of rattlesnakes inside."

"So those dark places on the ground are blood pools?"

"How do you know about the bloody ground."

"The young smiling Latino agent you had talked to before I got here had a camera on the dash of his truck this morning. When he asked you for a job."

"Damn, I didn't consider that. Whose idea was that?"

"Havelee's. We lost Desmond and M&M to the Tucson gang unit when several members of the five fifty-six gang and three nights ago there was a bombing. And everybody was pulled thinking it was a terror attack. Harris managed to talk to the Director, and he read in the Tucson ASAC, the Phoenix SAC, and ASAC. The Director told them about Bradford and our having a CI; your name is still a secret. Your last text said something about a balloon going down. Havelee quizzed a group of agents during a meeting yesterday if they knew what it meant. Ernie was the only one with the answer. When he told her his background, she called the Director and got him assigned to our team two weeks early."

"So I gathered. As young as Smith is, he must be a first office agent."

"He is assigned to the Phoenix Field Office. Sent to the terrorist task force after the bomb blew. He grew up on a ranch in Cochise County east of here. His family did business with Lyon Hamilton, and he met Hamilton the first time as a child. His family is in the horse business, and they used Hamilton's stud horse. The one Carson Bell says he has, and no one can get around. Ernie told me he worked his way through college as a rodeo clown, fighting bulls and doing comedy tricks with his horse. Poor TR believed the guy only looked like a cowboy. Ernie will be a really good agent one day. He has what it takes and one hell of a sense of humor."

"Where is Havelee now, screwing this TR guy in the pasture or something? Ernie said they were playing kissy face. And you were jealous."

"Damn, that guy doesn't miss a thing. And he was right too."

Vargas kissed Kroll again. After a few more minutes they came up for air.

"First off, only Bradford and his two thugs are at the ranch. One thug is injured. Nobody new is coming until the balloon goes down." Kroll turned and pointed toward the balloon floating high above the Huachuca Mountains. When that happens, Bradford collects everybody's phones. No communications. He wants me to lead a truck with some terrorists in it to Las Vegas. And he tells me not to make the call that arms the bomb until I get back to Nogales. He has offered five million cash and a new identity. El Jefe will fly the terrorists to the ranch, and others will bring the truck. I'm going to hide one of my phones so I can text you."

"Listen, Ron; we are subject to be pulled away for this trumped up terrorist investigation. They won't act on your word;

they want proof, not hearsay. They have us chasing our asses right now. If the Director hadn't reassigned Lane to a congresswoman in DC, we wouldn't even be here. Her ASAC, a guy, named Quarles accepted what the Director said and is supporting us. But if somebody sneezes we get called further away. You have to be careful. You are hurt, and we have no idea who removed the women. We have two children to show for it. No grownups. If somebody finds out anything, we will be pulled to find these women. What happened to the one who supposedly died? Do you know?"

"Yes, I found Porn Dude raping her. He had already choked her to death and was still pumping and moaning. When I first came upon them, I thought it was you. She looked just like you except for a tat on her left arm. I found a cattle prod in that shop and worked over Dumas' balls. I was losing control while I had him down and was getting ready to brain him when my lights went out. Whoever hit me, did a real number on him. I knew there were kids I didn't know what happened to them. I heard about the killings but not the bombs. The satellite TV system and computers are down. Bradford didn't pay the bill."

"Lupe's mother looks like me. No wonder she ran to me calling mother. After she had hugged me, she realized she was wrong. She looked at my left arm and then broke down in tears. Both girls are at the Double B. They act like Bell, and the Mexican couple that works for him are their grandparents. It is really sad."

"Ernie said you and Havelee had adopted them. When are you signing the papers?"

"That damn vaquero see's everything. Ernie just stands around and smiles."

"Ivalou, if I get out of this count on me help you raise Lupe."

"Kroll if you don't get out of this you won't be able to hide in hell. Because I'll lie my way out of purgatory to come whip your ass."

"I believe you will."

They heard the horses' hooves pounding the ground before they saw them. Havelee and Ernie galloped over a rise and up to where they stood.

"Kroll! Bradford and one of his thugs are looking around. They got into the SUV and started up the ranch road northwest of us. We need to leave now." Havelee said.

"Vargas you have what we need?"

"I do."

"OK turn that thing around and haul ass back to that gate. TR should be back there now with it open. Go!"

Vargas sped off, and Kroll started his machine.

"Get over the hill and empty the magazine in that rifle to the south. We will be running like hell north, Mr. Kroll." Ernie said with his perpetual smile. He spun Amigo and galloped after Havelee. They heard full auto fire a few minutes later.

The agents and TR made it back to the Double B Ranch without incident. Havelee dismounted and threw her horses lead rope to TR. She got into the ATV with Ivalou.

"Talk to me girl. What's happening?"

CHAPTER TWENTY FOUR

El Jefe was not satisfied with the results of the first bomb. The message sent to the five fifty-six upstarts was not complete. Their families needed to die. He sent for his Iranian bomb maker. El Jefe wanted a bigger bomb, like those he heard of in places like Bagdad and Beirut. After an hour long discussion with the Iraqi torturer interpreting, a plan was settled on. El Jefe's phone rang. It was Bradford calling.

"Senor Bradford, what have your bumbling idiots lost now?"

"Due to your impressive efforts, we have not been attacked again by this five fifty-six gang. My sources tell me there is no indication the women remain in southern Arizona. You may be interested to know that the FBI is not aware the women exist."

El Jefe quietly considered this. "Bradford, the last piece of equipment is in place for crossing when the balloon goes down. The men are in place as well. My accountants are double checking money as we speak."

El Jefe ended the call and walked into the large room next door. Fifty million dollars in US one hundred dollar bills neatly stacked on a large table. Half of this was El Jefe's fee for arranging the logistics involved in getting the device and the men to use it inside the US. The device was in the bed of a pickup truck and covered with a tarp. The men who came with it stunk and acted even stranger than his bomb maker. He watched as trusted men counted out twenty-five million and counted it the second time as they packed in large duffle bags for transport.

This cash was Bradford's fee for arranging the delivery of the device to the target city.

US news sources showed harried agents working the Tucson streets in search of the terrorists who set off the most recent bomb. And the gringos President ensured them their borders were safe. They were not safe from El Jefe and those like him. He grew up hating Americans and their wealth. He studied the history of his country and that of their northern neighbor the USA. What the terrorists planned for the device parked next to El Jefe's home did not bother him, unless it went off prematurely. The aftermath would certainly hurt his business for an unforeseen period. And eventually, the gringos would figure out who was behind it and who helped them. And they would come for them. If they still had the resolve.

Too many of younger generations lived on handouts from the US government. Large numbers of his countrymen went north to cash in. And the Americans paid and paid some more. Still, this bomb in his yard would hurt his bottom line for a time. He did not like Americans, but he loved their money and what it brought him. Bradford and his people would die. As would the terrorists who would arm and set off the device. El Jefe and along with his bodyguards and Iraqi torturer would load Bradford's twenty-five million back into the helicopter and fly south. Perhaps he would call the Americans and tell them where to find the mess.

Burns looked up from his computer as Jolene filled up their coffee cups. "My computer guru's facial recognition program identifies the newcomer as Ernesto Roberto Xavier Collazo Smith. Special Agent FBI. Number five in his academy class two years ago. The University of Arizona. Perfect shooting scores. Born and raised in Cochise County Arizona. Havelee managed to get a local boy on her squad."

"Is this the Collazo family you know?"

"Yes, they are all related. Ernesto is probably Manny's grandson. I'm surprised he wasn't on a rodeo scholarship somewhere."

"Real cowboys."

"As real as they get. I think Havelee's team went exploring yesterday. And Ernesto met Kroll. They hightailed back to this side of the fence when Bradford and his thug came looking. Kroll went back south and let go a magazine full auto for a distraction. The only thing I can't figure out is why aren't they putting all their resources on this? Sending in this new guy in his cowboy outfit is the first offensive move they've made."

"Maybe they have been waiting for a bigger fish, as in El Jefe, and they plan on trying for him and Bradford."

"That would make sense. Russell and Cruz have kept a tab on their sources that took the women. The women are no longer in this area. It is like it didn't happen. No one has looked so far. Harris and Vargas are keeping those little girls quiet."

"Maybe Havelee is not the team player she once was."

"Little girls can have a powerful effect on career women who don't have kids."

"Is that why you handed them off before I got to claim one?"

"That is not a fair question. You were the one hollering for me to find those kids. I did, and you didn't say anything about keeping one. And I sure as hell wasn't going to take that mountain lion kitten away from the cat brat. That would be a good way to wind up scalped."

"Don't worry. I wish the little one's mother hadn't died, but the Latina agent Vargas is planning on taking her home one day."

"Based on the DNA swapping, I watched her and Kroll doing she is planning on more than that."

"You don't miss much with that spotting scope."

Burns phone rang, and he saw it was Russell calling.

"What's up Half Breed?"

"New sheriff in town on the FBI gang. One of the Collazo boys, half-breed like me. You better keep that stud hid. I'm leaving Double B headquarters heading to Nogales. Ernie Smith is following me in a truck Cruz would like on his lot. I dropped some papers off for Carson Bell to give Harris and Vargas. Custody papers. I understand the FBI got a lead on the women's shelters. Thought you might want to know that. Carson thought he was going to have an extra hand for free courtesy of the FBI, while Butter Billy gets back on his feet. He got called back to Tucson while I was standing there. TR is glad to see him go. I think the kid out Cowboys him."

Burns laughed as he disconnected the call.

"What's that all about?"

"Spoke too soon about the shelters. FBI has a lead on them. I don't see any problems with it myself. But Havelee and company have moved out of the ranch again. And TR is jealous of the new cowboy. The kid is good I watched him take a steer down yesterday. He's riding a good horse too. I think I'm going to saddle up Don Cameron and take a look around. I want to talk to TR."

"Do you think TR is jealous of the young guy going for Havelee's affections?"

"No, he is jealous because he is a better cowboy. TR already has the girl. He just doesn't like to see a younger guy out do him on a horse."

"Why is he not jealous of you and Don Cameron?"

"He is but in that case I'm the old cowboy. I just need to keep that Collazo kid away from Don Cameron."

"Are you afraid of being outdone, old cowboy?"

"No, I don't want to see him get hurt."

Havelee assembled all of her team at the extended stay motel. The guys sat on the bed while Harris and Vargas occupied the chairs.

"Quick update guys, we've had some leads to work involving women's shelters. We received credible information that a large group of women destined for prostitution rings was intercepted and rescued by person's unknown. We want to know who those unknown persons are. We also want to make sure these women were not put back in the white slavery market by another gang. Des is there anything further on the six unidentified gunshot victims you learned about?"

"The medical examiner says they all suffered from one or more poisonous snake bites."

"That jives with something Kroll said. Lou, what were the details again?"

"Ron thinks whoever slugged him was the same person who put a couple of pillow cases full of rattlesnakes inside the bunkhouse and then barred the door on the outside."

Ernie giggled. "I bet that scared the shit out of them!"

"Ernie's radar detector video showed the bunkhouse. I remember seeing the door opened to the outside. It would have been easy to put a bar on it, while the guards were raping somebody. I hope Ron and his cattle prod ruined that scumbags sex life." Vargas said.

"Is it possible another agency has surveillance on that ranch that we don't know about?" M&M asked.

They all looked at each other considering the question.

"Expand on your reasoning for that question M&M," Havelee said.

"OK, somebody had to know the bunkhouse door opened out. Somebody knew where women were. The burning dope trucks came through that ranch. Were those trucks sabotaged before they left that ranch? According to forensics military-grade detonators with timers were used. Does a black ops team being involved sound farfetched?"

"What about these border watch groups, some of those guys are pretty radical. They are well armed and funded. They've been flying private drones on border ranches for years." Ernie said seriously without an accent.

"I knew Havelee had a good reason for poaching you." Desmond offered.

"There is something else we are missing?" Ivalou offered.

"What?"

"Remember the first time we visited Carson Bell. He told the story of the horse and dog that showed up. He said Miguel moved those animals to another part of his ranch. And he mentioned leasing part of the ranch with a small house on it. And when we were canvassing we stayed away from locked gates. Could it be possible a black ops team or some of these border watchers are staging out of that leased area?"

"That is the Double B Ranch northeastern casita. It was once only a line camp. Now it has a nice barn; the line shack made into a two-room cabin. Senor Bell leases it to people. Most are artists, or even some wanna-be cowboys and ranchers. He will lease it for as little as month or even a year. Whatever the client wants." Ernie said.

"Damn, it's good to have a homeboy on our team," M&M said giving the high five to Ernie.

"OK, maybe Quarles knows by now when that Aerostat balloon goes down. Let's work these shelter leads so we can get back to the San Rafael." Havelee said as she got up.

"Ivalou you work with Ernie. I've got to go to a supervisors meeting at the Field Office."

Later, dressed like FBI agents again and riding in Vargas Bucar, she queried Ernie some more.

"You said the casita has a barn. Would that be a good place to hide a horse like Hamilton had?"

"Si, someone would have to feed it. You are referring to Don Cameron of Lochiel. Only a top notch horseman can handle that animal. The dog, Jazz, is a champion herding dog, a border collie. He can move an entire herd of cattle by himself. Cam and Jazz are an inseparable team. Only Senor Lyon Hamilton could handle them together. An only Senor Lyon could ride Cam. I know the horse has thrown TR, and he has thrown three of my brothers."

"Has he thrown you?"

"Noooo, Ivalou he's not thrown me.' Ernie said grinning, very proud of himself, 'because I have more sense that to try and ride him."

"Ernesto you are too much."

"Si, I can be hard to take. But I'm worth it."

The last remark prompted Vargas to display her middle finger.

"Oh, you hurt a young vaquero such as myself."

"Ernie you're full of shit."

The elation of Havelee's team in finding a new investigative approach was short lived. El Jefe's Iranian bomb maker blew up an apartment building in Tucson, in a Hispanic populated neighborhood. Every available FBI unit went in that direction. Breaking national news was telling of the tragedy before Ivalou, Des, M&M and Ernie arrived on the scene. The White House resident assured the country with a classic statement, 'let me be clear, our borders are secure.'

Jolene and Andy watched the news on the motorhome satellite system. "Do you think El Jefe is behind this one?" She asked.

"I would bet on it. And I believe El Jefe has middle eastern contacts that built the bomb. If the locals can dig deep enough, they will likely find that apartment building housed gang members families. Mexican drug lords and terrorists like to remind those who are against them of their long reach."

"There had to be children in that building. Don't those people know that?"

"Yes, and it makes a bigger statement. It also provides an opportunity for the weak sisters to capitulate to the demands of the terrorist organization. Based on what we have seen coming into the Rocking H Bar and their prayer rugs, there is a bigger attack planned. The snakes in the bunk house and their AK47's have slowed that down some. And this last bomb is likely retaliation, but it could be a draw off, a maneuver to divert attention from the main event. The General send me a secure text saying the Aerostat balloon comes down for maintenance in forty-eight hours. I expect we will see an increased activity at the Lochiel border crossing and a low flying helicopter from the south.

"Then it will be time to stop this crap. The black team is awaiting the call. The General is not happy with the FBI Director. Next week the trips to his mistress and his relationship to a former Presidents shady dealings and subsequent cover-ups will be leaked."

"I would hate have the General mad at me."

"All he could do to you is have IRS audit your taxes every year and get an undercover game warden to follow your bass boat around."

"Such a dull life. And then I took up with you. Let me check this email message that just came up."

Burns watched Jolene as she read the message. "This is interesting. One of Lyon Hamilton's credit cards has just be used to pay the past due satellite TV and internet bill at the Rocking H Bar."

"Sounds like Bradford's thugs are getting bored."

"Well, there is one of them I don't think watches cartoons."

"Have you noticed him outside since we got the women out?"

"No, only Bradford, Kroll and the palooka looking dude, alias Numb Nuts, wonder how he got that handle. I haven't seen any Mexicans or jihadist either. I think they buried all of them."

"I expect Pauli Dumas is still on injured status. Kroll was working over his package with a cattle prod with I got to them. And I hit Dumas a hell of a lot harder than I hit Kroll."

"Lyle Thigman would appreciate your prowess using his blackjack."

"I wish there had been time to make a eunuch out that pervert."

"What are your plans when the balloon goes down?"

"I have an observation point on the Rocking H Bar, due north of the headquarters. I've used it a few times. I will move in there and watch. I will move Reid's team into the positions they used before. The biggest thing is catching El Jefe on the ground. He won't fax us his itinerary. I will lay there and wait for him to show up."

"I know Burrito and Buddy are busy for the next couple of days. I'm going with you. Get used to that idea."

"The only shade will be a camo net over us. And we will be laying on a tarp. Down on the ground with the snakes and the critters. You will need extra computer batteries and a black cloth to cover any light reflecting off that screen. Your personal hydration device with two extra bladders of water. Bring plenty of energy bars and beef jerky. If you don't want to squat on the ground, go to the store and buy some Depends. You will need your Glock and plan to carry one of the AR's with extra ammo. And it's all got to be in one small pack."

"I expected a plaid picnic blanket and a basket."

"Plan on being out there two days. Before we leave, this rig has got to be unhooked and ready to move the minute we get back. I will take care of that. We'll park the ATV's in the barn. I will let Miguel know he needs to feed Don Cameron and Jazz. I will tell Carson Bell we are going to take RV on a trip. And extend our lease the Casita."

"I gather once we do whatever we do over there, we leave ASAP. Are we coming back?"

"Yes. When I don't know."

"What about the Citation?"

"It will be ready when we get to the airport. I plan on taking this rig over to Bisbee for an overnight, then up to I-10 and loop back to Nogales. I will continue to rent the hanger and store this thing in it until we can come back for it."

"It sounds like a plan, except for the Depends part."

"I'm going to take Don Cameron out for a ride."

"Now that the feds have left I'm going to drive ATV over and visit with Estella. Are you planning on taking Don Cameron and Jazz when we go on our deployment?"

"I'm considering it. There is a copse of cottonwoods around the position. I doubt El Jefe's pilot would notice a horse on a high line in there. That is where we are going to hide the ATV."

"Sounds good, it looks like Kroll is going out patrolling on the ATV," Jolene said as she checked the camera feeds. "And Carson Bell is enjoying the company of his adopted granddaughters."

CHAPTER TWENTY-FIVE

With some sensitivity returning to his testicles, Porn Dude was in need of a sex fix. The internet like the satellite TV was off due to nonpayment. Dumas begged his boss to have it turned back on, and Bradford was having none of it. Porn Dude found Lyon Hamilton's credit card numbers on some old statements. It wasn't the bosses or Pauli's money, so what the hell. Dumas paid the bill with one of Hamilton's card numbers and ordered up a few porn flicks.

The next morning Pauli Dumas was surfing the net for anything sexual in nature. He heard Kroll leave on the ATV. It was an excellent opportunity to get even for the damage to his still back and blue balls. Porn Dude went to Kroll's room and began to search it methodically. It didn't take long to find the hidden cell phone. Pauli quickly realized from the stored messages this was the one Kroll used to call his whore. Dumas pocketed the phone and searched some more. He hit pay dirt when he found the undercover camera. Porn Dude took it straight to W. Ashton Bradford.

Ass Bradford recognized the camera as a model used by the FBI. Kroll was still on the payroll. Bradford considered his options. The ability of either of his henchmen to incapacitate Kroll without shooting him from ambush was doubtful. El Jefe was unhappy with what he viewed as Bradford's failures. The dope trucks catching fire and women being kidnapped right out of his barn. Even with the blame laid squarely on his Tucson competition. El Jefe told Bradford he had a spy on the inside of his operation.

And the Middle Eastern customers were due in the following morning with a significant payday for Bradford. The drug lord was flying in with the money and the jihadists. The bomb waited in a truck a couple of kilometers from Lochiel on the Mexican side of the border. The terrorists El Jefe was helicoptering in from his base. Included the bomb technician to arm the device and encode the cellular phones. Two suicide bombers to drive the truck and active the device on the Los Vegas strip at eight PM.

El Jefe was the key to getting Bradford getting safely out of the country. Kroll, up until this latest discovery, was the trusted lieutenant to see that plot was carried out. True to his first name, Welch. Bradford had planned on leaving Kroll holding the bag without his expected five-million-dollar payment. So why not cement his loyalty to El Jefe and the Middle Easterners by offering up Kroll as a traitor. Numb Nuts and Porn Dude could escort the bombers. They were expendable.

Ron Kroll riding one of the ATV's left at dawn to patrol the ranch perimeter. For the past two days, he'd been looking for the new FBI agent Ernie masquerading as Double B cowboy. Kroll wasn't aware of the latest bombing. The horseshoe camera recorded his departure and his return.

Kroll's operational background was city streets. Dirt roads and ranch trails were alien places for him. Ron was not looking for somebody hiding and watching him. Not that he would have spotted Burns, astride Don Cameron standing in a clump of trees. Andy considered getting the FBI agent's attention. This thought quickly went away. So far the fabulous bunch of intrepid crime fighters had not figured out his and Hadfield's involvement. Burns elected to keep it that way for the time being.

Andy got off Don Cameron at the motorhome and loosened the saddle cinch. He'd dropped the reins ground tying the horse.

"Nothing of interest so this morning. I guess you saw Kroll out for a ride." She said, "The head man is out on the porch having breakfast and coffee. It looks like he brought a pistol to the table with him. That is unusual."

Bradford stood up from his seat and removed something from the table top. He walked off the porch and watched Kroll approach.

"Somethings up," Burns said watching the screen. "That guy never gets up and walks out to greet Kroll."

Ron Kroll thought it was unusual too. He braked the ATV and coasted to stop by Bradford. He didn't have time to take the machine out of gear and shut it off. Ass Bradford pulled a Taser from behind his leg and fired the barbs into Kroll's chest.

"HE TASED HIM!" Burns and Hadfield yelled simultaneously.

Kroll fell off the ATV and spasmodically jerked as Bradford kept the current applied. The driverless ATV careened toward the porch and ran into Porn Dude and Numb Nuts running to help their boss. Unfortunately for Ron Kroll, it only slowed them down.

Limping over to where Ron jerked on ground, Porn Dude launched a weak kick into his balls. The Taser current probably kept Kroll from feeling the effects of the kick. Numb Nuts felt those effects when he grabbed Ron's arm. Bradford released the trigger so his goon could let go. Hadfield and Burns could only watch the screen.

Bradford let off the trigger, and the two thugs launched their attacks again. Kroll suffered another more effective kick in the nuts. Numb Nuts kicked him in the stomach. Bradford ordered the two men to secure Kroll. His hands were forced behind his back and secured with two large plastic ties. Two more plastic ties secured his ankles together.

The three men left Kroll laying in the dirt. Bradford was able to shut off the ATV before it did any more damage to the porch. Numb Nuts kicked Ron a few more times for catch up. Dumas ran to the shop and came back with the cattle prod. He repeatedly jabbed Kroll with it. After realizing it didn't work, he used it to beat Ron. Porn Dude kept this up until Bradford ordered him to quit.

"We're leaving early. The ATV is ready to go, fill the hydration devices and follow on the ATV, you have the GPS track. I'll be in position. Look directly south of the cottonwoods and move slowly in on my right side. Understand?" Burns said.

"Got it,' Hadfield answered as they watched the three hoods walked back in the house. Kroll was left laying on his side in the Arizona sun.

"When you cross the fence line drive slow, so you don't stir up a dust cloud. Unless I'm calling for help."

Jolene stood up and hugged Burns. He kissed her and then left. She watched from the door as he tightened the saddle cinch. When he mounted Don Cameron, she turned back to getting her gear together.

Burns watched through his rifle scope as the three hoods left the house. The freakish looking one with oversized penis urinated on Kroll. The other thug kicked him in the head and body while the boss watched. The three went to the SUV. Ashton Bradford gave instructions to his men and returned to the house. He paused and said something to Kroll, then went inside. Andy watched the SUV leave and turned his scope back to the undercover agent. With the scope dialed up to the highest power, Burns could see Kroll was breathing. For how long was another question. He relaxed got off the rifle and methodically rechecked the weapon.

Tethered between the trees behind him Don Cameron snorted. Jazz laying nearby growled. Unlike Burns the animals were in the shade of the stand of cottonwoods. Andy's only protection from the sun was the camo concealment netting laying over him. He heard the sound of the ATV. With deliberate moves, he turned to see Hadfield carefully and slowly approaching. She used the right amount of speed not to leave a dust cloud. Not that it made any difference. Burns' hide was seven hundred yards away from the ranch headquarters, making it unlikely that Bradford and company would ever know they were there.

Jolene settled in next to Burns and focused a high power spotting scope on Kroll. At sixty times magnification, she studied him.

"I can't tell how bad he's hurt. But those plastic ties have got to be cutting off circulation. His breathing appears shallow. I think he is trying to conserve what energy he has left. What are you planning to do?"

"The two underlings left in the SUV. The boss gave them instructions along with a lot of pointing and gesturing. He then went in the house. The thugs roughed Kroll up some more before they left. I expect they will eventually execute him. I'm not going to let that happen. Something is going down, and I believe we will soon learn. Right now we watch and wait."

"Kroll is suffering, and he may be in danger of dying. We can't wait forever."

"Check the porch now."

They both watched Bradford leave the house and approach Kroll. He a small device and glass. Bradford pulled Kroll upright and allowed him to drink out of the glass. Then he showed him the device and shoved him back to the ground.

"I wonder what that was about?" Jolene said.

"It appears the boss is making an effort to keep him alive. My guess is he showed Kroll something they found that tipped them off. Bradford is probably planning on handing him over to El Jefe and blaming him for all their troubles."

Another two hours passed when Burns and Hadfield watched a different truck turn into the ranch. Followed by the Suburban.

"I've got it,' Jolene said examining the truck with the spotting scope. 'There's a tarp covering something in the bed. It is overloaded, sitting low on the back end. Numb Nuts is driving it. The porn freak is following in the ranch truck. They must have picked up the loaded pickup when they crossed the border."

"I think whatever is expected just arrived. I believe as soon as the Aerostat goes down for maintenance, El Jefe will fly across the border and land on the ranch. I can take out any threat to Kroll and get El Jefe and Bradford in the process. Reid and his crew can get what's left."

Burns put his rifle scope on the two trucks arriving ranch. Bradford came out and greeted his men. Numb Nuts parked the truck beside the house. It's tailgate toward Andy's observation point. Ashton Bradford unhooked the tarp and examined the cargo. Burns commandeered the spotting scope from Jolene and zoomed in on the contents.

"Damn," Burns hissed. "It has Cyrillic markings and appears to be an explosive device. I hope the hell it is not what I think it is." He handed the scope back to Jolene.

"What is that?" Jolene asked.

"There has never been any proof those things exist except in the minds of spy novelists." Burns was back on his rifle watching Bradford raise the tailgate and replace the tarp.

"What the hell is it, Burns!"

"It appears to be a tactical nuclear device or what some call a suitcase nuke."

"You can't be serious. No not an A-bomb. They can't be that crazy. If they are, it's time to kill those bastards; cut Kroll loose and get the hell out of here."

"It could be a chemical device. But it is a weapon of mass destruction."

"If they set it off here Burns we're dead. I think it's time to stop asking questions and start shooting."

"Whatever it is. The terrorists are not going to set it off in this valley. There are not enough people to kill. We are dealing with terrorists they are going for a big hit. Not a few ranchers and cowboys. My guess is LA maybe Los Vegas. Phoenix is possible. They will want at least a couple million population to use it. This valley is just the point of entry. And those idiots aren't smart enough to set it off. We'll wait. There will be somebody else along shortly. Hopefully, it will be El Jefe. Then we do something."

"Burns that asshole with the donkey dick just peed on Kroll!! Damnit shoot that thing off!"

Porn Dude was jumping up and down shaking his member and laughing. Pointing at Kroll and making obscene gestures. Burns held him in the crosshairs briefly considering Jolene's request.

"No, I think Kroll should have that privilege."

Jolene talked and worried into the night. Finally, to Burns relief, she dozed off and slept soundly. Soon the sky began to lighten. Just before sunrise over the Huachuca Mountains, Burns looked and realized the balloon was not there. It was lowered twenty-four hours early!

Havelee wanted to look at the text that just arrived on her phone. She wouldn't because Quarles severely chastised another supervisor for checking their phone. The ASAC was being to feel the stress of the bombings. There had already been two police shootings since the bomb went off. It would be a while before she could locate her team. One thing for certain was they were nowhere near the San Rafael. Havelee casually wondered where the Tucson Field Office and FBI would be on the Chinese Fire Drill rating scale. And she wanted to pull out the phone and look at a cute picture of Larcena and her cat.

Vargas found time to call Estella and spend a few minutes talking to Lupe. That was when her Penelope phone started buzzing. To took a few minutes to get the child off the phone. The bonding process between Ivalou and Lupe was going well.

Pauli Dumas gleefully slapped Numb Nuts on the shoulder.

"I'm gonna fuck Kroll's Mexican ho! I cracked his phone I've already sent her a text!" He slapped Numb Nuts again.

"Stop it or I'll knock the shit outta you! Boss ain't gonna let you go to Nogales to see no whore!"

"I ain't going to Nogales asshole. The whore is coming to me! I sent her a text offering big bucks for an outcall to the ranch. Hell, that horny bastard Kroll even tells her how to dress! But he sure as hell ain't thinking about pussy now! Hell, I might drag him back to watch."

"You mean she is gonna come to us!"

"Not us dumb ass, me. I gotta call Willie and make sure he takes care of her pimps."

"You better check with Boss first."

"Screw him. He owes me big time for finding out Kroll."

"Yeah, that was good Pauli."

Ivalou Vargas was following orders. She drove flat out toward Nogales from Marana Arizona. The Penelope text she received was the undercover extraction code. They needed to get Kroll out ASAP. Ivalou sent a priority text to Havelee and Desmond Taylor and M&M. She didn't have Ernie Smith's number on the group dial. When she reached him, she learned he was in Florence AZ. He told her would get there as quickly as possible. Vargas along with Des and M&M were Kroll's only back up. And they all had to stop and change clothes. Des and M&M would have to transfer their gear to the Escalade. Vargas arrived at the motel in Nogales ahead of the guys.

Pauli Dumas was on the phone. He waited until Deputy Willie Hillman answered. Having been bought and paid for by Bradford and Pauli's promise of introductions to pornography makers Willie answered promptly.

"This is Hillman what ya want PD?"

"Willie I got a whore making an outcall to the ranch this afternoon. She should be here in the next hour or so. I've seen this bitch in Nogales and always wanted some of it. She was Kroll's ho, so I stayed back. She always has a couple of nigger pimps following her. They drive a black Escalade. How about running their black asses out of your county for me."

"Man, I'll do that! No problem. Think you could save a little of it for me? That is if you don't stretch her out too much!"

Porn Dude let out a high pitched giggle. "Yeah, Dude I'll film you fucking her and send to my buddy in LA. That will get you the start you need in the business."

"Great man! Do you know if those coons are coming over from Patagonia?"

"Yes, she works out of Nogales."

"I'll handle it PD! See you later!"

Dumas disconnected and played with himself in anticipation.

Ivalou Vargas was standing in the motel room wearing only a sexy lace bra and panties if you called the pink satin thong panties. Not her normal type, but if giving someone a peep show got Kroll out, it was bare butt time. Ivalou snapped the horizontal holster to her bra between the cups. It held the compact .380 pistol right under her breasts and above her abdomen. She wished she had a mini skirt and blouse with her. The blouse would make accessing the pistol easier. The mini dress was all she had time to grab. Ivalou picked up the next item she would carry.

It was a Benchmade assisted-opening folding knife with a pocket clip. Assisted-opening was a kinder and gentler term than switch blade. Ivalou stood sideways to the mirror and slipped the knife between her buttocks clipping it to the thong. Satisfied it would carry there. She pulled the tight dress over her head and wiggled it down on her body. Once in place, she realized the knife would stay concealed if she used perfect posture and didn't bend over. The curvature of her butt helped conceal the last ditch weapon. Ivalou would have to have a wardrobe malfunction to draw the pistol. You can't have everything working undercover.

She saw Desmond and M&M entering their room when she was getting into her car. Ivalou tossed a suitcase with street clothes and a decent pair of underwear in the back seat. When she got behind the wheel, she had to wiggle in the seat to get comfortable because of the knife. She thought about the time difference waiting on the guys and considered the consequences. They were behind already. She started the car and sped off toward the highway to Patagonia and the Rocking H Bar.

Desmond looked over at M&M. "Put the gas to this beast. Lou gonna be down there by herself, and we stuck in traffic."

M&M was a graduate of pursuit driving school and Bondurant's road racing school near Phoenix. He got all he could out of the Caddy SUV, making up time on the four-lane connector road to Highway 82 in Nogales. Both agents hoped the local police were on coffee break. Once on the narrow scenic highway. M&M adroitly steered the Escalade around the curves. Approaching Patagonia Desmond found his voice again.

"Slow down! This town got cops they call marshals. They ain't gonna look kindly on a couple of African American pimps masquerading as FBI agents."

Braking for a school zone, M&M grinned, "What is we first, pimps or FBI agents?"

"Depends on how she's dressed," Desmond said giving the high five to his partner.

They got through Patagonia without meeting a marshal. The road south was even narrower. Still, M&M drove as fast as he could. "Them marshal dudes they got cowboy hats and all that shit?" He asked.

"Don't know. I just saw the office and a car parked in front of it."

Soon the pavement played out, and the road turned to dirt. The dirt track was a little wider, so M&M gassed it and the SUV fishtailed. "Yahoo! Ride 'em cowboy!" He exclaimed.

"You gonna think cowboy if you wreck this thing. I'd hate to say who'd be worse to deal with Ivalou or Havelee."

Neither agent noticed the sheriff's SUV pull out behind them.

Willie Hillman felt the tightness in his pants. He didn't know if it were from anticipating the forthcoming encounter with Latina whore he'd spotted a few minutes earlier. Or roughing up a couple of smartass pimps. He closed on the Escalade and moved into the dust cloud it kicked up. Hillman turned on his lights and siren.

"Shit, one of the marshals you been talking about!" M&M said looking in the review mirror. He slowed the Caddy and turned on the emergency flashers. "This thing ain't got any cop lights to turn on."

"Just play it cool and let him rant. If he writes a ticket, accept it. We can't blow the cover. Kroll said they got a sheriff's deputy working for them. Be cool man it's a deputy."

Desmond watched Willie Hillman slowly exit his vehicle. Parked in the classic vehicle stop position Hillman used his PA system.

"YOU BOY DRIVING! GET YOUR BLACK ASS OUTTA THAT VEHICLE AND KEEP YOUR HANDS WHERE I CAN SEE THEM!"

"Oh shit, Ivalou gonna whip both our butts now," M&M said as he carefully opened the door and stepped out.

"ALL RIGHT BOY MOVE YOUR ASS AWAY FROM THAT DOOR AND KEEP YOUR HANDS UP WHERE I CAN SEE THEM! FUCK UP AND I'LL BLOW YOUR BACK ASS TO HELL!"

Desmond Taylor saw the shotgun Hillman pointed at M&M. The deputy racked a shell into the chamber for emphasis. Protocol be damned Des thought as he got out his creds and opened them. He held them extended in his left hand toward the open driver's door. Taylor would never be able to explain why he drew his Glock.

Hillman advanced toward M&M with the shotgun shouldered and ready to fire. The deputy yelled his next command.

"KEEP YOUR HANDS UP AND GET ON YOUR KNEES NIGGER! DO IT NOW!"

M&M complied, never taking his eyes off Willie Hillman. M&M left his open credentials pack on the driver's seat. He was very aware of the holstered Glock pistol under his shirt on the right side. An M4 carbine and a 12 gauge Remington 870 were in the rear seat floor board. There was no telling what would happen if this redneck deputy managed to spot those weapons through the tinted rear windows. Or what would happen if he spotted M&M's gun before seeing the creds?

Hillman advanced slowly, his finger on the shotgun's trigger. Desmond watched the man move out toward the center of the forest service road and away from the side of the SUV. He was getting into a position where he could peek into the front seat and keep M&M covered. Wounds from the shotgun would not be survivable at these distances. Desmond took a deep breath.

Willie Hillman stopped at the point where M&M was between him and the open door. Willie swung the shotgun toward the opening. Desmond yelled.

"FBI DEPUTY LOWER THAT SHOTGUN!"

"AIN'T NO FUCKING NIGGER WITH A BADGE TALKING TO ME LIKE THAT!"

Hillman aimed the shotgun into the truck. Desmond shot him twice. The first bullet struck him in the left eye. The second below his nose above his lip. Desmond puked.

M&M said, "shit shit shit."

M&M recovered first. He tried the radio in the car. It wasn't working. He pulled his cell phone out and dialed the Tucson Field Office. "You all right man?" He asked.

Desmond shook his head and puked some more. He laid his pistol on the driver's seat next to his credentials folder. Des leaned over to the dash and prayed as he cried.

The Tucson Field Office operator answered the phone. "FBI Tucson how may I direct your call?"

"This is Special Agent Mickey Morris connect me to the duty agent."

"Duty Desk, Special Agent McGowen speaking."

"This is Special Agent Mickey Morris, Bad Apple's team. We have an Agent involved shooting. A sheriff's deputy is down and based on wounds apparently deceased. We are south of Patagonia Arizona on an unnamed forest service road. We are in an undercover vehicle, and we are dressed for undercover. A sheriff's vehicle is behind us with emergency lights activated. You can get GPS coordinates from my phone."

Tucson ASAC Quarles bad day just got worse. And it wasn't intermission time yet.

Ivalou was focused on the ranch road when her Penelope phone beeped a text. She slowed and read it.

Turn right by the house. Go past the truck and SUV park between the shop and in front of the bunk house on your right

She responded with, 'k.'

She thought she heard a helicopter but wasn't sure. Vargas could not see the area where Kroll lay nor the front porch. She drove up to the shop and stopped. A shadow crossed over her car. Startled, Ivalou looked in the rear view mirrors and watched a helicopter land behind her. The aircraft was on the ground blocking her view of the ranch road. Four men got out of the helicopter. The pilot remained at the controls, with the rotors idling. The men walked toward the house.

Burns watched the chopper land and the men get out. A moment later two thugs exited the house. They all stopped where Kroll lay. There were some gesturing and two men returned to the helicopter and unloaded four large duffle bags. They carried them half the distance to the group of men and sat them down. They unzipped the bags. Bradford went over and inspected the contents. Burns increased his scope power and saw that each bag held stacks of bills. Hadfield yawned as she woke up.

Ivalou, watched the landing and the men get out of the helicopter. She was focused on the rear view mirror and did not see Porn Dude walking softly toward her car. The open driver's window worked well for his plan. Pauli struck her on the side of her head. He dragged the stunned agent out of the car by her hair and struck her in the head a couple of more times.

Ivalou was barely regaining her senses when she felt her dress being yanked down below her boobs. Her arms were pinned by the straps now at her elbows. Her hands felt a hard, rough surface. Dumas had lifted her onto the work bench. She felt this on her bare butt cheeks as the hem of her dress was yanked upward.

Pauli backhanded her and ripped her bra down. Effectively covering the pistol, he hadn't seen. The move allowed her to free her arms. Ivalou's breasts provided the distraction she needed.

She leaned back her right hand on the bench trying to push him off with her left. Ivalou's brassiere and dress were too bunched up for her to reach the pistol. Porn Dude got a look at the satin thong. It was too much for the mutant pervert. He grabbed at it with his left hand while he shoved down his sweat pants with his right.

Ivalou saw his massive appendage and grabbed it as Porn Dude began ripping off her thong. The pink fabric gave way the same moment her right hand found the assisted-opening knife.

Unaware of the drama involving Porn Dude, Ashton Bradford spoke earnestly to El Jefe. Numb Nuts stood nearby. El Jefe's bodyguard exited the chopper after the money was removed and stood nearby. Three other men, all Middle Eastern were between the money and Bradford. One of them held a briefcase that according to El Jefe contained the phones that would arm and set off the device. The Iraqi torturer stayed in the helicopter, aiming an M249 machine gun at the Americans. His Diehard battery and jumper cables were under a nearby seat. El Jefe promised he might get to use them.

"El Jefe, you correctly guessed I had a traitor on my team. Today I present him to you along with the evidence." Bradford showed El Jefe the undercover camera and told him Kroll was an undercover FBI agent.

"Because of your continued trust in me. I give you Ron Kroll to do with as you wish. I would like to strap him to that device and let him enjoy one last ride. However, it would not serve the purpose of warning his employers."

"Gracious Senor Bradford, you speak such fine bull shit. But I am pleased you found the traitor. Let me borrow the knife of one our Middle Eastern Brothers."

With that, El Jefe went over to one of the jihadists and asked for his knife. The man produced what looked like a small machete from under his loose hanging shirt. El Jefe smiled at the man, and he gestured like he wanted to behead Kroll.

El Jefe gestured for the man to come with him. He told Numb Nuts to lift Kroll up to his knees. The jihadist gleefully took his place behind Kroll. He held his hand out for the knife. El Jefe spoke.

"Senor Bradford, I wish you to do the honor of cutting the traitors throat first. Then our Middle Eastern friend will finish removing his head. In my country, we find that doing this slow makes the traitorous ones more aware of their foul deeds."

El Jefe handed Bradford the knife.

W. Ashton Bradford grasped the knife in his right hand. He stepped behind Ron Kroll and grabbed him by his hair. Bradford brought the knife under Kroll's chin to the left side.

Banshees from hell could not have emitted a more petrifying sound than the horrendous scream that resounded across the prairie.

Ivalou Vargas cut off Pauli Dumas's dick. She slashed downward. The blade cut the pulsing muscle the full length of its edge. The drop point ripped open Dumas's thigh and his femoral artery.

Andrew Burns placed his crosshairs on the bridge of Ashton Bradford nose and squeezed the trigger. A thirty caliber hollow point boat tail bullet streaked through the desert air. Bradford jerked his head left the instant Burns fired. The 300-grain bullet stuck Ass Bradford forward of his right temple shattering his skull. And turning the front portion of his brain into a mass of tissue and bone spewing from the large cavity on the left side of his head.

Burns shifted his aim as the rifle recoiled and settled the crosshairs on the jihadist. He died in a similar fashion when the next bullet entered his right eye. Numb Nuts brain hadn't finished registering the scream when the next round struck the center of his forehead.

Swinging the rifle onto El Jefe, Andy rushed the next shot. The drug lord was hit squarely in his neck a fraction of an inch below his head. The effect was the same as well carried out hanging, only messier.

The WMD Tech support jihadi died still holding his briefcase when the next shot struck him in his chest blowing apart his aorta. The remaining suicide bomber was struck under his left arm as he turned to run. Both men found out the 72 virgin business was BS at the same time.

El Jefe's bodyguard made a running dive into the rear door of the helicopter. The pilot was spinning up the rotors. The rifle, a modified AR10 of Burns creation' was capable of firing three shot burst via a selector switch. Burns thumbed the switch, placed the crosshairs on the pilot's head a mil-dot high, and squeezed the trigger.

The pilot managed to get the machine a few feet off the ground. The three round burst of bullets smashed the canopy and into his chest. He died with the throttle at max power. The helicopter spun around slinging the torturer machine gun and all out the door. The aircraft stalled flipping on its side smashing into the ground. The Diehard truck battery careened out and landed on the Iraqi's head. The bodyguard died instantly from a broken neck. Remarkably the machine did not catch fire.

Burns changing rifle magazines. The finely tuned weapon deposited the spent cartridge cases next to him. Casually, he picked up the brass cases and put them a pouch. Andy rose to his knees and picked up the rifle folding the bipod rest under the barrel. Hadfield didn't have time to use the spotting scope before Burns started shooting.

"Get the scope and the gear. Roll up the net. Now. We have to move. Clear the place like your cleaning up a crime scene."

"Who did you shoot Burns? Is Kroll OK?"

"The problems at the Rocking H Bar are over. Get all the gear packed now. I'll drive the ATV over to check on Kroll. Be ready when I get back. He reached for his encrypted laptop and entered several commands, shutting down all the cameras."

Ivalou Vargas ran bare ass from the shop to her vehicle. Her concussed brain could not think clearly. She could only focus on getting dressed. She watched the helicopter crash without comprehending what she saw. Ivalou stripped naked and methodically begin changing clothes. She breathed easier when clad in modest undies and bra. Slacks and blouse followed. Vargas holstered her Glock and put the 380 still holstered and attached to the torn bra into her bag. She put on a pair of walking shoes. Her heart rate was still extremely high. An ATV motor raced nearby. Ivalou just stared at the open shop. Porn Dude still bellowed as he tried to duct tape his dick back together without concern for the blood pumping from his femoral artery. Vargas lost consciousness and fell to the ground.

Ron Kroll dehydrated to confusion, was sure of one thing. He was alive. Ron was not sure what he saw when the ATV roared into view. A cowboy was driving it. Kroll thought the westerner was taking pictures. He walked back to the ATV and removed a water bottle. He came over to Kroll and pulled a knife from his belt to slice the plastic bonds. Ron greedily drank from the proffered water bottle. Before he could swallow too much water too soon, the cowboy took the bottle away from him. He walked over to where El Jefe lay and removed an ornate pistol from his body along with several magazines.

All Kroll would remember was the man worn leather chaps, boots with spurs, a tan shirt, a bandana and a cowboy hat. And he drove an ATV.

Burns carefully walked around the ranch house, weapon deployed. He saw Ivalou Vargas lying unconscious next to her car. He removed a glove and checked her carotid pulse. It was strong. Replacing his glove, he stepping into to the garage and watched Porn Dude bleed out. Burns smiled.

Jolene had the equipment ready Burns drove up in the ATV. Satisfied the area was swept clean of evidence Burns said.

"Jo, drive back to the RV. Load up this gear and get ready to leave. But it is important the RV is ready to leave."

"Andy, tell me that bomb is not going to explode."

"Sweetheart, everything is OK. The bomb will not blow up." He kissed her on the cheek.

Jolene hugged him tightly and would not let go for several seconds. Finally, she spoke.

"Burns. I'll see you at back at the RV."

"Watch for me at the barn. I've got to put up Don Cameron and Jazz. Then call Carson Bell and let him know we are leaving."

"I can call Carson. We are coming back, aren't we? This thing is still not solved."

"We are, but somebody else is going to sort it out."

"Got it. Let me get moving."

Burns watched her leave and then he saddled up Don Cameron. He rode to higher ground where he could observe the Rocking H Bar headquarters with his rifle scope. Kroll was still down but breathing. So was the female agent. Burns pulled out the sat phone from his saddle bag. Reid answered on the first ring.

"This thing went down a day early. Head for the Rocking H Bar headquarters immediately. There is a WMD in the back of a Toyota truck. Secure it. There are two FBI agents there. Both are seriously injured and need a medevac. Keep the scene secure until the General gets back to you."

"Will do, we will be airborne when the gauges are green."

The phone went dead, and Burns dialed the General's number. He downloaded pictures of the device. Burns was well on his way to the casita's barn when a Blackhawk helicopter with no markings swooped over the Huachuca Mountains and descended toward the Rocking H Bar headquarters.

"So you two are getting out of my hair?" Carson Bell asked.

Burns finished grooming the stallion and then got the shoeing tools. He removed all four shoes and turned the horse out in the barn paddock.

"Yes, have Miguel take of Don Cameron and Jazz. I'll keep the lease on the Casita until this thing plays out. We will be back when the dust settles.

"Burns I don't want to know what you've been doing. But I expect it needed doing. TR came up on those two black FBI agents near our fence on the service road. He said it looked like Willie Hillman is dead, and one of the FBI guys is sick. TR is trying to get in touch with his girlfriend. I don't suppose we will ever know what that was all about."

"You probably won't. But like you said, it probably needed doing. Thanks for continuing to keep our activities to yourself."

"Be careful Burns."

"Adios amigo."

Burns walked back to the RV. He finished unloading the ATV's contents into one of the outside storage compartments. Andy put the horseshoes he removed from Don Cameron in with his gear. He walked around the coach making sure it was ready to roll. A few minutes later he locked the Casita road gate behind him. Jolene sat quietly watching the valley.

"Burns this place is beautiful. I'm glad you kept it from getting blown up. I'm sorry I slept through all the excitement. Do I need to know what happened?"

"No, but a lot of folks who have been hurting people won't be doing it anymore."

"Good and I still love you."

"I'm glad."

Chapter Twenty-Six

A SAC Quarles and his Phoenix counterpart were going over the preliminary bombing investigation reports when the duty agent reported the shooting involving undercover agents assigned to the Bad Apple's Investigation. Quarles summoned Harris.

Havelee was desperately trying to find her team after having gotten the message from Ivalou about the need to extract Kroll forthwith. The briefing she'd spent the morning sitting through kept her from reading the text when it was received. Ernie was the only one she managed to find, and he was held up at a sheriff's roadblock south of Patagonia. Whatever Quarles needed for the bombing response would have to wait. She stepped into his office.

"Harris your people have been in a shooting involving a Santa Cruz Sheriff's deputy. We are unable to contact them. Have you been in touch with them?"

"Which ones were in the shooting and are they OK?"

"Taylor and Morris is all we know. Morris called it and indicated they were not hurt, and the deputy is deceased. The Santa Cruz Sheriff's Department will not return our calls. We are totally in the dark. What the hell is going on?"

"Mr. Quarles I received a text from Agent Vargas during this morning's meeting. I could not read it until a few minutes ago. It was an emergency request from Kroll for extraction."

"Kroll what the hell has he got to do with this? He got fired six months ago!"

"I misspoke; Kroll is the CI on Bad Apples."

"EXCUSE ME MR. QUARLES!" It was the duty agent again.

"What the hell is now McGowen?"

"We got a call from the Army Hospital at Fort Huachuca. They have two seriously injured FBI agents that came in by an Army medivac helicopter. One is a female named Vargas, the other's name is Kroll. Kroll does not have credentials Vargas does. All the Army would say was the call was for notification purposes only."

Harris was on the phone to Ernie. He picked up quickly.

"Can you get around that road block?"

"No, but I'm circling from behind. Ivalou said they had to do an undercover extraction on Kroll. I'm heading toward the Rocking H Bar, but I've got to go the long way around. The Sheriff's people were about to throw me in jail, but I escaped."

"Get to the Army hospital at Fort Huachuca. Vargas and Kroll are there. See what you can find out and call me."

"Now, what the hell are you talking about?" Quarles demanded.

"Smith, the only member of my team I can find. I just sent him to Fort Huachuca. We need a shooting team in route to where ever Des and M&M are."

"Our pilot and a forensics team are waiting on you, Agent Harris. The shooting review people are in route on another helicopter from Phoenix. I'll take you to the airport; there is room you on the chopper. You are Taylor and Morris's supervisor. Quarles why don't you go get a cup of coffee."

The Phoenix ASAC said, taking charge of the situation. He motioned Havelee to follow him. Which she did, glad to get away from Quarles who was overwhelmed by the situation.

"I'm not making excuses for Quarles. He is running like a chicken with his head cut off. Here is my card. I'm at this office for the duration. Go to the airport; everybody should be ready when you get there. The shooting team will fly out of Phoenix. They will be a few minutes behind you. Good luck. And take care of my man Ernie Smith. You poached a sharp young agent."

"Thank you, Mr. Nye," Havelee said reading the name on the card. Reluctantly she called Ransom Carter to brief him.

High on Special Agent Ernesto Roberto Xavier Collazo Smith list of flaws was that he drove too fast. Too damn fast was the way some of his colleagues described it. Another flaw on the list was his way of circumventing orders. Ron Kroll was his hero. But Ernie, unlike Kroll, would always cover the saddle side of his wranglers before breaking the rules. Fort Huachuca's rear gate was closer to the San Rafael than the main gate. At least he didn't side to a stop sideways when he arrived.

The young MP had never seen an FBI agent's credentials and the one showing them to him wasn't that much older either.

"Sir, I will have to contact my First Sergeant with your request to visit the hospital." The MP told Ernie.

Ernie smiled and waited. He didn't want to go to the hospital. And his reasoning was that Ivalou and Kroll were in the hands of medical professionals. And he, Special Agent Ernesto Smith, was not a doctor. He would just be in the way. The MP came out of the guard house and walked to Ernie's car.

"Sir, my First Sergeant says our hospital does not have your people. They were stabilized for transport and sent by a civilian medical helicopter to Tucson."

"OK, thank you," Ernie answered putting his issued Bu-car in reverse. Minutes later he was happily westbound to the San Rafael. His first stop the Double B Ranch bunkhouse where he could change into his cowboy duds. And then to the barn for his best friend.

The helicopter carrying Havelee and the forensic team circled above the shooting scene as one of the agents shot video. Several times sheriff's deputies waved them off and pointed weapons at the aircraft. They landed in a nearby pasture. The pilot thought it would not be prudent for all the agents to disembark until their status was known. Havelee, wearing a blue FBI raid jacket got off and approached the scene with her credential folder held high in the air.

Several Deputies approached her with rifles and shotguns aimed. Havelee was ordered to stop and keep her hands in view.

A man in uniform approached her.

"I am the Sheriff of Santa Cruz County. Get back on your helicopter and leave. If you don't, I will arrest you for interfering with a criminal investigation."

"I am Supervisory Special Agent Havelee Harris; I work for the FBI Director. You have two of our agents on the ground over there. I need to speak to them now."

"Get back on that helicopter, little lady and get out of my county. And do it quick."

The Sheriff looked at the closest deputy and pointed at the circling chopper.

"Take that M16 and fire a burst at that helicopter so he knows we mean business."

Havelee watched in horror as the deputy opened fire on the helicopter carrying the shooting team. Their pilot was better at his job than the deputy was a marksman. The aircraft flew out of harm's way.

"Now get your skinny little butt on that helicopter and get outta here!" The sheriff snarled.

Havelee took her time retreating to the aircraft. She noticed a familiar looking cowboy sitting a horse across the road from the crime scene and behind a fence. When the helicopter took off, it gave her a better look at the cowboy.

Ernie Smith didn't bother to look up; he just sat on his horse smiling, watching over his handcuffed colleagues laying on the ground.

Harris was dismayed that the young agent hadn't followed her orders, but was glad to see him where he was. One of the crime scene people handed her a headset. She put it on, and the pilot's voice came over.

"Agent Harris our second air unit has reported being turned away from overflying an area south and east of our position. They were contacted on the universal frequency by a US Army Apache Gunship and told the airspace was closed due to national security. I have eyes on the Apache they have not turned in our direction yet."

Can I talk to the Army helicopter with this headset?"

"Yes, but I will be able to hear what you say."

"No problem land on that ranch road and advise the other helicopter to land also."

The helicopter flew a descending circle east then south then west. Havelee watched the menacing Apache turn out of its orbit and speed in their direction. Her headset crackled with the transmission from the Army pilot.

"Descending rotor wing aircraft, you and the previously warned aircraft are in a closed airspace. Do not land, turn to a northerly heading, and leave this valley."

"This is Special Agent Havelee Harris of the FBI these helicopters are on official business. Have your commanding officer contact the FBI Director and confirm our status."

"That is negative; you are not authorized to fly over this area. You are subject to being shot down. Turn north immediately. Pilots follow those orders."

"Go ahead and land," Havelee said to the pilot.

"No ma'am, we are going to follow the Army's instructions. I am responsible for the safe operation of this aircraft and its passengers. Take it up with my SAC."

Both FBI helicopters followed the instructions. Once they turned northwest and over the Patagonia Mountains, the Apache turned back and joined another one patrolling the skies of the San Rafael.

"Pilot, can you land at Nogales?"

"Yes, ma'am."

"Ask the other helicopter to do so as well."

"Yes, ma'am."

Havelee was on the phone to Ransom Carter.

The lead agents of the respective teams on the helicopters were reporting to their bosses, while Havelee was reporting to hers. She was the last one to finish her call. The other agents were irritated at the delays. Havelee punched in another number.

"I was glad to see you where you were. But that is not where you were told to go. What do you have to say for yourself, Ernesto?"

"I went to Fort Huachuca's back gate. The closest place I could enter the fort. The MP told me that Vargas and Kroll were stabilized and sent by civilian helicopter to Tucson. I felt I could be of more use here. Besides the radar detector has internal batteries for the camera. It works well from inside a bag hanging on my saddle horn. I can send you the video. They have abused Des and M&M. I wanted to intervene but then there would be three of us in cuffs. Here I'm just a dumb vaquero watching the action. I will be checking out the Rocking H Bar when it is all over here. And your boyfriend wants you to call him in the worst sort of way. He says it's very important. And you won't answer his calls."

"Ernie, that is some of the most creative bullshit I have ever heard. But I will accept it for the time being. Just keep that camera rolling. And don't attempt to go to the Rocking H Bar, until I tell you it is OK. Comprende amigo?"

"Si, Ernesto comprende."

Havelee disconnected. She dialed TR's number. He answered on the second ring.

"I've been calling you for over an hour now."

"TR, I told you there would be times I can't take your calls. You need to understand that. If it involves Larcena, we will have to work out a text message system."

"Hav, it involves your agent M&M and what's going right now. I wouldn't have been calling for anything less."

"I'm sorry, I spoke out of hand. What is it with M&M and Des?"

"I was working the fence near the road. I heard a siren and a minute or two later I heard two shots. I rode up to see what was happening. Des was throwing up; Willie Hillman was laying in the road with the back of his head blown off, and M&M was in the front seat of Hillman's sheriff's unit. Des would not or could not answer me. M&M jogged over to me and gave me his phone. He told me to get the hell out of there and give to the phone to you and nobody else. He said to check the downloads."

"DO YOU HAVE THAT PHONE IN YOUR HANDS?"

"Yes."

"Turn it on and follow my instructions."

A few minutes later Havelee was looking at the video M&M downloaded off the dash cam in Hillman's police car. Her phone rang. It was the FBI Director himself.

"Agent Harris, you will leave your evidence team with the shooting team and have your pilot take you to the Tucson Hospital Trauma Center. Agents Kroll and Vargas are there. I understand the local Sheriff fired on one of our aircraft, and they will not let us on the scene. Carter is reaching out to the US Attorney in Southern Arizona to get a writ of habitus corpus so we can get our agents."

"Sir if I may."

"What do you have Agent Harris?"

"I have the video and audio from the deputies' dash cam I can forward. I also have an undercover agent on the scene. He is videoing what they are doing. Our detained agents are being abused according to my undercover agent. And the Sheriff doesn't know we have the dash cam video."

"Send me the video immediately. Is this agent you have on the ground in a position where I can call him?"

"He is hiding in plain sight. I have his phone number. But expect unconventional responses from him. I need to let him know to expect calls from someone other than me."

"I will call him myself after I see the video. What is his name?"

"Ernesto Roberto Xavier Collazo Smith, he is quick to say his father is a gringo."

"I remember him from his academy class. Report back when you have spoken to your agents in the hospital. We will get your other two out of harm's way."

Havelee when back to the group and spoke to the leaders. She made the shooting team aware of the dash cam video and that it was under review by the Director. When he authorized her to release it, she would send to them forthwith."

"Harris, have you seen this video?" The shooting team leader asked.

"Yes, I have."

"How did you get your hands on it?"

"M&M, that's Special Agent Mickey Morris, downloaded it to his phone. He was able to hand the phone off to a very close friend of mine who happened to be nearby. M&M made it plain to TR not to give it to anyone but me. He called me several times. I called him back since we've been on the ground here. I told him how to download the phone to my laptop."

"TR is?"

"Excuse me; everyone calls him that. Tobias Rutledge is his name."

"Is this Rutledge where we can interview him?"

"Yes, when we can get back into that valley."

"I suppose you know why the Army won't let us in there. And, if I may ask, why do you share evidence directly with the Director?"

"I work for the Director, and I supervise investigation codenamed Bad Apple's. We have an undercover agent in a criminal organization led by former FBI agent W. Ashton Bradford. That agent requested an emergency undercover extraction. My agents involved in the shooting were in route to back up the extraction. The agent doing the extraction and the undercover agent are in the hospital in Tucson. Somehow the Army extracted them. I don't know how they got involved. We do know a deputy sheriff from this county is an accomplice of Bradford."

"Wow. I don't suppose you would at least let me look at that dash cam footage?" The shooting team leader asked.

"I can let you look at it. If you bring your team to the office, they are letting us use."

Havelee found Ivalou in a wheelchair parked in Ron Kroll's room. Two Tucson police officers were in the hall guarding them.

Kroll was asleep. He was hooked up to monitors, and an IV line ran to the back of his right hand. His face was swollen and bruised to where he was almost unrecognizable. A female doctor was examining him.

"I'm Special Agent Havelee Harris, that man is one of my agents. How is he?"

"I'm Doctor Cordell, Agent Harris. He is beginning to respond to being hydrated. He has a severe concussion, and all his ribs are fractured. These injuries are consistent with his being beaten. We are still evaluating his internal injuries. He keeps worrying about the agent who is sitting over there guarding him. And her injuries are such that she should be in bed. But she will not leave him. I can't speak as to how clear his mind is, or hers for that matter. We have pain meds flowing into both of them. His call button is next to his right hand. Press it if you need us." The doctor took her chart and left the room.

Ivalou's face was swollen and beginning to change to ugly red and blue. Her eyes were black. Kroll wasn't the only one beat up. Havelee sat down in a chair next Vargas.

"I know you're hurting. But I need you to tell me everything you can for now. There will be an official statement later." Havelee said.

"I thought I was responding to Ron's texts for an undercover extraction. I went to where I was told to go on the ranch. I know I stopped the car and started to get out. Next thing I remember some ugly sonofabitch with bad breath was slobbering over me and yanking my dress down and trying to get my underwear off. I was wearing that damn hot pink thong. The dude was hung like a horse and trying to shove it in me. I remember getting my hand on my hideout knife. I cut the dudes' dick off. I ran to the car. And I remember trying to change clothes. My 380 was in my bra holster. My bra was ruined. I know I put it and the gun in my bag. I remember getting out my

Glock and my creds. The next time I woke up, paramedics were loading me in a chopper."

"I hope the hell this isn't my official statement. And I want my knife back that thing cost me close to two hundred bucks."

Havelee touched Ivalou's shoulder. "No, this isn't your official statement. That will come but not tonight."

"Are Des and M&M all right?"

"No, they are in the Santa Cruz County Jail charged with murdering a sheriff's deputy."

"WHAT THE HELL?" Ivalou shouted. The two officers from the hall to come in the room, alert for trouble. Havelee motioned them out.

"Apparently, they were pulled over in a traffic stop. The deputy was, well racially aggressive. Des shot him."

"Did they identify themselves?"

"Yes, an instant before the shots were fired."

"Did the deputy shoot at them?"

"No, and I really can't say any more right now. It will have to play out. The US Attorney is on our side. And the locals are stonewalling us on everything. We can't even get on the ranch crime scene. The only reason I know so much about the shooting is TR came up on it soon after it happens. M&M, bless his soul, managed to download the cops dash camera onto a cell phone. He gave the cell to TR and told him to get the hell out of there and call me."

"Good for M&M. Damnit Hav this is a major fuckup."

"You got that right," Kroll said in a weak voice.

Ivalou rolled her chair next to his bed and grabbed his hand.

Kroll's voice was barely audible.

"Porn Dude found the hideout camera. Bradford Tased me. They took my phones. Tied me up left me outside, all day and all night …. El Jefe flew in with some ragheads. They sent a nuke across …. They were going to set it off in Vegas. Bradford was going to behead me and …. And there was a godawful scream…

Never heard anything like it. I dropped to the ground. I heard thuds like bullets hitting. The helicopter crashed. A cowboy gave me water. Lou where are you?"

"I'm right here Ron; I'm holding your hand. You are going to be alright."

"I love you Ivalou."

"I love you too Ron."

"Ron do you remember when you sent the undercover extraction message?" Havelee asked.

"I didn't send a message."

Chapter Twenty-Seven

Tucson awoke to news images from Santa Cruz County showing two badly beaten black men being perp walked, dragged was more like it, into the county jail. The sheriff gave a press briefing and showed FBI raid jackets the two were purportedly wearing when deputies arrived at the scene. These men are being charged with the murder of Deputy Willie Hillman who apparently pulled them over in a traffic stop. A reporter asked the Sheriff if he knew why the men were being stopped. The sheriff referred them to photos of the Escalade they men were driving.

"Black men don't drive cars like that in the San Rafael Valley unless they are up to no good." The Sheriff said into the cameras.

"Do you have dash camera video of the traffic stop?" A reporter asked.

"Deputy Hillman's car was not equipped with one." The Sheriff answered.

"What does the FBI say about the raid jackets."

"No comment."

"Is that your no comment or no comment from the FBI."

"That is I don't know what they said. This conference is over."

The US Attorney for the Southern District of Arizona watched a recording of the Sheriff's press conference in the Federal Judges chambers.

The Judge addressed the US Attorney's motions.

"I will grant you a writ to remove those agents into Federal Custody. And I authorize the seizure of the deputy's vehicle. I will not grant your request for a warrant to search the Rocking H Bar Ranch. I suggest you appeal to the State Police and tell the FBI to be nice to them. I have a docket ready this morning. This matter is closed."

The US Attorney called Quarles who was in a meeting with Ransom Carter and the Director. Quarles took the call and listened to the lawyer. He thanked him and turned to the Director.

"Sir, the US Attorney has the order to release our agents into Federal custody and to seize the patrol unit the deputy was driving. He will not grant us search warrants for the ranch. He suggests, and I quote, 'we play nice with the State Police.' I have the State Police Commander's direct line if you wish to call him."

Quarles was interrupted by a knock on the conference room door. His administrative assistant responded when he asked who was knocking.

"Mr. Quarles, one of the agents assigned to Bad Apple's is here. He has video footage downloaded. He states Agent Harris instructed him to bring this to Mr. Carter and the Director forthwith."

"Send him in." The Director said.

Ernie Smith entered the room, dressed as an FBI special agent should be. He went to the laptop that operated the video monitors. Without comment, he inserted a SIM card and put the raw footage up on a screen.

After viewing footage of deputies and the sheriff himself beating and kicking Desmond Taylor and Michael Morris. The Director spoke.

"Get that US Attorney over here now. Show him that footage and I want Civil Rights charges against every officer who laid hands on my agents and Federal Assault Charges on them as well. Every one of those people will be in Federal custody by tonight. Quarles pull enough people to make that happen."

"Yes, Sir. We have been getting numerous press request for comment on the raid jackets our agents were wearing. I have been stalling them, but they will want something soon."

"Issue a statement, to the effect that we are investigating the issue and will hold a press conference when we have the facts."

Another knock, Quarles opened the door again.

"Sir, The Secretary of the Army is on the line for the Director."

The Director took that call.

When terminated the call, the Director addressed those in the room.

"The Army officially states, and I repeat officially, that a helicopter on a routine training mission observed a crashed helicopter on a ranch in the San Rafael Valley. They landed to give assistance. They discovered a male and female still alive. They identified the female as an FBI agent. She identified the male as being an agent also. The Army helicopter transported them back to Fort Huachuca and their medical people stabilized them. They were then transported to Tucson by a civilian medical helicopter. The Army dispatched a pair of armed helicopters to the ranch to keep it secure until the Arizona State Police Forensics Unit arrived."

"That sounds like they know more than what they are saying," Carter said.

"Yes and I was told not to pursue the Army's involvement any further. I will contact the White House."

There was another knock at the door. It was the US Attorney. Once he got in the room, the Director asked Ernie to start the video again. The lawyer signaled he'd seen enough as his cell phone buzzed. A very mad US Attorney answered it. He listed to the call and slammed the phone down on the table. Anger management was not his strong suite.

"That was the US Marshals service. The Sheriff in Santa Cruz County refused to comply with the writ and told the deputies he was going to use it for toilet paper. Director, if you will assemble your SWAT Teams, I will direct the US Marshal to do so as well. I authorize the arrest of every individual in those videos. Start with assault on federal officers and 1980 violations will follow. I've got to look up the statue on them shooting at the helicopters. And whoever got that video needs a raise and promotion. Now, if you gentlemen will excuse me, I need to get to work on this."

"Gracious Senor." Ernie Smith said.

Burns met with Russell and Cruz outside the rental hanger at Nogales airport. They briefed Andy on the recent events and lack of any news other than a deputy being killed. There was no news from the San Rafael Valley. The Sheriff did not make it known where in his county the shooting happened. Burns asked the two men to total up their bills for services rendered and submit it for payment.

"You good for it Cowboy?" Russell quipped.

"My accountant is, he will pay you in any color of beads you want, Half Breed."

"As long as he doesn't pay with pesos I'm happy." Burrito Cruz allowed.

They hung around and chatted with Jolene while Burns loaded the aircraft. He got a tow bar and a tug from the linemen and pulled the Citation onto the ramp. Burrito Cruz assisted by driving the RV into the hanger. Burns continued his contract to rent the hanger until he made arrangements for someone picking up the RV. Cruz said he would take the coach instead of payment for services rendered.

"Sure you would. But I think it's worth more than forty hours of minimum wage." Burns rejoined.

The linemen gave Burns a lift to the office so he could file a flight plan. They delivered him back to the jet, and he commenced his preflight inspection. After that, Jolene hugged the two PIs. Once they were on board, Andy closed the cabin door. Jolene buckled into the copilot's seat, and Burns began his checklist.

At 10:30 AM local time, Citation November Eight Zero X-ray taxied onto the active runway at Nogales. Burns applied power. Several hours later, at precisely the planned time the jet touched down at Mobile Aerospace. With the aircraft tucked safely away in a locked hanger. And all their gear and four extra bags loaded, Burns drove the truck to Baldwin County Alabama.

Burns carried all four duffle bags and his rifle into his shop. Hadfield went to her rooms unpacked and crashed. Burns carefully cleaned the rifle and then completely disassembled it. He selected a new barrel blank and installed it in the CNC lathe. After entering the contour parameters, Burns turned on the machine. He picked up the old barrel and went into the knife shop. Burns lit his forge and before long the barrel was glowing red. He used a power hammer to turn the round barrel into a flat piece of steel. He cut the piece into equal lengths. Satisfied he went back to the machine shop and began counting the money in the duffle bags. Burns did not have a bill counting machine. Drug people were precise at counting money. Mistakes got you dead. The bills were packaged in bundled stacks of banded one hundred dollar bills. Twenty bills in a stack, ten stacks in a bundle. Andy counted the bills in a stack and then the number of stacks in a bundle. Burns put the bills back in the duffle bag and went to bed. Pondering what to do with twenty-five million dollars of purloined drug money.

The Director and Carter along with Quarles got into the helicopter.

"Mr. Quarles, what is the status of Agents Kroll and Vargas this morning?"

"Sir, Vargas will be released. But, she is staying at the hospital with Kroll. They are keeping Kroll another twenty-four hours."

"Prognosis?"

"Vargas suffered a concussive injury, bruises and contusions, possible short term memory loss. According to Agent Harris, Vargas doesn't have total recall of what happened to her. She remembers parts of it. That is consistent with the medical reports. They expect her to have a full recall of memory at some time. They won't say when. Kroll was suffering from serious dehydration and numerous physical injuries. He had been beaten. They may keep him longer than twenty-four hours. They say he is not ready to be questioned extensively."

"Very well. Harris is their supervisor. Let her make the call on both of them. I don't want anyone pushing to get statements from them. Harris is meeting us at this ranch. When we conclude the meeting there with the State Police Commander, we will drive over to the next ranch. I want to meet the cowboy that got us that video."

When the FBI Director and his entourage landed at the Rocking H Bar, Harris met them. She introduced the State Police Commander.

The head of the state crime lab briefed them about the crime scene.

"There are ten deceased persons. Seven of them appear to have died from single shots likely fired from a sniper rifle. One was a victim of the helicopter crash a second person near the crash had his head crushed by a truck battery. Another bled to death from an unusual wound.

"We have been able to recover four projectiles. They appear to be thirty caliber rifle rounds. They are in good enough shape for ballistic comparison. We have recovered one large knife from the area in front of the ranch house and several handguns. We recovered an M-16 rifle from the helicopter wreckage and M249 machine gun was found on the ground near the wreckage as well.

"During subsequent search warrant service on all the adjacent buildings, we have recovered several handguns and assault weapons. Out of the ranch house proper, we found three assault weapons several pistols along with shotguns and rifles. The latter guns are the kind of firearms I would expect a rancher to have.

The SUV is shown registered to W. Ashton Bradford. The Ford F250 and Ford F450 belong to the Rocking H Bar ranch. A Nissan registered to Ronald J. Kroll. And another Nissan vehicle that has no record of registration.

"We have not found any evidence of the sale of this property by the owner Lyon Hamilton. Lyon Hamilton is a missing person. There is evidence of four males living in the ranch house. The bunk house has evidence of some persons having lived in it. There are numerous bullet holes in the bunk house as well as blood stains.

"The barn has evidence of marijuana storage and also a large number of people. We found female hygiene materials in the barn. We believe this ranch may have been a drop off point for persons smuggled into the country.

"We have teams searching the adjacent areas to this area. And another team working all the ranch trails. We have found an area that appears to be gravesites. Our cadaver dogs hit on this area, and we have a forensic anthropologist supervising the disinterment of human remains."

"Have any computers been recovered." The Director asked.

"Yes, several they have been taken to our lab."

"Will you share the information you find on them?"

"I'll defer that question to the State Police Commander."

"Director, we will share anything we find with the FBI. We will allow agents to inspect this scene. We will not relinquish jurisdiction to you. We will ask for your resources in identifying foreign nationals involved. Another helicopter is inbound from Mexico as we speak and will land here within ten minutes. It carries the head of the Mexican National Police force. He will confirm the identity of one of the deceased. Who we believe to be EL Jefe."

"El Jefe was involved with the target of this investigation and complicit in the smuggling operations happening here." Ransom Carter added.

"The FBI is well known in the law enforcement community for not sharing all it has during joint investigations. In the spirit of hoping, you can change that attitude, Director. I'm going to share something that will affect the investigation into the deputy's death."

"I would like to say I appreciate that. But it depends on what you are sharing."

"We recovered the cell phone of the deceased person who bled to death. He was in the habit of recording his calls. He called the deputy and asked him to stop a vehicle containing two pimps. And keep them out of this valley. Two other cell phones recovered indicate text messages to a prostitute using the name Penelope. Other conversations between the deceased and the deputy indicate some involvement down here by the deputy. I would appreciate enlightenment on the prostitute Penelope if you would. And you can have a copy of the deputy's conversation."

"The two agents were assigned to the undercover investigation. We have not been able to talk to them yet. They were in route to back up an undercover extraction. I understand they posed as pimps. The female agent posted as a prostitute the deep cover guy would visit. I honestly don't know the name she used. Our operation was code-named Bad Apple's. W. Ashton Bradford was the target. He was a rogue agent we terminated but screwed up the prosecution. The undercover agent, Ron Kroll, was playing the part of a terminated rogue agent."

"This guy Kroll must be one hell of an actor." The Commander said.

"Your tech mentioned one of the deceased bled to death from an unusual wound. Would you elaborate Commander?"

"The deceased suffered a wound at the hands of an unknown person or persons. This wound appears to have severed his femoral artery. The wound occurred when the unknown assailant severed the deceased's penis. The deceased bled to death while he was trying to reattach his penis with duct tape. The said penis was the largest our medical examiner claims to have seen. I suspect losing one that size might cause a person to overlook the fact he was bleeding out from a femoral artery.

"We also found a nice and bloody folding knife in the rear seat of the car apparently driven by your female agent. And it appears she changed clothes as well. Remind me to be nice to the ladies carrying federal creds."

"Thank you for your candor Commander," Ransom said. "I understand from that Agent's supervisor that she is concerned about her knife."

"Once we have her statement I will approve releasing it to her. She might want the pistol with a real interesting holster back as well."

"I think we are getting into an area we don't need to know. Commander, I heard your reminder about sharing. And what you have shared is most welcome. Thank you for your time. Supervisory Special Agent Havelee Harris ASAC Quarles are the agents assigned to inspect this scene. Quarles will remain here. We need Agent Harris to accompany us to a neighboring ranch. She will return when that detail is complete.

"I believe the Chief Federale has arrived."

They watched the Mexican helicopter land. A distinguished looking Latino with stone gray hair alighted from the aircraft. After introductions, he was directed to a body bag, which a technician unzipped for him. The man nodded as he said, 'that is El Jefe. May he rest in hell."

The Mexican official asked for a briefing on how the criminal died. The Official listened to everything. He spoke in accented English.

"When I was a young Federale I worked Sonora. Time and time again we were called to the bodies of narco trafficantes dead on our side of the border. They were always killed as they prepared to execute a hombre who told of their deeds. That was the work of La Migra El Con Riflie. He must still ride these hills."

The Mexican looked north and crossed himself saying, "Vaya Con Dios Mi Amigo, muy gracious."

With that, he shook hands and returned to his helicopter. As the noise of the departing aircraft subsided. The Director asked.

"Anyone know what that last part was all about?"

"Thirty years ago or there about, I was a rookie trooper working this sector. There was a legend about a border patrolman who used a long range rifle to shoot drug smugglers. They confiscated one of their guy's rifle and tried to match it to evidence the Mexicans found. No match. Most people believe that is a story the Mexicans cooked up to cover up for one of their people doing the killing." The State Police Commander said.

The Director, Ransom Carter and Havelee all sat on the verandah of the Double B Ranch headquarters house. Carson Bell and TR sat with them. Estella served tea, and two little girls came around. Larcena sat next to Havelee while Lupe enjoyed sitting Carson Bell's lap.

"Mr. Rutledge the FBI and two of its agents owe you a large debt of gratitude for your help with getting that phone to Agent Harris. If we can ever do anything for you, legal that is, all you have to do is ask." The Director said.

TR didn't waste any time asking. "Mr. Director, the first thing you can do is transfer Havelee to Tucson. She promised to marry me when this investigation is over. The second thing you can do is we are going to adopt that Apache girl is sitting next to her. Anything you can do to make that happen. I would appreciate. Your Agent Vargas plans on adopting Lupe, the little one sitting in Mr. Carson's lap. Add that one to your list as well. And I'm not done asking either."

"Ransom, make what he wants happen. Congratulations Agent Harris. Now, what else is on your list Mr. Rutledge?"

"I worked for Mr. Lyon Hamilton on the Rocking H Bar. Mr. Lyon would never sell the place. I believe those people killed him and buried him over there somewhere. Find his body. So his sister will know where he is."

"That is happening as we speak."

"Mr. Director, I have a question." Carson Bell said.

"Go ahead Mr. Bell."

"Sir I am a retired Air Force Colonel. This valley is my home. My late brother ran this ranch like our father and uncle did before him. I grew up with Lyon Hamilton. I too want him found. So do the rest of his friends in this valley. The next thing is, and I held a top secret security clearance when I was in the Air Force. So start telling me everything that happened at the Rocking H Bar. I can keep a secret."

The Director told him.

Back at the Rocking H Bar the Director and Carter started toward their helicopter. The Director paused and looked at Havelee.

"Transferring you out here will happen. My question to you, is, do you want greater responsibility? I think you can handle it."

"If I may be candid Sir."

"I would expect nothing less."

"I would love the responsibility, but I am afraid I would flunk the chick shit requirement."

"We need a lot less of that in management. The current Tucson SAC submitted her resignation to accept a job with a Congresswoman. When all the paperwork catches up, how would you like to be SAC Tucson?"

I would, but Mr. Quarles is ASAC, shouldn't he be given a chance?"

"Well said, Quarles will do a good job for you. Right now I need you as Tucson SAC."

"I will accept Sir."

"Good wrap things up down here and wait for the official notification."

"I want Taylor, Morris, Vargas and Smith assigned to my Field Office Sir."

"I can do that. Put this mess to bed Agent Harris. We will talk when your promotion becomes effective. The only person you can tell is your cowboy, TR.

"Yes, Sir!"

As the helicopter ascended north over the Patagonia Mountains, the Director, and Carter spoke through headsets, with the pilot's blocked from hearing their conversation.

"Are you going to follow up on Kroll's statement about a nuclear weapon El Jefe brought across the border for an attack on Los Vegas?"

"I would if we had any evidence it was there. I'm going the ask the President to have the Army come clean about what they know."

"How are you going to handle who killed the bad guys?"

"I'm going to spin it as being another Mexican drug cartel's work. Let them start killing each other. That will solve the terrorist bomb plot in Tucson as well."

"It will give the President a chance to say look what we have done to keep our borders secure."

"He will say that."

"One thing that bothers me. Carson Bell said the same thing in Spanish the Chief Federale said. La Migra con riflie or some such."

"Ransom, when we get back to headquarters, take a look at that legend and see if there is any truth to it."

"Yes, Sir."

There was no mention of this anywhere in the news media. The big story was as it happened. FBI and US Marshal Service SWAT teams descended on Santa Cruz County, arresting the Sheriff and seven deputies. The news media received the footage of their crimes. Video of deputies repeatedly kicking and beating the agents was shown over and over again. Along with footage of a deputy opening fire on an FBI helicopter. Agents Taylor and Morris were carried from the Santa Cruz County and loaded into an ambulance. Their condition was listed as guarded in a Tucson hospital.

A search warrant revealed the Agents credentials the Sheriff's desk drawer, along with their handguns. The Governor announced the State Police would take over the operation of the Santa Cruz County Sheriff's Department until a successor could be appointed. There only four deputies that were not involved in the debacle. Two of them were out of state on vacation, and two more hadn't answered their phones when called with orders to come into work.

The President held a press conference at the White House to announce the FBI had thwarted a major terrorist plot against the United States involving the notorious Mexican Drug Lord El Jefe. At the President's behest the FBI Director came to the podium and did the expected, the FBI took credit for the bust. Mexican drug cartels got the blame for assisting jihadists and blowing up rival gangs in Tucson. There was no mention of the San Rafael Valley.

Chapter Twenty-Eight

The Mexican Police and Military stormed El Jeffe's compound. The Iranian bomb maker got killed in the shootout, or so it was said. Evidence recovered from the Tucson bombs connected the deceased bomb maker to those devices. Another victory for international cooperation along the US Border with Mexico. After the reorganization, it would be business as usual. The press made a big deal about a sophisticated border tunnel between a massage parlor and a strip joint.

The former Santa Cruz Sheriff and most of his deputies and jailers faced indictment in US Federal Court for numerous charges stemming actions related to the shooting of Deputy Willie Hillman by FBI agents. The FBI shooting team found that Desmond Taylor acted within the agencies policy for using deadly force. The Santa Cruz County Prosecutor declined to take the shooting in front of a grand jury. Desmond and M&M would recover from their physical injuries. Taylor took leave and went home to Biloxi Mississippi where he spent time with Rev. Theodis Cleckler. M&M was transferred to the Tucson Field Office as was Ernie Smith.

Miraculously, with all the agencies involved, the Rocking H Bar was never mentioned in any media releases. There was no mention of the nuclear bomb. The President told the FBI Director it was not his need to know. And the Director was having problems with a scandal involving a mistress. The

General was not pleased with the Director claiming credit for what his Bureau didn't do.

Reid visited Burns place with several team members. They all shot the suppressed .338 Lupa rifle. Reid wanted three. Burns built them and never sent a bill. The team members that wanted Burns knives got them as well. During the visit, Reid briefed Burns about the bomb.

"Once we got medical help for the FBI people. We drove the truck with the bomb back to Fort Huachuca. We entered the Fort via the rear gate and drove to the airfield where a C-17 waited on the ramp. My people drove the truck directly onto the aircraft. We stood by and watched the bird leave for points unknown. The General told me later the bomb was Soviet approximately twelve megatons in size and rigged to detonate via cell phones. Exactly like your typical IED. It would have worked and Las Vegas as we know it would no longer exist."

Reid extended his hand to Burns. "Good shooting Cowboy. Damn Good Shooting."

Jolene drove her Nissan 350Z to the trendy cafe in Fairhope Alabama. She was not looking for to this meeting. Lois Hamilton Thornton was waiting at a private table. The older woman got up and hugged Jolene.

"I understand Sheriff Rabun needs to obtain a sample of my DNA. Can you explain that request?" Lois Thornton asked.

'Officially your brother was listed as a missing person by the Baldwin County Sheriff's Department. The State Police in Arizona has to make the request for DNA through the reporting agency."

"The FBI is not involved in this?"

"No, the General made sure they stayed out of the way."

"He's good at that sort of thing. What I want to know is, was Lyon involved in that mess?"

"No, there is no evidence whatsoever that indicates he was anything other than a victim."

"Can you tell me about what they found when they discovered his body and why they want DNA if they know it was him?"

"They are sure one body is your brothers due to identification found on it. They want the DNA sample to be one hundred percent sure. They can't leave anything to chance."

"You said one body. You mean there were more?"

"Yes."

"Tell me everything. Please."

"Lois, are you sure you to hear this?"

"Jolene that's my only sibling I have to know." Lois Thornton was crying now. Hadfield reached over and held her hands. She let Lois cry for a few minutes. Jolene teared up as well.

"Lois, your brother's remains, were discovered in a grave with three others. His cause of death was from a gunshot to the head. He died instantly. The medical examiner stated all those in that grave died almost at the same time. The other three's injuries were consistent with being struck by a shod horse. Two men had their skulls crushed; the third had massive chest injuries."

"Don Cameron." Lois Thornton said almost in a whisper. "Lyon always said that horse was as protective of him as a dog would be. The Border Collie Jazz was the same way. They would accept people who were with Lyon. But no one else could get near them. TR could feed them. And Miguel over at the Double B. I understand the horse and dog are over at the Double B. I don't know what I can do with them now."

"The subject of the FBI investigation hijacked the Rocking H Bar and killed your brother. The horse and the dog defended Lyon. There was canine bite damage on the other bodies. So I can imagine what happened when those people killed Lyon. Andy Burns believes their violent response was why they escaped and ran to a place of safety they were familiar with."

"What about the other graves?"

"Mostly people they can't identify and probably never be. There was one female, a Latina who was smuggled into the country believing her and her daughter would have a new life. Had she lived she would have been forced into prostitution. I understand the individual responsible died a very suitable death. The child was rescued and is in the process of being adopted to what will be a very good home."

"So they got everybody involved?"

"They think so. It's not likely anyone escaped."

"How do I give this DNA sample do they take blood?"

"No, Sheriff Rabun is a friend of mine. I have a swab kit. I will take a saliva swab from your mouth. Then seal it in a test tube and it will be sent overnight FedEx."

"How long before they know for sure?"

"I don't know."

"You told me from the beginning that your Andy Burns said someone stole the ranch. He was right. I've spoken with Carson Bell; he is impressed with Mr. Burns horsemanship. Lyon always said Don Cameron was a one-person horse. And Jazz, a one-person dog. Carson says Andy Burns handles them as well as

Lyon ever did. I understand Mr. Burns wishes to purchase those animals."

"Yes, he does."

"I guess that brings us to the question of your fee. What do I owe you?"

"You owe me the cost of the private investigators we used out there. Here is a copy of their bills. David Cromwell is Burns lawyer and accountant. He has already paid them. Just send a check to David and a copy of this bill."

"I want to compensate you Jolene for what you have done."

"Sell Andy Burns that horse and dog. I will consider us even. And if you decide to sell the Rocking H Bar, Buddy Russell one of the investigators we used is also a realtor out there who can handle the transaction on that end. Andy wants the ranch as well, and he can afford it. David Cromwell has an offer ready for you to look at."

Lois Thornton sat silent for a few moments. "Jolene let me think about this, I will call David. Meanwhile, let's have lunch. And I want you to tell what you think of the San Rafael Valley."

It was another six months before the books officially closed on the Bad Apple's Investigation. Ron Kroll got his retirement. The FBI Director presented him his retired credentials personally at the Tucson Field Office. The moment shared with his wife, Supervisory Special Agent Ivalou V. Kroll and their daughter Lupe Kroll. Havelee Harris SAC Tucson, Special Agents Desmond Taylor, Mickey Morris and Ernesto Smith watched the presentation. Not that it mattered that much to Ron. He struggled with images of that day he almost died. The cowboy who gave him water took on the status of an angel in Kroll's memory. And angels were real. A certified letter arrived at the apartment he where he with Ivalou Vargas Kroll and Lupe. It was from a bank in the Bahamas. On deposit in an interest bearing account was five million US dollars. The necessary instructions of how to transfer these funds to another bank. Kroll and Ivalou purchased an off the grid adobe home near Patagonia that overlooked the San Rafael Valley.

At the behest of Lois Thornton, Tobias Rutledge moved back to the Rocking H Bar and ran the ranch. Lois made it clear the sale of the ranch was pending, and TR would always have a home and employment there. So would Havelee Harris-Rutledge and her adopted daughter Larcena Sells Harris-Rutledge. Pepe, Larcena's tame mountain lion, roamed the ranch at will. And would come and go via a doggie door installed in a window. The cat slept in Larcena's bedroom.

Buddy Russell returned to his real estate business. Ron and Ivalou Kroll were his clients. And of course, Lois Thornton. The private investigation business closed. Benito 'Burrito' Cruz returned to his used car lot in Nogales. The Governor appointed Cruz Sheriff of Santa Cruz County. Russell was trying and not very successfully either, to avoid being Burrito's Undersheriff. Not that either one of them needed a job. Burrito and Russell both received certified letters from the bank in the Bahamas.

The sun was rising behind Citation November Eight Zero X-Ray as it streaked across Texas. Andrew Burns rode in the co-pilot's seat. In the left seat, a clean-cut young man piloted the aircraft. Burns hired him to bring the jet back to Mobile along with the passengers, the General, his wife, and her daughters. Burns would drive back to Alabama in the motorhome. When the aircraft touched down in Nogales, it was nine months since it last flew out of that airport. A brand new Sundowner horse trailer sat next to the motorhome in the hanger. Burns hitched it to the RV. Everyone else left in rental vehicles. Burns drove the coach to the Double B casita.

Carson Bell got out of Jeep FC170 truck at casita's corral. He got and walked over to the pipe fence. He leaned on the fence and watched Burns work Don Camron. The horse responded to Burns every cue. Lyon Hamilton would be smiling.

"How is he doing?" Bell asked when Andy rode the horse over to where he stood.

"Like I never left. Cam and Jazz were glad to see me."

"Where's your lady?"

"She declined to make this trip. There are a couple of fishing tournaments on her calendar."

"Well, I think Havelee has the idea we didn't tell her everything. But that little Indian gal changed her heart. All the adoption papers went through on both the girls. Larcena is officially Larcena Sells Harris-Rutledge."

"Harris-Rutledge? She and TR tie the knot?"

"Yes, they were married at sunset on that ridge above the Rocking H Bar headquarters. They rode off on a pair of matched geldings. The Collazo's provided the horses. Havelee's family came out from Oklahoma. It was a good wedding."

"Good I think both of them deserve that. So does the little girl."

"Burns I understand you want to buy this old jeep truck."

"Carson all you have to do is name your price. I'll have it shipped back to Alabama."

"TR, Butter Billy, Miguel and Estella all got an interesting letter from a bank in the Bahamas. You wouldn't know anything about that would you?"

"You know, Half Breed Russell said he got a letter like that. I thought he smoked something funny in his peace pipe."

"My doctor tells me I'm suffering from congestive heart failure. I could go anytime. I have updated my will. Lupe Kroll will inherit the Double B when she becomes of age. Miguel and Estella will be allowed to live out their lives here with a nice stipend. Butter Billy and his intended Bonita will be employed for life as well. Butter will run the ranch. Ron and Ivalou are happy with this. They bring Lupe by every few days. This casita and 180 acres around it are willed to you. So is the Jeep truck, I hate to see it leave this place. My daddy brought it new. The will stipulates it has to remain here. You made things right in this valley so you should be part of it. I hope Lois Thornton makes as good of arrangement for Rocking H Bar and Tobias. I understand she's sold the place. I hope it didn't go another holding company like the one that owns the CRM. But, the Ranch Manager over there and all the hands say the ranch has never been better."

Burns got off Don Cameron and removed his gloves; he extended his hand to Bell.

"Carson, I appreciate your bequest. I hope it is a long time coming. Lyon Hamilton would be pleased with the arrangement made for the Rocking H Bar. Lois is going to tell TR this evening."

"I hope so. I have the urn with Lyon's ashes. Lois asked me to bring it to you. I need to get back to the house so; I can get ready for this celebration she calls it. I think it is sad myself."

The San Rafael Valley was resplendent in the sunlight that afternoon. All the ranchers' wranglers' cowboys and cowgirls of the valley gathered at the Rocking H Bar, as were businesspeople from Nogales, Patagonia, Sierra Vista and other parts of Santa Cruz County. Horsemen from all parts of Southern Arizona were there. Arrangements were in place for a large ranch style lunch and gathering. Buddy Russell and Burrito Cruz hung close to each other. Ernie Smith was with the Collazo family. Havelee graciously suffered being introduced to all of them. Ron and Ivalou Kroll watched Lupe and Larcena play.

Lois Thornton struck the iron triangle hanging on the front porch.

"My brother Lyon would appreciate all of you being here today. I have asked a friend to scatter Lyon's ashes."

A bagpipe began to play Amazing Grace. The Piper, in full kilt, slowly marched from the side of the ranch house and past the crowd. He marched up the ranch road toward the ridge.

When he heard the pipes playing Andy Burns rode Don Cameron from the south to the crest of the ridge. He paused where those in attendance could not see him. Burns took his hat off and bowed his head for a moment. He replaced his hat and removed the lid from the urn. The sound of pipes was beginning to fade as the Piper reached the crest of the ridge.

Andy put his spurs to Don Cameron's flanks. The horse bolted forward with the dog in pursuit. Burns leaned forward and at the instant the horse crossed the ridge where the crowd could see them. Andy emptied the urn behind him. The gray cloud of ash took to the wind. It was at the spot where Lyon Hamilton liked to sit astride Don Cameron every evening and contemplate the day. Burns turned the horse out of sight and let him gallop north leaving the ranch that was once his home.

Burns was finished putting up Don Cameron when Lois Hamilton arrived at the Casita. She hugged Andy and went over to the horse and stroked his neck.

"There wasn't a dry eye in that crowd when you came across that ridge scattering those ashes. Everyone recognized Don Cameron and Jazz."

"There wasn't a dry eye on that horse either. I sure would have like to have known your brother. Don Cameron is the best horse I've ever ridden."

"There is still plenty of food. If you change your mind about coming over. TR and Havelee were overwhelmed when they learned the Rocking H Bar has been purchased by CRM Holdings and deeded to Larcena when she turns twenty-five. I understand that company has an educational fund for her and Lupe Kroll. That is most generous of them."

Lois Thornton handed Andy an envelope. "These documents have been properly executed. You are now the owner of Don Cameron of Lochiel and his sidekick Jazzman of Lochiel. These animals are my gift to you for your efforts on behalf of my brother, Lyon Hamilton. And Jolene said I could hug you."

Andy Burns enjoyed a peaceful night in the San Rafael watching the stars and listening to the ghosts of the past. He loaded Don Cameron and Jazz into the trailer at first light. Everything was hooked up and ready when two ATV's pulled up to the casita barn followed by the Jeep truck. TR, Butter Billy got out of one ATV, Russell, and Cruz the other. Miguel, Estella, and Carson Bell got out of the Jeep. They carried a couple of thermoses full of coffee. And a basket full of food.

"One goes with you on the road the other we drink now," TR said.

They all stood around the picnic table, and Burns handed each man a sheathed knife. The knife blades were etched with their name and the Burns Maker logo. Butter Billy reacted first. He grabbed Andy in a bear hug lifting him off the ground.

"THANKS, MAN I NEVER HAD ANYBODY GIVE ME ANYTHING LIKE THIS!"

Burns recovered when the big cowboy sat him back on the ground and said, "You're welcome."

"What kind of steel Cowboy?" Russell asked.

"Made them out of an old rifle barrel Half Breed."

"Andy I hope you make your way back to this valley sometime. I think you belong here." TR said.

"Thanks, TR, this place is never too far from my mind.' Burns handed TR an old book. 'It is your job to ensure that Larcena knows the legacy of this valley. I suggest you start by teaching her story of the first Larcena to live here. This book is her story." The book: With Their Own Blood: A Saga of Southwestern Pioneers.

Burns got a man hug from TR. The Cowboys went on their way leaving Russell and Cruz behind.

"How long before you get back traveling with the horse?" Cruz asked.

"Three maybe four days. I'm not in a hurry. I have corral reservations in several places. I won't keep Cam in the trailer over ten hours a day."

"I've got a question," Russell said.

"Ask."

"The holding company that purchased the Rocking H Bar, CRM Holdings. What does CRM stand for?"

"Charlie Raifield's Money."

"And what do you have to do with it?"

"That's two questions Half Breed."

"I'm an Indian what do you expect?"

Burns smiled. "I own it."

Burns prediction of four days was right. It was late afternoon when he pulled through the gate at his place. Jolene walked with Burns as he led Don Cameron to the pasture where Major's grave was. He opened the gate and let the horse go inside. Andy removed the halter and leaned against the gate. Jolene stood on the other side. Don Cameron looked around at his new surroundings. Jazz sat next to him scoping out the same things. The horse leaned down and cropped a mouth full of grass. He took a few more steps and took another bite or two. He lifted his head and shook like a dog and bolted off in the pasture.

He galloped to the far end and gracefully turned and thundered down the fence line toward Burns. Don Cameron made a sliding stop butt down mane and tail flying. He nuzzled Burns' arm and craned his neck across the fence and touched Jolene's cheek with his nose. He turned and cantered to the gravesite. The horse stopped and sniffed the ground then walked reverently around it. He whinnied loudly and trotted back to Burns. Andy stroked his head and neck for a few minutes and then led him back to the barn. After putting him in a stall, Burns left some hay for the horse and made sure his water bucket was full. Jazz got water and feed as well.

Jolene and Andy walked back to the house holding hands. "Burns I need to tell you something."

"What's that?"

"I redecorated the kitchen."

"It's about time."

"Burns!"

ABOUT THE AUTHOR

Tom Ellis is a retired police sergeant. As former contributing editor for Law Enforcement Technology Magazine he authored numerous articles on firearms, equipment, and training. He was a member of the Alabama Police High Power and Small Bore Rifle Teams, participating in the International Law Enforcement Games in Sydney Australia, Edmonton Alberta Canada, and Washington DC, USA. He lives in Saint Clair County, Alabama with his dog and two cats.

Visit the author's website: www.Brokenspurs.com

When the CEO of a local casino is fished out of a lake by former police officer Andy Burns, it sours his otherwise peaceful retirement. Something about the murder weapon, a custom-made knife jutting inches above the late CEO's silk tie, sticks in Andy's mind. He's seen this blade before and Andy is not happy about the implications his admission will mean for an old friend.

Sergeant Jolene Hadfield is assigned the case, and despite rampant racism, sexism and nasty inept department politics that hamper her investigation, she comes to suspect an unlikely motive for revenge may be the reason for the murder. Her boss on the other hand, insists she button the case up, and pin the whole thing on a too convenient suspect—compelling evidence to the contrary or not. For Hadfield solving the crime might become secondary to keeping her job.

Burns and Hadfield might make an unlikely team, but together they have a shot at finding the real killer, even if it's going to make them rather unpopular in this part of Mississippi. This is not a fight either of them were looking for, but it's not one they plan on backing down from.

— Available in paperback & ebook editions —